BRENDA JACKSON

is a die "heart" romantic who married her childhood sweetheart and still proudly wears the "going steady" ring he gave her when she was fifteen. Because she believes in the power of love, Brenda's stories always have happy endings. In her real-life love story, Brenda and her husband of more than forty years live in Jacksonville, Florida, and have two sons.

A *New York Times* bestselling author of more than seventy-five romance titles, Brenda is a recent retiree who now divides her time between family, writing and traveling with Gerald. You may write Brenda at P.O. Box 28267, Jacksonville, Florida 32226, by email at WriterBJackson@aol.com or visit her website at www.brendajackson.net.

BRENDA JACKSON

CANYON
& HIDDEN PLEASURES

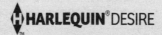
HARLEQUIN® DESIRE

Recycling programs
for this product may
not exist in your area.

ISBN-13: 978-0-373-83791-5

CANYON & HIDDEN PLEASURES

Copyright © 2013 by Harlequin Books S.A.

The publisher acknowledges the copyright holder
of the individual works as follows:

CANYON
Copyright © 2013 by Brenda Streater Jackson

HIDDEN PLEASURES
Copyright © 2010 by Brenda Streater Jackson

Printed in U.S.A.

CONTENTS

Dear Reader,

I love writing about the Westmorelands because they exemplify what a strong family is all about, mainly the sharing of love and support. For that reason, when I was given the chance to present them in a trilogy, I was excited and ready to dive into the lives of Zane, Canyon and Stern Westmoreland.

It is hard to believe that Canyon is my twenty-fifth Westmoreland novel. It seemed like it was only yesterday when I introduced you to Delaney and her five brothers. I knew by the time I wrote Thorn's story that I just had to tell you about their cousins that were spread out over Montana, Texas, California and Colorado.

It has been an adventure and I enjoyed sharing it with you. I've gotten your emails and snail mails letting me know how much you adore those Westmoreland men, and I appreciate hearing from you. Each Westmoreland—male or female—is unique and the way love conquers their hearts is heartwarming, breathtaking and totally satisfying.

In this story, Canyon is in for a shocker when he discovers his former girlfriend's closely guarded secret. And then he has to learn to forgive a woman who has a problem with forgiving herself.

I hope you enjoy this story about Canyon and Keisha Ashford.

Happy reading!

Brenda Jackson

CANYON

* * *

To my husband, the love of my life and my best friend,
Gerald Jackson, Sr.

To the members of the Brenda Jackson Support Team,
this one is for you!

A merry heart doeth good like a medicine:
but a broken spirit drieth the bones.
—*Proverbs,* 17:22

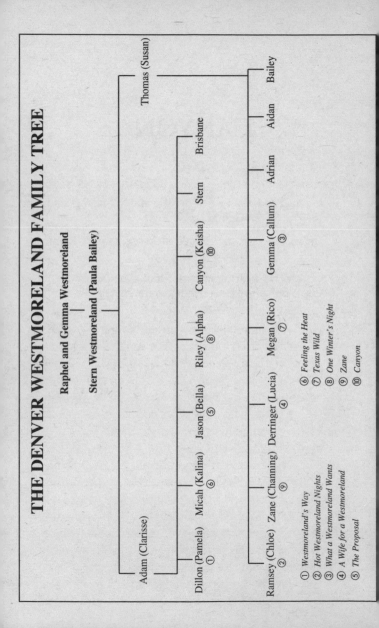

THE DENVER WESTMORELAND FAMILY TREE

Raphel and Gemma Westmoreland

Stern Westmoreland (Paula Bailey)

Thomas (Susan)

Adam (Clarisse)

Dillon (Pamela) ①　Micah (Kalina) ⑥　Jason (Bella) ⑤　Riley (Alpha) ⑧　Canyon (Keisha) ⑩　Stern　Brisbane

Ramsey (Chloe) ②　Zane (Channing) ⑨　Derringer (Lucia) ④　Megan (Rico) ⑦　Gemma (Callum) ③　Adrian　Aidan　Bailey

① *Westmoreland's Way*
② *Hot Westmoreland Nights*
③ *What a Westmoreland Wants*
④ *A Wife for a Westmoreland*
⑤ *The Proposal*
⑥ *Feeling the Heat*
⑦ *Texas Wild*
⑧ *One Winter's Night*
⑨ *Zane*
⑩ *Canyon*

One

Canyon Westmoreland was tempted to get out of the parked car and stretch his legs, but decided against it. The one thing he'd learned from watching cop shows was that when you were on a stakeout, you did nothing to give yourself away. You remained as inconspicuous as possible. And as far as he was concerned, he was on a stakeout, determined to find out once and for all why Keisha Ashford refused to give him the time of day.

He was very much aware that she hated his guts because she believed he had betrayed her with another woman. And he knew that assumption was the reason she'd left town three years ago, cutting all ties with him, and was also the reason why she felt that, upon returning to Denver, she had every right to act as if he didn't exist.

However, he had put up with it long enough.

They were both corporate attorneys, a profession which had brought them together initially, and a profession that still placed them together on a number of occasions. Since she'd returned to Denver ten months ago, they'd sat across from each other at the negotiating table for more than one business deal. And it bothered him when she acted as if they didn't share a past.

A number of times he had approached her about straightening things out between them, if for no other reason than so they could have closure, but she always turned him down.

Well, he'd had enough. He refused to allow another day to go by with her thinking he had betrayed her.

So here he was, parked outside the law firm where she worked. Canyon planned to follow her home and confront her. They would finally have that discussion she'd been refusing to give him.

His brothers Stern and Riley had warned him that she had the right to call the police if she felt harassed. But he hoped she wouldn't feel that way. He wasn't trying to harass her. He only wanted to talk to her.

He glanced at his watch. Since he wasn't sure what time she got off work, he'd been parked here for more than an hour now, leaving early from his job at his family's company—Blue Ridge Land Management—to make sure he didn't miss her.

He'd moved to switch channels on the radio when his cell phone rang. He pulled it out of his pocket and frowned when he saw it was his brother. He clicked the phone on.

"What do you want, Stern?"

"Just calling to see if you've been arrested yet."

Canyon rolled his eyes. "I won't be getting arrested."

"Don't be too sure of that. No woman likes being stalked."

Canyon's hand tightened on the steering wheel. "I'm not stalking her."

Stern chuckled. "So what do you call your plan of waiting in front of her office with the intention of following her home?"

Canyon adjusted his tall frame in the seat to find a more comfortable position. "I wouldn't have to follow her if she'd told me where she lives."

"There's a chance the reason she didn't tell you is because she doesn't want you to know," Stern said. "Her house is her territory, and you're forcing yourself into her space. She might not like that."

Canyon was about to tell his brother that at this point he couldn't care less about what she liked when he saw Keisha and another woman walk out of the building together. They were conversing and smiling, headed to their cars. Both were nice-looking women, but his gaze was focused solely on Keisha. He thought the same thing now that he'd thought the first time he'd met her. She was an incredibly beautiful woman.

She still had creamy brown skin that highlighted dark brown eyes, a perky nose and high cheekbones. And she still wore her silky black hair straight and parted in the center. It brushed against her shoulders. Just looking at her full lips made him remember how they tasted, which in turn made him hungry for them. He wished he didn't recall the many times he'd spent devouring her mouth.

But there was something different about her shapely body in that navy A-line skirt and pretty blue blouse. Was it his imagination, or did her hips really appear curvier and her breasts slightly larger than what he remembered?

Regardless of whether his memory was playing tricks on him or not, Keisha Ashford looked good.

He shifted in his seat again, thinking some things didn't change, even his desire for a woman who couldn't stand him.

But he had no problem remembering a time when she *could* stand him. Those had been the best times of his life. He'd never thought he would be ready to settle down with a woman before his thirty-fifth birthday, but he had fallen for Keisha quickly and had been ready to pop the question—before a lie had torn them apart.

He released a deep sigh as his gaze continued to soak her in, every single detail, especially those legs, which could wrap so firmly around a man's waist—

"Canyon, are you still there?"

He blinked upon remembering he still had Stern on the phone. "Yes, I'm here. But I have to go. Keisha just walked out and I need to follow her."

"Be careful, bro. It's been a long time since a Westmoreland was put in jail. I'm sure you remember those days."

He drew in a deep breath. How could he forget? There was only one Westmoreland with a jail record. As a teen, his baby brother Brisbane—known around Denver as *Badass Bane*—had gotten into enough trouble for all of them. Now Bane was serving his country as a kicking-the-enemy-ass navy SEAL.

"It won't get that far, Stern. I'm no threat to Keisha. I just want to talk to her."

"You weren't a threat to her before, but that didn't stop her from almost slapping a restraining order on you. Look, Canyon, it's your business but—"

"I know, I know, Stern. You don't want me to do anything to bring shame on the family."

Keisha and the woman had parted ways, and Keisha was now walking alone toward her car. She still had that walk that he thought was as sexy as hell. Although she moved like a model, she had the look of a cool professional in her four-inch pumps with her briefcase in hand.

"Canyon!"

He jumped. "Look, Stern. I'll call you later."

Without giving his brother a chance to say anything else, Canyon clicked off the phone. He watched as Keisha sized up her surroundings before opening her car and getting inside. Although she had glanced in his direction she hadn't seen him. He was parked behind a couple of cars.

He gave her time to start her car and pull out of her parking spot. Then, just as he was about to pull out of his own parking spot, a car darted out in front of him.

"What the hell," Canyon muttered, hitting his brakes. "What damn fire is he rushing off to?"

Not wanting to lose Keisha, he pulled in behind the black sedan, keeping her vehicle within his vision. After tailing her for a few blocks, he became uneasy. It seemed the car in front of him—the black sedan—was tailing her, as well.

As an attorney, Canyon was aware there were times when clients of the opposing council didn't like a court's decision and wanted to make that dislike known. That could be what was happening here. He didn't want to think of other possibilities, like a carjacking. They'd had a number of those lately around the city.

Canyon's protective instincts kicked in when Keisha turned a corner to head away from town and the driver of the black sedan did, too. He couldn't tell if the person driving the car in front of him was male or female because the windows were tinted. But he *could* make out the license plate number.

He pushed the phone button on his steering wheel. "Yes, Mr. Westmoreland, may I help you?"

"Yes, Samuel. Please connect me with Pete Higgins."

Pete was best friends with his cousin Derringer and was a deputy with Denver's police department.

"Please hold on for the connection."

It didn't take long for Pete to come on the line. "Deputy Higgins."

"Pete. This is Canyon. I need you to check out a license plate number."

"Why?"

Although Canyon knew Pete had every right to ask that question, he couldn't keep his irritation from escalating. "A woman is being followed."

"And you know this how?"

Canyon bit his lip to keep from cursing. His patience was stretched to the limit. "I know because I'm following her, as well."

"Oh. And why are *you* following her?"

Canyon had always admired Pete's easy, laid-back manner. Until now. "Now look, Pete."

"No, you look, Canyon. No one should be following a woman, not you or anybody else. That's harassment and I can bring you both in for stalking. What's the license plate number?"

A mad-as-hell Canyon rattled off the number while wondering why Keisha hadn't noticed she was being followed by not one, but two vehicles.

"Um, this is interesting," Pete said.

"What?" Canyon asked, annoyed.

"That license plate was stolen."

"Stolen?"

The driver in the sedan was smart enough not to follow behind Keisha too closely. But evidently he wasn't smart enough to pick up on the fact that he or she was being followed by Canyon. Maybe the driver was so busy keeping up with Keisha that he hadn't noticed what was going on behind him.

"Yes. According to our system, that license plate was reported stolen earlier today. Where are you?"

"Right now I'm going through the intersection of Firestone Road and Tinsel, and heading toward Purcell Park Road."

"You're way on the other side of town," Pete noted.

"Yeah." Canyon wondered if Keisha had deliberately chosen to live on the opposite side of Denver from where the Westmorelands lived.

"Is she driving a nice car?" Pete asked.

"Yes, looks like a pretty new Bimmer. Why?"

"I'm thinking that you might be looking at a possible carjacking. I'm on my way. Don't do anything stupid until I get there."

Canyon rolled his eyes. Did that mean he could do something stupid *after* Pete got there?

The thought of someone stalking Keisha angered him, and he quickly pushed to the back of his mind the thought that he was doing basically the same thing. The big difference was that Canyon didn't intend to hurt one single hair on Keisha's head. He couldn't say the same for the bozo in front of him.

The last thing the other driver needed to know was where she lived. If she was heading home, he didn't have time to wait for Pete. Pete's office was on the other side of town. There was no telling how long it would take him to get here. At that moment, Canyon made a decision.

He would handle the situation himself.

* * *

Keisha swayed her body to the music blaring out of her car radio. She loved satellite stations with continuous commercial-free music, and she especially liked this channel, which played her favorite hits nonstop. And today she needed to hear them.

It had been one of those kinds of days.

It had started at ten, in court. She'd barely had time to grab lunch before rushing back to the courthouse for another case at one. Around three, she had returned to her office only to be pulled into a meeting she'd forgotten about. She was glad to have left work to start what would be a busy weekend.

Even knowing everything she had to do over the next two days did not dampen her mood. She'd won three cases this week, and she knew her bosses, Leonard Spivey and Adam Whitlock, were pleased.

Three years ago, Leonard hadn't liked it when she'd given him only a week's notice before leaving Denver and moving back home to Texas. But because she'd been one of the firm's best attorneys, he'd been kind enough to give her a very good recommendation—and to welcome her back to the firm when she'd needed to return.

Sometimes things happened for a reason. When she'd moved to Texas, it hadn't taken her long to land another job at a law firm in Austin. And had she not returned home, she probably would not have found out about her mother's breast cancer scare.

Luckily, Keisha had been there for her mother during that difficult time. The two of them had always been close. Lynn Ashford was a strong and independent single parent. After the man who'd fathered Keisha denied she was his, Lynn had moved away from her hometown of Austin and settled with her daughter in Baton Rouge.

Then, when Keisha's grandfather had died when she was fifteen, she and her mother had returned to Austin to be there for Keisha's grandmother.

There had been many hard times while growing up. To compensate, her mother had worked two jobs, leaving Keisha in the care of her grandmother. But seeing how hard her mother had worked without the help of a man had shown Keisha that if push came to shove, she could do the same.

Her heart ached when she thought about the man who had proved that fact to her.

Canyon Westmoreland.

She'd fallen in love with him the first day she'd laid eyes on him, but that love ended when she discovered he'd been unfaithful to her. She could tolerate a lot of things, but the one thing she wouldn't tolerate was infidelity. Trust was paramount and a loss of it meant an end to everything…even a relationship that had held so much promise. Or she'd thought it'd had promise. Obviously she had been wrong.

Now, after three years, she was back in Denver. The scandal that had hit the law firm where she'd worked in Austin, and the firm's eventual shutdown by the Texas Bar and the justice department, had made leaving a necessity. She'd known she would miss her mom, and that she was taking a chance with her decision to return to Denver, but Spivey and Whitlock was the one law office where she wouldn't have to start at the bottom. She needed the money because she had more than herself to think about these days. However, to assure that she didn't run into Canyon, other than for business, she'd deliberately moved clear on the other side of town from Westmoreland Country.

She knew the story of how Canyon's parents, aunt and uncle had died in a plane crash, leaving fifteen orphans. Staying together hadn't been easy, especially since several of the siblings and cousins had been under the age of sixteen. But together, the Westmoreland family had weathered hard times and was now enjoying the good times thanks to the success of the family's land management firm, Blue Ridge.

Canyon's parents had had seven sons: Dillon, Micah, Jason, Riley, Canyon, Stern and Brisbane. His aunt and uncle had had eight children: five boys—Ramsey, Zane, Derringer and the twins Aiden and Adrian; and three girls—Megan, Gemma and Bailey. From what Keisha knew, the majority of the Westmorelands were now college educated and successful in their own right, either working for the family firm or in their chosen profession. She'd met most of them when she had attended the annual Westmoreland Ball while she was dating Canyon. The ball was a huge event in the city and benefited a number of charities.

Her thoughts shifted back to one Westmoreland in particular. Canyon.

The *Grand Canyon,* as she would sometimes call him during more intimate moments.

The memories of those times hurt the most. She had loved him and had believed he loved her. She had opened her heart, and her home, to him. He had moved in with her after they'd dated for six months. She'd assumed their relationship was moving in the right direction. He had proved her wrong.

The blaring of a horn prompted her to glance in her rearview mirror. *What in the world?* she asked herself, frowning.

The drivers of the two cars behind her were engaging

in some kind of road rage. It appeared that the driver of a burgundy car was trying to run the driver of a black sedan off the road.

Deciding the last thing she needed was to get involved in what was going on with those two drivers, she increased her speed and drove on ahead, leaving behind what she perceived as two hotheads vying to be king of the road.

Keisha checked the clock on the dashboard. She was eager to reach her destination and the person waiting for her there.

Canyon watched the black sedan speed off. Although he'd gotten pretty close to the car, the tinted windows had prevented him from determining if the driver had been a man or a woman, but he was leaning more toward a man.

He returned his attention to the road in time to see Keisha turn the corner a couple of blocks ahead. He continued to keep his distance, not wanting her to know she was being followed. It had been a long time since he'd been in this section of Denver, but because of the nature of his business, he knew about all the new development in the area. Several housing communities had been constructed, along with a number of shopping places and restaurants.

He watched Keisha put on her car's right blinker to turn into what he at first thought was a doctor's complex. Upon getting a better view of the huge sign out front, he saw it was Mary's Little Lamb Day Care. He frowned. Why would she be stopping at a day care? Maybe she was doing one of her coworkers a favor by picking up their child, or she could have volunteered to babysit tonight for someone.

He slid into a parking spot and watched as she got out of her car and went inside, smiling. That probably meant she was ready for the weekend to begin. Hopefully, her good mood would continue when she saw that he'd followed her home. His focus stayed on her, concentrating on the sway of her hips with every step she took, until she was no longer in sight.

He was about to change stations on his radio when his cell phone rang. He hoped it wasn't Stern again. He pulled it out of his pocket and saw it was his cousin Bailey, the youngest of the Westmoreland siblings and cousins living in Denver. Growing up, Bailey had been nearly as bad as Bane when it came to getting into trouble.

He clicked the phone on. "What's up, Bay?"

"Zane's back. He got in today."

Canyon nodded. His cousin Zane had left town a good three weeks ago on what Canyon had assumed was a business trip, only to discover later that his cousin was running behind a woman he'd once had an affair with by the name of Channing Hastings. Rumor had it that Zane was returning home with a wedding band on his finger.

"He's married?"

"Not yet. He and Channing are talking about a Christmas wedding."

A Christmas wedding? It was hard to believe Zane, a die-hard bachelor, was thinking about settling down.

"Didn't think I'd live to see the day."

"Well, I'm glad he came to his senses." Bailey paused and then said, "Don't forget this is chow-down night."

Every other Friday night, the Westmorelands got together at his brother Dillon's place. The women would do the cooking and the men would arrive hungry. Afterward, the men took part in a poker game and the women did whatever they pleased.

"I might be a little late," he said, since he wasn't sure how his confrontation with Keisha would go. If she was babysitting somebody's kid, he would follow her home just to see where she lived and then return at another time and try to talk to her. At some point, he needed to let her know about the person who'd been following her. It might be something she needed to check into, especially if it was related to a case she was working on.

"Why?"

He frowned at Bailey's question. "Why what?"

"Why will you be late? Dillon mentioned you left work early today."

For some reason Bailey assumed being the youngest automatically made her privy to everyone's business. Instead of answering her, he tapped on the phone several times and then said, "Sounds like we have a bad connection, Bay. I'll talk to you later."

He clicked the phone off in time to see Keisha walk back out of the building. Studying her face he saw she was still smiling, which was a good sign. She was also chatting with the little boy whose hand she was holding—a boy who was probably around two years old.

Canyon studied the little boy's features. "WTF," he muttered under his breath. The kid could be a double for Denver, Dillon's three-year-old son. In fact, if Canyon didn't know for certain that Denver was at home with Dillon's wife, Pam, he would think it was Denver's hand that Keisha was holding. An uneasy feeling stirred his insides as he continued to study the little boy whose smile was just as big as Keisha's.

Canyon took in a gasping breath. There was only one reason the little boy looked so much like a Westmoreland. Canyon gripped the steering wheel, certain steam was coming out of his ears and nose.

He didn't remember easing his seat back, unbuckling his seat belt or opening the car door. Neither did he remember walking toward Keisha. However, he would always remember the look on her face when she stopped walking and glanced in his direction. What he saw in her features was surprise, guilt and remorse.

As he got closer he watched defensiveness followed by fierce protectiveness replace those other emotions. She stopped walking and pulled her son—the child he was certain was *their* son—closer to her side. "What are you doing here, Canyon?"

He came to a stop in front of her. His body was radiating anger from the inside out. His gaze left her face and looked down at the little boy who was clutching the hem of Keisha's skirt and staring up at him with distrustful eyes that were almost identical to his mother's.

Canyon shifted his gaze back up to meet Keisha's eyes. In a voice shaking with fury, he asked, "Would you like to tell me why I didn't know I had a son?"

Two

Keisha drew in a deep breath while thinking about what she would say, and from Canyon's tone of voice she knew it better be good. She'd often wondered how he would react when he found out he had a son. Would he deny her child was his like her own father had done with her?

Instead of answering his question, she countered with one of her own. "Would it have mattered had you known?"

She saw surprise flash in his eyes just seconds before his lips formed a tight line. "Of course it would have mattered," he said with affront. "Now tell me why I wasn't told."

Keisha could tell by the way her son held tight to her skirt that he sensed something was wrong, and she knew how anxious he got around strangers. Although she wished otherwise, the time had come for her and Canyon to talk. But not now and not here.

"I need to get Beau home and—"

"Beau?"

She lifted her chin. "Yes. My son's name is Beau Ashford."

The anger that flashed across his face was quick. And although he muttered the words, "Not for long," under his breath, she heard them.

She slowly pulled in a deep breath and then carefully exhaled it. "Like I said, Canyon. I need to get Beau home to prepare dinner and then—"

"Fine," he cut in before she finished. "Whatever you have planned for tonight, I'm included."

Like hell he was. "Now look here, Canyon. I—"

She stopped talking when she saw Pauline Sampson, owner of the day care, approaching them. Pauline had been one of Keisha's first clients when she'd begun practicing law five years ago. She was also a friend of Mr. Spivey's wife, Joan. Pauline was smiling but Keisha saw deep concern in every curve of the woman's lips. There was also a degree of curiosity in her eyes.

"Keisha, I happened to glance out my window and saw you were still here. I just wanted to make sure everything was okay," Pauline said smoothly.

If everything wasn't okay, Keisha had no intention of letting Pauline know. "Yes, everything is fine, Pauline." She hadn't planned on making introductions, and she was aware that Canyon knew it. She really wasn't surprised when he took it upon himself to make the introductions himself.

Extending his hand out to Pauline, he said, "How are you, Pauline? I'm Canyon Westmoreland, Beau's father."

Keisha watched Pauline's brow lift in surprise. "Westmoreland?"

Canyon flashed Pauline what Keisha knew to be his dashing smile, one known to win over jurors in the courtroom. "Yes, Westmoreland."

She saw interest shine in Pauline's eyes. "Are you related to Dillon Westmoreland?"

Canyon kept his smile in place. "Yes, Dillon is my oldest brother."

Pauline's smile widened. "Small world. I can definitely see the resemblance. Dillon and I went to high school together and serve on the boards of directors of several businesses in town."

"Yes, it is a small world," Canyon agreed, glancing at his watch. "If you don't mind excusing us, Pauline, Keisha and I need to get Beau home for dinner."

"Oh, not at all," Pauline said, beaming. "I understand." She then glanced up at Keisha. "Have a good weekend."

Keisha doubted that would happen now. "You, too, Pauline."

She knew not to waste time talking Canyon out of following her home. He wanted her to answer his question—not tomorrow or next week, but tonight.

When Pauline turned to go back inside, Keisha moved toward her car and gasped in surprise when Canyon reached down and picked up Beau. Keisha opened her mouth to warn him that Beau didn't take well to strangers. She closed it when instead of screaming at the top of his lungs, Beau wrapped his arms around Canyon's neck.

Canyon adjusted their son in his arms. "I'll carry him to the car for you."

She frowned. "He can walk."

"I know he can, but I want to carry him. Humor me."

Keisha didn't want to humor him. She didn't want to have anything to do with him. Father or no father, if Canyon thought he could bombard his way into her or Beau's lives, he had another think coming. He'd made his choice three years ago.

She tried pushing her mother's warning to the back of her mind. When Keisha had discovered her pregnancy and shared the news with her mother, Lynn had warned her not to assume Canyon would be like Kenneth Drew. Lynn believed every man had a right to know he'd fathered a child, which is why she had told Kenneth. Only after his decision not to accept Keisha as his child had Lynn ceased including Kenneth in her daughter's life.

Lynn felt Keisha hadn't given Canyon a chance to either accept or reject his child, and he should be given that choice. Keisha hadn't felt that way. Knowing her father had rejected her had tormented her all through childhood and right into her adult life. It had been her decision to never let her son experience the grief of rejection.

When they reached her car, she opened the door to the backseat and moved aside to watch Canyon place Beau in his car seat. Then another surprise happened. Beau actually protested and tried reaching for Canyon to get back into his arms.

"It seems he likes you," Keisha muttered, truly not happy with it at all.

Canyon glanced over his shoulder at her. "It's a Westmoreland thing."

Keisha didn't say anything. If that was his way of letting her know his son should have been born with his name, he'd done so effectively.

"From now on, partner, I'll never be too far away,"

she heard him say to Beau and wondered if he realized he needed her permission for that to happen. When it came to her son, he would only have the rights she gave him.

As if Beau understood, he then spoke to Canyon for the first time. Pointing his finger at himself, he said, "Me Beau." He then pointed at Canyon. "You?"

Canyon chuckled and Keisha knew he had deliberately said the next words loud enough for her to hear. "Dad."

Beau repeated the word *dad* as if he needed to say it. "Dad."

Canyon chuckled. "Yes, Dad." He then closed the car door and turned to Keisha.

Ignoring the fierce frown on his face, she said, "You seem to be good with kids."

He shrugged. "Dillon has a son named Denver who's a little older than Beau, and I'm around him a lot. They favor."

She lifted a brow. "Who?"

"Beau and Denver. Although Denver is a little taller, if you put them in a room together it might be hard to tell them apart."

It was Keisha's time to shrug. She would know her son anywhere. Besides, she couldn't imagine the two kids looking that much alike. "Since you insist that we need to talk today, you can follow me home. But I don't intend to break my routine with Beau because of you."

"I don't expect you to."

She moved to walk around to the driver's side of the car when he reached out and touched her. Immediately, heat raced up her spine and she was forced to remember the raw masculine energy Canyon possessed. She'd have thought that after three years she would be immune to him, but it seemed nothing had changed in the sexual-chemistry department.

"Keisha?"

With her pulse throbbing, she fought to regain her composure. She lifted her chin. "What?"

He met her gaze and held it. "Is there any reason someone would be following you?"

"What are you talking about?" Keisha asked, frowning.

Canyon shoved his hands into his pockets. "I started following you from your job, but I wasn't the only one. A black sedan pulled out in front of me and whoever was behind the wheel followed you until a mile or so back. That's when I tried getting the driver's attention by driving close along the side of the car and forcing him or her to pull over. I don't know if the driver was a man or a woman since the windows were tinted. Instead of pulling over, the car made a quick right turn at the next corner and kept going."

Keisha remembered glancing in her rearview mirror and witnessing what she'd assumed were two drivers engaging in road rage. "You're driving a burgundy car?"

"Yes."

"I heard a horn blast and saw you trying to run that black car off the road. I figured it was nothing more than two drivers acting like fools."

"It wasn't. It was about me trying to find out why someone was following you. I even called the police to report it."

"The police?"

"Yes. Just so happens that Pete Higgins is a deputy and a friend of Derringer's. At the time, I only had a hunch you were being followed, so Pete checked it out as a favor. Then he got suspicious when he discovered the license plate had been reported as stolen. He's since phoned back to say they're still looking for the car."

Although Keisha had only met Derringer West-moreland once, during the Westmoreland Ball, she'd heard about him. Before marrying and settling down, he'd had a reputation of being quite the ladies' man. In fact, a number of male Westmorelands had claimed that reputation.

"Well, I have no idea why anyone would be follow-ing me. Why were you following me?"

"Because on a number of occasions over the past ten months, I've approached you, wanting to talk and you refused to give me the time of day. Now I know why."

Not wanting to get into it with Canyon about Beau now, because she was certain Pauline probably had her face glued to her office window, Keisha said, "We'll talk later."

"I'll be right behind you."

Canyon waited until Keisha had gotten into her car before crossing the parking lot to get into his. It was only when he had closed the door and snapped his seat belt that the impact of the past twenty minutes hit him hard.

He had a son. A son he hadn't known about until today.

With her heart pounding furiously in her chest, Kei-sha pulled out of the day care's parking lot. She thought about Canyon's assertion that a car had been follow-ing her. That didn't make sense. None of the cases she was working on were serious enough to warrant anyone wanting to harass her.

This was a new car she was driving, a very popular model. Perhaps the person had had carjacking in mind? Shivers raced through her at the thought.

When she came to a traffic light she glanced into the backseat to make sure Beau was okay. She couldn't get over how easily he had accepted Canyon.

And just how easily Canyon had accepted him.

Canyon hadn't demanded a DNA test for verification, instead he'd claimed that Beau favored Dillon's son. Had that been the reason why his acceptance had come without any hassles? Well, there hadn't been any hassles so far. They still had to talk, and someone who'd been as close to Canyon as she had been in the past knew that while he had a cool demeanor on the outside, he was simmering on the inside.

Keisha drew in a deep breath and exited onto the road that would take her home. Glancing in the rearview mirror her gaze met Canyon's as he seemed to look right at her. Gee whiz, did he have to look at her like that? With an intensity that had her dragging in more than one shaky breath and a rush of heat flooding her stomach, making it quiver. She gripped the steering wheel and refocused on her driving.

Canyon had always been able to get to her. At that moment, she couldn't help but remember the day nearly four years ago when they'd met…

"Excuse me. Is this seat taken?"

Keisha looked up from the papers she'd been reading. A shot of hard lust reverberated through her veins. Lordy. Standing in front of her had to be, without a doubt, a man who could get a "yes" out of a woman without even asking the first question.

He was tall, more than six feet, and she had to strain her neck to look up at him. He had smooth mahogany skin, dark eyes, a firm jaw and a too-delicious-looking pair of lips. Once she got past his facial features then she had to deal with his broad shoulders and a too-fine body in an immaculate business suit.

"So, is it?" he asked in a deep, sexy voice.

She self-consciously licked her lips. "Is what?"

"This seat taken? It seems to be the only one empty."

She glanced around the courthouse's lunchroom. He was telling the truth. "No, it's not taken."

"Mind if I join you?"

She had to bite her lips to keep from saying he could do anything he cared to do with her. Instead, she said, "No, I don't mind."

She watched as he pulled out a chair and settled his tall frame in the seat. She had to be in court in less than an hour. At any other time she would have been annoyed at being disturbed, but not this time. This man was worth the interruption.

Extending his hand out to her, he said, "I'm Canyon Westmoreland. And you are?"

"Keisha. Keisha Ashford." She accepted his hand and wished she hadn't. Her belly vibrated the moment they touched. And then, suddenly, it seemed the room quieted and they were the only two people in it. The only thing she heard was the sound of their breathing. The way he stared into her eyes made her breath catch. She felt the rush through her veins.

The sound of silverware hitting the floor made her blink, and she realized Canyon still had her hand. She tugged and he released it.

"So, Keisha Ashford, are you an attorney or a para-legal?"

She lifted a brow. "Does it matter?"

He shrugged broad shoulders. "Not with me. I'm sharing a table with a beautiful woman and I'm not complaining about anything."

She chuckled, appreciating his compliment. "You sound easy."

"Um, maybe."

A smile spread across her lips. She liked him. She had checked out his ring finger. It was bare, with no indication that a ring had once been there. "I'm an attorney."

"So am I," he said smoothly.

"I can tell. You look the part," she said.

He leaned over the table and she drew in his intoxicating male scent. "Let's meet later so you can tell me what you mean by that."

Oh, she thought. He was good. As smooth as silk. Any other time, and with anyone else, she would have brushed off what was definitely a flirtatious come-on. But not today. And, for some reason, not with Canyon Westmoreland.

Instead of agreeing to his suggestion, she said, "Canyon is an unusual name."

"Not according to my parents," he said, smiling. "I was conceived one night in the Grand Canyon, so they felt my name fit. I understand it was one hell of a night."

She tilted her head. "Your parents told you that?"

"No, but I heard them share a private joke about it every once in a while. It brought them fond memories for years."

"And what do they think now?"

She saw a flash of pain flare in his eyes. "I don't know. My parents were killed in a plane crash a little over fifteen years ago."

"Oh, I'm sorry," she said.

"Thanks. Now what about meeting me later for drinks? There's a place not far from here. Woody's." He

glanced at his watch. "Around five. Hopefully, if we win our individual cases, we will have reason to celebrate."

She smiled. "That would be nice. I'll be there."

He tipped his head and the smile that spread across his lips was priceless...and sexy as hell. "Good. I'll look forward to later, Keisha Ashford."

She swallowed as his gaze raked over her in a way that had her skin scorching. At that moment she was drenched in full awareness of him and could only respond by saying truthfully, "So will I...."

"Mommy."

Keisha's thoughts returned to the present at the sound of her son's voice. He had been busy playing with one of his toys while sitting in his car seat. Beau was just as high-spirited as any other two-year-old and typically never stopped talking except when shoving food into his mouth. But today things were different. She couldn't help wondering if Canyon's presence had something to do with it.

"Yes, Beau?"

"Dad gone?"

Was that disappointment she heard in his voice? Moving here from Texas had been hard for him. Her mother had become a regular fixture in his life and the first months away from his grandmother hadn't been easy. Beau had made her fully aware what tantrums were about.

"He's in the car behind us."

She looked in the mirror and saw Beau trying to twist his body around in his car seat. "Why?"

She lifted a brow. "Why?"

"He not here. Our car?"

Keisha felt a headache coming on and knew after

Canyon's visit she would have to have a talk with her son. "Because he has his own car."

"Go home with us?"

"Yes." Too late she realized how that sounded and quickly moved to clear it up. "He has his own home. Not ours."

"Not our house?"

"No, not our house."

He didn't say anything, but went back to playing with his toy. When they got home she would feed him dinner, give him a bath and then let him have a little playtime before putting him in bed. When it came to bedtime, she was lucky. Beau didn't have the issues some other kids did with fighting sleep. He eagerly went to bed each night as if it was his God-given right to get eight hours or more of sleep.

She glanced back into her rearview mirror at the car still following closely behind her. Her gaze connected with Canyon's once again.

She no longer loved him, she was sure of it. Her love hadn't dissipated immediately but in slow degrees. And just to think—she had planned to tell him about her pregnancy when she had returned home early and found him with Bonita.

She broke eye contact to face the road ahead, which is what she'd been doing since that night. And she didn't intend to look back again.

Moments later she was pulling into the driveway of the home she considered hers. The community was a new one, and most of the families were progressive couples or singles with small children. She'd already joined the homeowners association and knew several of her neighbors. It was a friendly neighborhood and she enjoyed living here.

She brought the car to a stop and then got out. She had moved around to the side of the car by the time Canyon got out of his. She glanced over at him and said, "I really wish you'd wait and talk to me at another time."

"We don't always get what we want, Keisha."

Feeling frustrated and annoyed, she narrowed her eyes at him and opened the door to get Beau out of his seat.

"I'll do that," Canyon said.

She stepped aside to let him, not wanting to make a scene in front of Beau. However, the main thing she intended to do when they talked was to make it absolutely clear that while he might be Beau's father, she would not allow him to bulldoze his way into their lives.

Pulling her keys from her purse, she moved up the walkway to her front door. Canyon followed with Beau in his arms. She was tempted to remind Canyon once again that Beau could walk, but decided to keep quiet for now.

The moment she opened the door, Keisha knew something was wrong. For starters, the chime from her security alarm didn't sound. And when she took a step inside and glanced around, she gasped in horror.

Someone had broken into her home.

Three

Canyon quickly went into action and handed Beau to Keisha. "Take Beau and get back in the car."

Already he was on the phone calling Pete. "This is Canyon. The woman who was being followed earlier today had her home broken into."

"What's the address? I'm still in the area. Don't mess with anything."

Canyon turned around, not surprised that Keisha hadn't gone back to the car like he'd told her to do. "What's the address?" He could tell from her dazed look that she was still in shock at what she'd found when she'd opened her door.

"Keisha?"

She looked at him. "Yes?"

"What's this address?"

She rattled a number off to him which he gave to Pete.

"Home messy, Mommy."

Their son's words made Keisha suck in a deep breath and Canyon saw how Beau's innocent words had crushed her. This was the home she had made for her and their son and someone had invaded her sanctuary. They had violated it.

"Come on, let's step outside, Keisha. The police are on the way," he said softly. When she opened her mouth to protest, he added, "We can't touch anything until they get here."

Keisha closed her mouth and drew in a deep breath, feeling the pain in her chest when she did so. Canyon, she knew, was intentionally blocking her view but she'd already seen her living room and could just imagine how the rest of her house looked. Had the intruder gone into her bedroom? Beau's room? What had been stolen?

"Keisha?"

"Yes?" The single word had been hard to get past her lungs.

"Come on, let's sit in the car."

She hesitated but knew what he was suggesting was reasonable. There was nothing they could do until the police arrived and Beau could tell she was troubled. She didn't want to upset him.

"Play, Mommy," Beau said when they reached her car. She placed him back in his car seat and gave him his favorite toy. When she went around to get into her seat, she noticed Canyon talking on his cell phone. Was he talking to the police again?

"Yes, Keisha's okay, Dil," Canyon told his oldest brother. He'd given Dillon a quick rundown on what had transpired over the past hour, including the fact that he had a son.

"Everyone is here for dinner, so how do you want me

to handle things?" Dillon asked. "I'm sure you'll want to be the one to tell them about Beau."

Canyon drew in a deep breath. "Yes, I want to be the one. Pete is on the way. When we finish here, Keisha and Beau are coming with me until we figure out who did this and why. I'm leaving my car here so I'll need someone to pick it up and drive it to my place later."

"I can do that. But will Keisha agree to go anywhere with you, Canyon?"

Canyon rubbed a frustrated hand down his face. He was more than certain she wouldn't. At least not at first. Keisha had an independent streak that she'd inherited from the single mother who had raised her. He'd always admired her ability to stand her ground and not depend on anyone for anything. But in this case things were different. She didn't have just herself to think about. She had their son.

Their son.

The thought sent an unexplainable thrill through his veins. "No, Dil, she's not going to go along with it, at least not easily. But I'm convinced what happened to her house and that car following her today are connected. My only ace is that she has Beau to think about. If it was just her she would dig in her heels."

At that moment three police cruisers pulled up and the one leading the pack was driven by Pete. "Pete's here now, Dil. I'll call you back later."

Keisha stared at the policeman in confusion. "What do you mean I was targeted personally?"

Pete leaned against the kitchen counter as he stood beside Canyon. "You've verified that nothing of value was taken, not even that container filled with gold coins sitting in plain view on the dresser in your bedroom. My only conclusion is that the person who did this didn't take anything because this is about you personally. It seems to be more or less a scare tactic."

None of this made sense. She had been grateful that her next-door neighbors, a couple with a set of twins a few months older than Beau, had come over and offered to take him to their place, feed him dinner and keep him entertained while she handled the break-in.

With Canyon and Pete by her side, she had gone from room to room taking in the devastation. Her sofa and chairs had been turned over, pillow cushions thrown about along with her magazines. In her kitchen, the person had opened a canister and floured her counters to the point where it looked like snow in August. Not one bedroom had been left untouched…not even Beau's room. Some of his favorite toys had been broken. And in her bedroom, in addition to her clothes, which had been pulled out of the drawers and strewn about, the intruder had left water running in the bathtub to flood the floors.

What Pete said was right. Nothing of value had been taken. Not the coin collection her mother had started for Beau, not the set of expensive purses in her closet or any of her big screen televisions. The only thing the person had done was trash every part of her home as if he'd been trying to make a statement. However, she was clueless as to what statement that could be.

"Think hard, Ms. Ashford. Are there any cases you're working on that someone would want to scare you away from?" Pete asked.

For the life of her she couldn't think of one case, past or present, where anyone could want to extract some kind of revenge. She had won all her cases lately, except for one, and none of the cases were such that either party would encounter any financial hardship.

"I honestly can't think of any case like that, Deputy Higgins."

Pete nodded and shoved his notepad into his pocket. "If you think of anything later, let me know. I'm turning this over to a detective who will contact you. There is also the issue of the car that was following you earlier today, the one Canyon reported."

She'd almost forgotten about that.

"You think the two are related?" Canyon asked before she could.

"Right now, Canyon, I'm not discounting anything. By the time I reached the area where the car was supposed to be, you had taken matters into your own hands and run the guy off. I should have known it was too much to expect a Westmoreland to do what he was told."

"Whatever," Canyon said, shoving his hands into his pockets and then releasing a deep breath. "So what's next?"

"We're still looking for the vehicle. I'm going to pull the videos from the red-light cameras and traffic-surveillance cameras in the area. I hope they'll reveal something. Although we already know the license plate was stolen and the car was a black Ford sedan, if we have a picture of the vehicle itself we can determine if there are any dents or scratches that might make the car stand out. If there are, then it will make locating the vehicle easier. I want to find the person who did this."

"So do I."

Keisha and Pete looked at Canyon. It wasn't what he'd said, but how he'd said it, in a low, threatening tone. In a way, she wasn't surprised by his reaction. She'd felt the intense anger radiating from Canyon as he'd gone from room to room with her. She'd felt the hostility even more when he'd seen the senseless destruction in her and Beau's bedrooms.

Instead of either of them addressing what Canyon had said, Pete looked over at her. "I wouldn't advise you to stay here tonight. Whoever did this was able to bypass your security system."

"She won't be staying here," Canyon said before she could respond. "She's coming with me and will be staying at my place for a while."

"That's a good idea," Pete said as if that settled it.

It didn't. "Whoa. Wait a minute. I won't stay here, but I'm checking into a hotel," Keisha said.

Canyon looked at her. "No, you're not."

She placed her hands on her hips, stiffened her spine and narrowed her eyes at him. "Yes, I am."

"No, you're not."

Pete cleared his throat. "I'll let you two hash out those details without me. But if you remember anything at all, Ms. Ashford, call the precinct. Detective Ervin Render will be handling your case." Pete quickly left, as if he didn't want to get in the line of fire.

Even before Pete had cleared the doorway that separated the kitchen from the dining room, Keisha turned back to Canyon. "Now, wait just a damn minute, Canyon Westmoreland. Why should I stay with you when I can stay at a hotel? Besides, what I do or where I go is none of your business, so back off."

Hearing her sharp tone, any sane man would not have hesitated to do what she'd suggested. However, instead of backing off, Canyon took a step forward. The fierce expression on his face and the laser-sharp look in his eyes had her dropping her hands to her sides.

"Probably, if it was just you, I might back off, Keisha, since your decision about me three years ago proved just how little trust you have in me. You had the gall to believe I would admit to loving you and then sleep with another woman…in *your* bed."

She tightened her hands into fists at her sides. "I know what I saw, Canyon."

His eyes flared with anger. "And just what did you see? Did you see me screwing Bonita? Wrapped in her arms or she in mine? No. What you saw was me, naked except for the towel wrapped around my waist, stepping out of the bathroom from my shower to find Bonita lying in your bed."

Keisha's own anger escalated. "She was naked!"

"I saw that fact at the same time you did. I told you what happened. Bonita came by your place looking for you minutes after I got in from the gym. She was upset about some argument she'd had with her fiancé, Grant Palmer, and I offered her a drink to calm her down. She asked me to share it with her and I saw no reason not to. Afterward, she thanked me, said she needed to pull herself together and asked if she could stay for a few minutes because she was too upset to drive home. I told her yes, but that I needed to take a shower. I expected her to be gone when I got out of the bathroom, because she'd said she would be."

He paused a moment and then added, "I had no idea she had stripped off her clothes and gotten into your bed until I walked out and saw you standing in the middle of the bedroom with an accusing look in your eyes. I told you the truth. But you didn't believe me. You preferred believing the lie your friend Bonita told you instead."

"Why would she lie about it? She was engaged to marry Grant."

"Maybe that's a question for you to figure out since Bonita isn't around any longer to provide answers."

His remark was a stark reminder that Bonita had been killed last year in an early-morning pileup on Interstate 70, an accident that had killed ten people.

"I'm not going to waste time discussing our dramatic past," Canyon interrupted her thoughts to say. "What I am going to discuss is my son…a son I didn't know I had, dammit. And if you want to go sleep in a hotel room tonight without all the facts about who's trying to scare you enough to follow you home and then do this," he said, gesturing to the mess in her kitchen, "then go right ahead. But my son won't be going with you."

"Who the hell do you think you are telling me where *my* son won't be going?" she asked, taking a step closer and getting in his face.

"His father. And I think once you put your misplaced hatred for me aside, you'll agree that both of you going to Westmoreland Country would be the best thing. Would you feel safe living here?"

She tempered her anger somewhat as she took in his words. "I said I would go to a hotel."

"And what if the person finds out where you're staying? You still don't know why you're being targeted. Hell, you don't even know if it's a man or a woman. I'd think you would care about Beau's life even if you want to take chances with your own."

Keisha nibbled her bottom lip. Was Canyon deliberately trying to put the fear of God in her? She drew in a deep breath and glanced around. All it took was one look at her kitchen and the memory of the condition of the other rooms in her house. Canyon was right. Until she found out who'd done this and who had been following her earlier that day, she needed to do everything she could to keep Beau safe. And he would be safe with Canyon.

But what about her? She knew Canyon would never hurt her physically, but what about emotionally? It seemed he was still proclaiming his innocence as if she was supposed to believe him. She knew what she'd seen that night.

Keisha remembered Bonita's tearful admission that she and Canyon hadn't meant to sleep together. It had just happened. Bonita had gone to Keisha's place looking for her friend after a tiff she'd had with Grant, only to discover that Keisha hadn't yet returned from her out-of-town trip.

Bonita had been upset and to calm her down Canyon had given her something to drink, which he'd shared with her. They'd both drunk themselves silly and the next thing Bonita knew they were having sex on the floor in the living room. Canyon had taken a shower afterward and had asked Bonita to wait for him in bed.

And that was when Keisha had returned unexpectedly to find Bonita naked in bed and Canyon walking out of the bathroom wearing a towel around his middle.

Oh, he had pretended to be just as shocked as she'd been to see a naked Bonita, but Keisha hadn't bought his story then and she wasn't buying it now. There had been two empty wineglasses and Bonita's clothes had been thrown on the floor all over the place, corroborating Bonita's story.

But what if there was a smidgen of truth in what he'd said just now? What if the scene had been cunningly crafted by Bonita?

"It's getting late, Keisha, and we need to leave here," Canyon said, interrupting her thoughts.

Keisha held his gaze. Could she and Canyon spend a single day under the same roof and be civil to each other? Tomorrow was Saturday, and she had scheduled appointments to take Beau to the barbershop, do laundry, buy groceries and get her car washed. Now she would need the entire weekend to arrange the cleanup of her place. Right now she felt violated, and her main concern was keeping her son safe.

"One night," she heard herself saying. "I'll agree to stay one night." Then she thought about all that needed to be done here. "Maybe two."

Canyon frowned in exasperation. "Fine, do your two nights, but the invitation is open for as long as you need it. There's some nutcase out there and until Pete and that detective figure out what he has against you then I intend to keep you and Beau safe."

She bit her tongue to keep from telling him that neither she nor Beau needed him because that would be a lie. At this moment, with so much uncertainty in her life, for the next day…or two…she and Beau did need him.

Four

"Make yourself at home."

Keisha stepped over the threshold of Canyon's house and thought he had to be kidding. This wasn't a home, this was a friggin' castle.

It had been dark when they'd arrived but she had seen the lighted marker that denoted Westmoreland Country. And she had seen another marker that said Canyon's Bluff. Because it had been dark, she'd barely made out the massive structure until the car's headlights had shined on it. She'd sat in the car for a full minute, amazed.

He had been in the process of having the plans drawn up for the house when she'd left town. She had heard the story about how, after his parents' deaths, he and his brothers—upon reaching the age of twenty-five—inherited one hundred acres of land each...all except for

Dillon. Since Dillon was the oldest, he had inherited the family home and the three hundred acres it sat on.

Canyon and several of his brothers had been perfectly content living in the main house with Dillon until Dillon had married. That was when all the brothers had decided to build their own places. Canyon hadn't been in any hurry at first. When he'd moved from Dillon's home, he and his brother Stern moved in with their brother Jason, who'd had plenty of room. Eventually, Canyon had moved in with her.

"So what do you think, Keisha?"

She glanced over at him. He was holding a sleeping Beau in his arms while standing in the middle of what she figured was his living room, although it was three times the size of hers. "Can I ask you something, Canyon?"

"What?"

"Why would a single man need such a large place?"

When he smiled she felt a stirring in her belly. "At the time, I didn't think of needs, just wants. Four of my brothers and I were building our homes practically at the same time, and we all wanted something different and unique. You think this place is big, you ought to see Micah's Manor, Derringer's Dungeon, Riley's Station, Stern's Stronghold and Zane's Hideout."

She couldn't help grinning. "I gather all of your places have unique names."

"Yes. It was Bailey's idea."

"I think the names are cute," she said, reaching for Beau.

"Whatever," he said, handing their dozing son to her.

"Those were some pretty nice neighbors to take care of him like they did."

Keisha agreed. "Yes, and I appreciate them." Janice and Everett Miles were super. Not only had they fed Beau, but they'd given him a bath and put him in a pair of the twins' pajamas. Now she held her sleeping child in her arms as she looked around a house that was too large for one person. And it was decorated for a king…and a queen. The furniture was expensive and the decor perfect.

"You must have paid a lot in decorating costs," she said.

Canyon, who was moving around turning on lights, looked over his shoulder at her and chuckled. "I wish I could say my cousin Gemma came cheap but she didn't. She made plenty of money off her brothers and cousins and wasn't guilty about doing so."

"She did a great job."

"We got what we paid for. And if you ask me, we even paid for what we didn't get. I think she deliberately overcharged us because she figured she could get away with it."

Canyon's gruffness wasn't fooling Keisha one bit since she heard the fondness in his voice. That was one thing she'd always admired about him and his family— their closeness. He had told her all about his family, and it had been her choice not to get to know them better. While Canyon had been great company, and the sex had been off the charts, she hadn't thought their relationship would last. Initially, she'd thought their physical relationship was all she'd wanted or needed.

But Canyon had had a way of growing on her, and it had seemed she had started growing on him, as well. Within six months, she had invited him to move in with her. While living together they'd gotten along fabulously and things had been going really well…until the night he'd betrayed her.

"My guest rooms are furnished but with no kiddie beds," he said, interrupting her thoughts.

"No problem, he can sleep with me."

Canyon nodded. "Okay. Right this way."

There were two spiral staircases. He moved up one and she followed, thinking his house looked even more impressive when seen from the stairs. High ceilings, crown moldings, colorful walls, hardwood and tile floors as well as intricate lighting. Everything served the purpose of complimenting the grace and style of the house. Definitely not anything a man would have had a hand in.

"Unfortunately, my place isn't childproof either."

She didn't say anything. It didn't matter since she and Beau wouldn't be staying here that long anyway. When they reached the next floor he moved into a hallway that seemed to branch out in three directions. Even this area was beautifully decorated and a huge light fixture hung from the ceiling.

He moved down a corridor containing three bedrooms. Opening the door to one of the rooms, he stood back for her to enter. This guest room, she thought, was simply stunning. There was no other word for it.

"This is the blue room," he said.

She could see why. The walls were painted sky-blue with white billowy curtains around the windows. Plaid blue-and-white coverings were on the king-size bed. A white leather love seat was on one side of the room and two beautiful white ceramic lamps sat on nightstands on either side of the bed.

"It's pretty," she said.

"Thanks."

She walked across the white marble tile to the bed, pushed back the covers and placed Beau in the center.

She glanced down at their son who looked so peaceful while sleeping. Little did he know that his mother's world had just gone topsy-turvy.

"I used to do that."

She nearly jumped. She hadn't known Canyon had followed her over to the bed. "What?"

"Sleep curled up with my face resting on my hands."

She smiled. "And he makes those sounds in his sleep like you used to do."

She watched Canyon's brow rise. His eyes, normally so dark and intense, seemed even more so in the bedroom's low light. "What sounds?"

Those sounds you used to make that turned me on whenever I woke up to hear them, she thought. *Not a snore—more of a groan, as if you were having some hell of a dream.*

"So, what sounds?" he asked again.

"Not important," she said, rubbing the back of her neck. This was not how she'd planned to kick off her busy weekend. With everything she'd had planned to do Saturday and Sunday, tonight she'd hoped to curl up on her sofa with a bowl of popcorn and a movie after putting Beau to bed. Instead she was here, at the home of the one man she didn't want to deal with again.

Yes, she'd run into him occasionally since returning to Denver. Her law firm represented several of his company's clients, and she would admit that the first time they'd sat across from each other as opposing council in a legal proceeding had been difficult.

All she could think about that day, and the ones that followed, had been his betrayal. So when he'd approached her, asking if she would join him for dinner so they could talk through their issues, she had turned him down. After that it had seemed that the more she turned him down the more persistent he got. And to think he'd assumed he could follow her home to force a conversation with her!

But now she would admit she was glad he had been there when she'd walked into the house and found her home in shambles. His take-charge attitude had helped when she'd become too emotional to think straight.

"Do you think he will fall out of the bed?"

Keisha chuckled softly. "No. He's out for the night. And he's not a wanderer so don't worry about him tumbling down the stairs during the night either."

"Good, because if you're up for it, we need to go downstairs and talk."

She appreciated that he was giving her the option to say no. But she knew they needed to talk, and she wanted to get it over with. "Okay," she said, turning around.

He was standing too close, and as she looked up into his face lust shot through her. She wasn't surprised. Canyon had that effect on women. It had been that way for her the day they'd met in the courthouse lunchroom. And it had been that way a month later when she'd attended a meeting regarding a land dispute with his company. Every time Canyon glanced across the table at her she felt her insides sizzle.

"I'll need to use the ladies' room first," she said, rubbing her hands down the sides of her skirt.

"Every bedroom has a private bath. I'll see you downstairs in a few." He then turned and walked out of the room, pulling the door closed behind him.

She let out a deep breath when she heard his footsteps move down the stairs. When she'd made the decision not to tell Canyon about Beau she had been pretty comfortable with it. But she had a feeling that

when Canyon finished with her she was going to wish
she had decided differently.

Canyon stood at the window in his living room and
looked out. It was dark, but he didn't need to see to
know what was out there: the one hundred acres he
had inherited.

From the time he'd been a kid, he'd known he wanted
to claim this spot, the one with a perfect view of Whisper Creek Canyon. He didn't have to be on Gemma's
Lake—the one named after his grandmother—or any of
the other lakes and streams in Westmoreland Country.
Nor did he have to be close to the valleys and meadows.
This was where he wanted to be.

He recalled those times when he would go hunting
with his father, uncle, brothers and cousins. They would
ride their horses here on this land and then camp out
near the canyon. When everyone would fall asleep he
would stay awake, wide-eyed while he stared up at the
stars. He was convinced only special stars shone on this
spot. And they were *his* stars. Over the years, whenever
he was bothered by anything, all he had to do was stare
up at them to find the answers he needed.

It was here where he had escaped almost twenty
years ago after finding out that his parents and uncle
and aunt had died in a plane crash. And it was here
where he'd come while in college when he'd made the
decision to change his major from medicine to law.

He'd thought he had wanted to follow in his brother
Micah's footsteps and become a doctor, but after two
years of medical school he'd known he had made a mistake. He'd been torn about what to do.

Dillon had sensed something was bothering him that
week when he'd come home for spring break. And it had

been Dillon who'd suggested Canyon take time away from school and come home to seek the answers he needed. So Canyon had taken a semester off.

For those four months, he had crashed with his brother Riley and had spent his days either helping Ramsey with the sheep or Zane, Derringer and Jason with the horses. Then, on the weekends, he'd camped out here, on this land.

When it was time for the next semester to start, he'd made his decision to switch from medical school to law school with his family's blessings. Although his family got mad at each other sometimes, whenever it came to major issues they stuck together and supported each other.

He took another deep breath as he recalled another decision he had made here on this spot under the stars. It had been the decision to ask Keisha to marry him. One evening while she was out of town on business, he had come here. He'd already decided to build a house on this land and had been gathering ideas for what kind of home he wanted to build and exactly where he wanted the structure to face. Then, out of the clear blue sky, a voice inside his head had said, *Keisha will be the woman to live here with you.*

He really hadn't been shocked or surprised by that revelation since he'd never had issues about falling in love like some of his cousins and brothers had. He didn't have a fear of losing someone the same way he'd lost his folks. His only reason for taking his time about getting serious with a woman was that he enjoyed being single and hadn't been ready to settle down. He'd figured that one day he would meet that special person, fall in love and marry. He was fine with that idea. He just hadn't figured it would happen so soon.

He had taken a horse and ridden down into the canyon, camping out that night on this land. He'd looked up at the stars and within minutes he'd known.

He could hardly wait for Keisha to return. He hadn't been expecting her for another two days. But she'd come home early, found Bonita in her bed and assumed the worst. And Bonita had intentionally led her to believe a lie.

That angered him more than anything else about the situation because the woman had never done anything to rectify the situation. Keisha had been her friend but Bonita had lied to her. Canyon never knew what the woman's true motive had been.

Canyon's thoughts returned to the present when he heard the sound of Keisha coming down the stairs. He turned around and moved toward her, pausing briefly to pick up the wineglass off the table where he'd placed it moments ago. "Here, I think you need this," he said, handing the glass of wine to her.

She accepted it and took a sip. He could tell from the smile on her face that she appreciated the taste. "This is good. Where did you get it?"

"My cousin Spencer and his wife own a vineyard in California's wine country. Russell Vineyard has been in Chardonnay's family for years and—"

"Chardonnay?"

"Yes, that's Spencer's wife."

"Her family owned a vineyard and named her Chardonnay?"

Canyon chuckled. "Yes, they did. I guess it's no different than my parents naming me Canyon after what they conceived on a pretty nice vacation."

He paused a moment and then asked, "How did you come up with the name Beau?"

He watched as she slid down to sit on the steps. "You don't have to sit down there when I have a perfectly good sofa," he added.

She shook her head. "No, I'm fine." She took another sip of her wine and then said, "Beau's full name is Beaumont. He was named after my uncle…my mom's only brother who died when I was a little girl. Mom and Uncle Beau were close and when I hadn't decided on a name, she asked if I would name Beau after her brother. So I did."

Canyon leaned against the staircase. "When did you find out you were pregnant?"

She took another sip of wine before glancing up at him. "I was already late when I left for Tampa but while I was there I took a pregnancy test." She paused. "The reason I came back to town early was to tell you. It was something I figured was too important to tell you over the phone. But then I found you with Bonita."

Canyon's stomach clenched in anger. Up until that moment he'd convinced himself that no matter the circumstances, he and Keisha could talk things out in a rational manner. But now, after hearing the truth from her—that she'd known she was pregnant before leaving town and had allowed her distrust to keep her from telling him he was going to be a father—was too much. He couldn't hold back his anger.

"Please come with me. I don't want to wake Beau."

Keisha followed. She'd known from the anger she heard in his voice that her words had infuriated him. It was best for them to have it out now, to get it over with. He led her through his dining room into the kitchen and she stopped in the doorway. Even the kitchen was huge and spacious. Since she knew Canyon wasn't any more of a whiz in the kitchen than she was, that meant this kitchen—with all its sterling-silver appliances, rich dark oak cabinets and beautiful granite countertops— was only a showplace.

He pulled out two chairs and remained standing as if expecting her to sit in one. She'd rather stand, but changed her mind when his glare deepened. He watched as she moved from the doorway to cross the kitchen and sit at the table. Once she sat down he claimed his seat, as well. She looked over at him and lifted her chin. "Are there any more questions, Canyon?"

She almost saw steam come from his nostrils. "You know damn well there are."

And, as if he was trying to rein in his anger, he didn't say anything for a moment. "I'm not going to restate my innocence as to what happened that night since you choose to believe a lie. And to be quite frank, I don't care anymore what you think. Because if you can be- lieve I did what you've accused me of doing that means you didn't deserve my love. I refuse to feel bad about what happened."

His words, spoken in barely contained rage, caused her to flinch. Not because of the harshness of his tone but because of what he was saying. Her gut clenched as his meaning sank in. Uncertainty flowed through her. What if she had been wrong? What if Bonita had lied? What if he was innocent of what she'd accused him of?

She hesitated, not wanting to consider that possibil- ity. Everything about Bonita's story had added up. But still, what if…

"You hated me so much that you felt I didn't need to know I had a child?" he asked, interrupting her thoughts.

She felt the tension growing between them. "We were no longer together and…"

When her words trailed off he lifted a brow. "And what?"

"And after a while, I figured if I told you I was pregnant, you might question whether or not Beau was yours."

Canyon stared at her for a long moment without saying anything, but she saw the fury building in the gaze holding hers hostage. "That's bull and you know it," he finally said with a degree of steel in his voice that had her shifting in her seat. "There was no reason for me to assume your baby wasn't mine. Unlike you, I trusted you. Unconditionally. Your excuse is unacceptable, Keisha. And what's really unacceptable is that you've been back in Denver for ten months and you've seen me a number of times yet you never told me I had a son. Didn't you think I had a right to know?"

She decided to be honest with him. "No. What you did was unforgivable and dissolved your rights where I or my child was concerned. Besides, the last thing I wanted was for my pregnancy to make you feel obligated to a woman you evidently didn't love."

He leaned in closer to the table. "But I did love you. I told you as much a number of times."

She leaned closer as well, until their noses almost touched. "But then you showed me that love was a lie."

He pulled back and Keisha knew he was trying to control his anger. "You kept me from my son for two years because you didn't believe I loved you, because you believed that I betrayed you. What you've done is unforgivable. One day you're going to find out that the only lie in this whole thing is what you've believed for the past three years. You were wrong about me and when you find out the truth, I want you to think long and hard about what you did to me and to Beau."

Her chin stiffened. "Beau had me."

"And you were supposed to be both mother and father?"

"A woman does what she has to do when there isn't a man in the picture. My mom did."

"But you didn't give me a chance to be in the picture." He leaned back in his chair. "Is that what this is about, Keisha? Your father not wanting you, so you assumed I wouldn't want my child? If that's the case, I'm holding two strikes against you. One for not trusting me and another for thinking I'm the jerk your father was."

His words stung and stung hard. She slowly rose to her feet. "I made a mistake coming here tonight."

He tilted his head back to look up at her. "You've made several mistakes, Keisha, but coming here wasn't one of them. I am confident that one day you will realize you were wrong about me and wrong for keeping me away from my son." He paused. "But be forewarned, Beau and I won't be separated again."

She suddenly felt uneasy. "What do you mean?"

"Just what I said. If you try keeping my child from me again I will take you to court and fight you for custody. Full custody."

She gasped. "You would take my child from me?"

"Didn't you take him from me? You kept me from the pregnancy, from being there when he was born, from watching him take his first steps and from hearing him say his first words. You denied me my right to all those things, Keisha, so yes, I would take him from you, without blinking an eye. I have the means to do it. Two can play your games."

She released a frustrated breath. "Fighting between us isn't the answer, Canyon."

"Didn't say it was. But now you know where I stand." He got to his feet. "Detective Render called while you were upstairs. He'll be coming by tomorrow around noon to talk to you." He paused. "And Pam called."

She knew Pam was Dillon's wife. "And?"

"We're invited to breakfast at nine."

"I don't think—"

"At the moment, I really don't care what you think. It's time my family met my son."

She lifted her chin. "I'll go, but I won't pretend."

His gaze turned to stone but his tone was dangerously calm when he said, "Pretend what? We're in love? That we're a family? That you don't hate my guts for thinking I betrayed you, to the point where you kept my son from me for two years? No, Keisha, the last thing I want you to do is pretend you feel anything for me, because I sure as hell won't be pretending I feel anything for you."

Keisha swallowed hard as her heart pounded in her chest. In other words, even his family would know how much he despised her. "Fine," she said in a shaky breath. "It's late, and I want to go to bed, so if you'll please grab those things out of the car I'd appreciate it."

She hadn't wanted to pack any of her things to bring with her. Her skin crawled every time she imagined anyone touching her belongings before tossing them out of the drawers and closets. Canyon had made a pit stop at a Target where she'd rushed in to grab some toiletries and an outfit for tomorrow and something to sleep in. Luckily, she kept extra clothes for Beau in a bag in her car's trunk in case of emergencies.

She would go shopping for him tomorrow before leaving for the hotel. And there was no doubt in her mind that after she talked to Detective Render she would check into a hotel.

There was no way she could stay here with Canyon another night.

An hour or so later Canyon went up to bed but he couldn't sleep. Anger kept him awake. It was fueling his mind and riling him to a degree that he'd never been before. He felt enraged. Infuriated. How dare Keisha deny him so much? Her love. His son. Her faith and trust. And all because she believed another woman's lie.

He eased out of bed and tried to put a cap on his anger. He couldn't. It was too deep. Too strong. And, to his way of thinking, too justified. He knew there was only one thing that could ease his anger: gazing through his telescope.

Because of his fascination with the stars, his cousin Ian, of the Atlanta Westmorelands, had given him this beauty after discovering Canyon's captivation with the galaxy. Like him, Ian was into stars. Canyon shook his head, thinking that was truly an understatement where his cousin was concerned. Ian was not just into stars, but the entire galaxy. He graduated from Yale with a degree in physics and had worked for NASA, as well as for a research firm, and had become the captain of his own ship, all before his thirty-third birthday. Now Ian owned the Rolling Cascade, a beauty of a casino in Lake Tahoe.

Canyon looked through the telescope, searching for one star in particular. He had first seen it at the age of ten and named it Flash. Now, twenty-two years later, Flash still had a soothing effect on him, and he really needed to see Flash tonight. It took him a full half hour before he found it and relief flooded through him as he took in the beauty of the universe.

Minutes later, he was about to get back in bed when his cell phone rang. He glanced over at the clock and saw it was almost one in the morning. "Hello?"

"I was calling to see if everything is okay."

Canyon settled in bed with his back against the headboard. When his parents, aunt and uncle had died, Dillon had become guardian to everyone under eighteen. And those over eighteen had still looked to him for guidance and leadership in keeping the family together. Canyon couldn't help but recall that the twins, Adrian and Aiden, as well as Bane and Bailey, hadn't made things easy when they'd gone through those terrible teen years.

But Dillon was still the fearless leader. He was someone they could go to for advice, knowing that with his level head he would give it to them straight. He had an uncanny sense of when one of them was troubled about anything. So, in a way, this phone call wasn't a surprise.

"Yes, Dillon. Everything is okay." He paused a moment and then added, "At least for now. But seeing how Keisha and I feel about each other tomorrow is another story."

"And just how do the two of you feel about each other, Canyon?"

Canyon released a deep sigh. "She hates me, and I hate her."

"Hate is a strong word, Can. Besides, you're not capable of hating anyone. It's not in your makeup. You might not like a person but you could never truly hate anyone."

Canyon frowned. It annoyed him that his oldest brother seemed to know him better than he knew himself. "Okay, I don't hate her. But I don't like her."

"No, because you love her."

Canyon rolled his eyes. "I *used* to love her. She destroyed that love."

"By doing what?"

"Dammit, Dil, I have a son. A son I didn't know about because she kept him from me. Even after she returned to Denver and I approached her all those times… I gave her the opportunity to tell me, and she didn't. Beau is a little over two and was born just shy of eight months after Keisha left town.

"What pisses me off more than anything is that not once did she pick up a phone, send an email, find me online or send a letter to let me know about him. And to top it off she feels she was justified because I screwed around on her. She actually still believes that. And because she believes it, she feels I had no rights where he's concerned. I missed out on the first two years of his life."

Canyon paused and then asked, "Can you imagine missing out on the first two years of Denver's life?"

There was silence on the other end before Dillon said, "No, I can't."

Canyon was certain that his brother knew how he felt. But he also knew Dillon Westmoreland was, and would always be, the voice of reason—even when no one wanted him to be.

"But look at another side of things," Dillon said.

"What other side?"

"What if she'd decided not to carry your child to term?"

Canyon closed his eyes at the thought of Keisha choosing that alternative. "Then I would hate her for sure."

"So, in other words, she's dammed if she does and damned if she doesn't."

"Don't try to defend what she did, Dil," Canyon said. His annoyance was turning to anger again, anger he'd gotten under control just moments ago.

"Not defending her, Canyon. Just giving you something to think about. Keisha thought you were unfaithful. I'm sure you'd even admit things looked pretty bad. The woman was naked in bed and you were coming out of the shower practically naked. That woman played the two of you."

"Yes, but Keisha should have believed *me*."

"I'm wondering," Dillon said, as if he'd given what he was about to say some serious thought.

"Wondering what?"

"If you had come home from a trip and found a naked man in your bed, with Keisha barely wrapped in a towel, what would you think?" Then, without missing a beat, Dillon said, "Looking forward to seeing you and your family at breakfast in the morning. Good night."

His family.

"Good night, Dil." After Canyon clicked off the line, he rubbed a hand down his face. Now he would spend the night thinking about what Dillon had said.

Five

"Wake up, Mommy. Big bed."

Keisha forced open her eyes, one at a time, to find her son's face right in front of hers. She blinked and then recalled where they were and that Beau had been asleep when they'd arrived.

She pulled up in bed and tumbled him into her arms, loving the laugh she got out of him. "Good morning, Beau. Yes, this is a *big* bed."

"Not Beau's bed."

"No, not Beau's bed," she said, running her hand through the thick curls on his head. Knowing he would have another question for her, she quickly said, "Potty?"

He nodded. "Yes, Mommy. Potty."

She eased out of bed to lead him to the bathroom and watched as he looked at everything for the first time. Beau was pretty smart for his age. He mastered his words well for a two-year-old and bathroom train-

ing hadn't been the horror story she'd heard it would
be. They had just come out of the bathroom when there
was a knock on the door. She quickly grabbed her robe
off the bed before saying, "Come in."

Canyon strolled in.

Keisha tried not doing a double take but it was hard
when Canyon Westmoreland was eye candy. Dressed
in jeans and a Western shirt, he was the epitome of a
fit male with a physique that would put most men to
shame. That body…muscled shoulders, perfect abs and
broad chest…and she of all people knew how hard that
chest was since she'd been intimately pressed against
it a number of times. The muscles of his upper thighs
would tighten whenever she gave him a—

"And how is everyone doing this morning?" he asked.

She was grateful for his intrusion into her thoughts.
The last thing she wanted to remember was any inti-
macy she'd shared with him. Her gaze moved from the
lower portion of his body and traveled up to his face.
He was smiling.

What on earth did he have to smile about? And why
did it appear he was in a good mood? Before going to
bed they'd had heated words, but you wouldn't know it
from the smile on his face. Then it hit her why he was
acting so nice. Beau. Canyon might not be willing to
pretend for his family, but he evidently had no problem
putting on a front for his son.

"Dad!"

Before she could stop him, Beau took off, racing
across the room and launching his little body right at
Canyon. Canyon's deep laughter filled the room as he
picked up Beau in muscled arms and lifted him high in
the air. That got a squeal of glee from Beau.

She just stood there and watched the interaction be-

tween father and son, still somewhat astonished with
how quickly Beau took to Canyon when it usually took
him a while to warm up to strangers. And before yesterday, Canyon had been a stranger.

While holding Beau high over his head, Canyon
glanced over at her. She saw a flash of heat pass through
his eyes and was convinced it had nothing to do with
anger. In fact, she was so sure that she tightened her
robe around her.

"How is everyone doing this morning?" he repeated
when the only sound in the room was Beau's laughter.

Heat stung her face at the thought that he'd caught
her staring. "We're fine. You're up early."

"Breakfast at the main house, remember?" he said,
lowering Beau to the floor. "You haven't changed your
mind about going, have you?"

As if he'd given her a choice. "No. You said nine and
it's barely seven."

"I know. I got up at five and worked out some. Now
I'm about to go horseback riding in the canyon, which
is something I do every Saturday morning."

"Big bed, Dad."

Canyon laughed at how wide Beau had stretched out
his arms.

"Mine is bigger," he said to his son, extending his
arms out wider.

Beau's eyes widened. "Bigger?"

Canyon smiled. "Yes, bigger." He then glanced over
at Keisha. "I'll leave you two to get dressed and will be
back in an hour to give you a tour of my home."

"That's not necessary," she said.

"Yes, it is. Beau will be spending a lot of time here

with me, and I want you to be comfortable that he's in a safe environment."

Tilting her head, she studied Canyon's features and saw the same handsome man she'd always seen. But there was a determination in his eyes that let her know that when it came to Beau he meant what he'd said last night. He would not let her come between him and his child again.

"I'll be ready for that tour when you get back," she said.

He arched his brow and continued to look at her as if surprised she'd given in so easily. She was smart enough to know which battles to fight and which ones to let go…for now. "Come on, Beau, we need to get dressed."

"Wanna see Dad's big bed, Mommy."

She was curious about Canyon's big bed, as well. "Later, Beau. We need to put our clothes on and get ready to go. Your daddy is taking us somewhere."

He looked at her confused. "My daddy?"

"Yes." Keisha knew that right now, to Beau, Canyon was Dad…as if Dad was Canyon's name and not the role the name represented. She needed to make Beau understand. "Mommy," she said, pointing at herself. "And Daddy," she said, pointing at Canyon.

Beau poked out his little bottom lip. "No, Mommy. He Dad."

Keisha smiled. "Yes, and he's Daddy, too."

Beau scrunched up his face. "Daddy?"

"Yes, Daddy." She knew Beau was trying to recall all the times he'd heard other kids use the word *daddy,* mostly during pickup at day care or when the twins next door talked to Everett. Beau had never been around a male for any long period of time, and he certainly hadn't been around one that he could call daddy. Until now.

Beau turned to Canyon and a big, wide smile spread across his lips. "Wanna see your big bed, Daddy-Dad."

Canyon couldn't help but laugh out loud before saying, "And you will, but not now." He looked at Keisha. "Thanks."

Canyon knew what Keisha had tried to do this morning with Beau, and he appreciated it.

After one hell of a sleepless night, he'd woken up determined to make this a good day. He would be introducing Beau to his family, and he was pretty damn excited about it.

An hour later, as Canyon returned from riding his horse, he was still filled with excitement. There was something about riding across his land and through the canyon that soothed him. Not only was it his heritage and his legacy, it was also his solace. And one day he would leave it all to his son.

Beau.

The realization that he had a son filled him in a way he hadn't thought possible. A child had never been a top priority for him. Hell, a wife hadn't either, until Keisha. But seeing Beau, holding him, touching him—that parental part of Canyon had come alive and had become so deep that he could feel it in every part of his body. He'd meant every single word he'd told Keisha last night. He didn't intend to be separated from his child ever again.

He wasn't sure how she would deal with it or how she would deal with him. That wasn't his concern. The only thing that mattered to him was building a strong relationship with his child, starting now. Today. He needed to make up for all the time he'd lost, and he refused to let her stand in his way.

He recognized the frigid looks she was prone to giving him and knew his responsive stare was just as bad. The only thing holding his temper in check whenever he thought about the two years he'd lost was to remember what Dillon had said last night. She could have made a different decision regarding Beau, but she hadn't.

He walked into his house, placed his Stetson on the hat rack and glanced up at the same time that Keisha and Beau were coming down the stairs. Beau grinned wide when he saw Canyon and was about to take off toward him, but Keisha held firm to his hand. "No, Beau. Remember. No running down the stairs."

"Yes, Mommy."

Canyon couldn't stop staring at Keisha. She had changed into a pair of jeans and a pullover blouse. To his way of thinking, she looked absolutely beautiful. He recalled yesterday when he'd seen her walk out of her office and noticed that her body had changed. Now he knew why. Because of Beau.

She'd always had a nice body, now it was even curvier. More enticing. More tempting.

He pushed those thoughts from his mind. He would not become involved with a woman who didn't trust him, and she'd proved just how much she didn't.

As soon as Beau's feet touched the floor, he took off running toward Canyon. "You know the rule, Beau," Keisha said. "No running in the house."

He stopped and looked back at Keisha. "Not my house."

Canyon had to cough to keep from laughing out loud and hung his head when Keisha shot him a warning look. "It doesn't matter, young man, whose house it is. No running in any house. Understand?"

He nodded and then walked as fast as his little legs

could take him to Canyon. He reached up his arms. "Pick me up high again, Daddy-Dad."

"See what you started," Keisha said.

Canyon chuckled as he hoisted Beau up in the air, thinking that he didn't mind. In fact, he loved hearing the sound of his son's laughter. "And for the record, this is your house, too, Beau." He glanced over at Keisha with a look that dared her to refute his words.

He placed Beau on his shoulders and said, "Now for that tour I promised you."

Keisha had already seen Canyon's living and dining rooms as well as the kitchen. But he showed all of it to her again anyway. "While I'm showing you around, note if anything is a red flag where a child is concerned and let me know so I can change it."

"All right," Keisha said as he led her up the second set of spiral stairs.

This was the first house she'd seen that had two beautiful spiral staircases, but the layout didn't look odd. The two staircases appeared to join at the top, when they really did not. The effect was simply breathtaking.

With Beau still perched on his shoulder Canyon turned when they reached the landing. "This is where my suite is located as well as other rooms for my pleasure."

For his pleasure? She wondered what kind of rooms they were.

It didn't take her long to find out. She entered the first room, the one he'd called his mini-gym. His personal workout room had every piece of weight-lifting equipment imaginable. Next was a game room with a dartboard, a pool table and a big flat-screen television that seemed to be over eight feet wide.

"Nice," she said. She could envision him in both rooms after a long and tiresome day at the office. He would probably work out first, shower and then go into his game room and unwind before calling it a night.

"This way to my bedroom," he said, leading her down a spacious hall that led to massive double doors made of dark oak. When he opened the door she just stood in the doorway and stared.

"Big, big bed, Mommy."

That was an understatement. She was familiar with a queen-size bed since she had one of her own, and of course she'd seen a king-size. But this one had to be a super-duper king. "Yes, this is definitely big."

"*Big, big,* Mommy," Beau reitcrated

She chuckled. "Okay, Beau. Big, big. Your daddy has a *big, big* bed."

"Let's see if it's too big for you," Canyon said, dumping Beau off his shoulders and into the center. Beau bounced up and down, laughing a few times.

"Fun, Mommy, fun. Come on bed, Mommy. Get in Daddy-Dad bed."

Keisha was certain her face tinted at the thought of her doing that. "No thanks. I'll just stand here and watch you." She didn't have to glance over at Canyon to know he was looking at her. She could feel the heat of his gaze all over.

Instead of looking at Canyon, she walked over to the huge wall-to-wall window. He had an amazing view from his bedroom, of the canyon as well as the Denver sky above it.

Her heart began pounding in her chest when she felt Canyon's heat and knew he had come to stand behind her. To take her mind off his presence, she said, "This is a beautiful view of the canyon."

"Yes, I think so, as well. That's why I designed the house this way so I could wake up to the canyon every morning."

She turned and noticed Beau still bouncing as if Canyon's bed was a trampoline. "And what about your guests? They don't have this view."

He shrugged as an impish grin touched his lips. "No, all the guest rooms have a view of the mountains. I don't think that's so bad."

She didn't think it was so bad either. In fact, she'd liked it, and when she'd woken up this morning, she couldn't help looking out the window at the mountains while getting dressed. This house, Canyon's Bluff, could grow on a person.

"Come on, let me show you the other parts of the house." He moved away, went to the bed and caught Beau in his arms as he bounced. Canyon then left the room.

She followed, taking a quick peek into his bathroom. She shook her head. The master bath was to die for and was bigger than the living room at her house. *Her house.* She then remembered why she was here and what someone had done to her home, her sanctuary. The place where she'd always felt secure. She couldn't push away the thought that someone had intentionally taken that security from her. Like the deputy had said, whoever had trashed her home had done so to make a point. But she had no idea what it was.

Fifteen minutes later, Canyon ended his tour in the room that housed an indoor swimming pool. Like the rest of the house, the room was beautiful, and no matter what the weather was outside—even if the grounds were blanketed in snow—you could have a nice swim.

"So did you see anything?" he asked in a voice that,

to her way of thinking, sounded way too sexy. They were leaving the pool room, and he took the time to lock the door behind him.

She lifted a brow. "Anything like what?"

"Anything I need to be concerned about when Beau spends the weekends."

His words reminded her that he intended to be a part of her son's life, her life, whether she wanted him to or not. "The only thing I saw that would concern me is the pool. Beau can't swim."

He nodded as he led them back to the living room. Beau was still riding Canyon's shoulders with his legs dangling around Canyon's neck. "No problem. I intend to start teaching him how to swim next week."

Keisha bit down on her lip to keep from telling Canyon he shouldn't make assumptions. Granted, upon seeing how well Canyon and Beau were getting along, a part of her was regretting keeping them apart, but she refused to let him run roughshod over her.

She was still Beau's custodial parent…although she had placed Canyon's name as the father on the birth certificate. That had been the one concession she'd given after being hassled by her mother. Lynn had regretted not putting Kenneth Drew's name on Keisha's birth certificate. Even though Kenneth had not claimed his daughter, she was his blood nonetheless. Acknowledging that kinship would have at least given Keisha the name of the man who'd fathered her.

"If you recall, I taught you how to swim," Canyon said, putting Beau down on the floor, watching as he walked quickly over to the huge aquarium and pressed his face against it.

Keisha felt an intense pull in her stomach. Canyon would have to remind her of those lessons. It had taken triple the length of time it should have taken…not that she hadn't been an adept student. But mainly because they had spent their time exploring the numerous positions a couple could use while making love in water. To this day she would never forget those swimming lessons on one of the lakes in Westmoreland Country, and judging by the way he was looking at her, he hadn't forgotten either. Just remembering sent sensual chills through her body. Chills she didn't want to feel.

Deciding not to respond to his comment about her swimming lessons, she said, "As to the other parts of your home, I didn't notice anything since we won't be staying long. However, I would like to take a more indepth tour later today on my own."

Being around him was unnerving her when it shouldn't. She'd accepted that the sexual chemistry was still there, even after three years, but she had expected to be able to handle it much better than she was.

"Help yourself. I want to make sure I do things right, and I want to make sure you won't be worried when he's here with me."

"But I *will* worry anyway, Canyon," she said honestly. "And when I do worry, please don't take it personally. It comes with being a mother. Now that you know about him, you'll worry, too, although you know I'm capable of taking care of him. It comes with being a father." She hesitated a moment and then added, "Although some men take that role more seriously than others." She smiled. "I even worried every day when he was with Mom. I used to call so much she would fuss at me for bothering her."

Canyon thought about what Keisha had just said. "Your mother took care of him every day while you worked?" he asked.

"For the first eight months. She took a leave from her job just to do it."

He'd never met her mother but had spoken to her once or twice on the phone when she'd called. He knew of Keisha and her mother's close relationship. He also knew Keisha had inherited her mother's independent nature. Keisha had told him the story of how her father had denied she was his child when her mother had told him about her pregnancy and how her mother had raised her alone without any involvement from him.

Canyon noticed when Keisha glanced at her watch. "I guess we need to leave if we want to—"

She stopped talking when he reached out and took her wrist in his hand and looked at the watch…remembering. "You kept it."

It was a statement more than a question and he was well aware that she knew it. He had given her the bracelet watch for her birthday a few weeks before she'd broken up with him.

"Yes, I kept it. Did you think I was going to throw it away?"

He shrugged. "That had crossed my mind."

She absently flexed her fingers and he knew she was nervous about something. "Are you nervous about Detective Render's visit later today?"

She glanced over at Beau before shifting her head back over to him. "No. That's not it."

He lifted a brow. "Then what is it?"

She nibbled on her bottom lip. "It's your family."

"What about them?"

She drew in and then released a deep breath. "You and I agreed we won't be pretending and I have a feeling they won't either."

He tilted his head. "Meaning?"

Lowering her voice so Beau wouldn't hear, she said, "You and your family are close, Canyon. You and I didn't part on the best terms, and I'm sure they know all about it. There's no doubt in my mind they'll be taken with Beau, but..."

"But what?"

"Maybe you should have found out for certain if they really want me there. I have done things they probably don't agree with. I'm sure most of them took your side about what happened. They probably figure I should have believed what you said. And that I was wrong for not telling you about Beau. Even you believe I was wrong on both counts so how can I expect them to feel any differently?"

Canyon didn't say anything for a minute. "First of all, please stop judging my family prematurely. You met most of them already—all of my brothers, except for Bane and Micah, and all of my cousins except for Gemma, since she'd already married and moved to Australia. You and I met the year after I returned home from law school, so you already know some of my brothers' and cousins' wives. You met Pam, Chloe, Lucia and Bella, because Dillon, Ramsey, Derringer and Jason had married them by the time you and I started dating."

Although she was three years younger than his thirty-two, they had finished their respective law schools at the same time, mainly because of the extra time it had required for him to change his major. He would never forget the day they'd met in the courthouse lunchroom. He had been an attorney for fewer than six months and had won his first case that day. She had won her case that day, as well. They had celebrated that night over drinks.

"My family," he continued, "will decide if they like you because of you and not because of me. They'll let our business be our business. The Westmorelands make it a point to stay out of each others' affairs." He chuckled. "The only time we didn't abide by that rule was when Derringer got involved with Lucia. She was Chloe's best friend and childhood friends with Megan and Gemma. So, unfortunately for Derringer, those of us who knew his reputation were overprotective where Lucia was concerned."

He paused. "When you and I were involved I tried to get you to spend more time with my family, but you declined all my invitations. If anything, they probably think you have something against them because you never wanted to get to know them before."

His statement sent an embarrassing tint across her cheeks. What he'd said was true. She had turned down invitations to his family's chow-downs and other little activities. But it hadn't been because she'd had anything against them.

Her grandparents didn't have any siblings and her mother had had only one brother. For that reason, the thought of a family as large as Canyon's was overwhelming to her. Luckily, he'd understood and hadn't pushed. When she'd attended that charity ball with him and finally met his family, she'd found them to be nice and very friendly. His sisters-in-law and his cousins-in-law—Pam, Chloe, Lucia and Bella—had invited her to lunch, but before she could take them up on their offer, she and Canyon had split up.

"I had planned to get to know them better," she said in her defense. "But both of us know what happened, don't we?"

The look in his eyes turned cold. "Yes, we know. You chose to believe a lie rather than the truth."

Keisha opened her mouth to give him a blistering

retort, when she felt a tug on her jeans. Beau pulled on Canyon's pants, too, and then glanced up at them with big pleading brown eyes. "Bouncy bed again?"

She knew Canyon was about to give in when he reached down to pick up Beau, but Keisha knew her son's antics better than anyone. He would use those beautiful eyes to wrap a person around his finger, and he'd figured out that Canyon was an easy target.

"No, Beau," she said firmly. "No bouncy bed again." She then switched her gaze back to Canyon. "I'm ready to go now."

Canyon nodded and, without saying anything, he led her toward the door.

"I don't believe it," Pamela Westmoreland said, staring at the little boy in Canyon's arms. She turned to her husband who was standing at her side. "Can you believe it?"

Dillon smiled. "Yes. That's how Dare and I knew we were cousins the first time we met because we looked so much alike. Strong Westmoreland genes."

Canyon chuckled. "I don't think Keisha believes us. I can't wait until she sees Denver. Where is he by the way?"

"In the back with Bailey," Dillon said, grinning. "Playing with Denver gives Bailey the excuse to act like a kid again. Come on in. Welcome to our home, Keisha."

"Thank you," Keisha said, glancing around. This was a big house, bigger than Canyon's. She knew all about the history of Dillon's home. It had been built by Canyon's great-grandfather and passed on to his grandfather who'd passed it on to his two sons. The house tripled in size when both sons, their wives and their families lived here—in what was considered the main house—

in harmony. Then the sons and their wives died and as the oldest grandchild Dillon had inherited the house and the three hundred acres it sat on.

"So good seeing you again, Keisha," Pam said, giving her a hug. That was something else Keisha had tried to get used to when it came to Canyon's family. They were such a huggy group. She and her mother were close, but didn't hug as much as the Westmorelands did.

"Canyon told us what happened to your home. That's just awful. If there's anything any of us can do, please let us know."

"Thanks." Keisha felt Pam's offer was sincere, and she appreciated it. Pam Westmoreland was a beautiful woman. Keisha had thought that same thing the first time she'd seen Pam on her husband's arm at the ball. And from what Canyon had told her, Pam, a former actress who'd lived in California at one time, was perfect for his brother.

"Where are the others?" Canyon asked. "I see the cars out front."

"They're out back, as well," Dillon said. "It's such a nice day that Pam and the ladies decided to set up things outside on the patio. And speaking of cars, yours is parked in the back, Canyon."

"Thanks for handling that for me."

"No problem. Everyone expects you to be here, and I didn't mention anything about Keisha and Beau. I decided to let you handle it."

Keisha felt her stomach tighten. She could just imagine how many of Canyon's family members were here. She inwardly prepared herself for a lot of cold stares. Things would be worse when they saw Beau. He was their family, and they would probably resent her for keeping him from them.

"Jill flew in last night, and I'm excited about it," Pam said, grinning from ear to ear.

"Jillian is Pam's sister," Dillon said, chuckling. "She's twenty-four and in medical school in Louisiana, with a goal of one day becoming a neurosurgeon. She couldn't make it home for Megan's wedding, so this is the first time we've seen her this year. We're all excited she was able to get time off to come home for a few days."

Dillon led them through a huge dining room and a very spacious kitchen. Keisha recalled what Canyon had once told her. When Dillon had married Pam she had been the guardian of her three younger sisters who'd come to live with them in this house, as well. It seemed fitting that a man who'd once made it his life's mission to be responsible for his younger siblings and cousins had married a woman who'd done practically the same thing.

Keisha drew in a deep breath when they reached the sliding glass door. Outside, she saw a beautiful patio with the most gorgeous view of a huge lake. She felt Canyon slip his hand in hers and she glanced up at him. The look in his eyes was unreadable, but she figured he knew how nervous she was and he was letting her know he was there for her. His actions were confusing. He'd said he wouldn't pretend, so why was he acting as if he cared?

"Look who finally got here," Dillon said, stepping out onto the patio with Pam at his side.

Keisha watched as everyone looked over at them. Her presence garnered only a little interest. The one who really snagged everyone's attention was Beau.

"Hey, guys. Most of you know Keisha," Canyon said. "I want to introduce you to our son, Beau."

Everyone stared without saying anything. Keisha

had known meeting Beau would be a surprise, but the crowd's response made her wonder why so much attention had been drawn to Beau. Were all the shocked expressions necessary?

Just then, a little boy raced across the room toward Dillon. "Daddy! Daddy! Look what Megan gave me."

Keisha glanced down at the little boy and her breath caught. Her hand flew to her chest. "My God!" she whispered in shock.

The little boy could be Beau's twin.

Six

"I tried to tell you," Canyon whispered in Keisha's ear. She felt her body tremble slightly from the heat of his breath so close to her skin.

Dillon swung his son up into his arms as pandemonium hit. Canyon's siblings and cousins rushed over to them. The ones she had met before gave her hugs and told her it was good seeing her again. She tried to keep surprise out of her features.

They cooed and aahed over Beau, who seemed to enjoy getting so much attention. No one questioned why they were just now meeting him for the first time. Keisha figured they were staying out of Canyon's business because they knew he would handle it.

"How old is he?" Bailey asked. She was the one holding Beau and didn't seem inclined to relinquish him.

"He's a little over two."

Bailey smiled as she looked back and forth between

Beau and Denver. "Denver is almost four. Except for their size, they have the same facial features. That's absolutely incredible."

Keisha thought it was pretty incredible, as well. If Denver wasn't taller and almost two years older, the little boys could pass for twins. And speaking of twins…

The Westmoreland twins stood in front of her, smiling, and she couldn't help but smile back. Identical twins. Even down to their handsome grins. She couldn't forget the identity trick they'd played on her the night she had met them.

"Aiden and Adrian." She lifted a brow then looked from one to the other. "Or is it Adrian and Aiden."

Their identical smiles widened. "We'll never tell," one of them said.

"Okay, guys, you've forced my hand now I'm forcing yours." She reached out and took one of their right hands and turned it over so that it was palm up. She nodded and then glanced back up at the man whose hand she held. "You're Adrian."

Both men shifted their gazes from her to Canyon and Aiden said accusingly, "You told."

Canyon shrugged, and Keisha couldn't help but grin. Yes, Canyon had told her that the only way to tell the two apart was by the tiny scar in the palm of Adrian's right hand just under his thumb. It had been a childhood injury caused by falling out of a tree.

"Move over guys, Keisha needs to come with us so we can girl talk," Ramsey's wife, Chloe, said, taking Beau from Bailey. Bailey then reached for Denver and when the two women stood side by side with both boys everyone just shook their heads. The two boys seemed as fascinated with each other as much as everyone was fascinated with them.

"Now Denver has a playmate he can do guy stuff with," Dillon said, grinning. "Susan is getting too prissy for him." Susan was Ramsey and Chloe's daughter who was a few months younger than Denver.

"I hope when they grow older they don't play those crazy games and go around tricking people like Aiden and Adrian used to do," Megan said, laughing.

"You mean those games they still like to play?" Riley Westmoreland said as he came to join them. "Keisha, I'd like you to meet my fiancée, Alpha Blake."

Instead of extending her hand, Alpha reached out and gave Keisha a hug. "Congratulations, and nice meeting you."

"Same here."

"Think I can have my son back now?" Canyon asked, reaching for Beau.

"I guess," Chloe said, smiling, handing Beau to Canyon.

With a huge grin on his face, Beau reached out eagerly to go to Canyon. "Daddy-Dad."

Canyon's brother Jason raised a brow. "Daddy-Dad?"

Canyon chuckled as he perched Beau on his shoulder. "It's a long story." He then glanced around and asked, "Where's Zane?"

Trying to keep a straight face, Riley said, "I guess he and Channing decided to sleep in this morning. We expect them later."

Canyon nodded. He then shifted his gaze to where the Westmoreland women had led Keisha off to a section of the patio. He knew how reserved Keisha was with new people and inwardly smiled. She was going to find out that when it came to the Westmorelands, the word *reserved* wasn't in their vocabulary.

"Hey, Can. You okay?" Stern asked his brother when he followed Canyon's gaze over to Keisha.

"Yes, I'm okay. Why wouldn't I be?"

Stern shrugged. "No reason. Just asking." He paused. "She looks good."

Canyon switched his gaze off Keisha and onto his brother. "I see your eyesight is still good. But I suggest you check out somebody else."

Stern laughed. "Getting testy, aren't we?"

Canyon shifted Beau in his arms, refusing to be baited. At that moment, Canyon's cousin Zane and his fiancée, Channing Hastings, arrived and stepped out onto the patio. Everyone greeted the couple and Channing couldn't resist holding Beau. She left to join the ladies with Beau in her arms. It was then that Zane pulled Canyon aside.

"I see you handled your business without my help," Zane said, glancing over at Keisha.

Canyon rolled his eyes. He had called Zane a few weeks ago when he'd gotten fed up with Keisha trying to avoid him. That was when he'd come up with the plan for following her home. "Yes, but it's not what you think."

"Well, I've got a feeling you're going to find out like I did that…once your woman, always your woman."

Canyon was about to tell Zane how wrong he was when Zane walked off to talk to Ramsey and Dillon. Feeling frustrated, Canyon moved across the patio to get his son, wanting to spend as much time with him as he could.

Despite Keisha's apprehensions about sharing an amicable relationship with the women surrounding her, she couldn't help it. They were so outgoing, friendly and

personable that she found it hard to resist their camaraderie. It had been the same way that night at the ball.

She had fond memories of that night even though
she had been a little overwhelmed by Canyon's family. He'd introduced her to not only the ones living in
Denver, but also the ones living in Atlanta, Montana
and Texas. The one thing she would always remember
about that night was how easily they had accepted her.
It was as if they'd made up their minds. If Canyon had
brought her with him then that meant something. Too
bad that she'd believed the same thing only to find out
months later just how wrong her assumption had been.

She glanced across the patio to the yard where Canyon was helping Beau go up and down a kiddie sliding board that was part of a cedar swing set. There was
also a sandbox, an outdoor playhouse and several other
pieces of playground equipment in a play area separated
from the lake by a high fence.

She could hear Beau's laughter and knew he was
having the time of his life. As if he felt someone looking at him, Canyon glanced over at her. His dark gaze
was neither friendly nor sensual as he stared back. But
that didn't stop the heat slowly inching across her skin.
The attraction that was still there between them was
frustrating. She was certain he didn't like it any more
than she did.

Holding back a sigh, she broke eye contact with him
to watch the women sitting around her. In addition to
Dillon's wife, Pam, Ramsey's wife, Chloe, and Ri-
ley's fiancée, Alpha, there were also Kalina, who was
married to Canyon's brother Micah; Canyon's cousin
Megan, who'd gotten married a couple of months ago;
Lucia, who was married to his cousin Derringer; and
Bella, who was married to his brother Jason. And then

there was Channing Hastings. From what Keisha had gathered, Channing and Zane had broken up a while ago but had patched things up and were now back together.

Also included in the mix were Pam's three gorgeous sisters. Jillian was twenty-four; Paige was twenty-two, had recently graduated with a degree from UCLA and was living in Los Angeles determined to follow in her big sister's footsteps and become an actress; and Nadia, who was in her second year of college at the University of Wyoming. It was easy to see that Pam adored her younger sisters and they adored her.

Keisha was drawn back into the conversation among the women. Jillian was talking about how hard medical school was and it was then that Keisha noticed Bailey staring at her.

While the other women would allow her and Canyon to deal with their issues in their own way, without taking any sides, she had a feeling Bailey wasn't prone to doing that. The youngest Westmoreland had immediately been taken with Beau and was probably resenting the fact that this was the first time any of them had seen him. Keisha wondered if the others felt that way but were just doing a better job of hiding their true feelings than Bailey.

And then, as if Pam had somehow picked up on the question floating through Keisha's mind, she reached out, touched her hand, smiled and said, "We're glad to have you as part of the family, Keisha."

Keisha swallowed hard. Although she appreciated Pam's words, Keisha knew she needed to set the record straight. "But I'm not part of the family. Canyon and I aren't together that way."

Pam waved off her words. "Beau is a Westmoreland and you're Beau's mother, so that makes you part of the family."

Keisha had news for her. Things didn't work out that way, and no doubt Canyon would make certain they didn't. Deciding not to disagree with Pam for now, Keisha took another sip of her orange juice.

Jillian excused herself to go to the ladies' room and Nadia stood to take Pamela's other son, seven-month-old Dade, out of Pam's arms. Paige gathered the other young ones together and herded them to the kiddie playground.

Keisha had been introduced to all the kids and it seemed a number of them were close to Beau's age. Ramsey and Chloe had three-and-a-half-year-old Susan, as well as two-year-old Rembrandt. Micah and Kalina had two-year-old Macon and Kalina was pregnant again with a girl. Derringer and Lucia had a two-year-old son named Ringo; and Jason and Bella had two-year-old twin daughters—Faith and Hope—and Bella mentioned that she and Jason wanted at least two more kids. Keisha felt good knowing that during those weekends Beau would spend with Canyon, he would have plenty of cousins to romp around with.

"Isn't Canyon's home just gorgeous?" Bailey asked.

Keisha wondered if anyone else had picked up on Bailey's snide question. Bailey was no doubt trying to make a point while fishing for information; specifically, whether or not Keisha had spent the night in Canyon's home. Although the others were too polite to ask, no doubt they were wondering how Canyon had found out about Beau and what status she held in Canyon's life.

Keisha decided that whatever information they got about Beau, Canyon would give them himself. However, she had no problem letting them know—once again—

that she and Canyon weren't sharing that kind of relationship. She didn't have any status in Canyon's life.

She held Bailey's gaze. "Yes, Canyon has a gorgeous home, and I appreciate him letting me stay there for the night considering what happened to mine."

Chloe arched her brow. "What happened to yours?"

Keisha frowned slightly. Had Canyon not told his family about why she had stayed with him? "My house got trashed."

"What!"

The single word of shocked surprise spouted simultaneously from every women sitting around her. "Yes, it got trashed." She then told them what had happened from the time she'd left work yesterday up to now.

"And the police have no idea who was following you or who trashed your house?" Lucia asked, clearly outraged.

"So far, no," Keisha said. Talking about it made her angry once again at what had happened. "A Detective Render is meeting me at Canyon's home at noon to go over everything and to ask more questions."

"I've met Ervin Render before," Megan said. "He's loaned his expertise to a couple of cases Rico has worked on. Rico says he's good." Rico Claiborne was Megan's husband and a private investigator.

"I'm glad to hear that. I plan to stay in a hotel tonight, and I want to feel safe doing so."

"Maybe you shouldn't say in a hotel, Keisha," Bella said. "At least not until they find out who trashed your house."

"They didn't take anything of value?" Bailey asked, as if to make sure she'd heard correctly.

Keisha shook her head. "No, they didn't. Not my

jewelry, my coin collection or anything. It's pretty darn obvious whoever did it wants to scare me."

There, she'd said it herself. The police deputy had said the same thing but this was the first time she'd said the truth out loud. Saying it sent a cold chill through her body. She couldn't think of one reason why anyone would want to do that. But evidently someone did.

Leaving Beau in the care of Paige, who had gathered the kids together to play several games, Canyon went into the kitchen and grabbed a beer out of Dillon's refrigerator. It was early, but he needed something stronger than orange juice to calm his libido.

Every time he glanced over to where Keisha was sitting on the patio with the Westmoreland women, he couldn't stop his body from revving up into a state of sexual desire. Why did she have to look so damn good? And why did his heart pound like crazy in his chest each and every time she opened her mouth to talk? More than once, he'd been tempted to leave the kids' play area, cross the yard and pull her into his arms for a kiss. He could just imagine tangling his tongue with hers like they did in the good old days.

Deciding to make a pit stop at the bathroom before grabbing his beer, he rounded the corner and slowed when he recognized the voices in the hallway. He was about to greet the two people talking, when the words being spoken between them made him stop.

Aiden released a deep sigh and tipped Jillian's chin up so that she was staring into the depths of his dark eyes. "It's time we tell them, Jill. I don't like sneaking around."

"I don't like sneaking around either, but you promised we would wait until I finished medical school. You said you understood," she murmured softly.

"I did at the time, but now I don't anymore. I think Dillon and Pam will be okay to know that we've fallen in love."

"But you don't know that for certain. As far as they're concerned we're family. Your cousin married my sister, and that makes us—"

"Legally no kin," Aiden said in a voice tinged with frustration.

"But Dillon tells me, Nadia and Paige all the time that we're part of the Westmoreland family."

"Because he married your sister. So to him, and to all of us, you are. But you're not a blood relative, and I've never thought of you as anything other than the woman I love and want. Nothing about that is going to change, Jill."

"Oh, Aiden, then promise me you'll wait a little bit longer. I don't want to cause a rift within the family."

"You won't."

"I might, and I don't want to take that chance," she said, fighting back a sob. "Please understand."

"Don't cry, baby. I'll wait a little while longer because you're worth waiting for. Always have been."

"Oh, Aiden."

He pressed a light kiss to her lips but a fierce longing and desire had him pulling her into his arms and taking her mouth with a hunger that sent a rush of need through him.

When Aiden lifted his head, he stared deep into Jillian's eyes for a long moment before lowering his mouth to hers once again...

* * *

"Damn," Canyon muttered under his breath as he quietly backed up.

When had this started? Hell. He didn't want to be around when Dillon and Pam found out. Dillon probably wouldn't have much to say because he'd gotten used to Bane and Crystal sneaking around. But Canyon wasn't so sure how Pam would take the news.

Jillian had been seventeen when Dillon married Pam and brought her and her sisters to Westmoreland Country. Canyon, the twins and Stern had mostly been away at college, and Bane had already left for the navy. So when had Jillian and Aiden gotten together? Over the holidays? During spring breaks? It sounded serious. He hoped so, for Aiden's sake. Everyone knew how protective Pam was of her three sisters, and Aiden had always had a reputation for playing women. If Pam thought some funny business had been going on under her nose all this time and that Aiden didn't mean Jillian any good, then there would be hell to pay.

Maybe Canyon ought to talk to Aiden. Then, on second thought, maybe he should tend to his own business, which was pretty messed up at the moment. He had a son he'd just found out about and a former lover staying at his house who still hated his guts.

His plate was full, and he didn't need anyone else's problems to add to it. Opening the French doors, he stepped back onto the patio and looked to where Keisha was still sitting and talking to the women in his family. He wasn't sure what they were talking about, but from their expressions, the conversation looked serious.

He glanced at his watch. It was almost eleven, and Detective Render was supposed to be at his place to question Keisha at noon. He moved to the playground to get Beau. After thanking Paige for entertaining his son and letting Dillon know he was on his way out, Canyon walked to where Keisha was sitting.

"I hate to break up this little party but Keisha, Beau and I have to leave," Canyon said.

Keisha glanced up at Canyon. He had Beau in his arms and stood tall with his Stetson on his head, which Beau seemed to find fascinating. "All right," she said, standing.

"Don't let her stay at a hotel tonight, Canyon." To Keisha's surprise, that directive had come from Bailey.

"I won't."

Keisha frowned at Canyon who merely stared back at her. He'd said it like he could stop her from leaving his home if that was what she wanted to do. She bit her lip to keep from setting him straight in front of his family.

"I think we should go shopping," Megan said quickly, as if that was the answer for anything and everything.

When everyone stared at Megan, she shrugged and said, "I figure you didn't bring a lot of your things over, and even if the detective says it's okay for you to return home, it's going to take a while to clean up the mess... which we'll all pitch in and help you do, of course. But regardless, Keisha, you're going to need a few items now."

"Whether you stay at Canyon's place or a hotel," Bella added, smiling.

"We can go after church," Kalina said excitedly, as if the thought of going shopping had stirred her blood. "I need to pick up some more maternity outfits anyway."

"Going shopping is a great idea," Lucia piped in to say.

Keisha saw she was outnumbered but decided not to

make any promises. "We'll see. Check with me tomorrow." She then bid everyone goodbye as Canyon led her off the patio.

Seven

Keisha checked her watch after putting Beau to bed for his nap. Detective Render would be arriving in a few minutes and since she hadn't heard anything from Pete, she could only assume the police didn't have any answers for her yet.

Canyon hadn't had much to say on the drive back home from Dillon's place. No comments and no questions. It was as if he had a lot on his mind or was deliberately ignoring her. She wished she could do the same and ignore him, but there was just something about a man with so much testosterone. He was sexy without even trying to be and her body responded.

Whenever she'd focused on his hands, which had gripped the steering wheel, she couldn't help but remember how those same hands had stroked her body, had fondled her and had masterfully caressed her breasts. She'd sat there, crossing her legs and then uncrossing them a number of times before they'd arrived at Canyon's Bluff. If he'd found her fidgeting in her seat unusual, he made no mention of it.

After freshening up in the bathroom for her meeting with Detective Render, she glanced over at Beau and saw he was still sleeping peacefully. Keisha couldn't help but smile when she thought about all the fun Beau had had today with his cousins. He'd barely made it back here before falling asleep.

And she would have to admit that he wasn't the only one who'd had a good time. Considering her and Canyon's strained relationship, she had been surprised by just how warm and fuzzy Canyon's family had made her feel. She hadn't expected their acceptance and although Canyon had tried to assure her that his family wouldn't be rude because of what was going on with them, she hadn't believed it. Everyone had gone out of their way to be kind to her.

The ladies had even offered to go shopping with her, although she didn't intend to take them up on the offer. When Beau woke up in an hour, she would pack up the things she'd brought here and check in to a hotel. She would call Mr. Spivey on Monday morning to let him know what had happened and ask for a few days off to return some order to her home. Instead of accepting Canyon's family's offer to assist her with that as well, she would hire someone from a cleaning company.

Although Bailey hadn't come across as warm and fuzzy as all the others, she had shown concern about Keisha staying at a hotel. But then, she could have been more concerned for Beau's welfare than Keisha's.

Shrugging and deciding not to dwell on it any longer, Keisha moved toward the window to appreciate the beautiful view of the mountains. Canyon's bedroom view might be of the canyon, but she thought this view was just as breathtaking. A movement made Keisha glance down into Canyon's yard. She saw him, near the barn, bending down while cleaning his saddle. In addition to teaching her to swim, he'd taught her to ride a horse. Those were two things he intended to teach their son to do.

And then, as if Canyon had radar where she was concerned, he glanced up to the window and snagged her gaze. Her breath caught. She could still see the anger in the dark depths but now she saw something else. She felt it. In every part of her body.

Canyon's look always unnerved her, which was why she never maintained eye contact with him for any length of time…especially when they were sitting across the table from each other during client negotiations. So far they'd never had to face each other in a court of law. And she hoped that time never came.

She drew in a deep breath as his gaze continued to hold hers like a magnet. Tight. Fixed. Unyielding. It was eerie, stimulating and stirring, in a sensual kind of way—all at the same time. Without breaking eye contact, he straightened. *Tall, dark and too handsome for his own good.*

There was such strength and masculinity in his tall form that her heartbeat increased and her nipples transformed to hardened nubs.

She recalled how he used to unbutton her blouse, undo the front clasp to her bra and suck her nipples between his lips.

Geez. Why were all her memories of him so sexual?

Because even though they had enjoyed each other out of bed, their relationship had been sexual. And boy had she enjoyed their bed time. Canyon could stroke her into a climax with just his hands and mouth, but she had really enjoyed those times when he would embed himself within her. Thrust in and out of her as if he had every right to do so, like her body belonged to him and him alone.

And in a way it had. That was probably why over the past three years, at some of the oddest times, especially late at night when she couldn't sleep, thoughts of him would inflame her mind, her body and her soul. She would ache with an unquenchable longing. She would whisper his name in want, in need, in desire.

Even now, she hadn't made love to another man since Canyon because she hadn't desired another man...not even a little. That had to be why her body was bubbling over with all these crazy hormones now. Why the desire to mate, to have Canyon buried deep inside of her, was so poignant—to the point that it was becoming an emotional thing. And she had promised never to do the emotional thing with any man ever again.

Especially not this man.

Canyon broke eye contact with her, and she followed the direction of his gaze to see a car pulling up the long-winding driveway. She glanced down at her watch. Noon. She moved away from the window. Detective Render had arrived.

After the introductions, Canyon plopped down into one of the living room chairs. Keisha sat on the sofa with her hands clenched together in her lap, and Render sat across from her in another chair. Instead of a notepad, he had opted to use a recorder with Keisha's permission. The man, who appeared to be in his late forties, seemed all business. He was talking into the recorder, giving the date, his location and the reason the interview was about to take place.

Under normal circumstances, one of the police department's sharpest detectives wouldn't waste his time following up on a blatant case of harassment. Not when there were murders to solve. But with Sheriff Harper being such a close friend of Dillon's, and Pete being best friends with Derringer, and Render and Rico sharing a close working relationship, it seemed priority had been given to the incident.

Canyon shifted his gaze from Render to Keisha. As if she'd known the exact moment when he'd done so, she looked over at him. Their gazes held for a long moment and a bond neither of them could deny flowed between them.

At that moment they both knew there was a deeper connection between them than there had been before. It was the result of the little boy sleeping in the bed upstairs. Before, they'd only been lovers. Now they were parents and that was a link neither could break, even if they wanted to.

"Now, Ms. Ashford, let's begin," Detective Render said, causing Keisha to break eye contact with Canyon.

"First of all," Render said, looking at her, "I want to share what I hope is some breaking news. The car that was following you that day as well as the driver of the car have been located. He has been questioned thoroughly."

"Who is he?" It was Canyon who asked before Keisha had a chance to.

Render glanced over at Canyon. "A guy by the name of Shamir Ingram. He has a rap sheet a mile long. We found the car first, with the help of the traffic videos we pulled. And then when an officer recognized the car during a regular patrol, he pulled it over. Ingram was still driving it around with the stolen plate."

"Why did he do it?" Canyon asked.

"Is he the same person who trashed my house?"

Render chuckled when he looked from Canyon to Keisha and then back over to Canyon. "It might be a good idea, Westmoreland, if you joined Ms. Ashford on the sofa so I don't get a whiplash."

"No problem," Canyon said, standing and moving to the sofa. He could have put space between them but decided to sit right beside her. Once he was settled in his seat, Render continued.

"Ingram claims he was paid to follow Ms. Ashford."

"By whom?" Canyon asked, feeling anger toward Ingram invade his body.

"He won't say," Render answered.

"Gone brain-dead, has he?"

"Seems that way. But his cell phone has been confiscated and we're obtaining a search warrant for his place so we can go through his belongings."

Render shifted his gaze from Canyon to Keisha. "Ingram claims he was only paid to follow you and nothing more. His instructions were to freak you out by bumping into your car and running you off the road, but he was not told to trash your house. He guesses someone else was paid to do that."

"I don't believe him," Canyon said angrily.

"I do," Render countered. "I was there during his interrogation. I saw the look of surprise in his eyes when he was questioned about Ms. Ashford's house. And he got riled up at the thought that we were trying to pin both things on him."

"Yet he won't tell you who hired him?" Keisha asked.

"No. He claims he never met the person. The hire was made through a third party."

"What's the name of the third party?"

"He won't say," was Render's reply.

Canyon leaned forward. "Give me some time alone with him and I bet he'll talk."

Render chuckled. "Don't be so sure. A few bruises from you would be nothing in comparison to what he'd get if he's labeled a squealer." Render glanced over at Keisha. "That's why I need to ask you some pertinent questions. Someone is trying to scare you and I need to know why and who."

Keisha nodded. "All right."

"At this point we'll start the recorder," Render said, turning it on. When he was satisfied the equipment was working properly he said, "Ms. Ashford, I understand you moved away from Denver three years ago. Why?"

Keisha frowned. "What does that have to do with anything?"

Render met her gaze without blinking. "I plan to cover all bases and leave no stone unturned."

Keisha nodded and then answered, "I decided Denver was not where I wanted to live any longer."

Canyon knew she had skirted around the real reason she'd left and he had a feeling Render knew it, too.

"Yet, you've returned," Render said.

Canyon felt her tense up beside him before she said, "Yes, I returned. I had to leave my last job and my former boss heard about it and called and offered me my job back here."

Canyon snatched his head around and looked at her. "Why did you have to leave your last job?"

"That's my question, Westmoreland," Render said,

grinning. "For the record, Ms. Ashford, why did you need to leave your last job?"

As Canyon and Render watched, Keisha licked her lips nervously. "The law firm was forced to close down."

Render arched a brow. "It went bankrupt?"

Keisha shook her head. "No. The Texas Bar and justice department shut it down."

"Why?" both men asked simultaneously.

Canyon then glanced over at Render and said apologetically, "Sorry."

Render smiled and then looked back to Keisha. "Why did the Texas Bar and justice department shut down the law firm where you worked?"

Keisha sighed. "It was discovered that several attorneys in the firm—all five partners—abused their power by encouraging their clients to agree to foreclosures and then charging those homeowners exorbitant processing fees. It was later found out that the attorneys were defrauding those clients when the attorneys were receiving kickbacks from the banks, who were reselling the homes at a higher price and making a profit."

"Who turned them in?" Render inquired.

"There were speculations, but the person who exposed them was never identified."

"Was anyone indicted?" Render asked.

"Yes. All five were indicted. My former boss heard about the scandal and knew any law firm in Austin… or Texas for that matter…would be reluctant to hire me on after that."

"Why?" Render asked.

"Although I had nothing to do with what happened and was quickly cleared of any involvement, another firm wouldn't want to bring on an attorney connected to lawyers who were convicted of defrauding clients. So, my former boss offered me my job back."

Canyon said nothing. He'd wondered why she had returned. He knew it hadn't been because she felt Beau needed to be close to his father.

"How long ago did all this happen?" Render asked.

"Ten months ago." Keisha paused. Tilting her head, she stared at Render. "Surely you're not thinking there's a connection between that and what's going on with me now."

With an unreadable expression on his face, Render asked, "Any reason I shouldn't?"

"Of course there is. In fact, there are several," she said, leaning toward him.

Holding her gaze, Render said, "Name them."

Keisha pulled back and nodded. "Okay. First of all, those fraudulent activities were going on before I was even hired there and I never worked any of the cases. I was one of three relatively new attorneys. Second, those who were indicted were all partners. The other two attorneys, like me, were freshmen attorneys, considered to be peons. We were clueless as to what the top brass was doing. Third, why would anyone connected with that incident want to scare me? Scare me away from what? Why me? And who would be orchestrating such a thing?"

Render smiled. "First of all, I never said I had made a connection. You're the one who offered reasons why there is no connection, and I just asked you to name them. My job is to gather the facts, Ms. Ashford. All of them. And I agree that the chances of what happened yesterday being connected to what happened with that law firm in Texas is farfetched. But like I told you, I'm leaving no stone unturned." He paused. "But before you completely discount the possibility of a connection, let me give you this to consider. The attorneys were indicted, but I assume they haven't gone to trial?"

Keisha lifted a brow. "How would you know that?"

He chuckled. "We're talking about attorneys." Then, as if he remembered both Canyon and Keisha were attorneys, he smiled and said, "No offense, but I'm convinced these particular attorneys would use their knowledge of the law to delay serving time for as long as they can. They would also use their knowledge of the law to build a defense…while they're putting the fear of God in the whistle-blower."

Puzzlement appeared on her features. "But I wasn't the whistle-blower."

Render smiled. "Would they know that? Which makes me wonder if the other two freshmen attorneys not involved in the crimes have experienced scare tactics, too? Do the three of you keep in touch?"

She shook her head. "No. I never developed any close relationships with them. They were single and partiers and I was a mother with a newborn at home."

"Give me their names. It would be worth checking to see if they're being harassed, as well."

She gave him the man's and woman's names. Render then leaned back in his chair. "And just in case that's a theory leading nowhere, let's talk about the cases you've handled since returning to Denver?"

Keisha's eyes widened. "All of them?"

"As many as you can remember that might have resulted in ill feelings with clients or plaintiffs."

Three hours later, Ervin Render stood and stretched his body. "Well, I think I have a lot of information to go on."

Keisha frowned. She thought he had more than enough. He had picked her brain dry while almost making her suspect that any of her clients could be the culprit. Beau had wakened a couple of hours ago and she now glanced over to where he was on the floor staring at all the species of fish in the huge tank.

"If I have any more questions, I'll reach you here," Render added.

"You can try my mobile number because I won't be here," she said, standing as well when Canyon came to stand beside her.

Render lifted a brow. "Where will you be?"

"Probably at a hotel until I get my house back in order. Is there a problem?"

He shrugged and glanced from her to Canyon and back again. "Not for me, but it might be for you."

"In what way?" It was Canyon who spoke up with the question.

Render shoved his hands into his pockets. "We still don't know who hired Ingram to scare Ms. Ashford or who was responsible for trashing her house. If I were her, I wouldn't go anywhere alone."

That was not what Keisha wanted to hear. Nor was that what she wanted Canyon to hear. "I have a life, Detective Render," she said. "I can't give in to scare tactics."

"No, and you shouldn't," the man said easily. "But then you shouldn't make yourself a target either, Ms. Ashford. Until we know who's behind this, you should stay low for a while."

"That's not possible," she said, lifting her chin. "I work and have a job to do."

Render didn't say anything. Instead he glanced at Beau and then moved his gaze back to her. "You also have a son to raise, and I'm sure you want to be around to do so. I suggest you take a week off from work and don't go anywhere by yourself."

Keisha slowly drew in a breath. "Surely you're not suggesting that someone would—"

"I'm not suggesting anything. I'm just letting you know the possibilities. Someone wanted to scare you off. The reason why is still a mystery. Until you know what or who you're dealing with, you should hang around people you know, ones who have your back. Think about it. No need to bother showing me out. I know my way."

Canyon walked the man to the door anyway, while a frustrated Keisha worked the kinks out of her neck. She had to go to a hotel. There was no way she could stay under Canyon's roof another night.

She glanced up when he reentered the room. She opened her mouth to tell him she was going to a hotel in spite of what Render had said when he stopped her.

"I heard what Render said, Keisha, and there's nothing to think about. You're staying."

He then turned and walked out of the room.

An angry Keisha followed Canyon to the kitchen but hung back to stand in the doorway so she could also keep an eye on Beau, who was still lying on the living room floor staring at the huge fish tank.

"You don't tell me what to do," she said in a near whisper. "And I'm leaving."

Canyon walked back to her. "No, you're not. Did you not hear what Render said? Why are you being so damn stubborn?" he asked in a low, infuriated tone.

She lifted her chin. "I am not being stubborn, just practical. I can't stay here."

"Can you give me one good reason why you can't?"

There was no way she would tell him the real reason, mainly that being around him did crazy things to her hormones and made her remember feelings she just couldn't shake.

"Well?"

She frowned. He was standing there with his arms over his chest, facing her down like she was an unruly child. "For all I know, you might be involved with someone who might resent my being here."

He stared at her as if she'd lost her mind and then he said, "I'm not involved with anyone, and even if I was, do you think I'd let that person sway me to put my son's life in danger? Or to put the mother of my child in danger?"

Keisha swallowed. In a way, it hurt that all she was to him now was the mother of his child. There once was a time when she had been more. But that was before he'd allowed another woman to come between them.

"I can't stay here, Canyon. And you can't force me to stay. Nor can you threaten to take Beau from me if I leave with him."

Instead of addressing anything she'd said, he informed her in a low tone, "You still haven't given me a good reason why you can't stay here, Keisha. I told you I wasn't involved with anyone. I live in this big house by myself. I'll have my side and you'll have yours. What are you afraid of?"

She bristled at his question. "I'm not afraid of anything."

He ran a frustrated hand over his face and sighed. "Then think sensibly for a moment. Sure you can go to a hotel, but Beau will have more space here. He has family here. Why are you so determined to keep him away from me? Do you hate me that much?"

Something twisted inside of her. There wasn't a grain of truth in his assumption, and there was no way she could allow him to think that there was. "No. I don't hate you at all, Canyon. I admit when I left here I was angry and hurt. I felt betrayed. And I kept feeling that way with all those emotions festering inside of me. Then one day something happened," she said softly.

He lifted a brow. "What?"

She drew in a deep breath. "I felt my baby move. The baby you had put inside of me. I realized it was a real life, and I knew I couldn't feel so angry with you anymore because, at that moment, regardless of how things ended between us, you'd given me something you could never take away."

Canyon dropped his arms. "Is that why you don't want to include me in your and Beau's world…because you think I'd take him away from you?"

She took a long, shuddering breath before narrowing her gaze at him. "You said as much just last night."

"We said a lot of things last night, Keisha. I'm sure today there are regrets on both our parts. I don't want to take Beau from you. I want to share him with you. But first I want to keep you both safe. Please let me do that. Stay here for at least a week to see how things work out. Hopefully by then Detective Render's investigation will provide more answers. Then, who knows, it might be safe for you to go home."

"And if it's not?"

"We will reevaluate your options then."

Keisha knew she shouldn't consider his offer. There was no way she could remain a week under his roof without fear of losing her sanity. But would it be fair to place Beau in danger just because she couldn't keep her hormones in check?

She switched her gaze from Canyon's intense features to Beau. He had finally grown tired of lying on his stomach staring at the fish tank and was now on his back playing with the toy Denver—by way of Denver's parents—had loaned Beau.

She loved her child more than life, and she had to keep him safe until she knew what she was up against. And there was only one way to do that.

Canyon.

She might not be his favorite person right now, but he would do anything to protect his son.

She looked back at Canyon and met his dark, penetrating gaze. "All right," she said softly. "Beau and I will stay for a week."

Eight

Keisha eased out of bed. No matter how tired she was, she just couldn't seem to fall asleep and now she had one of those headaches she often got when she was stressed about something. All she could think about was how Detective Render had cast suspicions that now stirred in her mind, from her last job to every case she'd worked since returning to Denver.

What if one of the attorney's at that law firm in Texas had actually thought she was the whistle-blower and was trying to get back at her? Or what if the harassment had something to do with the case she'd won last year when she'd proved her client was the owner of land that a huge car dealership sat on?

Her client hadn't accepted the dealership owner's offer to lease the property. Instead her client had wanted the property vacated immediately, which could have caused hardship to the owner of the dealership. Bryant

Knowles hadn't been happy with her and had accused her of intentionally advising her client not to negotiate with opposing counsel. That hadn't been true, but nothing she said could convince Knowles otherwise. The two finally reached an agreement that was satisfactory to both in the end, but what if Knowles still harbored ill feelings?

Keisha glanced over at Beau. At least one of them had no problem sleeping tonight.

After she'd made her decision about staying, Canyon had gone to the store to purchase a safety gate for the stairs as well as cabinet locks, corner protectors, electrical outlet covers and a number of other items. While he was doing that, she had placed a call to Pam, letting her know she would need to go shopping tomorrow after all since she and Beau would be down to their last outfits.

When Canyon returned, he immediately went to work childproofing his house. And he'd purchased toys that had kept Beau entertained for the rest of the day. While he was out, Canyon had picked up carryout from McKays, a popular restaurant in town, which had taken the guesswork out of what they would have for dinner.

Grabbing her robe off a chair, she left the bedroom, securing the safety gate in place before going down the stairs. Except for the night-lights Canyon had installed, the rooms were completely dark, but Keisha had no problem finding her way to the kitchen. Canyon had left the curtains open, which gave her a full view of the moonlit sky.

The first time Canyon had brought her to visit this piece of land it had been at night and except for a few grassy areas the land had been wooded. They had parked and talked under the huge sky dotted with beautiful stars. And later they had made out in the car under that same sky. That night they had initiated their own private lover's lane.

Now Canyon had built a home here, possibly on the same spot because it sure as heck looked like the same sky. She knew that sounded crazy, but she was convinced this portion of sky belonged only to Canyon's Bluff.

"Couldn't sleep either?"

Keisha swung around when Canyon walked into the kitchen. She was immediately slammed with an overabundance of lust when she saw what he was…not wearing. He was in his bare feet, shirtless with his drawstring pajama bottoms riding low on his hips and clinging to a pair of powerful thighs.

The moonlight coming through the window encased him in a sensuous glow. Tingling sensations bombarded the area between her legs. Heated lust flared through her bloodstream and instinctively she pressed her thighs together.

Drawing in a shaky breath, she said, "No, having one of those headaches."

"Oh."

He knew about her headaches since she'd had them in the past when things hadn't gone quite like she'd wanted at work and she'd gotten stressed out about it.

"Come and sit down," he said, pulling out a chair from the table.

She glanced at the chair and then back at him. She knew what he wanted to do. Whenever she'd had a headache, Canyon used to rub her temples and ease the nagging pain away. She didn't know how he did it, but he would do it every time.

"Keisha?"

She swallowed. At the moment, headache or no headache, the last thing she could handle was Canyon's hands on her. But even as she had that thought, a fierce, agonizing throb pierced through her head, propelling her to move toward the chair. As soon as she sat down, she inhaled his masculine scent and instinctively breathed in deeper to pull in the heady aroma.

"Now close your eyes and relax," he said in a low, throaty tone that sent a ripple through her. She released a low groan when she felt his fingers slowly rake through her hair. She closed her eyes when she felt the heat of him behind her, gently massaging her scalp and placing light pressure at her temples. He kept up the kneading, working out the pain and soothing the ache.

He leaned down. "Feeling better?" he asked in an incredibly sexy voice, while the warmth of his breath fanned the side of her face.

Unable to respond, she nodded. The gentle scalp massage sent delicious shivers through her, replacing one kind of ache with another. She recalled the last time he'd done this. It had been a little more than three years ago. She had been stuck in litigation with what she thought was the case from hell. The opposing counsel had tried more than once to belittle her in front of the jury and she'd fought to retain her cool, which had resulted in an overpowering headache.

When she'd gotten home, Canyon had sat her down at the kitchen table and massaged her scalp and temples. By the time it was over, he had gotten rid of her headache but had left her wanting him…like he was doing now. Back then, he'd pulled her out of the chair, stripped her naked, laid her out on the table and made mind-blowing love to her.

"You can open your eyes now. And if you follow

this up with an aspirin, you'll feel good as new in the morning."

Drawing in a shaky breath she slowly opened her eyes. *What about tonight?* Would she feel as good as new tonight, too? She didn't think so…not as long as the tingling between her legs continued.

"Thanks, Canyon."

"You're welcome."

Keisha eased up from her chair and he slid it back under the table. She turned toward him. "You have a special touch," she said and then wished she could bite off her tongue for saying so.

His lips slowly spread into a smile, revealing a dimple that was normally kept hidden. "You think so?"

There was that sexy voice again that made her shiver. "Yes."

He chuckled softly. "Glad you still approve…of my hands…and what they are capable of doing."

She swallowed, wishing he hadn't gone there. "Well, I guess I'll go back upstairs."

"All right."

Why was she still standing there? Keisha asked herself. Why couldn't her feet move? Why was Canyon pinning her with those gorgeous dark eyes? And why was she standing there staring back?

She didn't remember who made the first move, all she knew was that it was made. He slid his warm arms around her, drawing her to him. And knowing what was coming next, her lips twitched, eager to be joined with his. He lowered his head and the connection was made with a precision that sent shivers all through her. She wrapped her arms around his neck as his tongue eased between her lips.

She groaned when he deepened the kiss as hunger

sent blood rushing through her veins. She'd known after their first kiss that no man kissed like Canyon. This was his calling, and she was a willing recipient. Her mind was flooded with memories…but this kiss was even better.

Keisha forgot about her vow to never let Canyon Westmoreland get close to her again. To never let him hold her, kiss her or make her moan. Because, at that moment, he was doing all three. And she was powerless to resist.

He deepened the kiss and heat flowed from his body to hers, setting the lower part of her body on fire. She felt his strong thighs pressing against her and thought, *Lordy.* His thick, hard shaft was cradled between her thighs, feeling as if it belonged there. Right there. Only Canyon had the power to manipulate her desires to his will and play havoc with her emotions.

And then suddenly, he broke off the kiss and his hands fell from her waist. The disconnect was so sudden she almost lost her balance. He quickly reached out to keep her from falling and she gasped when it hit her full force what they'd done. What she had let him do. She had to get away from him, to put distance between them, and she needed to do it now.

"I'm going back to bed," she said, backing up slowly. "Thanks for the head rub." She turned and was almost out of the kitchen when his words stopped her.

"Trust me, Keisha."

She stopped walking, tightening the robe around her and turning around. "What?"

"If the reason you got that headache is because you're worried about all the suspicions Detective Ren-

der raised, then I want you to believe that I won't let anyone hurt you or Beau. I want you to trust me about that."

Trust him? She drew in a trembling breath. The same
man who'd betrayed her with another woman wanted her
to trust him? A frown lined her brow, but as she stared
at him, she saw something in the depth of his dark eyes
that made the frown dissolve.

He wouldn't let anyone hurt her or Beau. She could
trust him regarding that.

Without saying anything, she nodded before turning
and quickly walking out of the kitchen.

Canyon watched Keisha leave while licking his lips,
savoring the taste she had left behind. She'd left her
fragrance behind as well, and it was just as arousing. It
didn't help matters that when she'd tightened the robe,
she'd emphasized her full breasts, her trim waist and
her curvy hips. And then when she'd walked out of the
kitchen the material had stretched across one delectable-
looking backside.

His memory had been jogged, remembering scenes
of that same body in several other outfits…like that
short, slinky red dress she'd worn when he'd accompanied her to her firm's Christmas party several years
back, and that short, black lace dress she'd worn to the
Westmoreland Ball.

And then there was a flash from the past of that body
wearing nothing at all. Now, *that* was a memory that
had his body getting hard, making him want things he
was better off not having. Especially when those things
concerned Keisha. There was no place for this fierce
hunger or for the assault on his senses that had come
from kissing her.

But he could no more not kiss her than he could stop

his heart from beating. Touching her, running his fingers through her hair, listening to her moan had pushed him over the edge, had made hot, potent lust flare up within him. Desire had taken control of his brain. Yes, kissing her had been foolish, but it had also been a detriment to his peace of mind. If he'd thought he couldn't sleep before, he sure as hell wouldn't be able to sleep now.

Moving across the kitchen, he went to the refrigerator and pulled out a beer and popped the tab. Hell, he truly needed something stronger but he would settle for this. It had been one hell of a day and was moving into one hell of a night. He'd missed most of it already.

He glanced over at the clock on the stove and saw it was just about midnight. He'd thought it was later than that. But who could keep time when it was taking all his effort to keep a level head around Keisha. He'd known Detective Render's visit had left her pretty uptight. Hell, who wouldn't be uptight, considering someone had paid a pair of goons to send her into a panic.

Before going to the store, Canyon had made a pit stop at Dillon's to tell him about Detective Render's visit and what had transpired. Dillon agreed that keeping Keisha and Beau within arm's reach here in Westmoreland Country was the best thing. He figured it would be advantageous if the Westmoreland men met to come up with a plan. Dillon had made the calls and within half an hour his brothers and cousins had arrived. They'd decided that if Canyon couldn't be with Keisha, one of the other Westmoreland men would be.

Now, tilting the can of beer to his lips, Canyon took a long, pleasurable gulp, licked his lips and frowned. Why could he still taste Keisha? Hell. Would he ever find peace from the woman? Evidently not, and now she was under his roof and would be for another week. And it had been his choice. He had asked, and she had reluctantly agreed. Now she was here and he had to decide how he felt about it.

If tonight was anything to go by, then what he was feeling were emotions that he shouldn't be feeling. This was a woman who thought he had betrayed her, a woman who hadn't told him he had a son even when she'd had every opportunity to do so.

Yet at the same time, he thought, taking another gulp of beer, Keisha Ashford was a woman he would protect with his life if he had to. It would be easier to protect her if she was here…and if he could keep himself from kissing her again.

Nine

"So, what do you think of this outfit, Keisha?"

Keisha glanced over at the clothes. Lucia held up a pair of little boy's jeans with a miniature work shirt to match. It was cute, and she could see Beau wearing it. She smiled. "I like it. Do they have it in a 3T?" Although Beau was two, because of his height he was wearing a size larger.

"Yes, I'll grab one for you," Lucia said excitedly.

Keisha grinned as she watched Lucia. Keisha obviously wasn't the only woman who liked shopping for her child. She was convinced the Westmoreland ladies had her beat. They had shown up on Canyon's doorstep at one o'clock with Canyon's younger brother Stern following behind them. Stern was only twenty months younger than Canyon and also an attorney at their family-owned firm, Blue Ridge.

Stern had advised the women that he was their escort for the day, and since none of them had questioned what he'd meant by that, Keisha could only assume everyone had been told of Detective Render's visit and his warning. Until they found out who was responsible for the craziness going on with her, it would be best if she took every precaution when it came to her and Beau's safety. And she was discovering the Westmorelands believed in looking after their own. The idea that she was now included in the mix because she was Beau's mother was mind-boggling.

So now she was in Kiddies' World Boutique surrounded by five women, who if Keisha wasn't careful could become her new BFFs. She'd taken a chance on Bonita after they'd met at a spa when she'd moved to Denver the first time and look what had happened. It had taken her a long time to even consider making new friends again.

"Think we got enough things for Beau?" Pam asked, coming up to Keisha holding outfits she'd grabbed off the racks for her sons Denver and Dade.

Keisha couldn't help but grin. "We bought too much if you ask me."

"Well, you heard Canyon's orders to get whatever you wanted," Chloe said, tossing the outfit for Beau in Keisha's cart and a cute little dress for her daughter, Susan, in hers.

Yes, he had said that, but it hadn't made her happy. She couldn't help frowning at the memory. When Canyon had offered her his charge card, she had refused to take it, telling him that she could pay for Beau's things without his help. He'd merely slid the card into her shirt pocket and said, "Humor me," before walking off.

"For what it's worth, I agree you should humor him,

like he said, Keisha," Pam said softly. "He wants to feel he's doing something for Beau."

Keisha released a sigh. "He did something for Beau yesterday. You should see all the stuff he brought back from the store. He got plenty of safety items, but he also bought Beau a lot of toys he didn't need."

"Sure Beau will need them," a pregnant Kalina said, grinning. "Kids can't have too many toys."

"It's the grown men you have to worry about," Bella said, smiling. "Jason asked his cousin Thorn to build him a motorcycle."

"Um, you ladies ought to check out Micah's speed-boat back in D.C.," Kalina said, laughing.

Keisha was amused when each woman told a story about their husband's favorite new toy. She saw how easy it was for them to laugh at themselves and with each other, and she knew this was what she'd missed out on by not belonging to a big family—a special connection, a camaraderie and a closeness that extended to the women who had married into it.

She glanced to where Stern was sitting in a chair near the entrance of the shop, his legs stretched out in front of him and his Stetson riding low on his head while he talked on his cell phone. Like his brothers and cousins, Stern was tall and ultra-handsome. He had long lashes to die for and a smile that could snatch a woman's breath right out of her lungs.

He didn't seem the least perturbed at having to hang out with a bunch of women today. And he hadn't gotten in the way. This was the second store they'd visited and at both locations he'd hung back, grabbed a chair and sat near the entrance while talking on the phone. But she was fully aware of his alert gaze, which had checked out all the people moving in and out of the store. His actions reminded her of just how serious her predicament was. It might be a while before the police found out who'd targeted her, and she couldn't expect a member of the Westmoreland family to be her bodyguard that whole time.

"Keisha?"

She shifted her gaze back to the women and found them staring at her. "Yes?"

"We're not trying to get in your business, because heaven knows all of us have had our ups and downs with Westmoreland men. But is there a reason you didn't want Canyon to know about Beau? We know about that incident you walked in on with that woman. We're not judging. But still, didn't you think he had a right to know about Beau?" Pam asked softly.

Keisha tried not to be defensive. She bit back the impulse to tell them to mind their own business. These women had befriended her when they didn't have to. They had been nothing but kind to her. Even Bailey, who'd joined them at the first shop they'd visited before leaving to meet a friend for lunch, had been nicer to her today.

All of the women before her had married Westmoreland men. Megan, the only married Westmoreland sister who still lived in Denver, hadn't been able to join them because she'd been called to the hospital this morning as the anesthesiologist for an emergency surgery.

Keisha wondered how she could explain her reasons so that they would understand. "When I left Denver three years ago, I was hurt and felt betrayed. I didn't want to see Canyon ever again, and I wanted no contact with him. I was determined to have my child without any man's help, like my mother did. I thought at the time that Canyon didn't deserve anything from me. As far as

I was concerned, he'd lost any rights to his child." She paused. "I now admit that I was wrong to feel that way."

Admitting she was wrong about something she'd believed so strongly at the time was a big move for her. "If I had to do it again I would handle things differently. No matter how or why our relationship ended, I should have told Canyon about Beau."

There, she'd said it. All it had taken was to see Canyon's interactions with his son over the past forty-eight hours to know how good they were for each other. Beau's acceptance of Canyon had been quick and absolute, and the same thing could be said of Canyon's acceptance of Beau.

Pam gently touched Keisha's shoulder. "That's a start, Keisha."

Was it? Keisha asked herself more than once over the next four hours they spent shopping.

There was still the issue of Canyon's betrayal. She had forced that nightmare out of her mind and had refused to consider that she'd been wrong. But what had she really seen? Although she hadn't caught Canyon and Bonita in bed together, Bonita had been naked, and Canyon had walked out of the bathroom with a towel around his middle.

Hadn't that been enough? Why would Bonita lie and say she and Canyon had slept together when they hadn't?

"You okay, Keisha?" Pam asked with concern in her voice as they made a turn onto the road leading to Canyon's Bluff.

"Yes, I'm okay," Keisha replied, but she wasn't. She felt a headache coming on, similar to the one she'd had

last night. The same one Canyon had relieved her of…
before he'd kissed her.

She took her tongue and licked her top lip, still feeling the aftertaste of pleasure. After she'd gone back to bed, the ache in her head was gone but the ache between her legs had been almost unbearable. It had been an hour later before she'd finally drifted off to sleep with dreams of endless sex with Canyon flowing through her mind.

"We're here. Looks like your guys are waiting on you."

Keisha glanced out the car window and felt a flutter in her stomach when she saw father and son sitting side by side on the porch, leaning back on their arms with their legs swinging simultaneously while watching the car pull up. Both had similar huge smiles on their faces. She understood why Beau was smiling. He was glad to see her. But why was Canyon smiling?

She couldn't imagine that he was glad to see her. She knew he'd been kind enough to provide shelter to her and Beau for the next week, but she knew the only reason he had was because he wanted to protect his son. She just happened to be part of the package.

As soon as she opened the car door, Beau charged across the yard to her. "Mommy! Mommy! You home, Mommy!"

She raised a brow. *Home?* Beau had only been here for two days and he already thought of Canyon's place as home. What about her house? Granted the last time he'd seen it, it had been a mess, but still…

"Yes, Mommy is here," she said, smiling down at him. "Were you a good boy?"

"Yes, good boy. Daddy-Dad has horse. Big horse," he said, widening his arms. "I ride."

Keisha chuckled. "Did you?"

"Yes." He turned toward Canyon. "Didn't I, Daddy-Dad?"

"You most certainly did."

Keisha watched as Canyon eased off the porch, and she felt a tingling in the pit of her stomach when his jeans stretched tight across his muscled thighs. She couldn't ignore the rush of desire that poured through her as she stared at him walking toward her with a stride so sexy she felt flushed by its heat.

"Well, we'll be going now," Pam said, reclaiming Keisha's attention.

She glanced at Pam and all the other women staring at her with a "we understand" smile on their faces. "Okay, and thank you all for everything."

"No problem. Jill is leaving early tomorrow morning, and she and I plan to do a movie tonight. At least I don't have to get up and take her to the airport. Aiden is such a sweetie. He volunteered to take Jill for me," Pam said, getting back behind the wheel of the van.

"I bet he did," Keisha heard Canyon mutter under his breath as Pam drove off. She glanced at him, wondering what he meant by that. He had come to stand beside her. He looked good, and he smelled good. It was a powerful combination.

Keisha then looked at Stern who'd gotten out of his car to help the ladies remove the shopping bags. "Thank you, Stern."

He gave her a sexy smile. "My pleasure."

"Looks like you bought a lot," Canyon said in a throaty voice, moving past her to take the shopping bags from Stern.

"I took your advice and decided to humor you."

Canyon threw his head back and laughed. "Thanks."

"Well, I hate to run, but I'm meeting JoJo in town.

We're attending that Muscle Car Show," Stern said, opening the door to his car and sliding inside.

"Thanks, Stern," Canyon said.

"No problem. Lucky for all of you that I didn't have a date or anything," Stern said, grinning. Giving them a wave, he then drove off.

Keisha glanced over at Canyon. "Who's JoJo?"

"His best friend, Jovonnie Jones. They have been friends since they were kids in middle school. Her father owned an auto mechanic shop in town, but she took things over when Mr. Jones passed away."

Keisha lifted her brow. "She's a mechanic?"

"The best. She works on all our cars," he said, turning toward the house. "Where do you want these?"

"Up in my bedroom. I mean the bedroom you're letting me use," she corrected.

"I knew what you meant, Keisha. Did you buy something for yourself, as well?"

"Yes, but I didn't put it on your charge card. I used my own, but thanks for the offer." She glanced down at Beau, whose hand she was holding firmly in hers as they went up the steps to the porch. She looked back at Canyon. "Was Beau a good boy?"

"Of course. All Westmorelands are good," he said, grinning.

She rolled her eyes. "So you say."

"So I know. And speaking of Westmorelands, there's something I want to discuss with you," he said, opening the door and gesturing for her to go in front of him.

She released Beau's hand when he tugged for her to let go. She watched him scamper off to the living room where he flipped down on his stomach to stare at the huge fish tank, which was becoming his favorite pastime. Canyon had purchased several fish to add to the tank yesterday and that had fascinated Beau even more.

When Canyon returned from placing the bags upstairs, he found her sitting down at the dining room table. "So what do you want to talk with me about, Canyon?" she asked, wondering what his discussion would involve.

Instead of sitting down across from her, he shoved his hands into the pockets of his jeans and leaned back against the huge breakfast bar that separated the dining room from the kitchen.

"It's about Beau."

Her stomach knotted at the serious look in his eyes and the firm set of his jaw. "What about Beau?"

"I want my son to have my name, Keisha."

She swallowed. "Your name?"

"Yes. He's a Westmoreland, and I want his last name to reflect that."

Canyon knew he had a fight on his hands, but he was ready for the battle. He had thought about it from day one and felt justified in what he was asking. There was no reason for his son not to have his name.

He waited and watched Keisha study the floor before looking back up at him. "All right."

He blinked, surprised at her response. "All right?"

"Yes, all right." She stood. "I'm sure Beau hasn't had a nap yet so I'll take him up—"

"Whoa. Wait a minute," he said, straightening away from the breakfast bar.

"Yes?"

"Why?" he asked.

She lifted a brow. "Why what?"

He gave her a level look. "Why are you being so charitable all of a sudden?"

She stiffened her spine. "Did you think I wouldn't agree to it?"

"Yes."

She held his stare and then turned away for a second before turning back to find his gaze searching her face. "Well?" he asked, staring her down.

She eased down into her chair. "I owe you an apology, Canyon."

More surprise flashed in his eyes. "Do you?"

"Yes. Beau is your son and no matter how things ended between us, I should have told you about him."

Canyon froze. Of all the things he had expected her to say, that wasn't it. She was right. She should have told him about Beau. "Is that the only thing you're apologizing for?"

He watched her lift her chin. She fully understood what he was asking. Was she also apologizing for believing he had betrayed her?

"Yes, that's the only thing I'm apologizing for."

He stared at her for a long moment. In other words, she still believed him to be a cheating bastard. One day she would realize just how wrong she was about him. When that day came, what would she do? Would she think any words of apology could erase what she had put him through? Had put them both through?

Holding in the anger he was feeling, he said, "I'll contact a man who handles all the Westmorelands' legal affairs. He will complete the paperwork for the change."

"That's fine."

He bit back the words to tell her that she was wrong. It wasn't fine. At that moment, he wasn't sure if things between them could ever be fine again.

* * *

"Honest, Mom. Beau and I are okay," Keisha said, talking into her cell phone. She and her mother made a point of talking every Sunday afternoon and Keisha knew she should tell Lynn what was going on.

"And the police have no idea who's responsible?" Lynn asked.

"Not yet, but they're on top of this."

"So you and Beau are living at a hotel?"

Keisha nibbled on her bottom lip. "No, we aren't at a hotel."

"Then where are you?"

Releasing a deep sigh, Keisha spent the next fifteen minutes telling her mother everything, including her recent apology to Canyon for not telling him about Beau.

When she finished, Lynn didn't say anything for a long moment. "I'm glad everything's out now, Keisha. I never felt you should keep Beau a secret from his father."

"I know, Mom, but during that time the pain was more than I could bear."

"I know, baby, but he had that right. Even I knew better than to do that to your father."

"Yes, but what good did it do?" Keisha asked curtly. "How could he have believed I wasn't his?" It was something she had wondered about, but had never asked.

"Because I was supposed to be on birth control, and he didn't want to believe it hadn't worked. And, unfortunately, at the time a woman had accused his older brother of the same thing and they'd found out she was lying."

"But he loved you, so he should have believed you," Keisha said fiercely.

"Um, that's easy for you to say. You loved Canyon,

yet you didn't believe him when he denied sleeping with that woman."

Her mother's words were a blow that Keisha felt in her belly, nearly knocking the wind out of her. "My situation was different," she defended softly, while her insides struggled for normalcy.

"Was it?"

"Yes." Keisha glanced out the kitchen window, again wondering if she'd done the right thing by staying here and not at a hotel. It was getting dark, but Canyon was still outside. She could see him working in his yard. Earlier, he had washed down the barn with a hose and before that he had washed his car. He was working off his anger. She understood and accepted his actions.

"I don't see how. You never saw them in bed together and only went with what that woman said. Getting back to your father, when he saw you for the first time, he knew you were his."

"Yes, but I was fifteen by then." She had gone over this with her mother plenty of times. Granted, her mother had moved away from Texas, which had made it impossible for her father to see her, but as far as she was concerned the timing and the distance had been his fault. All he'd had to do that day when they'd run into him and his brother in a restaurant was to look at her to know how wrong he'd been. He had spent the past fourteen years since that day trying to undo that wrong. But she'd refused to meet him halfway. A part of her couldn't let go of how he'd rejected her before she'd been born.

Needing to change the subject, she asked her mother how things were going at the hospital where she'd worked for more than twenty years. Keisha then inquired about the ladies who'd worked with her for years and whom Keisha considered honorary aunties. The same women who'd been there to give their support during Lynn's breast cancer scare. She knew her mother wanted to return to their discussion of both Canyon and her father, but Lynn knew when to back off. After all, Keisha was her mother's daughter, and although the mother might have mellowed over the years, her daughter had not.

When Keisha heard the kitchen door open and close she didn't have to turn around to know Canyon had come inside. "Okay, Mom, we'll talk again later. It's time for me to put Beau to bed."

"All right, sweetheart. Tell Beau that Gramma loves him. And say hello to Canyon for me."

Keisha nodded. "I will."

Keisha clicked off her phone and slowly swiveled around. Canyon was leaning against the refrigerator with his hands shoved in the pockets of his jeans, staring at her. A rush of awareness swept through her. It sizzled her insides and sent a gush of blood through her veins. "That was Mom. She told me to tell you hello."

He nodded and said nothing.

"Beau wanted to wait until you came in to eat."

Canyon glanced around. "Where is he?"

"Sitting at the dining room table listening to his books." Canyon had bought Beau a stack of audio storybooks with colorful pictures, which he was enjoying. "I'll let him know you're here so he can eat and get into bed at a reasonable time."

She made a move to walk past Canyon and he snagged her arm. When she glanced up at him, he moved to stand directly in front of her.

"I accept your apology."

Ten

Keisha was still mulling over Canyon's words hours later, even after she'd taken a shower and gotten into bed. Why did his acceptance of her apology make her feel worse instead of better? And why did her mother have to bring up her father?

A mental image of the man who'd fathered her flashed through Keisha's mind. The physical resemblance was there for even a half-blind man to see. She had her father's eyes, nose, lips and forehead. He'd seen it that day, and she had seen it for herself. That day he had discovered just what a fool he'd been to think her mother had betrayed him. The sad thing was that it had taken him fifteen years to realize the truth.

Since then, he'd made several attempts to reach out to her, but she didn't want anything to do with him. She'd even gotten upset when she'd found out her mother had given in and let him back into her life. Her mother didn't think Keisha knew, but she did.

Easing out of bed, Keisha decided to go downstairs and grab her ereader off the coffee table where she'd left it earlier. It was past midnight, so she would read a novel until she got sleepy. She didn't have any court cases this week, which was good, and she had spoken to Mr. Whitock. After explaining the situation, he had agreed that she should take the week off.

Sliding into her robe, she checked on Beau one last time before leaving the room to go downstairs.

Canyon stood at his bedroom window, staring up at the sky. He resented the seesaw of emotions coursing through him. One minute he was filled with so much anger about all Keisha had done, and then the next minute he was overcome by a need for her that could erupt into desire with very little effort.

And that kiss last night hadn't helped matters. It had only proved that the physical chemistry between them was stronger than ever. His need had flared up so swiftly he could have taken her then and there. That was why he had ended the kiss the way he had. His desire for her had been so sharp it had cut into everything, including his common sense. She could ignite desire in him without even trying.

Like earlier that day, when he'd come in from outside and she'd been talking on the phone to her mother. He had stood leaning against the refrigerator, feeling tightness in his loins. A warm rush of heat had flowed through him. She looked damn good in her jeans, which emphasized her lush curves and shapely backside. He could have ogled her for hours. And when she'd turned around he'd been captured by her incredibly beautiful face. His senses had been reduced to mush.

And then he had accepted her apology. While he was working off his anger outside, he had remembered how he and his brothers used to fuss and fight and how his mother would make them apologize to each other. His mother always told them not to apologize or accept an apology if they didn't really mean it.

Canyon rubbed a hand down his face. He had accepted Keisha's apology because he believed she'd been sincere in making it and regretted keeping Beau from him. To continue to feel bitterness and anger toward her wasn't healthy, not for him and not for his son. And very quickly Beau had become the most important person in his life.

As far as the issue of Keisha still believing that he was a cheating bastard, that was something that would not keep him up at night. She could think whatever she wanted, he didn't care anymore. As long as she didn't keep him from his son then he could deal with anything else. Besides, he no longer loved her. But he did want her. Lusty thoughts were keeping him up, making it hard to sleep. He'd already told Dillon he was taking tomorrow off. He had spoken with Roy McDonald, who had agreed to meet with him and Keisha at noon tomorrow to complete the paperwork to change Beau's last name.

When he'd mentioned the appointment to Keisha earlier tonight she'd said she would need Beau's birth certificate, which was at her home. So he would take her there in the morning to get it. He'd gotten the okay from Pete earlier yesterday that all prints had been lifted and it was okay for Keisha to bring order to her home. Canyon had already made arrangements to take care of that, as well.

He stretched his body, deciding to go downstairs and walk outside for a while. Seeing the sky from his bedroom window was nice, but on a night like this he preferred being beneath it.

Keisha made it across the living room before she collided with a hard muscled body. A spark of desire flashed through her the moment they touched. When she reached out to grab Canyon, to stop herself from falling, she touched his bare chest and heard his quick intake of breath. His arms went around her waist to steady her.

"Oh, sorry, Canyon. I didn't know you were still up."

"I wasn't. I couldn't sleep and thought I would take a stroll outside," he said in a deep, husky voice.

"Oh. And I came downstairs to grab my ereader off the table where I left it earlier."

"Couldn't sleep again?" he asked.

"No, I couldn't sleep again." Why were they still standing here with her hands on his chest and his hands around her waist? And why was his heart beating so fast beneath her palms and why was hers beating just as rapidly? And why were so many too-lusty thoughts flowing through her brain, causing heat to stir and making every cell in her body throb as she inhaled his manly scent?

"You want to go with me outside?" he whispered.

She swallowed. She couldn't. She shouldn't. But in an instant, she knew that she would. Dropping her hands from his chest, she said, "Okay."

He let go of her waist and entwined his hand with hers. "Come on." He led her across the room and out the door.

The moment they stepped onto the porch Canyon stopped to breathe in the warm August night air. He then glanced up at the sky and a sense of calm flowed through him. Something else flowed through him, as well. An affirmation of the thoughts he'd had earlier this evening.

"This sky still holds special meaning to you, doesn't it?"

He glanced over at her. "You remember?"

She chuckled softly. "How could I not. Because of you, I've grown fond of the sky, as well. I haven't gone so far as to buy a telescope or anything like that, but I find myself staring up at it a lot."

"Still certain you'll see the man in the moon?"

She snickered. "Yes."

One night he had brought her up here and she'd been convinced that if she kept looking hard enough then she would see the man in the moon. It had all been in jest, the kind of fun they'd enjoyed together. They'd shared all their secrets…even the silly ones. Later they had made love in the backseat of his car. "Let's sit down on the steps."

Other than the sound of crickets chirping, the night was quiet. There was a gentle breeze coming off the mountains, twirling around the canyons and valleys. He had a feeling it would rain later in the week. He could deal with any kind of weather, other than a heavy snowstorm. All Westmorelands detested snow, except for Riley. His brother actually looked forward to blizzards.

Canyon glanced over at Keisha. He hadn't allowed himself to think that one day she would return to Denver and sit beside him under his sky again. Underneath Flash. But she was here. Now if she could only get beyond the hurt and anger she felt were justified.

She was leaning back on her arms and staring up at the sky. What she was thinking? How she was feeling?

There had been so much animosity between them, but he hoped they could continue to find common ground without hostility and bitterness, for their son's sake.

"What are you thinking?" he decided to ask her.

When she glanced over at him he saw a semblance of regret in her eyes. "I was thinking of how things could have been."

If you hadn't screwed up, he figured she didn't add. He was fully aware that she still placed the blame for their three-year separation at his feet, but it wasn't justified. However, he refused to think about that tonight. "Sometimes it's best not to go back, Keisha. The best plan of action is to let go and move on."

"Is it?"

He gave her a tight smile. "I think so. It's a matter of forgiveness on all accounts…especially if it's a past you can't change."

She arched her brow, but didn't say anything as she stared at him. He knew how that analytical mind of hers worked. She assumed he was hinting that she should forgive him…but that was far from the truth. As far as he was concerned he hadn't done anything that needed to be forgiven. And to give himself credit, unlike Zane who hadn't tried getting Channing back when she left town, Canyon had done everything he'd known how to do to get Keisha back.

He figured she had run home to her mother in Texas, and he had tried calling but she'd changed her cell phone number. He'd even gone to see Bonita and pleaded with her to contact Keisha and tell her the truth but she'd refused. Bonita wouldn't even tell him why she had blatantly lied about the entire situation. And when he had sought out Bonita's ex, to see if Grant could shed light on why Bonita had done what she'd done, he'd only learned that Grant had moved away.

Finally, bitterness and resentment had settled in and he'd decided that if Keisha assumed the worst about him so be it. He would not try to run her down and plead his innocence. If she didn't trust him, then he was better off without her.

But then she had come back to town. As far as he was concerned, her return had been a game changer. Especially since he'd found out she'd given birth to his son. Now he couldn't help raising his hand and smoothing out the frown that had settled around her brow.

"What are you doing?" she asked in a quiet tone.

He smiled. "You're working yourself into another headache by thinking too much, about all the wrong things."

"Am I?"

"Yes."

Several moments of silence hovered between them. He felt it, that physical chemistry that was always there. They could try to ignore it, try to put a cap on it or they could give in to it. No need to think it would ever get out of their system because that wasn't possible. No matter the time or the situation, he would always want Keisha.

He felt the pounding in his heart and, of their own accord, his fingers moved from her brow, brushing a lock of hair from her face before slowly sliding down to her lips. The tips of his fingers grazed softly across her mouth, and he heard the breathless sigh in her throat when her lips parted.

Old habits die hard. In the past, whenever her lips would part on a breathless sigh, he'd known just what to do about it. The same thing he was about to do now.

Shifting his position, his arms slid around her waist

as he lowered his head and took her mouth with a possession that rocked him to the core.

Acting on instinct and insatiable hunger, Keisha's tongue mated passionately with Canyon's. For now, she was willing to do what he suggested, let go and move on. And she refused to question why something she'd thought impossible was now feasible. Canyon made sure she continued not to question by kissing her such that her yearning for him came back into focus. Her desire for him manipulated her emotions in a way she couldn't combat. He was reducing her to a ball of urgency and need. An entreaty for more escalated through her. He deepened the kiss, taking control of her mouth with firm strokes, making even more intense moans flow from deep within her throat.

Canyon stood and drew her up with him, not breaking their kiss. His hands moved to her backside and eased her closer to the fit of him, flexing his hips against her. She could feel the hardness of his erection, pressing against the juncture of her thighs, triggering more greed within her. It was a greed she'd kept dormant for three years, and the slow yet urgent strokes of his tongue were bringing that greed back to life.

He slowly pulled his mouth from hers and she knew the need to breathe was the only reason he'd broken off the kiss. She saw how his handsome face was bathed in the moonlight and the way his gaze held hers hostage while her body churned and blood rushed hotly through her veins.

Suddenly, as if neither of them could withstand the lust overtaking them, Canyon swept her into his arms and carried her back into the house and upstairs to his bedroom.

* * *

No man should want a woman this much, Canyon thought, putting Keisha down. She looked like a tempting miniature morsel in the ocean of covers on his huge bed.

While he watched, she scampered to her knees to remove her robe and then her nightshirt. He couldn't help but stand and watch her undress. When she had tossed aside the last piece of clothing, leaving her naked and totally exposed, the bulge in his pajama bottoms hardened, swelling to gigantic proportions.

When she eased up, stretching her body, she showcased a pair of firm breasts, a small waist, a flat stomach and curvy hips. His gaze dipped lower to the juncture of her thighs and his mouth watered.

Growling with primitive savagery and a feverish hunger, he eased his bottoms down his thighs as his gaze remained focused on her. He knew every measure of that body. Had touched it. Tasted it. Devoured it. Emotions clogged his throat when he saw where her interest lay as he stood before her totally naked.

"You're still the Grand Canyon, I see."

He couldn't help the smile that spread across his lips. At that moment, it didn't matter what she believed or didn't believe. Tonight his sheets would get scorched to oblivion when he made love to her. "Glad you think so."

He moved over to the bed and joined her, pulling her into his arms and easing her onto her back against the pillows, intending to lick every inch of her skin, starting at her lips. He whispered, "I missed you and I intend to show you how much."

And then he began his feast, holding her hips when she squirmed in pleasure beneath his mouth. By the time his tongue reached her breasts and supped on the protruding nipples, he felt them harden even more in his mouth. She called out his name but he only continued his sensuous assault, determined to remind her how good they were together and what they had once meant to each other.

Keisha shuddered with sensations as Canyon's mouth moved across her body, leaving no area untouched. His hand moved from her hips and drifted lower. She gasped at the feel of his fingers settling between her legs, sliding through her curls. At the same time, his mouth licked circles around her naval, causing a moan to rise in her throat.

And just when she thought there was no way she could take any more, he parted her womanly folds, slid a finger inside of her and began stroking her intimately. No woman could survive his skillful hand and she closed her eyes against the sensual torture.

Moments later, when she felt his tongue replace his finger, her eyes flew open. "Canyon!"

If he heard her scream his name he didn't let on, instead he deepened the kiss and intensified her agony, stroking his tongue in the right places, using his hands to lift her hips off the bed to get his mouth closer to her. Every nerve ending in her body strummed with intense pleasure.

Her body jerked when an orgasm tore through her and she screamed his name again and again. When the last spasm left her body, she slowly opened her eyes and watched Canyon reach into the nightstand and pull out a condom pack. He quickly sheathed himself, eased his body over hers and gazed down at her, his eyes filled with absolute possession and passion.

"Look at me, Keisha," he said in a low command.

"Look at me and see the man I am, the man you've always known. One day you'll know that I could not have betrayed you. Not when I have loved you from day one. Not when after all that's happened between us, I still love you."

She held his gaze and her heart pounded. And as she read the truth in his eyes, she felt her own fill with tears. Because she knew at that moment she had been wrong. "Oh, Canyon…"

He leaned down, licking the tears that flowed down her cheeks before taking her mouth in another ferocious kiss. Cupping her hips, he lifted her and entered her in one long, hard thrust, going deep, all the way to the hilt. And then he began moving, stroking, thrusting in and out—making love to her with an intensity that snatched her breath from her lungs.

Lifting her legs, she wrapped them around his waist, tightening them in a firm grip as another orgasm ripped through her. She knew the exact moment the pinnacle of a climax consumed him, as well. He released her mouth and threw his head back. His growl permeated the air as he continued to stroke deep inside of her.

Then his mouth returned to hers and blood surged through her veins. He kissed her with an intensity that made her shiver inside. Moments later, he released her mouth and she whispered, "I'm sorry," in a broken tone. "I am so sorry."

He cupped her face in his hands, kissed the side of her lips and said softly, "I accept your apology, sweetheart."

Canyon wasn't sure why he awoke in the middle of the night. But when he opened his eyes and shifted in bed the clock on the nightstand indicated it was almost

four in the morning. And the spot beside him was empty.
He would have thought he'd dreamed last night had it
not been for Keisha's feminine scent that was infused
in his bedcovers.

When he heard a sob, he glanced over at his bedroom
window. Keisha stood there, staring out into the night.
She was crying. Concern tugged at his heart and he slid
out of bed, walked over and put his arms around her.
As if she needed his strength, she turned in his arms
and buried her face in his chest, wetting his skin with
her tears.

He tightened his arms around her. "Shh. Don't cry.
It's okay. It doesn't matter anymore."

She pulled out of his arms and looked up at him with
tearstained eyes. "Why did she lie, Canyon? Why did
she deliberately tear us apart?"

He pulled her to him and wrapped his arms around
her again. "The only person who could answer that is
Bonita, sweetheart. Unfortunately, she took the reason
to the grave with her. We might never know."

She tossed her head back and looked up at him.
"How?"

He lifted a brow. "How?"

"Yes, how can you stand the sight of me after all I
did, all I said and believed? How can you forgive me
when I'm having a difficult time forgiving myself? How
can you think you love me?"

Canyon sighed deeply while tracing a path up and
down her back with his hands. He wondered what he
could say to help her understand. "I was hurt and angry
for a long time, Keisha. I convinced myself that I hated
you for what you did to us. And then when I found out
about Beau, and realized what you've deliberately de-

nied me for two years, I became furious." He paused. "But Dillon made me realize a few things."

"What?"

"First, that you had a choice. You didn't have to keep Beau when you found out you were pregnant. You hated me and thought I had betrayed you. He was a reminder of what you thought I did. Yet you chose to have him and for that I am grateful. And Dillon made me see that if the roles had been reversed, and I had come home to find another man in bed with you coming out of the bathroom in just a towel, I would have thought the worst, as well."

"But Bonita lied through her teeth. She intentionally wanted me to believe the worst about you."

And you did. He forced that thought to the back of his mind. "Doesn't matter, you know the truth now. I had convinced myself I didn't love you. I even thought I hated you at one time. But all it took was kissing you, holding you in my arms and making love to you to show me what my true emotions were. I discovered the truth that there is a thin line between love and hate."

Not giving her a chance to say anything, he swept her off her feet and into his arms. He carried her over to the bed.

"I checked on Beau, and he's sleeping peacefully," she said, looking at him.

"Good, because for the next hour, you won't be." Then he captured her mouth with his.

Eleven

The next morning, Keisha rushed downstairs. She had woken up in Canyon's bed and upon realizing how late it was—after eight already—she'd quickly slid back into her nightgown, grabbed her robe and fled from the room. Beau was an early riser, and from the moment he opened his eyes, he could be a force to reckon with. He was at that age where he assumed food should be at his beck and call.

As she rounded the corner leading to the kitchen she heard voices. Canyon was standing at the counter sipping a cup of coffee while Beau sat at the kitchen table eating eggs, bacon and toast, and drinking milk while talking nonstop, telling Canyon about the *big* horse he wanted.

When he detected her presence, Canyon turned sensual dark eyes on her. Immediately, her nipples puckered beneath the robe, the juncture of her thighs tingled and shivers of desire raced through her. After a full night of hot-and-heavy lovemaking, one would think sex would be the last thing on her mind this morning. But it wasn't. And from the look in Canyon's eyes, it wasn't the last thing on his mind either.

"Good morning, Keisha," he said in a voice singed with a sexiness.

She swallowed. "Good morning." She then moved to the table and kissed the tip of Beau's nose. "And how are you, Beau?"

Beau smiled. "Beau good. Food good. Daddy-Dad good, too."

Keisha chuckled. *Yes, Daddy-Dad is definitely good. Better than good,* she thought. She had indulged in hours and hours of lovemaking last night and he had proved that he hadn't lost his edge. In the bedroom, Canyon Westmoreland was still the best. She glanced down at Beau's plate. It seemed Canyon had also improved his cooking skills since the last time they'd been together.

She glanced up at him. "You did a good job dressing him."

Canyon smiled and his dimple oozed with rich sensuality. "I've been getting a lot of practice with Denver. I've been known to babysit a time or two."

She nodded. "And who taught you how to cook?"

His smile widened. "Chloe. When Ramsey's cook Nellie decided to move away last year, Chloe took on all the cooking for Ramsey and his men and let Lucia run the magazine company. Chloe enjoys getting up at the crack of dawn and the men loved her cooking and enjoyed seeing her pretty face in the morning.

"Chloe also felt all the single Westmorelands without cooking skills could benefit from a basic cooking class. Ramsey and Dillon seconded that notion, so now I can fend for myself."

He moved away from the counter and pulled her into his arms. "Now to kiss you good-morning properly."

By the time he released her mouth, Keisha was weak in the knees.

"Daddy-Dad, you bit Mommy!" Beau exclaimed.

Canyon chuckled as he rubbed the top of his son's curly head. "No, Beau, I *kissed* Mommy. You're going to see a lot of that around here."

Keisha swallowed. Canyon had said it as if he expected her to be hanging around a lot. Maybe this was not the time to tell him that although she now knew how wrong she'd been about him and he had admitted to still loving her, she couldn't rush into anything. She still had to return to her home when the seven days were up. She and Canyon needed to restart their relationship but rushing into things was not the way to do it. They had a lot of history to work through. They should take things one day at a time.

"Eat up, Beau. Aunt Pam is on her way."

She glanced up at Canyon. "Pam is coming for Beau?"

"Yes. We have a lot of business to take care of this morning, and I called and asked if she'd mind watching Beau. She thought it was a wonderful idea. The other day Beau and Denver played well together."

"Yes, but she has one in diapers. Three might be a lot for her to handle."

"Not for Pam. Dade isn't walking yet so he doesn't get in as much trouble. She mentioned that Chloe would be coming over later with Susan and Rembrandt and they plan on making it a fun day for the kids."

"Oh."

Canyon didn't say anything for a long moment. He just stood there studying her with intense eyes. Finally he asked, "You don't have a problem with the plans I made for Beau today, do you?"

A part of her did. She hoped she could make him understand. "I'm just used to making decisions about Beau on my own. Before, it's just been me and him."

He nodded. "I understand, but now there's the three of us. And if I ever do anything you don't agree with or that you're not comfortable with, let me know."

Keisha knew she was being silly. There wasn't a single mother out there who wouldn't want the father of her child to take an active role…especially if that role was a good one. And there was no doubt in her mind that Canyon and his family would be good for Beau.

"Keisha?"

She saw the concern in his eyes. "No problem. I'll just go upstairs and change. What time are we meeting with the attorney?"

"At noon. But I need to take you home first to get Beau's birth certificate."

"All right. I'll go upstairs and get dressed and be right back."

She was quiet, Canyon thought, glancing over at Keisha. They were in his car, on their way to her place and she hadn't said much. Keisha had been okay when Pam had arrived for Beau, but it seemed that once they'd driven away from Westmoreland Country, she'd withdrawn into her own thoughts.

He'd been trying to keep the conversation going by talking about the man who'd been elected mayor of Denver during the time she'd been gone, and what a great job the guy was doing. He'd even brought her up to date on his great-grandfather Raphel and how Megan's husband, Rico, was involved in investigating his great-grandfather's past. It seemed Raphel had been involved with other women before marrying their great-grandmother, and one of those women had borne him a child. That meant they could have more cousins out there somewhere. Westmorelands were big on family and they hoped Rico's investigation would shed light on who those cousins were and where they were now.

"You okay?" he asked her.

She glanced over at him. "Yes, I'm fine. Just feeling a little disgusted again about my house and the condition it's in, and worried because the police are still clueless about who did it."

He heard the frustration in her tone and understood it. He hadn't mentioned that he'd spoken to Pete this morning because there hadn't been anything new to report. "Well, I think we have the best police force around, if that makes you feel any better," he said, reaching over to take her hand in his when they came to a traffic light.

A small smile touched her lips. "I'll take your word for it."

His hand returned to the steering wheel when the traffic light changed. "So tell me how your mom is doing. Is she still a radiologist at that hospital?"

"Yes, and she doesn't plan to retire anytime soon." She then told him about her mother's breast cancer scare and how she was glad she had been with her during that time. "She took a leave of absence when Beau was born because she refused to let anyone else keep him while he was so young," she added. "So she kept him for eight months, and I appreciated it." She paused a moment and then said softly, "I think she might be seeing my father again."

Canyon was certain if he hadn't needed to come to a stop at another traffic light, he might have slammed on his breaks anyway. He looked over at her. "Your mother and your old man?"

"The man who got her pregnant? Yes," she clarified. She drew in a deep breath and then added, "I never told you this, but my father saw me when I was fifteen. It was then that he realized my mother hadn't lied after all."

No, Canyon thought. She'd never told him that. In fact, she'd only told him how the man had denied the baby was his when her mother had told him about her pregnancy. "So what did he do when he realized you were his child?"

"He tried making up for lost time, but it was too late. I knew the whole story of how he'd broken my mother's heart, and I decided that I didn't want to have anything to do with him."

So in other words, Canyon thought, she had totally dismissed her father and kept him out of her life—just like she'd done with him. "So what makes you think your mother has hooked back up with him after all this time?"

"Because as I got older I realized something."

"What?"

"That she never dated another man. She had friends and work, but she made me her life. For years I just assumed she enjoyed being independent, but now I can see things differently. She was hurt by his rejection, which is why we moved away from Texas. But now I believe the reason she never dated is because she couldn't give her heart to another man."

Canyon didn't say anything. What she said was probably true because he'd once walked that same road.

When Keisha had left Denver believing the worst about him, he'd been hurt and it had taken him a while to get back into the dating scene. But even then he'd known he would never love another woman the way he'd loved her.

"And lately," Keisha said, breaking into his thoughts, "she's been bringing him up each and every time we talk. It was subtle at first but now she's been trying to convince me that he regrets not accepting me as his, he regrets turning his back on me for the first fifteen years of my life."

He imagined that wasn't going over well with her since she tended to see things as black or white. "How do you feel about that? About your mom getting back with him?" he asked.

She shrugged. "I want to think I have no feelings one way or the other. It's her life. However, I don't understand how she can be so forgiving."

"Why? Because you wouldn't be so forgiving?" he asked, trying to keep his voice calm when frankly, he was getting annoyed with her attitude. "In that case, it's a good thing that you thought I betrayed you and not the other way around."

At her confused look he explained, "If I had been the one seeking your forgiveness because I mistakenly thought you betrayed me, chances are I wouldn't have gotten it."

Canyon's words left Keisha speechless. What could she say? Her own mother had made a similar assertion to her yesterday. Okay, she would admit that forgiving didn't come easily for her. And she would even concede that her inability to forgive easily was the reason she'd kept Beau from his father for two years. However, she'd been wrong to go that far and had admitted that, ask-

ing for Canyon's forgiveness. And he had forgiven her.
Was she being too hard on her father? Did he deserve
to be forgiven like she had been?

"We're here."

She snapped out of her reverie and glanced around.
They had pulled up in her driveway and there were several vans already parked there. "What's going on?" she
asked, already opening the door to get out.

"The cleaning team I hired is here."

When she reached his side, she turned to him with
a look of surprise on her face. "You hired a cleaning
team?"

"Yes. I had to talk Pete into giving me your key and
he only did so after I told him what I planned to do. I
didn't want you to worry about cleaning up the place
and it had to get done. A few years ago there was a fire
at the home Bella inherited from her grandfather. This
same company came in and did an awesome job, so I
figured they could do the same here. I contacted them
Saturday and I think you're going to be pleased."

Keisha couldn't say anything. Saturday hadn't been
a good day for them and they hadn't been on the best
of terms. Yet he had cared enough to hire some company to come in and get her house back in order. She
took his hand in hers and held his gaze. "Thank you."

She meant it more than he would ever know. She
hadn't looked forward to coming here today, knowing
what she would find. But he'd been kind enough to take
care of it for her.

"You're welcome." He tightened his hand on hers.
"Come on, let me introduce you to everyone."

Keisha met the owners of the company—Mr. and
Mrs. Helton—and their crew. From the moment she'd
walked over the threshold she'd seen firsthand what

a great job they'd done. Already they had righted her house to the extent that she couldn't tell it had been trashed. A new coat of paint had been applied to her walls and new carpeting had been installed throughout the house. All of the colors matched her original interior design choices. The kitchen was spotless and the floor tile was a gleaming white. She thought her house looked better now than it had before.

"The clothes that were thrown all over your floors have been taken to the cleaners or have been washed," Mrs. Helton said. "Are you pleased, Ms. Ashford?"

"Yes," Keisha said without hesitation. She glanced around her bedroom, amazed. A new coverlet and new fluffy pillows were on her bed. The new carpeting, a shade of tan darker than what had been there before, was the perfect blend. She'd seen Beau's room and her office and those rooms looked incredible, as well. "Your company did a fantastic job."

The woman beamed. "Thanks. Mr. Westmoreland said to make it special for you because you were special."

Keisha glanced over to where Canyon stood in the hallway, talking with Mr. Helton. "Well, you followed his instructions by doing an outstanding job."

"Thank you. Unless there's something else you think we need to do, we'll be leaving now."

Keisha nodded. "No, everything looks great."

The woman nodded with a smile on her face. "If you see anything we've missed after we leave, just give us a call. Our card is on your dresser and another on your kitchen counter."

"Thanks, I will."

The woman left and Keisha went into her bathroom and marveled at the new set of towels, matching throw rugs and shower curtain. A beautiful vase of artificial spring flowers that looked so real—she leaned down to sniff to make sure they weren't—looked perfect sitting on the new vanity.

"Keisha?"

"Coming," she said, leaving the bathroom to find Canyon standing in the middle of her bedroom. Did he always have to look so good? Have so much testosterone oozing from every pore? Her heart began pounding like crazy in her chest as she slid her gaze over the full length of him.

"Looks good, doesn't it?"

"Most definitely," she said, fully realizing they were talking about two different things.

He looked at her and smiled. "I'm glad you're pleased."

"I definitely am. However, I might have bad memories of how this place looked, unless…"

He raised a thick dark brow. "Unless what?"

She didn't say anything for a moment while toe-curling desire trickled through her. And then she moved, walking over to stand in front of him. "Unless the bad memories are replaced with good ones."

No one could credit Canyon with being slow. But then it could have been the way her hardened nipples pressed against her shirt that gave her away. He took a step closer and wrapped his arms around her waist. "Need my help doing that? Replacing those memories?"

She leaned in closer to him. "Are you volunteering, Canyon?"

"Yes, I'm volunteering."

She nibbled on her bottom lip. "Do we have time? There is that matter of our appointment with an attorney at noon."

"We'll make time."

Pulling his cell phone out of his pocket, he punched in some numbers without taking his eyes off her. Moments later he said into the phone, "Hey, this is Canyon. We're running late, Roy."

There was a pause and then. "How late?" He smiled down at Keisha as he continued to speak into the phone. "At least a couple of hours. Maybe three." Then, "Fine. We'll see you then." He clicked off the phone and slid it back into his pocket.

Keisha felt her pulse beat wildly near her throat. "The front door?"

"Locked."

She sighed in anticipation. She knew that look in his eyes. It had been there each and every time he'd made love to her.

He cupped her face between strong hands, leaned closer and whispered huskily, "I want you."

She whispered back, "And I want you."

Within seconds, his hungry mouth was devouring hers, mating with her tongue like he owned it. Possessing it. Claiming it. All in the sweep of his tongue as he took her mouth with a skill that was all consuming. No other man could make a kiss so stimulating and erotic. A moan of lust she couldn't contain forced its way out of her throat.

With their mouths still locked together, he backed her toward the bed. When they reached their destination, he lifted his mouth from hers and began removing her clothes. Lifting her blouse over her head, he proceeded to slide her skirt down her hips. She was left in only her bra and panties. He reached behind her and unhooked her bra. Eager, he cupped the twin globes of her breasts in his hands, his fingers brushing across the nipples. As though on cue, her body flamed at the juncture of her legs and she moaned deep within her throat.

Then he released her breasts, crouched down on his haunches and pressed his face to her feminine mound and drew in her scent.

Keisha knew what he planned to do, and when he licked her through the silk of her panties, she tightened her hands on his shoulders. "Canyon," she said, whispering his name on a shivering moan.

Canyon pulled back to ease Keisha's panties down her legs, barely able to contain his hunger. Before she could take her next breath, he parted her feminine folds and put his tongue inside her.

One of the things he'd missed most was this. Her delicious taste. She trembled hard and he held her firmly by her hips, intending to have his fill and give her pleasure. Over and over, he flicked his tongue over her and lapped up the taste of honey.

She moaned and arched forward. He continued to hold her hips as he felt pleasure ripple through her, making her say his name. The sound infiltrated his brain, intoxicated his soul and whipped him with just as much pleasure as it seemed she was feeling. When the last tremble passed through her, he slowly stood, gathered her close and then tumbled her down on the bed with him.

"You still have your clothes on," Keisha mumbled, when he slid off her to stand by the bed.

"Something I'm about to remedy," he said, pulling his belt through the loops of his jeans.

She rested against one of the huge pillows and

watched him while aftershocks of pleasure strummed through her. With her gaze glued to his body, she watched him undress. First his shirt. "Mmm," she said as he eased his jeans down his legs along with his briefs. The man was so well endowed. "It's always nice to re-visit the Grand Canyon."

"Glad you want to," he said in a deep, sexy voice.

"Oh, I do."

After sheathing himself with a condom he'd taken from his wallet, he returned to the bed. When his knees touched the mattress, he dipped his head and brought his mouth straight to her mouth, mating with it in slow easy strokes. Moments later, breaking the kiss, he pulled her to him, placing her back to his chest.

A shiver of anticipation stirred through her. There had never been a dull moment with Canyon in the bed-room and she had a feeling he was about to reacquaint her with some of those times.

After pushing her up to her hands and knees and turning her to face the headboard, she felt him caress the contours of her back, thighs and backside. She sucked in her breath when his fingers eased between her legs and found her wetness. Then he replaced his hands with feathery kisses.

When she thought she couldn't handle it anymore, he mounted her from behind, sliding into her, clamping her back to his front, thrusting in and out of her with slow, measured strokes. She closed her eyes, wonder-ing if she would survive all the pleasure.

And then the tempo changed. He pounded into her harder, faster, while stroking his hands over her breasts. The sound of flesh slapping against flesh pervaded the air and she couldn't help but moan. Her muscles, greedy for his invasion, clinched tight with each inward thrust.

A shiver began in the pit of her stomach and spread. She tried forcing it back, not ready for an explosion just yet. Not wanting this to end. Her body was ready, but she wasn't. She wanted to go on and on, and enjoy each powerful thrust.

"Let go, baby," Canyon whispered close to her ear as he increased the tempo even more. "I won't let go until you do and the pleasure is killing me," he muttered the words in a savage growl.

She let go. Screaming at the top of her lungs while he rode her hard, their bodies locked together. He let out one hell of a sensuous snarl, before roaring out her name. Moments later, as they tumbled down in the bed, he gathered her close.

She felt the aftershocks leave his body and hers and knew it would be a while before either of them had the energy to move.

Twelve

"Glad the two of you were finally able to make it."

Keisha nervously nibbled her bottom lip, totally embarrassed. Their appointment had been at noon and it was now four o'clock. She and Canyon were sitting next to each other, across from the man's huge desk. "Sorry, we're late, Mr. McDonald."

Canyon muttered softly, "I'm not."

She gave him a warning look and hoped Roy McDonald hadn't heard what he'd said. She felt bad all the way around. She'd even called Pam and apologized. After telling Pam this morning that they would be by to get Beau before two o'clock, they were late for that, as well. Pam had understood and told her not to worry. Beau was fine and was having fun with Denver. Pam had even suggested that she and Canyon grab something to eat while they were out because Beau could eat dinner with Denver.

"You did bring the birth certificate with you so we can start the paperwork?"

"Yes," she said, handing him the document. Roy Mc-Donald appeared to be in his mid-fifties and, according to Canyon, he had handled business for the Westmore-lands for a number of years.

She studied the bracelet on her wrist so she wouldn't be tempted to look over at Canyon. The last thing she needed to remember was what had happened back at her house. Not once, but twice. To say her home was now filled with good memories was an understatement.

"Well, the paperwork will be easier than I thought. All I need is your signature on a piece of documentation, Canyon."

Canyon lifted a brow. "Why will it be so easy?" he asked.

"Because you're already showing as Beau Ashford's biological father on his birth certificate, so all I'm doing is a simple name change."

"What?" He turned to Keisha, confused. "You listed me as Beau's father?"

Keisha nodded slowly. "Yes."

"Why?"

Roy McDonald didn't understand Canyon's question and interrupted to ask. "The child isn't yours?"

Canyon frowned at Roy. "Of course he's mine. What makes you think otherwise?"

Roy shrugged. "By the nature of the question you just asked Ms. Ashford."

Canyon drew in a deep breath. "I'm not asking because I think Beau isn't mine, I'm asking because I'm surprised she would have acknowledged it that way."

"Oh." Roy then stood and headed for the door.

"Where are you going?" Canyon asked.

Roy turned around and smiled. "To the break room to watch CNN. Evidently the two of you need to talk about a few things without me." He then left, closing the door behind him.

Canyon turned his attention back to Keisha. "Why?"

She nervously nibbled her bottom lip. "Mom always said that was the one thing she regretted not doing, naming my father on my birth certificate. If anything had happened to her I would not have known anything about him. I didn't want that for Beau in case he wanted to find you someday."

He nodded. "Thank you for doing that."

"You don't have to thank me."

"Yes," he said, standing and pulling her up from her chair, as well. "I do."

Then he kissed her with an appreciation he felt in every cell of his body. Last night and this afternoon had proved that their three-year separation hadn't eradicated the passion between them. If anything, their passion was more intense than ever. It wouldn't take much for him to place her on Roy's desk and take her here and now. Kissing her with slow thoroughness had a way of making him lose control.

There was a quick knock on the door and Roy stuck his head in. "I take it we're going to proceed as planned."

Canyon chuckled. "Yes, that wasn't the issue, Roy."

Roy lifted a brow as he returned to his desk. "Then what was the issue?"

Smiling, Canyon continued to hold Keisha's hand as they returned to their seats. "It doesn't matter anymore. From here on out, we're moving forward."

"Welcome to McKays. Will there be just the two of you dining this evening, Mr. Westmoreland?" the waitress asked.

"Yes, Priscilla, just the two of us."

Smiling, Priscilla said, "Then please follow me," as she led them to a table that had a gorgeous view of the mountains.

Once seated, Keisha glanced over at Canyon. "Are you sure it's okay for us to take time to eat here? I would have been okay if we had grabbed something from one of those fast-food places. I'd hate for Pam to think we're taking advantage of her kindness with Beau."

Canyon shook his head, grinning. "Believe me, no one in my family will ever think that. Besides, it's a way for Beau to start getting to know everyone since they'll become a vital part of his life."

Keisha took a sip of the water the server placed in front of them, deciding not to ask what he meant by that. However, eventually she and Canyon would have to talk. More than once today he'd hinted at something permanent between them as if it was a done deal. And it wasn't. Although he was willing to leave the past behind them and move ahead, she wasn't sure she could do it so easily. There were still some things she needed to work through—specifically, her guilt.

She had accused him wrongly, which had resulted in her treating him unjustly. And whenever she thought about what he had missed out on, what Beau had missed out on…she could only lay the blame at her own feet. He might be willing to forgive her, but forgiveness had never come easy to her. This time, it was *herself* she wasn't sure she could forgive. Her actions had cost him two years of his son's life. It had cost her three years of anger and pain that she'd let fester inside of her for no reason. Before she could consider getting back together with Canyon, she had to figure out her own issues.

Moments later, after the server came back to give them menus, Canyon said, "I think I'm going to order us a bottle of champagne."

She raised a brow. "Why?"

"Because we have reasons to celebrate. We have a son and we're moving forward—"

"It's nice running into you two."

Keisha glanced up and stared into the face of Grant Palmer.

Canyon stood. He wasn't sure what lie Bonita might have told Grant about that night three years ago. If the man planned to make a scene, then Canyon was ready. He'd only met Grant once before, and that was when he had accompanied Keisha to a birthday bash Bonita had given her fiancé. "Grant. You're back in Denver?"

"Only for a short while. I flew in this weekend to attend a cousin's wedding," Grant said, smiling and offering Canyon his hand in a hearty handshake.

Canyon knew his surprise showed on his face as he accepted the man's hand. Grant wasn't acting like someone holding a grudge. When Canyon glanced over at Keisha he could tell she was just as baffled as he was.

It was Grant's next statement that muddied the waters even more. "I'm glad the two of you are back together and relieved Bonita was able to make things right with you before she died."

Canyon glanced over at Keisha who had a *what is he talking about* look on her face. Keisha asked, "What do you mean, Grant?"

"I mean what happened that night…when it looked as if Bonita and Canyon had slept together."

Canyon felt as if he'd just been delivered a sucker

punch to the gut. "You knew it wasn't true?" Canyon asked in an incredulous tone that had a bit of a bite to it.

Grant's smile faded. "Yes." He glanced at Keisha. "Didn't she explain everything? She said she would."

Canyon shook his head, wondering what the hell was going on here. Before he could ask Grant to elaborate, Keisha spoke up with a slight tremor in her voice. "Bonita didn't explain anything to me, Grant. But Canyon and I would be most appreciative if you would."

Grant joined them after telling the friends he was dining with that he would rejoin them later. After Canyon told their waitress they weren't ready to order their meals but did want to order Grant a drink, a perplexed Grant sat down and said, "I think I'll start from the beginning."

"Please do," Keisha encouraged, smiling. She knew Canyon was just as bewildered as she was.

"It was the night I broke off our engagement," Grant said.

"You had broken off your engagement that night," Keisha repeated his words in surprise.

"Yes. I found out some disturbing news about Bonita." He paused when the waitress placed his drink in front of him. "She had a split personality." He paused. "In her dominant personality, she was the woman I fell in love with and wanted to marry, but in her subordinate one, she was a totally different person."

"When did you find out about her two personalities?" Canyon asked.

"Not soon enough. The reason I broke off with her is because I found out the other Bonita was having an affair with another man. The wife suspected something and had a video camera installed in her home. It showed

Bonita and the man together one weekend while the wife was out of town. It was filmed two weeks after we'd become engaged but, according to the wife, the affair had been going on for quite some time."

He didn't say anything else for a minute. After taking a sip of his drink, he continued, "When she came home from work, I confronted her and she denied it, claimed it wasn't her. But it *was* her. I had already gone through her drawers and found stuff I'd never seen before. All kinds of sex toys and crap. I even found her journal, which pretty much corroborated the wife's story about how long the affair had been going on. When I explained all of that, Bonita burst into tears and denied everything."

Grant paused again. "I didn't believe her and moved out that night, told her the engagement was off and I never wanted to see her again. And I didn't. But then two years later she showed up in Florida at the college where I'm teaching. That's when she told me the truth about her split personalities and that she was getting treatment from a mental-health professional. It was then that she confessed to what she'd done to you—at least what the other Bonita had done to you—the night I broke off our engagement."

"And what did she tell you?" Keisha asked quietly.

"She told me how the dominant Bonita was upset, distraught over our broken engagement. She drove across town to see you, Keisha, needing a friend, a shoulder to cry on because she couldn't understand how I could accuse her of such things. She said it was only after Canyon came to the door that she remembered you were out of town. He saw how distraught Bonita was, let her in, offered her something to drink and even shared a drink with her."

"I take it she had no memory of changing roles?" Canyon asked.

Grant shook his head sadly. "No. None. Although she saw the video of her affair for herself she denied knowledge of any of it. She even claimed those items and the journal weren't hers."

Grant took another sip of his drink before continuing. "She said she was fine at first…the normal Bonita. But then after Canyon excused himself to go take a shower that's when the other Bonita emerged. She's the one who undressed and got into your bed with plans to seduce Canyon when he finished with his shower. The only thing was, he walked out of the shower the minute you walked into the bedroom, Keisha. And you assumed you had caught Bonita and Canyon in an illicit act."

Keisha found Canyon staring at her with penetrating dark eyes. She didn't have to imagine what he was thinking. The shame of guilt was more powerful than ever. She could clearly recall that night, how he had pleaded with her to believe him and how Bonita had pleaded with her not to believe him. Keisha had been so hell-bent on believing the worst that she hadn't taken the time to notice that Bonita's behavior was different. Keisha had said some god-awful things to the both of them, told them they had better be out of her place before she came back. She had specifically told Canyon to clear everything he owned out and not to try to contact her or else she would put a restraining order in place. She had ended up driving to the mall and sitting in the parking lot in her car for hours just crying. By the time she had returned home all traces of Canyon were gone.

She never saw Bonita alive after that night, and she had refused to take Canyon's calls. She'd even changed her phone number. She had heard Bonita and Grant had ended their engagement, and she'd assumed he'd found out what had happened. Less than two weeks later, hurt, alone and pregnant, she had resigned from her job and moved back to Texas.

Drawing in a deep breath, Keisha asked softly, "When did Bonita realize there were two of her?"

"Not until she was arrested for shoplifting."

"My God," Keisha said, her hand flying to her chest in shock.

"The court required that she receive mental-health treatment and she did. When she realized the full impact of what she'd done to us, and to you, Keisha, the two people she had trusted the most and who had trusted her, she was devastated. That's why she came to see me in Florida and why she had planned to fly to see you in Texas. I assumed she had when I saw you and Canyon together.

"I guess she was killed before she had a chance to tell you anything. Her mother mentioned you attended the memorial services, so I assumed Bonita had confided in you, told you the truth, and that you had forgiven her. Had I known that wasn't the case and that you were still under the assumption that Canyon had betrayed you, I would have made it my business to make sure you both knew the truth."

Keisha nodded. "I went to her funeral out of respect for her family and noticed you weren't there," she said.

Grant ran a frustrated hand down his face. "No, I couldn't make myself go and see her that way. A part of me felt that I had failed her. I thought the worst of her but had I known the extent of her mental illness, I would have forgiven her and gotten her help. But I didn't know," he said brokenly.

Keisha didn't say anything because, at that moment, she felt as if she had failed Bonita, as well.

Canyon woke up for the second night in a row and found the spot beside him empty. Pulling himself up in bed he ran a hand down his face before glancing over at the window where he knew Keisha would be. She was standing in front of it, staring up at the sky like she'd done the night before.

Once Grant had left to rejoin his friends, the mood for celebrating with champagne had vanished. Instead they had ordered dinner and exchanged few words. He figured both of them were wondering if there was some way they could have detected Bonita's mental condition and he was sure there wasn't.

But he had a feeling Keisha believed otherwise. Keisha and Bonita had been good friends, and a part of Canyon was saddened about how the friendship had ended. But the last thing he would let Keisha think was that what had happened with Bonita was her fault. Easing out of bed he walked behind her and wrapped his arms around her, drawing her close to his solid chest.

"I didn't mean to wake you," she whispered.

"You didn't. I woke up and found you gone. Now that I have you back in my bed it's hard for me to think of you not being there with me." When she didn't say anything, he tightened his arms around her. "Talk to me, Keisha. Share your thoughts."

He heard her deep sigh. "I was thinking about Bonita, the one I knew and considered my friend…until that night. I was so full of hurt and anger that I refused to consider something else might be wrong. I was mistaken about you and wrong about her, as well."

He turned her around to face him with hands firmly

on her shoulders. "There was no way you or any of us could have known about her mental condition."

"But I was her friend, I should have known," she said.

"You aren't a mind reader. Grant lived with her, and he didn't have a clue. What happened to her was sad, but we have to move on and—"

"Forget the past," she snapped, pulling out of his arms. "That might be easy for you to do, but everyone isn't as forgiving as you, Canyon."

He frowned, dropping his hands from her shoulders. "What are you talking about?"

"I hurt you. I kept Beau away from you, yet you've forgiven me. That's all well and good, but I can't forgive myself, Canyon. I can't. Every time I see you and Beau together I'm reminded of what I did, of how much pain I caused both of us. And now I see how I wronged Bonita—"

"Whoa. I won't let you take the blame for that. Bonita had a mental illness that you didn't know about. Will you stop allowing misplaced blame to rule your life? To rule our life?"

She wiped a tear from her eye. "There's no *our life*, Canyon."

He stared at her. "What do you mean?"

"I mean that until I can come to terms with what I did and let it go there can't be an *us*."

He shook his head, as if dismissing what she'd said. "Of course there can be an *us*. We had a son together. You love me, and I love you."

She lifted her chin. "Do you really? How can you when I find it hard to love myself."

Canyon drew in a deep breath in an effort to make some sense of what she was saying. "Correct me if I'm wrong, but did we not make love in that bed last night?

Did we not make love at your place today? And in that bed over there again tonight?"

She turned away with slumped shoulders, but not before she said, "Doesn't matter."

He turned her back around to face him. "Yes, it does matter," he said fiercely. "And when things matter, you don't give up. You make it work. I refuse to let you become a victim of negativity and guilt. I refuse to let you punish yourself for something that wasn't your fault."

Canyon looked out the window at the sky to find the strength he needed where she was concerned. He loved her with all his heart, and he refused to let her give up on them.

He looked back down at her. "Do you love me, Keisha?"

She swiped back tears. "Yes, I love you," she said softly. "But this is one of those times when loving someone might not be enough."

"I love you, and I have it from the best—my married brothers and cousins—that loving someone will always be enough," he said. "More than enough," he added, cupping her face in his hands.

"But, baby, you have to believe it. You have to get off this guilt trip you're on, and stop believing you're to blame for every damn thing that goes wrong. You're not perfect and neither am I. We've both made mistakes. Everyone has."

His eyes held hers. "What I want more than anything is to marry you. Not because of Beau, but because of us. We're back together for a reason, Keisha, and I want to believe it's because that's where we should be. I want more than just Beau. I want us to have other kids, more Westmorelands to one day rule this land. Tell me you'll marry me."

He watched how her lips trembled and the look in her eyes reflected uncertainty.

When she didn't answer, he dropped his hands and took a step back. "I need to get away for a while. I'm going over to Stern's Stronghold. I'll be back later."

"But it's almost midnight," she said.

He shrugged as he slid into his jeans and put on his shirt. "He's a late-nighter." After slipping into his shoes, he said, "Go to bed and get some sleep."

Canyon left the room, taking the stairs two at a time. Before walking out the door he grabbed his cell phone off the table and saw he'd missed several calls. Only then did he remember that he'd placed it on vibrate while they'd been at McKays. Deciding he would check the missed calls later, he breathed in the mountain air the moment his foot touched his porch.

Lord knows he was trying to be patient with Keisha, but she was wearing him thin. He didn't want her for a lover. He wanted her as his wife. Canyon figured that until she came to terms with the issue of her father she would be weighed down by her inability to forgive, even when the only one needing that forgiveness was herself.

As he unlocked the door and got into his car he knew he would do whatever it took to make her see that while he'd gone without her for three years, now that she and Beau were in his life, he didn't intend to do without either one of them again.

Canyon's mind was so full of thoughts of Keisha and the marriage proposal she hadn't accepted that he didn't notice the dark vehicle deliberately hidden behind the tall sagebrush as he left Canyon's Bluff.

Thirteen

Keisha slid into her robe, tightening the belt around her waist when she heard the sound of Canyon's car driving away. The last thing she would be able to do was take his suggestion and get some sleep, so she decided to go downstairs for a cup of tea. She grabbed her cell phone off the nightstand planning to chat with her Mom. Knowing how her mother kept late hours, Keisha figured she would still be up.

She saw she had missed a couple of calls from Detective Render and wondered if he'd tried calling her because there was a new development with her case. It was too late to return his call tonight, but she would do so first thing in the morning. She had promised Canyon that she would stay here a week and she had four days left. Her plans were to return home on Saturday. Thanks to Canyon her home was back in order, along with a new security system. She was glad because she refused to live in fear that someone out there wanted to do her harm.

Yet, you're willing to live in another kind of fear, her mind mocked. *Fear of your own vulnerability.*

Keisha took a sip of the tea she'd just brewed and sat down at the kitchen table. *And what about your inability to forgive? That's the root of your problem. Are you trying to hold yourself to a higher standard than most people? Forgiving yourself for mistakes isn't a crime. Maybe you ought to try it.*

Keisha sighed as she clicked her phone to call her mother. Lynn picked up within two rings.

"Keisha? You okay?"

She knew her mother found it odd that she was calling so late and Keisha quickly assured her she was fine. "Yes, I'm okay. I couldn't sleep."

"What's bothering you?"

Keisha then told her mother what Grant had told her and Canyon about Bonita.

Lynn said, "It wasn't your fault, what happened to Bonita, and Canyon has forgiven you for the other mistakes, so why are you tormenting yourself? Why is it easier to deny yourself the man you love than it is for you to forgive anyone who you feel has done you wrong?"

"Someone like Kenneth Drew?"

There was a moment of silence on the other end of the phone and Keisha figured it was time she and her mother had *that* talk. "So, tell me, Mom, when was the last time you saw him?" She'd never asked her mother anything about the man who was her father.

"I saw him today in fact."

Keisha nodded. That didn't surprise her. "So you've forgiven him?"

"Yes, I had to move on."

"Move on? Is that why you're seeing him again?"

She heard her mother's sharp intake of breath. Keisha drew in a deep breath of her own and then said softly, "You gave yourself away without meaning to and that's okay. You don't need my permission do anything, you know. I just don't want you to get hurt again."

"It might be hard for you to understand now, baby, but one day you will see that life is something you won't be able to hang on to forever. That cancer scare three years ago showed me that. You should embrace life every day, with no regrets. Kenneth and I both made mistakes and he knows he's hurt me. He knows he's hurt you. He has tried to make things right."

"How? Just by claiming me as his because I look like him? Where was he when I was in school and you had to struggle to support me? What about when I was in college and law school and—"

"He paid for that."

Keisha stopped talking. "Excuse me?"

"Kenneth never wanted me to tell you, but he's the one who paid your college tuition. All of it. Including law school. At first I wasn't going to accept his offer, but I knew it was something he wanted to do. He and I both knew it wouldn't erase the first fifteen years of your life, but he was hell-bent on giving you everything he could during the years after that."

Keisha was silent. All this time she'd assumed her mother had been too independent to accept anything from anyone, especially from a man who'd turned his back on her when she had needed him the most.

"And another thing, Keisha," her mother said. "He never married and neither did I. You're his only child, and he says I'm the only woman he ever truly loved. He wants a life with me and doesn't think it's too late."

Keisha swallowed. "And what do you want, Mom?" she asked softly.

There was a pause and then, "I want him, too. But then, I don't want to lose my daughter."

Keisha hung her head. She should not be placing her mother in a position where she felt she had to choose. Could Keisha handle being the cause of her mother's unhappiness?

"Mom, I want you to be happy. Do what makes you happy. And no matter what, I will always be your daughter. Nothing will ever change that." Keisha stood. "I made some tea and I need to finish it off and get back to bed. We'll talk again later this week."

"Okay. They still haven't found out who trashed your home?"

"No, but I feel certain that they will. It's just a matter of time. Denver has a wonderful police force."

After ending the call to her mother, Keisha headed for the front door with her cup of tea. She had enjoyed sitting on the porch last night. But then of course Canyon had been with her. Tonight he had been in a hurry to flee her presence. Opening the door, she drew in a deep breath. This was something she'd missed while living in Austin. The air was fresh, as well as calming and comforting, things she needed right now.

Leaning against a post, she sipped her tea, watched the sky and tried to put her conversation with her mother to the back of her mind for now. She marveled at Canyon's fascination with the solar system and knew there was a star up there he claimed as his. Well, now she would claim it as hers, as well. He believed the star had helped get him through a number of rough times in his life. Maybe that same star could help her.

There was a moon tonight and stars aplenty. She wondered which one was Canyon's. She figured it had to be the one that was the biggest and the brightest since he was known to do things on a grand scale.

She'd never wished upon a star but hopefully it wasn't too late to do so. Closing her eyes she made a wish, one that was her heart's most ardent desire. She loved Canyon, and he loved her. They had a son to raise together, and tonight he'd asked her to marry him.

Opening her eyes she looked up at the star and said aloud, "One of you up there is Canyon's star and I'm making you mine, as well. I will be more forgiving, and I won't blame myself for everything. I forgive myself. I am not to blame."

She smiled, feeling renewed. Rejuvenated. Taking another sip of tea, she turned around and then gasped, dropping the cup. She tried to steady her breath and calm her heart rate. She recognized the man standing there.

Keisha opened her mouth to ask him what he was doing there, but stopped when he said in an accusing tone, "You're wrong. You *are* to blame. You're to blame for everything that has gone wrong in my life."

"Is there a reason why you're visiting me at this hour?"

Canyon ignored Stern's question as he studied the picture frames lined across the fireplace mantel. He asked a question of his own. "Do the women, the ones you bring here to the Stronghold, ever ask why you have so many photographs of you and JoJo around this place?"

Stern chuckled. "Trying to change the subject, are we? Okay, I'll give you this one. First of all, it's none of their business. And second, they don't question me because they know better. My friendship with JoJo is never to be questioned."

Now it was Canyon's turn to chuckle as he turned around to face his brother. "Why? Because then you'll have to explain how she kept Steven Edison from beating you up that day when the two of you were in middle school. Or how the only reason you won that high school swim trophy you still like to brag about is because she was on your team? Or how she is responsible for keeping your Corvette running like a charm? Or how—"

"Now, why are you here again?" Stern interrupted to ask.

Canyon plopped down into the chair. "I like visiting you after midnight."

"That's bull and you know it. You have a tendency to hang out at the Bluff as if you're guarding the place." Stern smiled. "But that was before it was invaded by Keisha and my man Beau. I like him by the way. I plan on teaching him how to race cars when he grows up."

Canyon rolled his eyes. That was when he remembered those missed calls. It was too late to return them, but at least he could check to see who'd tried contacting him earlier that evening. Shifting his body, he pulled the phone out of his back pocket and noticed all three calls had been from Detective Render. There was also a text message...Call me when you see this text. No matter how late.

"Detective Render wants me to call him," he said to Stern.

"Now?"

Canyon shrugged. "The text said no matter how late.

Must be important." He clicked on the detective's number and after two rings Render answered.

"Render, this is Canyon."

"I tried calling earlier," Render said.

"I went out to dinner and had my phone on vibrate and didn't hear it. What's up?"

"First, none of Ms. Ashford's coworkers in Austin are being harassed so we don't feel it's connected to her former job. But there is something else we're checking out. Ms. Ashford's neighborhood has one of those monitoring video cameras at the entrance, and we noticed this car on her street the same day her house was trashed… and we also noticed it returned the day after and the day after that, as if checking the status of her home."

Canyon nodded. "Possibly a visitor to someone in Keisha's neighborhood."

"That's what we assumed but we pulled license plate records and this person made us curious."

"Why?"

"Because he works at the law firm with Ms. Ashford. We did some further checking, and although he's a model employee, his personal life turned to shambles a few years ago when his wife discovered he was involved in an illicit affair and filed for divorce. She actually caught him on a video having sex in their bedroom one weekend when she was out of town. She filed a restraining order last year when he kept harassing her, trying to get her to take him back."

Canyon rubbed his jaw, feeling tired and wondering where Render was going with this—until this particular story started to sound familiar. Mainly the part about a man being caught by his wife on video, having an affair. "Wait a minute," Canyon said, straightening in his chair. "What's the man's name?"

"Michael Jarrod. We went to his place to question him, and he wasn't home. Talked to his neighbor, who said she hadn't seen him all day. And we found out that he left early from work, claiming he'd gotten sick. You know him?"

"No, but today someone mentioned a man who had an affair with his fiancée and the details were oddly similar. I need to check on something, and I'll call you back."

Canyon clicked off and went through the contact list on his phone. Lucky for him he had exchanged phone numbers with Grant before the man had left their table to rejoin his friends. Canyon clicked on the number. It was late but...

"Hello."

The man answered in a very sleepy voice. "Grant, this is Canyon. Sorry to bother you at this hour but something important came up, and I wondered if you can tell me the name of the married man that Bonita had an affair with."

"Yes," Grant said groggily. "His name was Michael Jarrod."

A funny feeling settled in Canyon's stomach. "Thanks, and again I'm sorry I woke you."

Canyon then called Render back and told him of the conversation with Grant at dinner. "I don't know why a man who works with Keisha who had an affair with a woman who was once Keisha's best friend would be coming into her neighborhood, three times in one week, but I'm going to find out. Maybe Keisha can shed some light on it," Canyon said, standing. He ended his call with Render.

Stern stared up at Canyon when he saw the concerned look on his brother's face. "Something's wrong?"

Canyon was headed for the door. "No. I just need to talk to Keisha about something. I'll talk to you later."

"Michael? What are you talking about and what are you doing here?"

Michael Jarrod came to stand in the moonlight and the look on his face was so serious that for the first time since knowing him, Keisha felt uncomfortable. "I'm talking about your friend. Bonita," he said.

Keisha lifted a brow. "Bonita? What about Bonita?" She vaguely recalled introducing Bonita and Michael several years ago, when Bonita had dropped by the firm. As far as she knew, their paths never crossed again.

"That day you introduced us, she seemed nice and well mannered. Someone with class. So imagine my shock when I was at a club one night with friends and she walked in, ready to sleep with the first man she saw. We ended up having an affair that lasted three months before my wife found out. Linda divorced me and refuses to take me back, and it's all your fault for introducing me to that woman."

Keisha thought she'd heard everything. But never had she heard anything so ridiculous in her life. Even *she* wouldn't claim blame for that one. "Michael, think about what you just said. *You* are responsible for your own actions. Introducing Bonita to you didn't push you into betraying your wife by sleeping with her. That was *your* doing and not mine."

She tried keeping the anger out of her voice. Her going on a guilt trip of her own doing was one thing, but she refused to let someone else send her on one unjustly.

"Besides," she added. "Bonita had a split personality. That's the reason she displayed one personality when you met her that day and another when you ran into her that night at the club."

"And you want me to believe that?"

"It's true."

He frowned. "Then you should have told me."

"I just found out recently." She'd never known Michael to display anger. He'd been a really nice guy when she'd lived in Denver before. But she had noticed since she'd returned that he'd been less friendly and more withdrawn. One of the other attorneys at the firm had mentioned that Michael had gotten a divorce but hadn't provided any details. Keisha figured the divorce was the reason he had started keeping to himself.

"But that's not the only thing I'm blaming you for." Michael broke into her thoughts.

Keisha was feeling more uncomfortable. Michael had no reason to be here, at one in the morning, standing outside on Canyon's porch. Why was he here and how did he know where to find her? She hadn't told any of her coworkers or Mr. Spivey where she was staying. Had he followed her? And why had he showed up when Canyon wasn't here? Was that deliberate?

"You left the firm right before I started going through my divorce," Michael said, interrupting her thoughts. "To deal with the mess my life was in, I threw myself into my work and took on cases nobody else wanted. I felt I had a good shot at making partner. Then you messed things up by coming back. You were Spivey and Whitlock's golden girl before. They thought you walked on water, and they were overjoyed when you decided to come back. They brag about the job you're doing just because you've won a few cases. Now rumor around the firm says that you'll make partner before I do. I was there when you got there. I was there when you left. It's not fair, and it's all your fault."

Keisha knew there was no sense wasting her time telling Michael just how ridiculous he sounded. The man had issues, which only made her more concerned about him and why he was here. "There's nothing I can say that will make you see how unjust your claims are. I suggest you leave now."

His smile sent chills up her body. "Oh, I'm leaving, and I'm taking you with me. I tried sending you warnings by paying that guy to scare you on the road and I, along with a friend who knew how to bypass your alarm system, even wrecked your house, hoping you would get scared and hightail it back to Texas. But this morning Spivey announced you were out and would return in a week. That's not good enough."

Fury fired through Keisha's veins. "You're the one who did those things? How dare you! I never did anything to you, and you trashed my house, turned my and my son's world upside down because of misplaced blame? How dare you?"

"Yes, how dare me?" he mocked. "You can get mad but it doesn't matter. I saw your boyfriend leave and since you didn't take my other warnings I'm getting rid of you once and for all. I'm not going to kill you. I plan to turn you over to some people I know involved in human trafficking to Central America. They'll toy with you a while, shoot you up with drugs and destroy that sharp mind of yours, the one that Spivey and Whitlock admire so much. No one will able be able to find you."

Keisha took a step back. Michael wasn't thinking straight. "I'm not going anywhere with you."

"You don't have a choice. I don't want to hurt you," he said. "But I will."

And then she saw it. The steel blade of the knife he was holding glinted in the moonlight. Fear rose in her throat. "Michael, please. You're not thinking straight. Nobody can place all the blame on others for their own actions." *Like nobody should place all the blame on themselves either. Or not forgive others, or themselves, when they have the chance to do so.*

"Let's go. No telling when your boyfriend will return," Michael said.

Keisha had hoped she could keep him talking until Canyon came back. All she could think about was Beau upstairs sleeping. She had to keep him safe. "Michael, please. I am not to blame for all your problems. We were once friends and—"

"No! A friend would not have ruined my marriage or taken away a job that should be mine! Now move!"

Knowing she had no choice, Keisha began walking down the steps from the porch. She knew she had to think of something fast when she saw his car. Once he got her inside it she might never get away.

An idea came into her head when she saw the weed edger that Canyon had used the other day, resting against a tree. It was a chance she had to take. Pretending to almost stumble, she quickly grabbed hold of the edger and twirled around fast, swinging it wide, feeling victorious when the knife was knocked out of his hand.

Instead of retrieving it, Michael lunged for her. She swung again, going low with all her might, hitting his knee hard and sending him to the ground. He scrambled to get up and she swung again. He was almost successful in grabbing the edger from her hand, but she kicked him below the belt. He yelped, releasing the edger. But he was looking around for the knife. She thought of running for the house but wasn't sure she could make it. So she continued to use the tool she had, swinging it back and forth. When he tried charging for her, she hit the power switch and set the blades in motion.

"Put that down, bitch!" he screamed, backing up when she almost shoved the blades in his face.

"I won't! And I'm not to blame. Do you hear me? I am not to blame!" She screamed at the top of her lungs, moving closer to his face with the blades.

She didn't notice when Canyon arrived, but he was there, coming up behind Michael and knocking him to the ground with one hard blow. Michael tried to get away from Canyon but that meant staring into the edger's blades.

So he turned and tried fighting Canyon, who with another single hard blow, knocked Michael out cold. It was only then that Keisha cut the switch to the edger and ran straight into Canyon's arms.

"You okay, baby?" he asked, holding her close.

"Yes, I'm okay. His name is Michael Jarrod and I work with him. He's the one who trashed my house and paid that guy to scare me on the road."

"I know, baby. I know."

She leaned back. "You know?"

"Yes. I had several missed calls from Render on my phone and called him. I figured things out and came back to ask you about Jarrod. I had no idea he was here. I should not have gotten mad and left tonight, leaving you and Beau alone. I don't want to think what could have happened."

She cupped his face. "Don't blame yourself. Michael was crazy, blaming me for things that were his fault. He blamed me for introducing him to Bonita, which resulted in an affair and his divorce, and he blamed me because Mr. Spivey is considering me for partner, a position he felt he deserved."

Canyon nodded, pulled out his phone and punched in Render's number. When Render answered, he said, "I think you need to come to my place and bring the police with you. Michael Jerrod tried to kidnap Keisha."

Canyon then called Stern. "Bring your rope. I need your help in tying up the man who tried to kidnap Keisha."

Putting his phone back in his pocket, he saw Jerrod was still out cold. He then turned his attention back to Keisha. "You meant everything you were screaming at Jarrod?"

She lifted an arched brow. "What?"

"Basically, that you won't blame yourself for anything again?"

She drew in a deep breath and nodded. "Yes, I meant it. I was saved by your star."

He looked at her oddly. "What?"

"I'll tell you later. Right now I just need you to hold me some more."

Canyon gathered her close and wrapped her in his arms.

Fourteen

Keisha learned that night that nobody in their right mind messed with a Westmoreland. Michael learned that lesson as well when he'd regained consciousness. Stern and Canyon had approached to tie him up, and he thought he could use that same edger on them that she had used on him. Not only had they taken the edger from him, but they had whipped his behind doing so.

Other Westmorelands had arrived as well as the police and Detective Render. She had felt sad watching a handcuffed Michael placed in the back of a police cruiser. He was a brilliant attorney who'd lost his bearings and she hoped he got the help he needed. Yes, she even felt she had the ability to forgive him for what he did. Like Bonita, he was mentally unstable.

"You okay?"

She glanced over at Canyon. After everyone had left,

they had taken a shower together and gotten into bed. Beau, bless his heart, had slept through it all.

"I'm fine," she said, cuddling closer to him. They had made love in the shower but she knew they would be making love again before either of them drifted off to sleep.

"Canyon?"

"Yes, sweetheart?"

"I love you so much, and I know I won't be able to change completely overnight. But I know I can accept things I wasn't able to accept before. My faults as well as others'. Making a wish upon your star helped."

"You mentioned my star earlier, and I wondered what you meant."

She told him what she'd been doing outside on the porch before turning around to find Michael. "I know I'm not perfect and will make mistakes, but I won't accept the blame for everything." She paused a moment and then added, "And I will do better in the forgiving department. I've sort of forgiven Michael already."

"What about your father?"

She didn't say anything for a minute, thinking of the phone call she'd had with her mother earlier. "I want to move forward with him, as well. It won't be easy but I'm willing to try. Mom has, and if she can forgive him then so can I. She's the one he hurt more than anyone else."

Canyon then turned her to face him. "I hate to say I'm saving the best for last, but now, what about me? Earlier tonight I asked you to marry me and you didn't give me an answer. Are you ready to give me an answer now?"

She smiled. "Yes. I'm more than ready."

He took her hand in his. "Keisha Ashford, would you marry me? Be my wife? Live here with me, share my life, give me more babies and love me as much as I love you?"

She fought back her tears. "Yes, I will marry you, Canyon. I want all those things that you want and more. I love you and I need you more than I ever thought was possible."

A huge smile spread across Canyon's lips. "Riley and Alpha are getting married next month, and Zane and Channing will tie the knot at Christmas. I want us to marry now. My son will have my name and I want his mother to have my name, as well. If you want a big wedding then we—"

"No, I don't need or want a big wedding. I prefer something small with your family and mine. Here at Canyon's Bluff." Her eyes lit up. "At night. Under the stars. Our star."

Canyon leaned down and covered Keisha's mouth with his and she knew from this day forward. She was his, completely.

Epilogue

Two weeks later

"When one mentions a wedding night, Canyon, this is not exactly what comes to mind," Stern said, glancing over at his brother.

Canyon chuckled as he glanced up at the sky. It was a beautiful August night and the moon was full, adding light to the lit torches that lined his driveway and decorated his huge porch.

Someone, and he'd figured it had been his female cousins, sisters- and cousins-in-law, had decorated the porch with huge white ribbons and sky-blue latex balloons. The balloons represented the color the sky would have been had they gotten married during the day. But they had chosen to get married at night.

"I see Flash," he said and then gave Stern his attention. "Tell Pam to let Keisha know Flash is here so we can begin."

Stern arched a brow. "Who's Flash?"

"Our star."

Fifteen minutes later Alpha Blake had everything ready. Canyon thought it was pretty damn nice to have an event planner in the family. Although she was in the middle of planning her own wedding, Alpha had gone right to work when Keisha had told Alpha of her desire to have a nighttime wedding. He was amazed at what had been done in just two weeks.

They had only invited family and close friends and a reception would follow. Tomorrow he and Keisha would leave to spend a few days in Vegas and return to Denver to get Beau for a trip to Disneyland.

He had asked Dillon to be his best man, and Keisha's mother was her matron of honor. Her father would he walking her out of the house and down the porch steps to where Canyon was standing. Canyon liked Kenneth Drew and knew the man was sincere in wanting to reconcile with his daughter. Kenneth was already overwhelmed with Beau.

Canyon was speechless when Keisha had told him that the world-famous attorney Kenneth Drew was her father. Drew's reputation rivaled that of Johnnie Cochran. He was best known for winning a number of notable cases.

Canyon held his breath when his front door opened and Lynn walked out to the instrumental rendition of "Music of the Night" from *Phantom of the Opera* flowing softly through the air. Ramsey's daughter, Susan, followed, carrying a small basket of flowers and tossing them to and fro. Then came Beau and Denver who grabbed more than a few chuckles when once their little feet hit the last step, they raced across the yard to their fathers, clearly disobeying the orders Alpha had whispered to them earlier to walk and not run. Everyone had been concerned the wedding would take place way past the kids' bedtimes and the parents had made sure the kids had taken an extralong nap today.

Keisha appeared in the doorway on her father's arm. She had decided to wear a beautiful light blue tea-length dress. At that moment, Canyon thought she was the most beautiful woman he'd ever seen. Her father walked her to the last step and then she crossed the yard to Canyon alone. When she reached him, he took her hand, stared at her for a moment, lifted her hand to his lips and kissed it. Then together they both stared up into the sky, saw Flash and then smiled at each other before turning to the minister to be joined as man and wife beneath the beautiful Denver stars.

Canyon nibbled kisses along the side of his wife's neck. Keisha turned her head and whispered, "Canyon, behave. There are people looking at us."

He chuckled. "Let them look. Maybe they will take the hint it's time for them to leave. I'm beginning to think having the reception here in our home wasn't a good idea."

Flutters raced through Keisha. *Their home.* She was now the mistress of this, Canyon's Bluff. She had taken a two-month leave from work and Mr. Spivey and Mr. Whitlock understood. Everyone had been as shocked as she'd been over Michael's behavior, and everyone was glad he was getting the mental-health treatment he needed.

"I hate to interrupt this unprecedented show of passion, but Pam would like to talk to Keisha in the house for a minute," Stern said.

Canyon gave Keisha a kiss before she left and then he turned to Stern. "So, you're on vacation next week. Got anything planned?"

Stern shrugged. "I'm headed for the lodge to do some elk hunting in Woodland Park."

Canyon lifted a brow. "Alone?"

"No. JoJo is going with me."

Canyon nodded. A few years ago Stern had purchased a run-down hunting lodge that he had since restored. It was now a beauty and Stern rented it out except for those times he used it himself. "Well, don't let JoJo outhunt you, like she did the last time."

Stern smiled. "I'll try not to, but you know JoJo, anything a man can do she can probably do better."

At that moment, Keisha returned. She had changed into a green pantsuit. She slid car keys into Canyon's hand. "I'm ready to go."

Canyon lifted a brow. "We're going somewhere? Tonight?"

Keisha chuckled. "Yes. That was my surprise for you. I made reservations for us at a hotel in town. Our bags are packed already and in the car. Mom and Dad will take care of things until we return tomorrow."

Grinning, Canyon took Keisha's hand. The idea of sneaking off from his own wedding reception was an awesome surprise. "Then, what are we waiting for? Let's go, baby."

He turned to Stern. "Enjoy your vacation, and I'll see you when you get back."

Canyon then tightened his hand on Keisha's as they

walked to his car. He was more than ready to get her alone. She was his heart and his soul. His everything. And when he got her into that hotel room, he intended to prove it.

* * * * *

Don't miss the next Westmoreland novel
by Brenda Jackson!
STERN
When Stern Westmoreland helps his best friend with a makeover, he never expects sizzling attraction to ignite between them. Now there's only one way to make her his—have one long, steamy night together as much more than friends!

HIDDEN PLEASURES

To the love of my life, Gerald Jackson, Sr.
This year marks my fifteenth anniversary as a published author
and I want to thank all of you for your support.
To my readers who have been with me since my first book,
this seventy-fifth book is especially for you.
To my good friend and classmate Valeria Stirrup Jenkins of
the Chloe Agency Finishing and Modeling School in Memphis,
Tennessee, for her feedback on proper etiquette and manners.
Thanks for your help. It was truly appreciated.

Hear thou, my son, and be wise,
and guide thine heart in the way.
—*Proverbs,* 23:19

One

"Holy crap!" Galen Steele muttered as he turned away from the bank of elevators and raced for the stairways of the Ritz-Carlton Hotel in Manhattan. A high school soccer team was checking out and filling all the elevators going down to the lobby. Galen could not be late for this wedding. His cousin Donovan would kill him if he were.

All the other groomsmen had left for the church a good thirty minutes ago, but he'd lagged behind when a woman he'd met at the bar last night had unexpectedly knocked on his hotel room door just when he was about to walk out. Not one to turn down a booty call, he'd thought he could make it quick. He had no idea Tina What's-Her-Name didn't believe in a quickie. A smile split his lips as he recalled how she'd made it worth his while.

And now he was late. He'd heard of weddings being

held up for the bride or the groom, but never for a groomsman.

He vividly remembered Donovan's warning last night at the bachelor party. His cousin, who'd been engaged two months shy of a year, had made it clear that he'd waited long enough for his wedding day and he intended for it to go off without a hitch. And that meant he wanted all twenty of his groomsmen to be at the church on time. As he spoke, he'd looked directly at Galen and his five brothers—not so affectionately known as the "Bad News Steeles from Phoenix."

Hell, it wasn't Galen's fault that his father, Drew Steele, had actually gotten run out of Charlotte over thirty years ago by a bunch of women out for blood— namely his. Drew's reputation as a skirt chaser was legendary, and although the old man had finally settled down with one woman, his six sons had been cursed with his testosterone-driven genes. Galen, Tyson, Eli, Jonas, Mercury and Gannon didn't know how to say no to a willing woman. And if she wasn't willing, they had the seductive powers to not only get her in a willing mood, but to push her right over the top. Or let her stay on the bottom, depending upon her favorite position.

Galen glanced at his watch again as he reached the main floor. Hurrying toward the revolving doors, he prayed a taxi would be available. This was New York City, the Big Apple, and yellow cabs were supposed to be all over the place, right?

He smiled. One was pulling up as soon as he exited the hotel and he ran toward it, thinking he might be on time to the wedding after all.

Not waiting to be assisted by a bellman, he opened the cab's door, slid in the seat and was about to direct the driver to the church when he felt a tap on his shoulder. He looked up and his gaze collided with a face he could only define as gut-grippingly beautiful. Eyes the color of caramel, naturally arched brows, a cute little nose and a pair of too-luscious lips.

The beauty he'd finally gotten out of his room less than ten minutes ago had nothing on this woman. It was like comparing apples to oranges. Both were good fruit, but one was sweeter.

He found his voice to speak. "Yes?"

"This is my cab."

He couldn't help but grin when he asked, "You own it?"

Her frown gave him a warning. It also gave him one hell of a hard-on. "No, I don't own it, but I called for it. It's here to take me to the airport. I have a flight to catch."

"And I have a wedding to attend and I'm late."

She crossed her arms over her chest, and the shapeliest pair of breasts he'd ever seen pressed tight against her blouse. The sight of them made his mouth water. "Sorry, but your lack of planning does not constitute an emergency on my part," she said in a haughty voice. "The proper thing for you to have done was to allow yourself ample time to reach your destination."

"Well, I didn't and as much I've enjoyed chatting with you, I have to go." He regretted saying so, because he would love to spend more time with her.

She dropped her arms and arched her shoulders. Once again his attention was drawn to her breasts. "This is my cab!"

"It was your cab, lady, and I really do have to go." He turned his attention to the driver and said, "I need to get to the Dayspring Baptist Church in Harlem in less than twenty minutes."

The driver shook his head, reluctant to move. "I don't know, man," he said with a deep Jamaican accent. "I was called to take a lady to the airport."

Galen took out his wallet, pulled out a hundred-dollar bill and offered it to the guy. "I'm down to nineteen minutes now."

The man almost snatched the bill out of Galen's hand and shot the woman an apologetic look. "Sorry, miss, I have a large family to feed. I'll call in and have another cab sent for you."

Satisfied, Galen reached over to close the door, but the woman—the sinfully beautiful but very angry woman—was blocking the way. He tilted his head back and looked up at her. "Do you mind?"

"Yes, I do mind. You have to be the rudest man I've ever met. Someone needs to teach you some manners."

He smiled. "You're probably right, but not today. Some other time, perhaps."

She glared at him as she moved out of the way, but not before saying, "And for heaven's sake, will you please zip up your pants."

He glanced down. "Oops." He quickly slid up his zipper before closing the door.

The cab pulled away then and he couldn't resist glancing back through the window at the woman they'd left at the curb. She was not a happy camper. In fact she looked downright furious. And he should give a damn why? Because he *had* behaved like an ill-mannered brute, which was not his typical behavior, especially when it came to beautiful women. It was definitely not the impression he would want to leave with one. If he'd had the time he would have charmed her right out of her panties and bra. It was the Steele way.

Oh, well. You win some and you lose some. And he'd

much preferred losing her than his behind, and there was no doubt in his mind that Donovan would kick that very part of his anatomy all over New York if he was late for his wedding.

"I now pronounce you man and wife. Donovan, you may kiss your bride."

Donovan Steele didn't waste time pulling his wife into his arms and giving her a kiss many probably thought was rather long. And if that wasn't bad enough, when he'd finally pulled his mouth from hers, he whispered, "I love you, sweetheart."

Natalie Ford Steele smiled up at her husband and said, "And I love you."

And then she was swept up into her husband's arms and carried out of the church.

Galen swallowed to keep from gagging as he watched the entire scene. Even though Natalie was a nice-looking woman, a real beauty, he'd still had a hard time believing that Donovan had decided to hang up his bachelor shoes and take a wife. Donovan's reputation as a womanizer was legendary; in fact, he'd been so infamous in Charlotte that there were some who thought he was one of Drew Steele's sons instead of a cousin. Galen figured Charlotte wouldn't be the same without a bachelor Steele to keep things lively. Maybe he ought to consider leaving Phoenix and moving east.

He kicked that idea out of his mind real quick. His older Steele cousins in Charlotte would probably give him a job in their Steele Manufacturing Company. He much preferred remaining in Phoenix doing what he loved, which some people thought was trivial.

And his father topped that list of critics. Drew Steele believed that a man was supposed to get up at seven o'clock, Monday through Friday, and work at some job until at least five. It had taken Drew a long time to buy into the Principles According to Galen Steele, which said that a man was supposed to work smarter, not harder. That was why at the age of thirty-four Galen was a multibillionaire and was still building an empire, while working less than twenty hours a week and having fun at what he did.

Fourteen years ago while attending the University of Phoenix, pursuing a degree in engineering, he and his two roommates decided to do something to make money, something different than what their friends were doing—like selling their blood or their sperm. So they began creating video games. After their games became a hit on campus, they formed a business and by the time they graduated from college two years later, they were millionaires. The three of them were still partners today.

Their business, the SID Corporation, was represented by three CEOs, Galen Steele, Eric Ingram and Wesley Duval. Their only employees were their art team. He, Eric and Wesley shared duties as game designers and programmers and leased a suite in an exclusive area of Phoenix's business district for appearances' sake and as a tax write-off. They preferred designing their games right in the garage of their homes. Simple. Easy. Shrewd.

He shook his head. He and his brothers had inherited the old man's penchant for women, but they'd been born to excel. Drew's expectations for his six sons had been high, and all of them had become successful in their own right.

Seeing the other groomsmen move forward, Galen brought his attention back to the ceremony in time to stay on cue and file out with the rest of the wedding party. He took the arm of his partner, Laurie, one of

Natalie's friends from college. She was pretty—and she was also very much married.

Outside in the perfect June day, he couldn't help but chuckle as he checked out the faces of his brothers and a number of Donovan's still-single friends. They had stood up there and witnessed the entire ceremony and they looked as if they were in shock. Galen understood how they felt. There wasn't a woman alive who'd make him consider tying the knot. He got shivers just thinking about it.

"You barely made it."

Galen came out of his reverie to glance over at two of his brothers, Tyson and Gannon. "Doesn't matter, Tyson. I made it," he said, smiling. "With a minute to spare."

"Should we ask why you were almost late?" Gannon asked with a curious look on his face.

Galen chuckled. He was the oldest and at twenty-nine Gannon was the youngest. Galen knew he was his youngest brother's hero and because of that he tried walking a straight-and-narrow path. Doing the role-model thing wasn't always easy, especially when you were the offspring of the infamous Drew Steele. But on occasion Galen liked pulling his youngest brother's leg. Like now.

"I'll be glad to tell you why I was almost late," Galen said, leaning close to his brothers as if what he had to say was for their ears only.

"I got caught up in a foursome and lost track of the time," he lied. And just so they would know what he meant, he said, "It was me and three women in my hotel room. Get the picture?"

"No kidding?" Gannon said, easily impressed.

Tyson rolled his eyes. "Yes, he's full of it, Gannon.

Don't believe a word he says. It might have been one woman, but it wasn't three."

Galen could only smile. There were only eleven months' difference in his and Tyson's ages. A lot of people thought they were twins, but they were as different as night and day. Dr. Tyson Steele tended to be too serious at times.

"Tell him the truth, Galen, or Gannon is going to go around believing you're superhuman or something," Tyson said.

"All right." He gave Gannon his serious look. "There were two women. I took care of one and the other one got away," Galen said, thinking of the woman whose cab he'd been forced to hijack. He could still see the anger on her gorgeous face, especially the fire that had lit a striking pair of eyes.

"Was she good-looking?" Gannon had to ask.

Galen lifted a brow. "Who?"

"The one who got away."

Galen couldn't help but smile. "She was more than good-looking. The woman was absolutely stunning."

"Damn, man. And you let her get away?" Gannon looked clearly disappointed.

"It was either that or get my behind kicked by Donovan if I was late for his wedding."

"Okay, everyone, let's go back inside the church for pictures," the wedding director said, interrupting their conversation. "Then we'll return to the Ritz-Carlton for the reception."

Galen's thoughts shifted back to the woman. The one who got away. Like he'd told Gannon, she was more than good-looking and for some reason he could not get her out of his mind.

And at that moment he thought he'd give just about anything to see her again.

Brittany Thrasher tucked a loose strand of hair behind her ear after bringing her car to a stop in front of her house. It was nice to be back home after attending that seminar in New York.

A few minutes later she was walking through her front door wheeling her luggage behind her. The first thing she planned to do was strip off her clothes in deference to the Tampa heat that flirted with the hundred-degree mark.

She looked at the stack of envelopes on the table and couldn't help but appreciate her neighbor and friend Jennifer Barren for coming over every day to get her mail and water her plants. This was Brittany's busiest travel time of the year. As CEO of her own business, Etiquette Matters, she and her ten employees traveled all over the country teaching the basics of proper etiquette to businesses, schools and interested groups. Last week her students consisted of a group of NFL players who'd been invited to the White House for dinner.

Kicking off her shoes, she went to her bedroom and her mind went to the man in New York, the one who'd had the audacity to take her cab from right under her nose. And with his pants unzipped. He hadn't seemed the least bit embarrassed when she'd brought it to his attention. The jerk.

She shook her head. Another thing she remembered about him other than the open zipper was his eyes. He had Smokey Robinson eyes, a mossy shade of green that would have taken her breath away had she not been so angry. The man had no manners, which was a real turn-off. She would love to have him as a student for just one day in Etiquette Matters. She would all but shove good manners down his throat. In a gracious and congenial way, of course.

She flipped through the stack of envelopes, sorting out the junk mail that needed to be trashed. One envelope in particular caught her attention. The handwriting on it was so elegant, she'd give just about anything to have that kind of penmanship.

The envelope had no return address, but the postal stamp indicated it had been sent from Phoenix. She didn't know a soul in Phoenix and it was one of the few places she'd never visited. Using her mail opener, she opened the letter and her eyes connected to words that had her gaping in shock.

Ms. Thrasher,
I have reason to believe you are the daughter I gave up for adoption twenty-eight years ago.

Two

Six months later

"Will any of my sons ever marry?"

Galen refused to look up from reading the documents that were spread out on his desk. He didn't have to glance at Eden Tyson Steele to know she was on a roll. Ever since Donovan's wedding, his mother had been swept away by wishful thinking. She had witnessed the ceremony, heard the wedding music and seen how happy the bride and groom were. Since then she'd felt something was missing in her life, especially because Galen's kinfolk in Charlotte could now claim that all the North Carolina Steeles, both male and female, had gotten hitched.

He'd gotten a call earlier from Mercury warning him that their mother was making house calls to each of her sons. Her message was consistent and pretty damn clear. She wanted daughters-in-law. She wasn't pushing for grandbabies yet, but the brothers figured that craving wouldn't be long. First she had to work on getting them married.

"Galen?"

He breathed out a deep sigh. There was no way he could ignore her question any longer. Besides, he figured that the sooner he gave her an answer, the quicker she would move on to the next son.

He glanced up and gazed into eyes identical to his and those of his five brothers. They might have Drew Steele's features and most of his genes, but their eyes belonged to Eden Steele all the way. And Drew would be the first to admit that it had been Eden's eyes that had captured his attention and then his heart. "Yes, Mom?"

"Will any of you ever marry?"

He fought back a smile because he knew for his mother this was not an amusing moment. She was as serious as a heart attack whenever she broached the subject of her sons' marital status.

Galen leaned back in his chair and gave her his direct attention, which he felt she deserved, even if she was asking him something he'd rather not address again. "I can't speak for everyone else, but my answer to your question is no. I don't ever plan to marry."

Her expression indicated his response had been one she hadn't wanted to hear. Again. "How can you say that, Galen?"

"Easily."

Seeing her agitation, he went on to say, "Look, Mom, maybe saying I'll never marry is laying it on rather thick, so let's just say it's not in my immediate future. Dad was almost forty when the two of you married, and everyone had given up on the idea he'd ever settle down and stop chasing skirts. So maybe there's hope for me yet."

He couldn't help but smile. What he'd said sounded good and should hold her for a while, but with the scowl on her face, he wasn't so sure. His mother was a beautiful woman and he could see how Drew Steele had taken one look at her and decided she was the best thing since gingerbread. There was a ten-year difference in their ages and according to Drew, the former Eden Tyson, a fashion model whose face graced a number of magazines worldwide, had made him work hard for her hand. And when they'd married, Drew had known his womanizing days were over and that Eden would be the only woman for him for the rest of his life.

Galen doubted such a woman existed for him. He had yet to meet one who could knock him off his feet…unless it was to make him fall flat on his back in their bed. He enjoyed women. He enjoyed making love to them. He enjoyed whispering sweet nothings in their ears. There was not one out there he would sniff behind other than to relieve the ache behind his zipper. What could he say? He was one of Drew's boys.

Most people in Phoenix either knew or had heard about "those" Steele boys. While he was in high school, most mothers had tried keeping their daughters behind lock and key. It never worked. Chances were those he missed out on had fallen for the likes of Tyson, Eli, Jonas, Mercury or Gannon. No female was safe from that lethal Steele charm.

That lethal Steele charm…

Too bad he hadn't had the time to lay it on that woman in New York. The same woman he couldn't get out of his mind. When they'd gotten back to the hotel for the reception, he'd actually glanced around for her, hoping that perhaps she'd change her mind about leaving. He'd even gone so far as to wish that perhaps she'd missed her flight and had to come back. No such luck. But just for him to hope that much bad luck on anyone proved what an impact the woman had made on his senses.

"You and your brothers are not your father, Galen."

"No, but we are his sons," he said, holding his mother's gaze. "Dad didn't marry until he found that special woman, so I'd say the same will hold true with the six of us."

"And I hope when she comes along, the six of you won't screw things up."

He chuckled. "Like Dad almost did?" Of course he'd heard the story about how their father had refused to accept his fate and ended up pushing Eden away. By the time he'd come to his senses, she had left the country to do a photo shoot somewhere in Paris. Panicked that he had lost her forever, he had tracked her down and asked her to marry him. To some the story might sound romantic, but to Galen it was a good display of common sense on his father's part. His mother was world-class.

"So, Mom, where's your next stop?" he asked, throwing out the hint that their little talk had come to a close.

She sighed in resignation and tossed back the hair from her face. "I guess I'll drop by and see Tyson. This is his day off from the hospital."

Galen smiled. "You might want to call first. He probably has company." Usually any day off for Tyson meant a day spent in bed with some woman.

His mother made a face before waving her hand at his words. "Whatever," she said it in that I-don't-care-what-I-catch-him-doing voice.

He stood and came around his desk to give her a

hug. "You do know that I love you and enjoy your visits, don't you, Mom?"

His mother sighed. "I won't give up hope on any of you, especially you because you're the oldest."

He lifted a brow and wondered what that was supposed to mean. She would have it easier marrying Gannon off than him. Galen had been out in the world the longest and still enjoyed sampling what was out there, whereas Gannon was just getting his feet wet. His mother would best grab him now before he discovered the true meaning of women.

"I'll make a deal with you, Mom," he decided to say, reaching out and gently squeezing her hand. "If I ever meet a woman who can hold my interest, you'll be the first to know."

Brittany sank into the chair opposite the man's desk. Luther Banyon was the attorney who'd sent her the recent letter, advising her that Gloria McIntyre, the woman who'd sent her that handwritten letter over six months ago, had died of ovarian cancer at the age of forty-four. That meant Gloria had only been sixteen when she'd given birth to Brittany.

Her tongue pressed against her sealed lips as she thought about how unfair it was to lose the mother she'd only just found. The letter from Ms. McIntyre had answered a lot of questions Brittany had always had. She'd known she had been given up at birth. That had been evident from her trek from foster home to foster home during her adolescent years.

There had been a time in her teens when she'd desired to find her birth mother, but after a while she'd gotten over it and had accepted things as they were. She'd moved on with her life, finishing high school at the top of her class and going on to college, then taking out a loan and opening Etiquette Matters.

"Now, Ms. Thrasher, we can begin."

Mr. Banyon pulled her out of her reverie. She had arrived in Phoenix a couple of hours ago, picked up a rental car and had come to his office straight from the airport.

"As stated in my letter, Gloria McIntyre died last month. I hadn't known she'd hired a private investigator to locate you until after she'd passed. That explains some things."

Brittany raised a brow. "What does it explain?"

"What she's been doing with her money for the past five years. When she died, her savings account was down to barely anything. And her home, although it has been paid off for years, was almost in foreclosure due to back taxes."

The man paused and said, "The doctor gave her five years to live and she used every day of those five years trying to find you. I'm so sorry her time ran out before the two of you could meet. She was a fine woman."

Brittany nodded. "Were you her attorney for long?"

"For over twenty years. She was married to Hugh McIntyre, but he died close to eight years ago. They never had any children. I guess it was after Hugh died that she decided she wanted to find you, the child she'd given away at sixteen."

Brittany didn't say anything. And then, "Mr. Banyon, your correspondence said she left a sealed letter for me."

"Yes, and she also left something else."

"What?"

"Her home. Though I must tell you that although it's been willed to you, there's a tax lien on it and it's due to be auctioned off tomorrow."

Brittany's chest tightened. "Tomorrow?"

"Yes. So if you want your mother's home, you arrived in the nick of time."

Brittany nodded. Yes, she wanted her mother's home because it was the key to who her mother was and why and how she'd made the decision that she had over twenty-eight years ago.

"And the items in the house?"

"Everything is still intact. However, house and contents are due to be auctioned. If someone else outbids you, you will have to negotiate with them and reach some sort of agreement or settlement as to the contents. All the city is concerned about is making sure the back taxes are recovered."

"I understand. Where will the auction take place tomorrow and what time?"

"I'll have my secretary provide you with all the information you need. Now if you will excuse me, I'll get that letter."

Brittany pulled in a deep breath at the same time she felt her heart soften. She'd known from the last letter that Gloria McIntyre wasn't one to say a lot, but what she did say had a profound impact. This letter was no different.

To my daughter, Brittany Thrasher, I leave my home and all my worldly goods and possessions. They aren't much, but they are mine to pass on to you with the love of a mother who always wanted the best for you.
Gloria McIntyre

"Are you all right, Ms. Thrasher?"

Brittany glanced up and met Mr. Banyon's concerned

gaze. "Yes, I'm fine. Do you know how much the back taxes amount to?"

"Yes, we're looking at almost five years' worth," he said, browsing through a stack of papers. "Here we are. It comes to close to seventy thousand dollars."

Brittany blinked. "Seventy thousand dollars!"

Mr. Banyon nodded. "Yes. Although the house itself isn't all that large, it sits on a whole lot of land and it has its own private road."

Brittany swallowed deeply. Seventy thousand dollars was more than she'd expected to part with. But it really didn't matter. She'd manage it. The business had had a good year. Paying the back taxes to gain possession of her mother's house was something she had to do. Something she wanted to do.

Her mother.

The thought made her quiver inside. Her only regret was that they'd never met. She could only fantasize about the type of relationship they would have shared if there had been more time. Just the thought that the reason the taxes had gotten delinquent in the first place was because her mother had placed locating her as her top priority was almost overwhelming.

"Is there a way I can get inside the house?" she asked Mr. Banyon.

He shook his head. "Unfortunately, there is not. It's locked and the keys have become the property of the city of Phoenix. They will be given to whoever becomes the new owner tomorrow. Ms. McIntyre's home is a rather nice one, but I can't and won't try to speculate as to who else might be interested."

Nodding, she stood. "Well, I intend to do everything in my power to make sure I become the new owner tomorrow."

"I know that's what Ms. McIntyre would have wanted and I wish you the best."

A few moments later after leaving Mr. Banyon's office, Brittany punched Gloria McIntyre's address into the car's GPS system. The directions took her a few miles from the Phoenix city limits, to a beautiful area of sprawling valleys.

She turned off the main highway and entered a two-lane road lined by desert plants. When the GPS directed her down a long private road, she slowed her speed to take in the beauty of the area covered in sand and tumbleweeds. Although this was the first week of December, the sun was shining bright in the sky. When the private road rounded a curve at the end of the drive, she saw the house with a wrought-iron fence around its ten acres of land. With all the cacti and a backdrop of a valley almost in the backyard, the scene looked like a home on the range.

She stopped the car and a feeling of both joy and pain tightened her chest. This was the house her mother had lived in for over twenty years and was the house she had left to her.

Mr. Banyon was right. It was modestly sized but it sat on a lot of land. The windows were boarded up; otherwise, she would have been tempted to take a peek inside. Several large trees in the front yard provided shade.

Something about the house called out to her, mainly because she knew it was a gift from a woman whom she'd never met but with whom she had a connection nonetheless. A biological connection.

As she put her car in gear to drive away, she knew whatever it took, when she left the auction tomorrow, this house would be hers.

Three

Galen had never been one not to take advantage of golden opportunities. Plus, he'd discovered a fascination with the auction mart since the day he'd bid on his first old muscle car. Snagging another one cheap was what drew him to the newest Phoenix auction today.

In addition to the car auction going on, there were several other things up on the auction block. Foreclosed homes, jewelry, electronic equipment, music memorabilia and trading cards. None of those items interested him. All he wanted was that classic 1969 Chevelle he'd heard about. After which, he would return home and continue to work on Sniper, the video game SID planned to unveil at the Video Game Expo in Atlanta in the spring.

Right now the biggest thing on his, Eric and Wesley's minds was the success of Turbine Force, the game they had debuted earlier that year. Because of an extremely good marketing campaign—thanks to his brother Jonas's firm—at present Turbine Force was the number-one-selling video game this holiday season.

He slowed his pace when his cell phone went off and pulled it out of his back pocket. "Yes?"

"Where are you?"

Galen rolled his eyes. "If I wanted you to keep up with me, Eli, I would be tweeting on Twitter."

"Funny. So where are you?"

Galen glanced at his watch. The auction for the Chevelle was starting in twenty minutes and he needed to be in place. "I'm at the auction mart. That Chevelle I was telling you about goes on the block today. What's up?"

He engaged in all-about-nothing chitchat with his brother for all of five minutes. Eli was the attorney in the family and handled SID's business concerns.

After putting away his cell phone, Galen headed toward the auction area. Adrenaline rushed through his veins. There was no telling how many car enthusiasts would be there waiting to buy and—

"Brittany Thrasher! I can't believe it!"

"Nikki Cartwright! I can't believe it, either."

Galen couldn't believe it, either, when the two women held their little reunion right in the middle of the floor and blocked the aisle. Anyone trying to maneuver around them had to squeeze by the huge decorated Christmas tree standing front and center.

He was about to follow the crowd and walk around the two when something about one of the women caught his attention. He slowed his pace and stared. He knew the one in the business suit. She was the woman whose cab he'd hijacked in New York six months ago. He'd recognize her anywhere, although now she was smiling instead of frowning.

Hell, he'd had a mental snapshot of her since that day. There were some things a man couldn't forget and for him a gorgeous woman topped the list. At that moment a primitive instinct took hold of him and he drew in a deep breath, absorbed in the implication of what it meant. Whatever else, he was no fool. He knew the signs, fully understood the warning, but it was up to him if he wanted to heed them. Desire was a potent thing. Too much of it could get you into trouble.

He'd desired women before, hundreds of times. But there was something about this woman that was tempting him all the way to the bone.

He stepped out of the flow of the crowd and moved off to the side, feigning interest in the rack of brochures in front of him. As he pretended to read a brochure that listed over fifty Elvis items being auctioned, he listened to the women's conversation. Okay, eavesdropping was rude, but hadn't this same woman told him he needed to be taught manners?

He would consider it research. He wanted to know who she was and why was she here causing all sorts of crazy thoughts to go through his mind. He glanced over at her. She had tilted her head to the side while talking and he thought there was beauty in her neck, a gracefulness. And he liked the sound of her voice. Hell, he'd liked it that day in New York. He'd just been in too much of a rush to truly appreciate it at the time.

The last thing he wanted was to be seen, in case she remembered him, more specifically his lack of manners. And he knew firsthand that some women had long memories. They also were driven to get even. Galen wasn't up for that today. To be honest, he was distracted. He had a project in his garage that needed his absolute attention, so technically he had no business being here. But he had to bid on that '69 Chevelle.

The Chevelle.

He glanced at his watch and moaned. The bidding had already begun and more than likely the entry doors had been closed. He had missed out on the opportunity to own the car he'd always wanted because of his attention to this woman. Now he'd be forced to do an off-bid for the car, which meant if others were interested, the bidding war could go on forever. He pulled in a disgusted breath. They said payback was a bitch. Was losing out on that Chevelle his payback for the grief he'd caused the woman six months ago? He wasn't ready to accept his punishment.

He wasn't ready to do anything but find out who she was and why their paths had crossed yet again. Not that he was complaining. He listened more closely to their conversation to try to find out as much as he could about her.

There was a reason he was drawn to her. A reason why such a cool, calm and reserved sort of guy like himself would love to cross the floor, interrupt their conversation and pull her into his arms and kiss her. To be quite honest, he wanted to do more than just kiss her.

He figured he was going through some sort of hormonal meltdown. Over the years he'd learned to deal with an overabundance of testosterone. But he was definitely having trouble doing so today.

After finding out who she was, he might decide to come out of hiding and make a move. They were not in New York, squabbling over a cab. She was in Phoenix, the Steele neck of the woods, and for her that could be a good thing or a bad thing.

* * *

Brittany couldn't help but smile as she stared at Nikki. It had been over twelve years since they'd seen each other. At fourteen they had been the best of friends and had remained that way until right before their sixteenth birthdays when Nikki's father, who'd been in the navy, had received orders to move his family from the Tampa Bay area to San Diego.

They had tried staying in touch, but in Brittany's junior year of high school, when Mrs. Dugan got sick, Brittany had been sent to another foster home. During that first year with the Surratts, she had been too busy getting adjusted to her new family and new school to stay in contact.

"You look the same," she couldn't help but say to Nikki. She still had her curly black hair and her energetic chocolate-brown eyes. She truly hadn't aged at all.

"And so do you," Nikki replied on a laugh. "Are we really twenty-eight already?"

Brittany chuckled. "Afraid so. So what are you doing in Phoenix?"

"I live here now. After I graduated from high school in San Diego I followed a group of friends to the university here. I got a job with a photography firm after I graduated and I've been here since."

"How are your parents?"

"They're fine and still living in San Diego. Dad's retired now and driving Mom nuts. My brother Paul got married and has two kids, so the folks are happy about that."

Brittany nodded. "Well, I'm still single. What about you?"

"Heck, yes. I'm building a career in freelance photography and not a career of heartache due to men. And that's all the single guys in this city will give you. Now tell me about you, and please don't say you've been living in Phoenix all this time and our paths never crossed."

Brittany smiled. "No, I just arrived in town yesterday. In fact this is my first visit to Phoenix." And because Nikki had been her best friend during that phase of her life when she'd wanted to know her mother, she couldn't help but say in an excited voice, "And I'm here because of my mother."

Nikki's face lit up like a huge beam of light, and the smile and excitement made her face glow. "You found her?"

"No, actually she found me." Then sadness eased into Brittany's eyes when she added, "But we didn't get a chance to meet before she died."

"Oh, Brit," Nikki said, giving her a huge hug. "I'm sorry. What happened?"

Brittany found herself telling Nikki the entire story and why she was in Phoenix and there at the auction.

"Well, I believe things will work out for you. There are so many foreclosures out there, you might not have much competition in the bidding. I wish you luck because I know how much getting that house means to you. It's your only link to your mother."

Brittany nodded. "I'll do anything to get it. I already got my loan approval letter, so the money is not a problem. I just hope things go smoothly."

Nikki smiled. "And they will. I'll keep my fingers crossed. Now tell me, are you still living in Tampa? And what do you do there?"

"I'm still in Tampa and I own Etiquette Matters, a mobile etiquette school. I and the ten people I employ travel all over the country and hold seminars and teach classes. Each of us is assigned a certain section of the country. Things are going great because a number of corporations have begun introducing business etiquette and protocol as part of their corporate image training."

"Wow, that sounds wonderful. So when can we get together? There is so much that we need to catch up on," Nikki said.

"What about dinner later? If everything works out— and I'm keeping positive that it will—I'll have reason to celebrate. And I plan on staying for a couple of weeks when I get the house. I want to move in and spend time there, knowing it was where my mother once lived."

Shivers of excitement raced up Brittany's spine when she added, "And what you said earlier is true. It is my one connection to my mother."

Galen waited until the women had exchanged contact information by way of business cards and hugged for what he hoped would be the last time before they finally headed in different directions.

The conversation between them had lasted a good twenty minutes. They had been so busy chatting away, catching up on old times as well as the new, that they hadn't even noticed him standing less than ten feet from them in the same spot, eavesdropping the entire time. It had been time well spent, because he'd gotten a lot of information about her.

Her name was Brittany Thrasher. She was twenty-eight, she lived in Tampa and she owned some sort of etiquette school that taught proper protocol and manners. He shook his head. Go figure.

He also knew all about the house she would be bidding on and why she wanted it so badly. It was a house on a private road off Rushing Street. He knew the area. Galen glanced at his watch and figured he would hang around after all and make sure he and Brittany Thrasher got reacquainted on more pleasant terms. It was time she saw that he wasn't such a bad guy. He'd just had an off day that time in New York. He would just throw on the Steele charm, talk her into taking him along when she went and took a tour of her new house. No telling where things would lead from there.

He was about to head in the direction she'd gone when another conversation caught his ears. This time between two men who were standing together talking.

"Are you sure the house off Rushing Street is going on the block today?" the short, stocky man asked his companion, a taller bald-headed guy.

"I'm positive. I verified it was listed in the program. If the rezoning of the area goes as planned—and I have no reason to believe that it won't with all the money we're pouring into the rezoning commissioner's election campaign—I figure that within a year, that property will be approved for commercial use."

The short, stocky man chuckled. "Good. Then we can tear the house down and use all that land to build another one of our hotels. We just need to make sure no one else outbids us for it."

Galen watched the men walk off. Evidently they wanted the same house Brittany would be bidding on. He shrugged, thinking it wasn't any of his business. That was the nature of an auction and there was no reason for him to get involved. Then he released a short laugh. Who in the hell was he fooling? Even when she had been in New York he'd made her his business. Time just hadn't lent itself for anything more than a confrontation between them.

He glanced at his watch before pulling his cell phone

out of the back pocket of his jeans. The push of one button had his phone connected to Eli.

"What do you want, Galen?"

He smiled. Eli was the moody brother. Ready for chit-chat one minute and a grouch the next. "I'm still here at the auction mart. I need you to fax me a loan approval letter with an open line of credit."

"What do you think I am, your banker?" his brother snapped.

"Just work miracles and do it and stop whining."

"Dammit, what's the fax number?"

"How the hell do I know? Just look it up." He quickly hung up the phone before Eli decided to get real ugly.

Galen made his way toward the auction area. Following the crowd, he wondered just when he'd begun rescuing damsels in distress. It was a disconcerting thought for a Steele, but in this case it was one he was looking forward to doing.

Four

Brittany got nervous as she glanced around the room. It was crowded, wall to wall. She knew there were fifteen homes being auctioned off today and she hoped none of these people were interested in the one she wanted. She would do as Nikki had suggested and think positive.

She smiled when she thought of how she'd run into her friend again after all these years. Although she'd had other friends, she'd never felt that special closeness with them that she'd felt with Nikki. And now they had agreed to do a better job of staying in touch and would start off rekindling their friendship by going out to dinner tonight. They had so much to catch up on.

She checked her watch. The auction would start in less than ten minutes and she was already nervous. This was the first time she'd ever attended an auction and hoped it wouldn't take long to get to her house.

Her house.

Already she was thinking of it as hers. She couldn't wait to go inside and look around. And she bet if she tried hard enough she would be able to feel her mother's presence. She shifted in her seat at the same time the hair on the back of her neck stood up. She scanned the room, wondering about the reason for her eerie feeling. But she didn't know anyone in the room, and no one here knew her.

The announcer at the front of the room hit his gavel on the table several times to get everyone's attention. She glanced down at the program and saw her house was listed as number eight. She pulled in a nervous breath when the auctioneer announced the auction had begun.

Galen was satisfied to sit in the back where he could see everything going on, and had a pretty good view of Brittany Thrasher. He also had a good view of those two guys who wanted her house. Of course he didn't plan to let them have it. Hopefully she had enough cash on hand to handle her own affairs, but in case she didn't, then unknowingly she had a guardian angel.

The thought of him being any woman's angel had him chuckling. He didn't do anything without an ulterior motive, and in her case he didn't have to dig deep to find out what it was. He wanted her in his bed. Or, if she preferred, her bed. It really didn't matter to him at this point.

He leaned back in his chair as he thought about all the heat the two of them could and would generate. But he had a feeling that with Brittany Thrasher he would need to proceed with caution. There was something about her and this intense desire he was feeling whenever he looked at her that he just couldn't put his finger on. But he would.

"Now we will move on to house number eight," the auctioneer was saying, interrupting his thoughts. For now it was a good thing.

"Who would like to open the bid?"

Brittany's heart raced when the bidding had officially begun on her house. She had gone on the Internet last night and visited the Web site that outlined the most effective way to participate in an auction. Rule number one said you should not start off the bid. Instead you should scope out the bidders to see if and when you could enter the fray. The key was knowing how much money you had and working with that.

The minimum bid had been set and so far the bidding remained in what she considered a healthy range with only three people actually showing interest. The highest bid was now at thirty-five thousand with only two people left bidding. She decided to enter at forty-six thousand.

She kept her eyes straight ahead on the auctioneer and didn't bother looking back to see who the other bidders were. That was another rule. Keep your eyes on the prize and not your opponents.

"We have a bid of fifty-two thousand. Do I hear fifty-three?"

She lifted her hand. "Fifty-three."

"We have a fifty-three. What about fifty-five?"

"Fifty-five."

Brittany couldn't resist looking sideways and saw a short, stocky man had made the bid. A nervousness settled in the pit of her stomach at the thought that the man wanted *her* house.

"We've got fifty-five. Do I hear fifty-seven?"

She lifted her hand. "Fifty-seven."

"The lady's bid is fifty-seven. Do I hear a sixty?"

"Seventy."

Brittany gasped under her breath at the high jump. Her approval letter was for a hundred thousand. She'd figured since the taxes were less than that it would be sufficient. Now she practically squirmed in her seat.

"We have seventy. Do I hear a seventy-two?"

She raised her hand. "Seventy-two." There were only two people left bidding, and she wondered how far the man would go in his bids.

She couldn't help but turn at that moment and regard the man. He flashed a smile that didn't quite reach his eyes. He wanted her house and—

"We have seventy-two. Can we get a seventy-five?" the auctioneer interrupted her thoughts by asking.

"Seventy-five," the man quickly spoke up.

The room got silent and she knew why. They had reached the amount of the taxes that were due, but the auctioneer would continue until someone had placed the highest bid.

"We have seventy-five. Can we get eighty?"

Galen sighed, getting bored. The bidding for this particular house could go on all evening and he was ready for it to come to an end. It was obvious to everyone in the room that both of the two lone bidders wanted the house and would continue until someone conceded. He seriously doubted either would.

"We have eighty-six. Can we get an eighty-eight?" the auctioneer asked.

The short, stocky man raised his hand at eighty-eight.

"Can we get ninety?"

Brittany raised her hand. "Ninety." She had sent a text message to her banker for an updated approval letter asking for an increase but hadn't gotten a response. What if he was out of the office and hadn't gotten her request? She couldn't let anyone else get her house.

She glanced across the room at the man bidding against her. He appeared as determined as she was to keep bidding.

"We have ninety. Can we get ninety-two?"

"Two hundred thousand dollars."

Everyone in the room, including Brittany and the short, stocky man gasped. Even the auctioneer seemed surprised. Brittany closed her eyes feeling her only connection to her mother slipping away and a part of her couldn't believe it was happening.

"We have a bid of two hundred thousand dollars from the man in the back. Do we have two-ten?" No one said anything. Both Brittany and the short, stocky man were still speechless.

"Going once, going twice. Sold! The house has been sold to the man in the rear. And I suggest we all take a fifteen-minute break."

The people around her started getting up, but Brittany just sat there. She couldn't believe what had just happened. She had lost her mother's house. Her house.

She glanced over at the short, stocky man and he seemed just as disappointed as she felt. He nodded in her direction before he and the man he was with got up and walked out. The room was practically empty now with everyone taking advantage of the break. There was nothing left for her to do but leave. However, she couldn't help wondering the identity of the individual who had won her house. She really needed to get that person's name and if nothing else, hopefully she could negotiate with him to purchase her mother's belongings and—

"Fancy running into you again."

With so much weighing heavily on her mind, it took Brittany some effort to lift her head up to see who was talking to her. As soon as her gaze collided with the man's green eyes, she knew. Her mouth gaped open as she stared at him while he stood there smiling down at her.

"Wh-where did you come from?" she stuttered as she tried recovering from shock.

This was the same man who, even with all his less-than-desirable manners, had been able to creep into her dreams once or twice. She swallowed knowing it had been more often than that. And just thinking about those times sent a shiver through her. Fantasizing about him in her dreams was one thing, but actually seeing him again in the flesh was another.

What was he doing in Phoenix, and better yet, why did their paths have to cross again? Especially now?

"Where did I come from?" he asked, repeating her question as if he'd found it amusing. "I came from my house this morning and don't worry I came by car and not by cab."

She glared at him. If he thought that line was amusing he was wrong. All it did was remind her of just how impolite he'd been that day. That's really what she should be remembering, not thinking about the way the smile touched his lips, or what a gorgeous pair of eyes he had, or why even now when she had just lost the one thing she'd ever wanted in life, that she could feel the charge in the air between them. The heat. She'd felt it that day in New York, too, even with all her anger.

She hadn't taken the time to analyze it until a few days later, in the privacy of her bedroom when every time she would close her eyes she would see him looking so extremely handsome and dressed in a tux. And his pants had been unzipped. A sensation stirred in her belly at the memory.

Automatically, her gaze lowered to his zipper and she was grateful he was more together this time. Boy, was he. He was wearing a pair of jeans and a white Western shirt and a pair of scuffed boots. He was holding a dark brown Stetson in his hand, and she appreciated that at least he didn't have it on his head. Someone evidently hadn't told a couple of the men who'd attended the auction that it was bad manners to wear a hat inside a building.

And he was tall. She had to actually tilt her head back to look at him. He was built and she particularly liked the way his jeans stretched tight across his thighs. His shoulders were broad beneath his tailored shirt. She could tell.

The sight of him could make a woman drool, and as she continued to study him she remembered how his eyes had captured her from the first. Although she hadn't wanted them to. Those gorgeous Smokey Robinson eyes. She'd thought that then and was thinking the same thing now.

"Small world, isn't it?"

His statement made her realize she was still sitting down. The shock of losing her house hadn't worn off. She slowly stood up and didn't miss the way the green-eyed gaze traveled over her when she did so. She rolled her eyes. She was a big girl and could handle lust for what it was. He was a man and, she presumed, a single man. At least he wasn't wearing a ring, not that it meant anything these days. Besides, no matter how good he looked she couldn't forget that he was the epitome of rude.

And she was quick to size him up. He was a man

on the prowl. She'd met more than one in her day and had always managed to convince them to prowl someplace else, in some other woman's neck of the woods. She'd discovered long ago that the whole idea of sex was overrated. She certainly hadn't gotten anything out of it so far.

"So, what about you? Where did you come from?" he prompted.

She thought that perhaps they were standing too close. Had he taken a step closer and she hadn't noticed it? She glanced around. The room was completely empty except for them.

"Doesn't matter where I'm from because I'm on my way back there." She glanced at her watch. "If you will excuse me, I need to find someone."

"Who?"

She tightened her lips to keep from saying it wasn't any of his business but decided not to. Besides, if he had been in the room during the bidding, there was a chance he might know the identity of the person who'd won her house.

"The man who placed the winning bid on the house I wanted. I really need to see him," she said.

"Okay."

When he didn't step back she moved around him. "Have a nice day," she said, throwing the words over her shoulder as she headed for the exit door.

"Where are you going? We haven't been introduced."

She stopped and turned to him. She refused to be rude even if he had a history of doing so. "I'm rather in a hurry. Like I said, I've got to find—"

"Me."

Brittany tilted her head slightly. "Excuse me?"

A slow, sinfully sensual smile touched his lips. "I said

in that case you're looking for me. I'm Galen Steele and I'm the person who placed the winning bid on house number eight."

Brittany took a step back thinking that couldn't be possible. This man, this rude man, could not be the new owner of *her* house. Not a man on the prowl. The man whose high testosterone level spoke volumes, to the point where even she—a person who'd never enjoyed sex—could read it. She guessed you didn't have to enjoy the act to feel the effect. Case in point, the way her heart was thumping in her chest.

"You have *my* house?" she asked, taking a deep, steadying breath. She still didn't want to believe such a thing was possible.

He nodded. "Signed, sealed and delivered. But it could be yours. I'm definitely willing to negotiate, Ms....?"

"Thrasher. Brittany Thrasher." She brushed her fingers against her throat trying to keep up with him. "Are you saying that you might want to part with the house?"

He shrugged. "Why not? It serves me no purpose. I already have a house that I happen to like."

She threw up her hands in frustration, anger and total confusion. "Then why did you bid on it?"

He chuckled. "Because I saw how much you wanted it and I figured it would be a good bargaining tool."

Her brows furrowed in confusion. "A bargaining tool for what?"

"For when we make a deal. I'm going to make an offer that I hope you can't refuse."

She pulled in a deep breath. Did he think she wanted the house that bad that he could make a quick profit right here and now? Evidently that's just what he thought. And unfortunately, he was right. She wanted that house.

"How much?" she decided to cut to the chase and ask.

He lifted a brow. "How much?"

"Yes, how much do you want for it?"

"A week."

"Excuse me? I must have misunderstood you."

He smiled. "No, you didn't. I won't take money for the house, Ms. Thrasher, but I will take a week. Just one week of your time, on my terms, and the house is yours, free and clear."

For a stretch of more than a minute, the only sound in the room was their breathing, and then Brittany spoke and she tilted her head back and her gaze locked with his as she stared up at him. "Let me get this straight. You will turn over that house to me if I spend a week with you?"

He nodded slowly and the gaze holding hers didn't flinch or waver. It was steadfast and unmovable. "Yes, but on my terms, which includes living under my roof."

Galen watched as she crossed her arms over her chest, just like she'd done that day in New York, reminding him what a nice pair of breasts they were. Standing this close to her again was calling his attention to a number of things about her that he'd missed that day. Like how her bottom lip would start quivering when she was angry or how her eyes would darken from a caramel to a deep, rich chocolate when things weren't going her way. He wondered if that same transformation took place while she was in the bedroom making love.

Her eyes narrowed on him. "Mr. Steele, you've lost your mind. What you're proposing is preposterous."

"No, it's not. It's what I want and personally, I think it's a rather good deal considering what you'll be getting," he pointed out. "In the end you'll get what you want and I'll get what I want."

Fire leaped into her face and he actually got aroused watching it. He wondered if anyone ever told her how hot she looked when she was angry. "How can you even suggest such a thing? A decent man would never talk that way to a lady. How dare you."

He chuckled again. "Yes, how dare me."

"And why in the world would I want to live with you for a week? Give me one good reason."

He shrugged. "I'll do better than that. I'll give you two. First, you want that house, so that should be incentive enough. Because it's not, there's the issue of what you said that day in New York about someone teaching me some manners."

"Well, they should!"

"Then do it. I dare you. I dare you to stay with me for a week and teach me manners." He reached into his back pocket and pulled out his wallet. And then he handed her his business card.

"You have only forty-eight hours to make your decision to contact me. If I don't hear from you, then I will donate the house, the land and all its contents to charity. Goodbye, Ms. Thrasher."

Then he walked off and didn't look back.

Five

The maitre d' greeted Brittany with a smile. "Good evening and welcome to Malone's. May I help you?"

"Yes. I have dinner reservations with Nikki Cartwright."

"Ms. Cartwright has already been seated. Please follow me."

Brittany glanced around while the man led the way. Nikki had suggested that they meet here and Brittany was glad Nikki had when the man stopped at a table next to a window providing a majestic view of the Sonoran foothills.

Nikki beamed when she saw her and stood and gave her a hug. "Well, did you get your house?" she asked excitedly.

Brittany fought to hold back the tears that had been threatening to fall since she'd left the auction mart. "No, I was outbid," she said as she took her seat.

"Oh, Brit, I'm so sorry. I know how much getting that house meant to you. Have you talked to the new owner to see if you can at least get your mother's belongings because the house was willed to you?"

Brittany shook her head in disgust. "The man and I talked about a lot of things, but we never got around to that. He was so busy telling me how I'd be able to get the house from him free and clear."

"Really? How?"

"I have to live with him for a week."

Nikki nearly choked as she sipped on her water. "What?"

"You heard me right. He offered to sign the house over to me if I'd agree to spend a week with him."

Nikki looked aghast. "Just who is this guy? Of all the nerve."

"His name is Galen Steele and I have—"

"Galen Steele?" Nikki sat straight up in her chair. "Are you sure?"

"Yes, I'm sure. He gave me his business card and I have forty-eight hours to get back to him with my decision."

Nikki shook her head. "I can't believe he actually approached you like that, a complete stranger."

"We're not exactly strangers," Brittany said and then went on to explain how they'd met over the cab. "Luckily, I was early for the airport and another cab was dispatched within minutes. But still, before he left I told him that someone should teach him some manners. So now he wants me to move in with him and do just that."

"To teach him manners?" Nikki asked.

Brittany gave her friend a straight look. "I wasn't born yesterday, Nikki. I'm sure a class on manners isn't all he's expecting."

Nikki nodded. "Knowing those Steeles, it's probably not."

She raised a brow. "Do you know him?"

"Not personally, but there aren't many single women in Phoenix who don't know of the Steeles. There are six of them. All handsome as sin with green eyes that can make your panties wet if they look at you long enough. The green eyes are from their mother's side of the family. She used to be a fashion model and was well-known in her day. I heard that even now she's still quite beautiful."

"And Galen has five brothers?"

"Yes, and all of them were born within a year of each other. Galen is the oldest. It seems their father was serious about keeping his wife pregnant. And in addition to being handsome, all those Steeles are very successful. The only one I've ever said more than two words to is Jonas. He owns a marketing firm and I've done freelance photography work for him once or twice. Jonas is a pretty nice guy, but all those Steeles have one thing in common besides good looks, success and green eyes."

"What?" Brittany wanted to know.

"They are hard-core womanizers, all six of them, which is why women consider them the 'Bad News Steeles.' People claim they got their womanizing ways from their father. I heard he used to be something else before settling down and marrying Eden Tyson."

Nikki then leaned over the table. "With you owning an etiquette school, you'll be the perfect person to teach him manners. Are you going to take Galen Steele up on his offer?"

Brittany pushed a lock of hair out of her face. "Of course not! He doesn't even know what I do for a living."

Nikki chuckled. "There's a joke around town that a

woman hasn't been bedded unless she's been bedded by a Steele. They're supposed to be just that good."

No man was that good, Brittany thought. At least none in her past had been worth the trouble. "Well, I plan on contacting him tomorrow. There has to be another way."

Nikki shrugged as a half smile eased across her lips. "I don't know. I understand when they see a woman they want, they go after her. Of course they drop her after a while, but there are a lot of women who would love to be in your shoes right now, including me. Not for Galen, mind you, but I've always had this thing for Jonas. He's a hottie."

Brittany stared across the table at her long-lost friend. "Let me get this straight. If given the chance you would accept his terms of an affair?"

"Of course," Nikki said without any thought. "I'm a career woman and I've pretty much given up the notion of finding Mr. Right because it seems they're already taken. What you have out there now are men like the Steeles, the Hard-Ons, the Idiots and the Dawgs. They are the men who want one thing and one thing only. I'm prepared for them because personally, I want only one thing myself. I no longer have any grandiose ideas of settling down, marrying a man who is my soul mate, having babies and living happily ever after. All it takes is for me to watch divorce court on television to know it doesn't work that way. At least not anymore and not for most people."

Brittany felt sad for her friend. When they were teenagers, Nikki had dreamed of a knight in shining armor.

"What about you?" Nikki interrupted her thoughts by asking. "I remember you weren't in a rush to ever marry. You wanted to see the world first. And," she added, lowering her voice, "you were sort of against men because of what that man tried to do to you that time."

Nikki's words suddenly yanked Brittany out of the present and pushed her right smack back into the past when she'd been thirteen and Mr. Ponder, a male friend of one of her foster parents, had tried forcing himself on her. He would have succeeded had she not bit him hard enough for him to let her go. It was the first time she'd run away from a foster home. After telling the police-men who'd found her what happened—or almost hap-pened—the authorities had placed her in another foster home right away.

That move had been a blessing because that's when she'd met Nikki. Nikki's family had lived across the street from the Dugans. At first the trauma of what the man had tried doing left Brittany withdrawn, confused and alone. But all that changed when Nikki became her friend. At some point she'd felt comfortable enough with Nikki to share her secret.

"Brit, maybe I shouldn't have brought it up," she heard Nikki saying. "I'm sorry."

She met her friend's apologetic gaze. "No, I'm fine, although I haven't thought of it in years. But now I'm wondering if that episode has anything to do with why…"

When her words faltered, Nikki raised a brow and asked, "Why what?"

Brittany glanced around to make sure no one was lis-tening to their conversation, leaned over the table and whispered, "Why I don't enjoy sex like most women."

"It might and then again, it might not. Some men are just selfish in the bedroom. It's all about them and they could care less if you get your pleasures or not. You might have been involved with those types."

Nikki smiled and then continued. "What you need is a man who has the ability to tap into those hidden pleasures. And if that's true, based on what I've heard, a Steele is just the man who can do it. I know several women who had short-term affairs with them and their only regret was missing out on all that pleasure. They claim that when it comes to fulfilling a woman's fantasy, those 'Bad News Steeles' are top-notch."

Brittany waited while the waiter placed menus in front of them. When the man walked off, she said, "And what if I don't have any hidden pleasures for anyone to tap into?"

Nikki gave her a somber look. "If you don't enjoy sex at the hands of a Steele, then I would suggest you get some serious counseling. Although that pervert didn't succeed in doing anything, I can imagine it was a traumatic experience for you to go through at the time. You were only thirteen."

Yes, Brittany thought. She'd been only thirteen. Now she understood those looks Mr. Ponder used to give her and why she wasn't comfortable when she received those kind of looks now from men.

"Do you know what I think, Brit?"

Brittany glanced across the table at Nikki. It was hard to believe they hadn't seen each other in over twelve years. That special bond they'd always had seemed to just fall into place. Nikki had been there to help her through some rough times in her life and when Nikki had moved away, she had truly lost her best friend. There hadn't been anyone she could talk to, share her innermost fears and secrets with. She had felt truly alone.

"No, what do you think?" she asked.

"Of course it needs to be your decision, but in a way you can practically kill two birds with one stone. If you accept Galen Steele's offer, not only will you get your mother's house free and clear, but you'll also find out if your dislike of sex is something you need to explore professionally. But I have a feeling Galen Steele will unlock all the hidden pleasures locked away inside you. It takes a man with an experienced touch to do that, and I hear that's what Galen Steele has."

Brittany shook her head, not convinced the suggested approach was the right one. "I don't know, Nikki. The couple of guys I slept with before...I could only do it because I liked them, although I never fancied myself in love with them. I'm not sure I can have casual sex with anyone just for the sake of sex. Besides, I'm not all that certain I even like Galen Steele. Both times when our paths crossed he didn't impress me as someone with good manners."

Nikki threw her head back and laughed. "Manners are the last thing you'll think about when the big 'O' strikes. And trust me, Brit, you won't be doing it just for the sake of doing it. You'll be doing it for pleasure, and there's plenty of pleasure out there waiting for you. I think you just need the right man and I'm totally convinced Galen Steele is that man. Think about it."

Brittany nodded. She certainly had strong motivation for doing so—her house was at stake. However, like she'd told Nikki, she wasn't sure if she could engage in casual sex and enjoy it. Then again, she'd done it a couple of times with guys she was involved with at the time and hadn't enjoyed it, either.

She picked up her menu and eyed her friend over the top. "All right. I'll think about it."

Eli Steele glared at the man sitting on the opposite side of his desk. He'd often wondered about his oldest brother's mental state and this was one of those times. "Let me get this straight, Galen. You rushed me to fax that damn loan approval letter to you yesterday so that you could bid on some house you really don't want? A house you are now signing over to some woman you really don't know?"

Galen nodded slowly. "Yes, that sounds about right to me. You have a problem with any of it?" Eli was son number three and there was barely a two-year difference in their ages. It amused Galen how their father had kept their mother barefoot and pregnant for six years straight. She'd given birth to a son each year. They'd grown up close, and they still were, but that didn't mean they wouldn't rattle each other's cages at times. He often wondered how his mother had handled living in a house filled with so much testosterone.

"No, I don't have a problem with it because it's your money," Eli said.

"And you're my attorney," he reminded him, which his brother seemed to forget sometimes. In addition to being the corporate attorney for SID, Eli was legal counsel for several other private companies and was doing quite well for himself. Which was probably why a couple of years ago, right before his thirtieth birthday, he'd bought the perfect building for his law practice in downtown Phoenix: the hub of business activities, and right in the heart of the valley. Prime real estate property if ever there was any.

Galen would be the first to admit the high-rise building was a beautiful piece of architecture and had been a wise investment for his brother to make. It was huge, spacious and upscale. Eli's firm took up the entire twentieth floor. The other floors were leased, which brought him in a nice profit each month. Another plus was the view from Eli's office window. He saw straight into a penthouse fitness center across the street, and Galen could just imagine his brother sitting behind his desk checking out the women.

"I'll have the papers ready for you to pick up later this evening," Eli told him.

"Go ahead and overnight the deeds to her because I won't be seeing her again."

He decided not to tell Eli about the outlandish proposition he'd made to the woman, probably because knowing Eli, he wouldn't consider it outlandish at all. And under normal circumstances, neither would he. But again, he knew how much that house meant to Brittany Thrasher so for once he'd given in to his soft spot and not his hard-on.

He smiled thinking there were women who wouldn't believe he had a soft spot, and very few could touch it like Brittany Thrasher had.

Chances were she was on her way back home to Florida. He'd have loved to be there to see her face when she received the papers giving her the house, property and land, free and clear.

"Do you have her address?"

Galen rolled his eyes. "Why would I have her address? I met her only twice."

"Yet you're giving her a property worth a lot of money?"

Leave it to Eli to try and make things difficult. His brother had a habit of rationalizing things too much. "No, the house was already hers. I've already explained that it was willed to her by her biological mother."

"Gotcha. You're such a nice guy, a real champion of good causes," Eli said sarcastically. And then he added,

"It's hard to believe there won't be anything in this for you."

It was hard for Galen to believe that, too. He'd made her that outlandish proposal, but hadn't really expected her to go for it. Not with her being Miss Manners and all. She probably figured his offer was just another display of his ill-mannered and brutish side. But he couldn't help but wonder how things might have been if she had accepted his offer.

He could just imagine spending a week behind closed doors with her. She would teach him manners and he would teach her how to let her hair down, live for the moment. He would love to see those caramel-colored eyes turn chocolate-brown from something other than anger. A full-blown orgasm would do the trick.

"Is there anything else? You're just sitting here not saying anything."

Eli's words whipped Galen's mind back on track and he quickly stood. "No, that's about it. If possible I'd like the papers sent today, so she'll get them tomorrow. She might want to return to Phoenix and go through her mother's belongings."

A part of him was counting on her doing so and he intended to make it his business to be around when she did. Maybe all wasn't lost after all.

"Excuse me, Galen, but I have work to do. Now you're just standing there, staring into space and smiling."

Galen shook his head. To know Eli was to love him. He could be such a pain in the ass. "You're going to the folks' for dinner tomorrow night?" he decided to ask before he left.

"Of course. Who could be brave enough to miss it? If we don't show up for Mom's Thursday-night family dinner hour, there's no telling what will happen the next day. She might decide to come around snooping."

Galen knew that to be true. Mercury hadn't shown up one night last month and before he could wake up Friday morning, Eden Steele was on his doorstep. She'd told him that because son number five had missed such an important family activity, she was duty-bound to spend the whole day with him. Unfortunately, Mercury hadn't been alone when their mother had shown up. By the end of the day, after driving their mother around town—to do some mother-and-son bonding as she'd called it— Mercury hadn't been too happy.

"Then I will see you tomorrow night." He turned to leave and then stopped and said, "And by the way, I like your new administrative assistant. She has nice legs."

Eli grunted. "I wouldn't know. I haven't noticed."

Liar, Galen thought. He happened to know Eli was a leg man. Chances were he'd not only noticed, but he'd already been between those same legs. If he hadn't gotten that far already, there was no doubt in Galen's mind that Eli was finalizing his plans to get there.

Galen couldn't help chuckling as he walked out the door. He wasn't mad at Eli. That was the Steeles' way. And why did another part of him wish things had worked out differently between him and Brittany Thrasher? It would have been nice had she agreed to his proposal. Just as well that she hadn't, though, because he had plenty of work to do back at his garage. He needed to get his mind back on track and finish working on his latest video game project.

But when it came to a woman who looked like Brittany Thrasher, he would trade in a bunch of electronic parts for her real body parts any day.

* * *

Brittany sat staring at her cell phone and the business card she had placed beside it. She had a decision to make and doing so wasn't easy. She had enjoyed dinner with Nikki; it'd been like old times as they'd reminisced and caught up on each other's lives. They had agreed to do lunch before Brittany returned home…if she didn't take Galen Steele up on his offer.

Drawing in a deep breath, she reached for her phone and then quickly snatched her hand back. She was not ready to do anything just yet. She glanced over at the clock. Only sixteen hours had passed since Galen Steele had made his offer and he'd given her forty-eight. That meant she had thirty-two hours to go. Because she hadn't been sure what to expect with this trip to Phoenix, especially how long she would have to stay, she had purchased a one-way ticket. One of her employees was covering her etiquette training classes for the next couple of weeks, so she didn't have to worry about work, either.

She stood and decided that no matter how much she wanted her mother's home and the belongings inside it, she would not make any hasty decisions where Galen Steele was concerned. It was quite obvious the man wanted only one thing from her and it had nothing to do with teaching him manners like he claimed. Mind you, his manners could use some improving, but she wasn't that gullible to believe he wanted her to stay under his roof for seven days to perfect his pleases and thank-yous.

She lay across the bed and grabbed the remote to flick on the television. She was not a television person, but for lack of anything else to do for now, she would see if there was anything on the tube worth watching. She had thought of driving back out to her mother's house, but there would be no purpose served in doing that.

As she lay there looking at the television without actually seeing it, she couldn't help wondering about the pros and cons of staying with Galen for a week. He didn't come across as the type of man who would try and force a woman to do anything she didn't want to do. But still...

Would she have a guest bedroom, or did he assume she would be sharing his? And just what type of manners did he want to be taught? Most people knew the basic manners; they just didn't use them. And then there was the issue of her little problem... If she spent an entire week with him, would Galen cure her of her sexual hang-ups? Her low libido had never bothered her. Now she was beginning to wonder if it should have.

She pulled the pillow from under her head and then smothered her face with it. It swallowed up her groan. This was all Galen's fault. The man not only had her thinking, but he also had her feeling things she'd never felt before. Nikki would think that was a good sign.

She removed the pillow off her face, tossed it aside and stared up at the ceiling. She thought about the last serious relationship she'd been involved in with Gilford Turner. For an entire year he would arrive after church on Sunday like clockwork and stay until Tuesday. They never discussed marriage and that had been fine with her as much as it had been with him. His mother had been the only one bothered by their lack of motivation to get to the altar. For them, there had been no big rush.

She hadn't fooled herself into thinking that she was in love with him or vice versa. They liked each other and that was as far as it went. That's why when he'd dropped by one day during the week to announce he wouldn't be coming back, with a smile on her face she'd gathered up all of his belongings, placed them in a box and walked him to the door and wished him well. In the days, weeks and months that followed, she hadn't pined after him, nor had she missed his presence. She had carried on with her life and her Sundays through Tuesdays had once again become her own.

And as for the sex…

She could honestly say she hadn't missed any of it because there hadn't been anything inspiring about it.

A year after Gilford, she'd tried getting back into the dating thing again and it took less than a month to decide she hadn't wanted the hassles, the aggravation or the drama of getting to know another man. Most tried to be slick and only had one thing on their mind. Sex. At some point she realized she'd rather have a root canal than to contemplate having sex with a man.

Would Galen be different? She was attracted to him, that much was a given. And around him she'd felt a sexual interest that she hadn't felt toward a man before, which could be considered a plus. And for the first time in her life she could admit to dreaming about hot, sweaty sex. Galen himself had crept into her dreams during those times.

Indulging her nervous habit, she bit her bottom lip. She had decisions to make and for now she needed her full concentration. She turned off the TV. She had to think. Boy, did she have to think.

Six

His cell phone rang and Galen absently pressed the Bluetooth in his ear without taking his gaze off the sixty pieces of software components in front of him. It was the middle of the day and he was in his air-conditioned six-car garage working on what would be the brain of his next video game. He had worked on what he considered the senses last night.

"This is Galen."

"Mr. Steele, this is Brittany Thrasher."

He shifted his gaze to a copy of the FedEx receipt Eli had dropped off earlier. Because he'd been busy at the time, he had placed it on his desk. He wasn't surprised she was calling. Evidently she'd gotten the overnight package and was calling to thank him.

"Yes, Ms. Thrasher?"

"I was wondering if we could meet somewhere and talk."

He lifted a brow, surprised. "You're still in Phoenix?"

"Yes."

He put down the pliers he'd been holding. If she was still in Phoenix that meant she was unaware he'd signed the house over to her. "And what do you want to talk about?"

"Your proposal. I have some questions about it."

He drew in a deep, steadying breath as he tried to get his heart rate under control, while at the same time ignore the throbbing in his groin. Was she seriously contemplating taking him up on his offer? He definitely hadn't expected her to do so. The decent thing to do would be to come clean and tell her that he'd signed the house over to her, so there was no need for them to discuss the proposal. But he couldn't help being curious about her questions.

"What kind of questions?" he heard himself asking.

"First of all, I want to know where I'll be sleeping while I'm under your roof."

Several visual images flashed through his mind. Maybe now was not a good time to tell her that if he had his way, she wouldn't be doing much sleeping. "Where would you want to sleep?" he decided to ask her.

"In a guest bedroom."

He smiled, not surprised. "That could be arranged for the first couple of days." There was no reason to tell her that if that's where she slept, then that's where he would also be sleeping.

"And I know granting this request might be a little difficult, especially for a man I'm teaching manners to, but I'd like you to promise to keep your hands to yourself."

He couldn't help but throw his head back and laugh. "When?"

"Excuse me?"

Oh, he wouldn't excuse her, not even a little bit. "I asked when am I supposed to keep my hands to myself?"

"At all times."

His smile widened. He hadn't done that since grade school when Cindy Miller had squealed to the teacher on him for kissing her neck. "Sorry, I can't make you that promise because I *do* intend to touch you," he said, deciding he might as well tell her the truth.

"Mr. Steele, this is only a coincidence but believe it or not, I teach manners for a living."

He chuckled. "You don't say."

"I do say. I own Etiquette Matters and I take my work seriously. If I decided to accept your proposal—and that's a big 'if'—my sole purpose would be to teach you manners."

"In that case, Ms. Thrasher, maybe the first thing on your list should be to teach me how to keep my hands off you." He leaned back in his chair, clearly enjoying this. He could imagine she was pretty damn annoyed with him about now.

"Is there any way we can renegotiate your offer?"

She had to be kidding. "No. I have something you want and you have something I want. You either come to live with me for a week or the house and its contents go to charity."

"You are being difficult, Mr. Steele."

He smiled. Now that she had surprised the hell out of him by showing an interest, she hadn't seen anything yet. "There's no reason for me to make it easy for you, Ms. Thrasher. I gave you my terms. You can either accept them or reject them. You have less than ten hours to decide."

He wished they were talking face-to-face. He figured her bottom lip was quivering in anger about now, and he would love to see, even better, he'd love to taste that anger.

"I'd like to make a counteroffer."

He shook his head. She didn't know when to give up. She was definitely persistent and he liked that about her because he was the same way. He didn't say anything for a while, deciding to let her statement hover between them for a minute. And then, "Because I consider myself a fair man, I'll let you do that. But we need to meet in person," he said. He rubbed his chin. "I can come to your hotel."

"I prefer we meet someplace else."

"If you insist. Let's meet at Regis. It's a coffee shop in downtown Phoenix, walking distance from your hotel."

"I never told you the name of my hotel."

He thought quick on his feet. "I didn't say that you did. I assume you're staying at one of the hotels downtown."

Not wanting to give her time to think about his slipup, he asked, "Are you not staying at a hotel downtown?"

She hesitated a quick minute before saying, "Yes, I am."

"Fine. I'll meet you at Regis in an hour. Goodbye." He then quickly ended the call before she could rethink it.

Brittany thought it was a beautiful day for walking. Besides, it gave her some extra time to think before actually meeting with Galen. Even though it was lunchtime and the sidewalk was crowded with people, she couldn't help being fascinated with downtown Phoenix.

Earlier that day she had gone on a tour of the state capitol and had checked out the Phoenix Art Museum. She had arrived in time to see a small play on the history of the state; however, she'd been so preoccupied with her thoughts that she hadn't really paid attention.

When she saw the sign for Regis up ahead, she began nibbling on her lips. Meeting with Galen Steele wouldn't be so bad if he wasn't so darn handsome. Her attraction to him had taken her by surprise, because no man ever captured her interest the way he had.

Annoyance seethed through her when she remembered that he was a man with only one thing on his agenda. It would be up to her to try and sway his mind about a few things. If he didn't go along with what she was going to suggest, what did she have to lose?

Her house, for starters.

That realization made her heart sink as she opened the door to the café. She only had to scan the place a few seconds before her gaze locked with his. In an instant she was drawn to the most captivating pair of green eyes anyone could possess. They would be her downfall if she wasn't careful. But how could a woman be careful around the likes of Galen? Just seeing him issued an invitation to take every risk and then some.

He stood when he saw her and she was impressed that he could display some manners when he wanted to. Only thing was, now that he was standing, her gaze shifted from his eyes to encompass all of him. He was wearing a pullover shirt and a pair of khakis. His stance was sexy as sin.

The sunlight pouring through the windows struck him at an angle that projected brilliant rays on his skin, which was the color of mahogany. And if that wasn't bad enough, his shoulders looked broader in that particular shirt.

She continued to hold his gaze as she released the door to step inside. This meeting was utterly ridiculous, really. His proposal had been absurd. And the thought that she was here to negotiate anything was absolutely crazy. What she should do was turn right around, open the door and leave. But she couldn't do that. This man stood between her and the one thing she wanted more than anything. A connection to her mother. He was the key. To be even more specific, he *had* the key.

She broke eye contact with him long enough to note that the café was packed but somehow he'd grabbed a table. Sighing deeply and with a tight smile plastered on her face, she moved toward him.

There would be nothing proper or graceful about the way he would take her the first time, Galen decided as he watched Brittany stroll in his direction. It didn't have to be in a bed. Any spot in his house would suffice. And they didn't have to be lying down. Taking her against a wall would be fine. He should be downright mortified with the direction of his thoughts. Definitely ashamed. But he wasn't.

He kept his gaze trained on her. She walked with confidence, grace and style. And the look on her face was that of a woman on a mission. A mission not to change the world, just his mind.

His eyes scanned her. She was wearing a denim skirt that hit below the knee and a modest blouse. Who did modest and below the knee these days? he wondered. Still, he had to admit that both items of clothing looked rather nice on her. The skirt did an awesome job of showing her curves, and the blouse emphasized the firmness of the breasts pressing against it. And those legs he'd admired yesterday were still looking pretty damn good today. He could imagine those legs wrapped around him after he got between them.

Was that sweat he was beginning to feel on his brow? No matter, the lustful thoughts running through his mind were exhilarating. Hot and potent at their best. But that was okay because at some point he intended to turn those thoughts into reality.

As she got closer he couldn't help noticing that she had a prissy look, too prim and proper. For some reason he felt that a bout of hot, heavy and sweaty sex would suit her. He wanted to see her perfectly done hair get mussed up a bit. He wanted to be the one to nibble on that bottom lip, and he wanted to be the one to make love to her without an ounce of finesse.

When she reached his table, she held out her hand to him. "Mr. Steele."

Such formality. She had to be kidding, he thought, just seconds before saying, "Ms. Thrasher." And then he took a step closer and lowered his mouth to hers.

Before Brittany could move, his mouth was there, dead center on hers. And when she parted her lips in shock, it gave him the opening he needed to slide his tongue inside her mouth.

For a split second she forgot how to breathe, especially when she felt Galen's tongue giving her mouth a quick sweep before he pulled back, ending the kiss. In less than a minute he had taken the term *short and sweet* to a whole other level.

A quick glance indicated a number of people had witnessed the kiss. She narrowed her gaze at him. "It is not good manners to kiss in a public place."

He smiled, evidently amused. "It's not?"

"No."

"Do you want to go outside and continue, then?"

"Of course not!"

"A pity," he said, pulling a chair out for her. He brushed his fingers on her arms while doing so and she shivered, wondering if the touch had been accidental or if he'd meant to do it. She glanced over at him and from the smile on his face she knew he'd meant to do it.

And this was the man who wanted her to stay under his roof for a week. If he was taking these kinds of liberties in public, she could just imagine what he'd do in private. There was something about him that made her unbalanced, shaky, and she had to wonder if she had completely lost her mind to even be here with him.

"People are staring at us," she said in a low voice.

He shrugged. "Let them stare. They probably think we're lovers who didn't get enough of each other last night. They're just jealous."

She wondered if he was always this quick with a comeback and if his mind continuously revolved around sex. If nothing else, she was picking up on some heated vibes just sitting across the table from him. She wondered if he felt them or if her senses were the only ones under siege.

"You wanted to make a counteroffer."

His words had cut into her thoughts and she looked into his green eyes. Good Lord, the man was handsome. "Yes, that's right," she said, almost stumbling over the words.

"Would you care for something to eat and drink before we get started on the negotiations?"

"Coffee, please." What she needed was something stronger, but coffee would have to do.

She watched him motion to the waitress who came over with the coffeepot in her hand and ready to pour. After the woman walked away, he gave Brittany a chance to add her sweetener and take a sip before asking, "So, what's your counteroffer?"

Brittany breathed in deeply, shifted in her seat and said, "That I teach you manners for a week but I live in the house."

Galen immediately knew what house she was referring to, but decided to ask anyway. "And which house is that?"

"The one you won at the auction two days ago."

"Why? Once you carry out the terms of my offer it will be yours in a week to do whatever you want with it, so what's the hurry?"

"If I told you I doubt you'd understand."

"Try me."

"I'd rather not."

Galen knew that even if she had shared her reason, he would not have changed his plans. "I prefer that you stay at my place. In fact, I insist on it. However, I'd give you the key to go there whenever you want when you have some free time."

Genuine surprise touched her eyes. "You would?"

"Yes."

He thought her smile perfection and it almost made him feel like a heel for playing her this way, when all he had to do was tell her that as of ten o'clock yesterday morning, the house had become hers anyway. But for some reason he couldn't do that. He'd never expected her to consider such an outlandish offer and now that she had, he couldn't back down.

She took another sip of her coffee and he took a sip of his, wishing it was a sip of her instead. That quick taste he'd gotten of her when they'd kissed wasn't enough, especially because he knew there was more where that had come from. Locking lips again with her was not something he was willing to pass up. And then there was her perfume. The scent was as luscious as she looked.

"So, are you ready to give me your answer?" he asked, while trying not to sound overly eager.

She looked up at him. "No, not yet. I have to think this through to the end."

He could only think of one reason why she was drawing this out and the thought of it annoyed him. "Why? Do you have a boyfriend back home?"

"Of course not! If I did, I wouldn't be here contemplating your offer. Just what kind of woman do you think I am?"

One who put too much emphasis on manners, he thought but didn't say. She wanted to teach him manners, and he wanted to show her that there was a time and a place for manners, and there was a time and a place *not* for them. "I don't know. What kind of woman are you?" he responded.

He wondered how long he was going to last, sitting here engaging in idle chitchat with her when all he wanted to do was take her somewhere and feel her body pressed next to his and indulge once more in the taste of her mouth. He knew he needed to proceed with caution with her, but he was finding it hard to do so.

"I'm a woman who takes life seriously," she said, frowning over at him.

His gaze automatically went to her lower lip. Seeing it quiver sparked a low burn in his groin and had his erection pressing hard against his zipper. She was annoyed, angry and probably frustrated and her facial features were letting him know it and turning him on in the process. He figured now would not be a good time to ask when was the last time she'd gotten buck-naked and wild in the bedroom. He knew for a fact that that was a good way to release tension and stress.

"I'm a man who takes life seriously, as well," he said, and from the look on her face, he could tell she doubted his sincerity.

"So what kind of manners do you want me to teach you?" she inquired before taking another sip of her coffee.

"What kinds are there?"

She took another sip of her coffee. "There are the basic manners about not putting your elbows on the table and what fork to use while eating. Then there are the business manners, party and entertainment etiquette, gift-giving etiquette, and the—"

"What about bedroom etiquette?"

He watched her lips tighten and enjoyed seeing that, too. Anything she did with her lips aroused him. He took a sip of his coffee and noted she hadn't responded to his question. Had he hit a sore spot with her or something? That possibility called for further investigation.

"Bedroom etiquette?" she finally asked.

A slow smile touched his lips. "Yes, you know, the dos and don'ts while a couple is in the bedroom making love. I'm curious as to what's proper and what's not. Surely there are some specific manners governing that sort of thing."

"I'm sure there are."

"But those are the manners that you don't teach?" he asked. He had her swimming in unfamiliar waters—and he was enjoying it. He was good at reading people and he could tell this topic of conversation had her somewhat flustered. Was she one of those women who thought a discussion of sex should only take place behind closed doors and not over coffee in a restaurant?

"Ms. Thrasher?" She had clamped her mouth shut and now he was forcing her to open it again.

"I've never done so before, Mr. Steele."

"Please call me Galen, and why not? Are you saying no one has ever approached you for such instruction?"

She held his gaze and lifted her chin. "That's exactly what I'm saying. You are the first."

Galen took another sip of his coffee. She was upset with him and her features showed it. In addition to the quivering of her bottom lip, her brows arched in a cute formation over her eyes and her nostrils seemed to flare. Why did seeing all of that make adrenaline flow through his veins? If that wasn't insane, he didn't know what was.

"In that case, I'd love to be your first student, Brittany. I can call you Brittany, can't I?"

"I prefer you not be my first anything, and yes, you can call me Brittany."

Brittany took another sip of her coffee. He had turned those green eyes on her and she felt trapped by them. If he was playing some sort of game with her, then he was winning. The man had her tied up in all kinds of knots.

"But I am your first in at least two things that I know of, Brittany. Has anyone ever hijacked a cab from you before me?"

"No."

"Has anyone ever made a proposition like the one I have?"

"No."

"Seems like we're on a roll. We might as well continue."

She much preferred they didn't. "Why would you want to learn bedroom etiquette?" she decided to ask, more out of curiosity than anything.

"I might decide to date a real lady one of these days, and I wouldn't want to run her off with my less-than-desirable behavior behind closed doors. Right now I like to keep things simple, and simple for me is delivering pleasure beyond measure. In a rather naughty and raunchy, hot and sweaty sort of way. The women I'm into now enjoy it, but I need to know how far I can go."

Naughty and raunchy? Hot and sweaty? She swallowed tightly at the thought of that description given to sex. "I really wouldn't know."

His mere words were causing more havoc to her body than Gilford's touch ever did. She actually felt a heated sensation between her thighs that made her cross her legs.

"If you want me to teach you manners, Galen, I prefer sticking with those areas I'm familiar with," she said in a clipped tone.

He leaned back in his chair thinking he so liked ruffling her feathers. "Okay. And when will you let me know if you plan to teach me any manners at all? When will I know for certain that you've accepted my proposal?"

She placed her coffee cup aside. "You've given me forty-eight hours. If you don't hear from me within that time frame, then you'll know my decision."

He nodded slowly. "And if I hear from you?"

"Then we can go from there." She stood. "Thanks for the coffee. Goodbye, Galen."

He stood, as well. "Goodbye, Brittany, and I'll look forward to your phone call."

She turned and walked away, and he continued to stand there and stare at her, appreciating the sway of her hips with every step she took.

* * *

An hour or so later Brittany was pacing her hotel room. Every time she slowed her pace and closed her eyes for a moment, she could see Galen Steele's arrogant smile in her mind.

Of all the nerve for him to ask her about bedroom manners. As far as she was concerned, there wasn't such a thing. What a couple did behind closed doors was acceptable as long as they both agreed and were comfortable with it, even if it meant swinging butt-naked from a chandelier. Of course he'd only asked to rattle her, she was sure of it, and it didn't help matters that she didn't have a clue as to what he was talking about. She wouldn't know naughty and raunchy or hot and sweaty if they came up and bit her on the butt.

A tingle went up her spine at the thought of someone, namely Galen, doing that very thing—biting her on the butt. Why on earth would she think such a thing? She didn't have a sadistic bone in her body. When it came to sex, she'd always gone for the traditional. Could that be her problem?

There was definitely one way to find out. She sat on the edge of the bed to think about what was at stake here. First and foremost was ownership of her mother's home. The offer was out there. One week under Galen's roof and he would sign it over to her, free and clear. Of course she would make sure he put it in writing. And then there was the issue of her not liking sex. Nikki was convinced it was her sex partners and not the sex act itself that was to blame. Or it could very well be the incident that happened when she was thirteen that had turned her off sex completely.

If something was wrong with her, then she owed it to herself to find out and seek professional help if she needed it. After all, she was twenty-eight and most women her age were involved in healthy relationships with men.

At that moment something clicked inside her mind. A sign, perhaps? Was it a coincidence that the house her mother had left her was now tied to Galen Steele? Had fate brought them together if for no other reason than to fix a personal problem she'd tried ignoring? Was Galen, without his knowledge, being used as a tool to right a wrong?

Okay, that thought might be taking things too far, but then, what were the chances of her crossing paths in Phoenix with the same man she'd met six months ago in New York? And then, not only did their paths cross again, but he had something she wanted. Back in New York, she'd had something he wanted—a cab.

She threw her head back. Maybe she was putting way too much thought into this, trying to find excuses to validate what she needed to do. She would be the first to admit that Galen Steele was different from any man she'd ever met. What was there about his brashness and arrogance that pulled her to a different level? All the guys she'd ever dated had impeccable manners, she'd made sure of it. So why was she now drawn to a man whose manners left a lot to be desired?

She reached up and touched her lips with her fingertips, remembering the exact moment he'd kissed her. It had been short but thorough, and she had tasted his tongue. Sensations had jolted her the moment their tongues had touched. None of her former boyfriends were much into kissing. They thought it unnecessary foreplay. But she had a feeling Galen took as much time with a kiss as he did with the sex act itself.

Regardless, it was inappropriate for him to kiss her

in a restaurant, and maybe that should be the first thing she covered with him—how he should behave out with a woman in public. It was quite obvious that he was used to doing whatever he wanted, whenever he wanted and wherever he wanted. Her instructions would definitely nip that in the bud.

She felt her heart race at the thought that she had a game plan. Regardless of what he figured he was getting, the only thing she would be delivering to Galen Steele was exactly what he'd asked for, what he definitely needed. A crash course in manners.

And before she could get cold feet, she picked up the phone off the nightstand.

Seven

Galen very seldom went online for anything other than to check out the competition. But here he was surfing the Internet for information on Etiquette Matters.

A half hour later he couldn't help but smile. What he'd just read was pretty darn cool. In his opinion, Brittany Thrasher was a highly intelligent woman. With an idea she started in college—pretty similar to how he, Eric and Wesley had gotten started—she had created Etiquette Matters. And over the years it had become a very profitable business. According to her bio, she'd had a fascination with the use of proper etiquette and had been considered an Emily Post wannabe. She'd started off with a small column in her university's newspaper and later she gave private classes to young women who'd come from the wrong side of the tracks, had made it to college and were determined to improve their social standing by getting a firm grasp on manners, etiquette and protocol.

She'd found her niche and within a year of graduating she'd hired five people to assist her. Now there were ten in her employ and the business seemed to be doing well. There was always some company or organization that wanted to know the right way to do things. Last year she'd even included a department on international protocol.

She had a waiting list of parents wanting private lessons for their children. And the contract she had snagged with the NFL was definitely impressive. He didn't have to be reminded that she was a professional. The shocked look on her face when he'd kissed her in the café proved that. Any other woman would have been ready to take it to the next level then and there, and would have thought it was a feather in her cap to be kissed in public by a Steele.

But not Brittany Thrasher. She'd been concerned they'd behaved inappropriately. He'd never forget the look on her face when he'd brought up the idea of her teaching him bedroom manners. It didn't take much to make her blush whenever he discussed a couple being intimate, which made him wonder about her sexual experience.

He tapped his fingers on his desk, thinking his mother would probably like her because Eden Steele was big into all that etiquette sort of stuff. She thought the women he was drawn to didn't have any class. How would his mother react knowing he had the hots for a woman who not only had class but was a master at teaching it to others?

He glanced at the clock on the wall. She had only a couple of hours left to call and he honestly didn't think she would. If that kiss hadn't scared her off, then he was certain the discussion of bedroom manners definitely had. The only thing he could hope now was that once she got home and found the package she'd realize the proper thing to do would be to at least call and thank him for his generosity. And when she made that call he would be quick to suggest they get together when she returned to Phoenix to take ownership of the house. From there he'd move things forward.

A short while later, he had finished getting dressed for dinner at his parents' house when the phone rang. He quickly picked it up because he was expecting a call from Eric.

"Yes?"

"I will accept your offer, Galen."

It took him a full minute to find his voice. He truly hadn't expected her to accept. "I'm glad to hear that, Brittany." Surprised, as well.

"I'd appreciate it if you'd have your attorney draw up the papers."

He lifted a brow. "The papers?"

"Yes. I want it stated in writing just what I'm going to receive after the seven days."

He pulled in a deep breath. She was concerned with what she would be getting after the seven days and his mind was already focusing on what he'd be getting *during* those seven days. Horny bastard.

"No problem," he heard himself say. "I'll have my attorney draw up the papers immediately." There was no doubt in his mind he would have to practically kick Eli in the rear end to do it. No matter. Whatever it took.

A part of him—that decent side—figured he should

end this farce by telling her that she already owned the house, but something was keeping him from coming clean. Probably the thought of her in his bed.

"When can I come pick you up?" he asked. Already he was feeling aroused. He shook his head. When had he wanted a woman this much? She had him intoxicated. He wished like hell that he could sober up but he couldn't.

"I think tomorrow morning will be soon enough," she said. He felt his stomach tighten in disappointment.

"That will give me time to check out of the hotel and shop for a few items of clothes I'll need. I hadn't planned to stay in town but a few days." Then she added, "You don't have to pick me up because I have a rental car and I prefer keeping it."

He clamped his mouth shut after coming close to saying he preferred she turn the car back in. After all, there might be a time when he wasn't available to chauffeur her and he'd never let a woman drive any of his cars. "That's fine. Here's my address."

"Hold on, let me grab a pen."

Moments later she was back on the phone and he rattled off his address to her. "If you need directions I can—"

"I don't need directions. The rental car has GPS."

"So I can expect you around noon tomorrow?" he asked, trying to keep the eagerness out of his voice.

"Yes."

"Good, I'll see you then," he said.

"All right, and don't forget to have the papers with you."

"I won't. Goodbye."

He hung up the phone and rubbed a hand down his

face. One part of him felt like a total bastard. The other part of him still felt like a total bastard, but a very happy and excited one.

Eli glared at his brother on the other side of his desk. "Whatever you're involved in, Galen, Brittany Thrasher will end up screwing you."

Galen smiled. Hell, he hoped so.

"You're thinking with the wrong head," Eli went on to add, clearly on a roll. "And don't be surprised if that head gets smashed with all of this."

Ouch! Galen couldn't help flinching at that. Like their old man, Eli had a way with words, especially while reminding you there were consequences for the actions you took.

"Just prepare those papers, Eli. She wants them tomorrow."

Eli shook his head, still not ready to let it go. "This doesn't make sense. She thinks she has to spend a week with you for a house you've already given to her."

"When she finds that out she'll be surprised and happy, now won't she?"

Eli grunted and then said, "Yes, but your ass still might be grass. Women don't like men taking advantage of them."

Galen rolled his eyes. "And those words are actually coming out of your mouth? You, who have more notches on your bedpost than I do."

"Yes, but I got them honestly."

Galen shook his head. Now he'd heard everything. Instead of arguing with Eli, he moved away from his brother's desk and went to look out the window. The gym across the street had closed hours ago.

He and Eli had come straight from their parents'

home where everyone had congregated for dinner. All six sons had been present and accounted for, grudgingly or otherwise. Over the years he and his brothers had figured their mother insisted on her Thursday-night dinners as a way to show her sons that although their father had once behaved like them when it came to women, after meeting her all that had come to an end. In other words, she was allowing them to see with their own eyes that a man who'd been known for his whorish ways could fall in love one day, marry and be true to one woman for the rest of his days. Like Drew Steele.

It didn't take long being in their parents' presence to see just how much in love they were. He and his brothers had always known from the time they were able to walk and talk that Drew adored his Eden. And after nearly thirty-five years of marriage nothing about that had changed.

But what his mother refused to understand was that in her sons' eyes, she was one in a million. The woman who'd brought Drew Steele to heel. She was in a class by herself and there wasn't another woman like her. But most important if there was, the Steele brothers weren't looking for her at the moment. They enjoyed their womanizing ways. There were benefits to not settling down with one woman, but Eden Steele refused to see that.

"Here."

Galen turned his head. Eli had prepared the paper and was holding it out to him.

He couldn't help but smile. "Thanks, man," he said, taking the paper and scanning it. The wording was simple and legal. All he had to do was sign it.

"Whoa, hey, you owe me big. And don't think you won't get billed. For after-hours services, too."

"Whatever."

"And I'm beginning to question your logic when it comes to women, Galen. Are you sure this woman doesn't mean anything to you?"

Galen lifted his head and glanced over at his brother. "Very funny. She's a woman. They all mean something to me."

Eli rolled his eyes. "I'm not talking about *all* women. I'm referring to this particular one. Brittany Thrasher. The one you signed over a house to. The same one whose name I've seen a lot over the past couple of days."

Galen was silent for a few moments and then he leveled with his brother. "Okay, she's different, Eli. I can't put my finger on why, but I need this week with her."

"To teach you manners?"

Galen smiled. When he'd spelled out the terms of the agreement to his brother, Eli had looked at him like he was crazy. Any son of the eloquent and sophisticated Eden Tyson Steele had impeccable manners. Whether he displayed them or not was something else.

"Manners and whatever else she wants to throw into the class sessions," Galen replied.

Eli rubbed his jaw. "Hmm, maybe I need a class in manners, as well."

Galen's eyes darkened. "Don't even think it. We've never shared before and we won't be doing it now. If you even make an attempt, *my* head won't be the one that will get smashed. Yours will. I'll personally see to it."

Eli laughed. "Sounds like someone has acquired a jealous streak."

"Think whatever you want. Just remember what I said."

A few minutes later, after leaving Eli's office, Galen got in his car and stretched his neck to work out the kinks. He did not have a jealous streak. If anything he had a protective streak. Who wouldn't after hearing the tear-jerking story Brittany had shared with that other woman? He knew the story, although he'd eavesdropped to hear it.

He knew what the house meant to her, her biological mother's last gift, and although he had a reputation when it came to women, he still had a heart. He could still be compassionate when it came to some things, thanks to having Eden for a mother. So for him to have signed the house over to Brittany made perfect sense. At least to his Eden Steele genes. On the other hand, pursuing Brittany for the purpose of sharing his bed was true to his father's genes.

Galen knew he and his brothers had been blessed to have their parents. Brittany had never known her mother, and the house was her only connection to the woman. Seeing her come so close to losing it had brought out protective instincts in him. It didn't matter that he never knew he'd possessed those protective instincts until now. If any of his brothers had been placed in the same position, they would have done the same thing....

Well, maybe not.

The important thing was that he was the oldest and he needed to set good examples for the others to follow. And he'd told Eli the truth. As much as he and his brothers joked around, when it came to certain things, they were dead serious.

Eli thought he was thinking with the wrong head.

Maybe he was. If so, he needed to know why Brittany Thrasher had such pull on not only that part of him but his common sense, as well. He needed to know why he'd thought about her all evening through dinner, and why he couldn't wait to see her tomorrow at his home.

The thought that she would be with him for an entire

week filled him with an emotion he didn't understand, and he figured the only way to understand it was to be around her. Spend time with her.

Oddly enough, as much as he wished otherwise, his mind and body didn't transcend into a sex-only mind-set when he thought about her. He chuckled as he put his car into gear and headed home. No wonder Eli was concerned about him. The bottom line was that he had invited Brittany to his home to be his lover. He knew it and she knew it.

Knowing it made an unfamiliar sensation settle deep within him, and for some reason he welcomed the feeling.

Brittany tilted her head back to gaze up at the house. The sprawling two-story Tuscan-style structure sat on a hill with the mountains for a backdrop and looked like something that would be showcased in a magazine for the rich and famous.

Although Nikki said all six of the Steeles were successful, Brittany didn't have a clue what Galen did for a living. It was quite obvious that whatever he did paid well.

She glanced around the house and figured it had to be sitting on at least four acres of land. Fittingly, the house had sort of an arrogant look about it. She could see Galen living here, making this place his castle, his home on the range, his haven against the outside world.

And he was bringing her here to it.

To spend a week with him. Although he claimed she was supposed to teach him manners, she knew what side of the bread was buttered. To get her mother's house she had to be his lover for seven days.

The thought of that had bothered her until she'd

talked to Nikki again. They'd had breakfast that morning. "Remember you'll be there for therapeutic purposes," Nikki had said. "No matter why he thinks you're there, Brittany, you're going to use this week to find out some things about yourself. You need to know if there's more to your inability to enjoy sex than what you think."

With that belief firmly planted in her head, Brittany told herself she was on a mission. She needed to see if there were hidden pleasures in her life and if so, Galen was just the man to find them. She was well aware that he had a mission as well—getting her into his bed. Wouldn't he be surprised to discover it wouldn't be as hard as he'd thought? But like Nikki had said, it was only for therapeutic purposes.

She began walking up the walkway when suddenly the huge front door, which looked to be made of solid maple, was flung open. And there he stood, in his bare feet with a pair of jeans hanging low on his hips, and an unbuttoned shirt that showed a hairy, muscular chest and broad shoulders.

"You're early. I just got out of the shower," he said, leaning in the doorway.

She could tell. Certain parts of his skin still looked wet and he had that unshaven look. And as she continued walking toward him, that spark of attraction that had taken hold of her senses six months ago, amidst all her anger and frustration, was back. She'd never experienced anything like this before. Maybe Nikki was right with her hidden-pleasures theory.

He was watching her approach with those deadly green eyes pinned directly on her. He looked as good as good could get and was stirring something within her with every step she took.

"Yes, I'm early," she found her voice to say. "I didn't

need to shop for as many items as I'd thought I needed."
She felt butterflies in her stomach flapping around. She
hadn't known until him that a man's presence could do
that to a woman. The idea slid over her and for some
reason she felt good about it. Maybe what she'd heard
about his abilities was true. A part of her hoped so. She
would hate living the rest of her life denying the part of
her that was woman.

She came to a stop in front of him. A combination of
soap and man plus the scent of cactus gave him a masculine aroma. She studied his face. There was a firm
set to his jaw, and the smile on his lips, best described
as predatory, only added to the activity going on in the
pit of her stomach.

"Come on in. I'll get your things later," he said, stepping back to allow her entrance. "First, I want to show
you around and then I want you to relax."

She glanced back at him. "Relax?"

"Yes, you're uptight. I can feel it."

Brittany didn't understand how he could feel anything, but he was right. She was uptight. Who wouldn't
be under the circumstances? She had dated Samuel Har-
old a full six months before they'd slept together and
Gilford even longer than that. And here she was, contemplating sharing Galen's bed when he was a virtual
stranger. It didn't matter one iota that their paths had
crossed six months ago. That time meant nothing and the
words they'd spoken to each other had been cross ones.

"I promise not to bite."

A thought occurred to Brittany and she had to fight
not to laugh out loud. But she couldn't stop her gasp
when she stepped over the threshold and looked around
his house. If she'd thought the outside was beautiful, the
inside was downright gorgeous. The Venetian plaster

ceiling along with the hardwood hickory and stone flooring looked extravagant in a rustic sort of way. And the design of the travertine stairway was an artistic dream come true.

He led her from the formal foyer into a huge living room with a fireplace. She glanced up. The Venetian ceiling in this room was dome shaped and the back wall was made of glass, a wall-to-wall window that provided a forever view of the majestic Black Mountains and the pristine northeast valley.

"There's a fireplace in all the bedrooms," he was saying. "And a view of the Black Mountains can be seen from every room."

He glanced over at her when he said, "But my bedroom gives the best view of all."

Brittany kept looking around, refusing to acknowledge what he'd said. Had he added that tidbit for a reason? She followed while he gave her a tour of the downstairs, which included a spacious kitchen with granite countertops and stainless-steel appliances, a wine cellar, a huge family room, three guest bedrooms, three bathrooms and an office.

Brittany was impressed with his furniture as well as how orderly everything was. She followed him up the stairs and tried not to concentrate on what a nice backside he had in his jeans. As soon as she reached the landing, she let out a sigh. A huge floor-to-ceiling window in the hallway afforded a panorama of the mountains. The view was breathtaking and one you captured as soon as your feet touched the landing.

She could only stand there and stare out.

"I know the feeling," Galen said, smiling. "Sometimes in the evenings I stand in this very spot and watch the sun go down. The rugged terrain makes you appreciate not only the land but the entire earth."

He gestured to a telescope that was mounted in front of one of the windows. "Normally on a clear day you can see up to ten miles with the naked eye, but I use that when I want to see farther than that. I've seen a number of bobcats, mule deer, coyotes and fox. It's quite interesting to observe them in their habitat."

"I can just imagine," she said. Back home she'd seen plenty of sunsets over the Gulf of Mexico. It, too, had taken her breath away. But the only wildlife she'd seen were the ones at Busch Gardens.

She turned her attention away from the view and back to Galen. She hadn't known he was standing so close and tried to avoid looking into the depths of his green eyes by lowering her gaze to his chest. That wasn't a good thing because his shirt was open and all she could see was a sculpted hairy chest. Neither Samuel nor Gilford had hair on their chests and she wondered how it would feel for her breasts to come in contact with it. Or better yet, how it would be to peel off his shirt and then trail her lips down his chest, all the way to where the hair line flowed below the waist of his jeans.

Heat stained her cheeks and she snatched her gaze back to his face, not believing she'd thought of such things. She nervously licked her lips and couldn't help noticing how his eyes followed the movement of her tongue. The way he was looking at her mouth reminded her of their kiss yesterday. It had been short, but it had left a lasting impression on her.

"So what else is up here?" she asked after feeling a tightness in her chest.

He leaned down and placed his mouth near her ear

to whisper, "Right now I couldn't care less about what's up here except me and you."

She figured had she been capable of speech he might not have made his next move. But she hadn't been able to talk with the warmth of his breath close on her skin. And when she tilted her head to look up at him, he took that opportunity to swoop his mouth down on hers.

This kiss was a lot different from the one yesterday. She still detected a sense of hunger, but it was as if he'd decided he had no reason to rush. They didn't have an audience and she was not going anywhere. It didn't take long for her to realize that he wasn't just kissing her. He was consuming her, every inch of her mouth and then some.

He angled his mouth in a way that provided deeper penetration and swirled his tongue with hers. And then her tongue started doing something it had never done before: it began mating with a man's. Her world started to spin and she felt grateful when he wrapped his arms around her and brought her body closer to his. Through her blouse her nipples pressed against the cushion of his hairy chest, and just the thought of the contact had her moaning deep in her throat.

Before she realized what he was doing, he had backed her against a wall while his lips and tongue continued to engage hers in a deep, hungry kiss that threatened to push her over the edge of madness. She wrapped her arms around his neck, kissing him back while blood roared like crazy through her veins.

She would be the first to admit she was experiencing some of those hidden pleasures Nikki had warned her about. They were coming out of hiding and she seemed incapable of concealing them again. Whether she liked it or not, she couldn't deny how Galen was making her feel. She stirred with an emotion she had never felt before. Passion. And she knew he was pushing her toward pleasure that only he could deliver.

But it was pleasure she wasn't quite ready for.

She broke off the kiss and pulled in a deep breath. He leaned over and kissed the corners of her mouth. "Is there a reason you stopped it?" he whispered against her moist lips. And it was then that she noticed his hand was underneath her skirt, actually on her thigh and squeezing it. How had it gotten there without her knowing it?

"Is there a reason you started it?" she countered. The man made seduction a work of art.

He lifted his head and smiled. Those green eyes were sexy as sin, totally irresistible. "Yes, there is a reason. I got a sample of you yesterday and I liked the way you taste and couldn't wait to kiss you again." His voice was so husky and deep, goose bumps were beginning to form on her arms.

"Do you always say what you think?"

He flashed an arrogant smile. "I always say what I feel. No need holding anything back."

She doubted he could do that even if he tried. He had the ability to render a woman mindless, make every cell and molecule in her body suddenly feel wicked. It would have been so easy to let him take her right here. Get it all over and done. But a part of her knew her experience with him would not be like the others. There would be no "over and done." He would take her slowly and deliberately. She would feel things she'd never felt before. Be driven to want to do things she'd never done before. And heaven help her, she wanted the experience. Yet at the same time she needed more from him. She needed to know more about him.

"You can let go of my thigh now, Galen."

"You sure?"

"Positive."

He let go and took a step back, and her traitorous thigh was tingling in protest from the loss of his touch. "Come on, let me show you the rest of the house. And just in case you're wondering about that kiss, the answer is no, I didn't get enough."

He led the way and she followed thinking, neither had she.

Eight

Galen kept walking, very much aware of Brittany beside him. He had expected her to ask for the legal papers of their agreement before she entered his home, but she hadn't.

And she hadn't seemed bothered by the impromptu kiss. He could tell she had enjoyed it as much as he had. A part of him wished she hadn't stopped things. No telling what they might be doing now if she hadn't. He could imagine them getting downright naughty and raunchy, hot and sweaty, and tearing off each other's clothes, doing it against the wall and then moving right to the floor.

"How long have you lived here?"

He glanced over at her the exact moment she was pushing a lock of hair out of her face. The brightness of the sun coming in through the window was making her squint, but he thought at that moment she had to be the most beautiful woman he'd ever seen. In a way he found that hard to believe because he'd been involved with a number of gorgeous women in his lifetime. He still found it rather strange that Brittany Thrasher hit him on such a visceral level.

"I've lived here for four years," he replied. "Although my partners and I have a suite downtown, it's only for window dressing to make our business appear legit. Few would imagine we do most of our work out of our garages."

She glanced over at him. "What kind of work do you do?"

"I design video games."

"Video games?"

He turned to her, studied her features to decipher what she was thinking. His occupation got mixed reaction from people. Those who didn't know about the millions he made annually considered his occupation frivolous, certainly not a career a man of thirty-four could take seriously. Of course no one in his family agreed with that assessment, especially because they knew the vast amount of his wealth as well as the hard work it took to create and design a successful video game.

"Yes," he finally said. "That's what I do for a living."

He'd noticed that a smile would first start in her eyes and then extend to her lips before spreading over her entire face. Understandably, he hadn't seen that side of her in New York and hadn't really seen much of it here, except for when he'd witnessed that little reunion with her friend at the auction mart. Now he was seeing it again and the transformation sent his pulse throbbing.

She lifted a brow. "So, are you any good?"

He couldn't help but throw his head back and laugh.

This woman was something else. He really liked her spunk once she stopped being angry and uptight.

"Well, are you?"

He shook his head as he finished off a chuckle. "There aren't too many things I'm not good at, Brittany."

She frowned. "It's not nice being conceited, Galen."

A smile touched his lips. "Bad manners?"

He could tell she was fighting hard not to return his smile when she replied, "The worst."

Their gazes tangled and he had to admit he was enjoying the moment. "I guess that's something I need to work on."

"I suggest that you do. Now back to the video games. Are there any out there that have your name attached to them?"

He started walking again and she fell in line beside him. There was something comforting about having her here with him. "There are a few. You ever heard of Time Capsule?"

"Yes."

"What about Wild Card?"

"Yes, I've heard of that one, too."

"And what about Turbine Force?"

"Of course." She stopped walking and turned to him. "Are all those yours?"

"All those are SID's, a corporation that I own along with two college friends. All three of us can claim success of the company."

"See there," she said as a huge smile touched her face. "You're a fast learner. You could have been conceited and taken all the credit for the success of your company, but you didn't. You shared the spotlight. You remembered your manners. I'm proud of you for doing so."

Galen shook his head. For the first time in a long time a woman had left him speechless.

So instead of saying anything, he began walking again while wondering for the first time what he had gotten himself into.

Brittany couldn't help but notice that Galen had suddenly gotten quiet on her. Just as well because she needed to think a minute. One thing she'd learned over the years was to respect another's need for a quiet moment. So while Galen seemed to be indulging in his, she glanced around, thoroughly pulled in by the appeal of his home.

It had a charm about it that spoke volumes. Whether Galen realized it, his house revealed a lot about his personality. A segment of it at least. She doubted very few, except those close to him, knew the real Galen Steele.

She'd never considered herself an outdoorsy person, but evidently Galen was. Most of the paintings on his wall indicated his appreciation for nature, in that they captured the natural beauty of the outdoors. And then she couldn't get over the view outside the window they were walking by. It literally took her breath away. In Tampa she was mostly surrounded by water, but here in the desert, she was surrounded by mountains. Mountains out of which Galen had mapped his space. One he was comfortable with. One that was totally him.

He stopped when they came to another room and she did likewise. When he stood back she stepped inside. It was another bedroom and Brittany thought it just as nicely furnished as the others she'd seen so far.

She glanced over at him. "You have a lot of house for only one person."

"I like my space."

She'd figured as much and wondered if he was giving her a hint. But then she dismissed the idea when she recalled that her being here was his idea. She had offered to stay at the other house, but he'd turned her down.

Moments later after showing her three other guest bedrooms, several spacious bathrooms and an upstairs library stacked with numerous books and video games, they walked down a hall that jutted into a wing that was basically a separate extension of the house.

Galen glanced over at her and said, "In addition to my space I also like my privacy. I have five brothers and once in a while we get together and play video games until dawn. When I want to retire for the night I prefer not hearing their excitement from winning or their strong, colorful expletives from losing. They tend to be rather rowdy."

"You and your brothers are close."

"Yes, although we pretend not to be at times. Tends to be more fun that way and with us, there's never a boring moment, trust me. Our parents are our rock. They have a strong marriage, a solid one. And I think what I admire about them most of all is that they're best friends."

"That's impressive."

Galen nodded. He'd always thought so, and he knew his brothers had, as well. But to hear an outsider confirm it pretty much validated their feelings. He hadn't asked her anything about her family and he couldn't help wondering if she found that odd. No odder than her not asking for those papers when she had insisted on them just last night. He couldn't help speculating why.

He pulled in a deep breath wondering if she knew how good she smelled. He guessed it didn't matter, because he did. He covertly studied her profile and wondered why he was even bothering when he was used to openly checking out any woman he was interested in. Any woman he wanted. But he wanted to watch her when she wasn't aware she was being watched.

It didn't take long to decide the side of her looked just as nice as the front. Her nose seemed rather short, but her full lips made up for it, and when you tacked on a sexy-looking chin, what you got, in his opinion, were nearly flawless features.

His gaze returned to her lips and lingered, and he remembered the feel of them pressed against his while he took her mouth in a kiss that even now had him aching. He was so engrossed in her lips that it took him a moment to realize they were moving and she was asking him a question.

"Excuse me?" he asked.

She met his gaze and there was an inquiring look in them when she repeated her question. "Does this door lead to your bedroom?"

He then noticed they had reached his bedroom door. "Yes, this is my private haven, but I give you permission to enter it at any time."

She gave him a weak smile. "Do you?"

"Yes." He wanted to reach out and touch her, to see if this moment was real. Had he really just given her something he'd never granted another woman—the right to invade his space whenever she wanted to? That was so totally unlike him.

He opened the double doors and then stepped aside. He wanted to see her reaction. He smiled when she glanced around, totally in awe of his bedroom. It had a masculine overtone while at the same time captured so much of the outdoors with the one solid wall of glass that showcased the beautiful mountain scenery. And then there was his see-through ceiling where he could wake up any time of night and look up at the stars.

He followed her gaze up after seeing the look of astonishment on her face. At that moment he could imagine her sharing his bed beneath those same stars. He would love making love to her one night while lightning flashed in the sky or the rain poured down. He had seen such a ceiling in his travel to Paris one year and knew he had to have one for his own. When he had the house built, this ceiling was the first design he made sure was in the plans.

"This is truly awesome, Galen. I've never seen anything like it before. I bet sleeping in here is an adventure."

He could only smile at that assumption. "Yes, you can say that."

He then watched as she crossed the room to take a closer examination of his bed. His bedspread was white, not the usual color a man would choose, and he hadn't. His mother had. In fact after buying the house, he had gone skiing one week to come back and discover she had decorated his bedroom.

It had taken a while for the white coverlet to grow on him and those days when it didn't, he would swap it out with a black one he kept in one of the closets. This morning while making the bed he'd decided to go with the white, thinking it would make a better impression. He propped against his bedroom door wondering when he started caring about making an impression on a woman.

He looked at her and knew it had been since meeting her. His first impression hadn't gone over so well, so now he was trying to win her over. That was even more so unlike him.

There was a momentary silence as she turned around

slowly, taking it all in, the furnishings and the view outside the window. She then turned to him and said, "This room is simply beautiful."

"I'm glad you like it. This is where you will sleep every night while you're here."

She stared at him. "Why do you want me in here?"

Without taking his eyes off her he moved away from the door. There was no way he would tell her that the thought of having her in his bed was an arousing one, even if he wasn't in that bed with her. "Do I really have to go into details as to why I want you in here, Brittany?"

She broke eye contact and looked out the window. She returned her gaze to his and said, "No."

"Good. Now if you'll excuse me, I'll go bring in your luggage."

Nine

Brittany stepped back from the dresser after placing the last of her unpacked items into the drawers. She glanced around the bedroom, still amazed at what she saw. She'd honestly never seen anything like it. Even the furniture was massive, as if specially made for a giant. On one side of the bed was a foot step to use when getting into the bed because it was so high off the floor.

She glanced up and saw the sky in all its brilliant blue. Galen had shown her the switch to use when she wanted a sliding shade to block the view, but she couldn't imagine not wanting to lie in bed and stare up into the sky.

He had delivered her luggage to her and without saying anything—other than telling her about the switch and indicating the top two drawers for her use—he'd left her to her own devices.

She figured he was having one of his quiet moments

or he was one of those moody people who preferred being left alone when they had a lot on their minds. But because he was the one who insisted that she come live with him for a week, she assumed he wouldn't mind the company. She headed downstairs.

She didn't have to go far to find him. He was in the kitchen. At some point he had buttoned his shirt, but his jeans were still riding low on his hips and he was once again barefoot. He looked both sexy and domesticated standing at his kitchen sink.

"When can I go check out the house?" she asked.

It was easy to see from his expression that he hadn't known she'd been standing there and he waited a moment before he replied. "I'm ready when you are, but I'd think you'd want this."

He picked up a legal-size envelope from the table and handed it to her. "It's the papers you demanded yesterday."

She took the envelope from him and pulled out the legal document and read it silently. Everything was as it should be. She placed it back inside the envelope and glanced over at him. He had returned to the sink. "Your brother is your attorney?"

"Among other things. Usually a pain in my rear, mostly. But I can say the same thing about the others, as well. Being the oldest isn't all that it's cracked up to be."

He glanced at his watch and said, "I guess now is as good a time as any to check out that house. We can stop somewhere on the way back and grab lunch."

She smiled. "All right. I'll just go upstairs and get my purse."

Galen watched as she hurried toward the stairs. He knew why that house meant so much to her, but she didn't know that he knew, and for some reason he wanted her to feel comfortable in telling him herself. He drew in a deep breath thinking he'd much prefer staying here and getting something going with her, but he knew the best thing to do was to get them out of the house for a while. Just the thought that she would be sleeping in his bed, whether he was in it with her or not, had his heart beating something crazy in his chest.

He'd been close to the breaking point when he returned with her luggage and found her standing there, still checking out his bed. There had been something about the overwhelming look in her eyes that touched him in a way he'd never been touched before.

And that wasn't good.

"So tell me about your brothers, Galen."

Galen briefly glanced across the seat of the car to meet her inquiring gaze. After she indicated that she preferred they take the rental car, he suggested that he drive. He'd promised himself never to let another female behind the wheel while he rode shotgun after an angry Jennifer Bailey had taken the Sky Harbor Expressway at over one hundred miles an hour—all because he refused to make her his steady girl. He didn't care that he'd been a senior in high school at the time. Some things you didn't forget.

He tilted his Stetson back from his eyes. "Why do you want to know about them?"

"Because there seems to be so much unity among you, even though the six of you might disagree sometimes. I lived in a foster home while growing up and although there were a number of us, unity didn't exist. It seemed everyone had their own separate agenda."

"And what was yours?"

She hesitated a moment before answering. "Survival, mostly. And hoping the people who were my foster parents would want to keep me. I hated moving from place to place, making new friends, attending different schools. There was no stability."

Anger flashed within Galen at the thought that she'd never grown up with real parents, siblings or a home to call her own. Now more than ever he was grateful he'd made the decision to turn her mother's home over to her. Still, he wanted her to talk to him. Tell him why the house meant so much to her.

"Is that why you wanted that house so much?" he prompted. "Did you live there at one time as a foster child? Did you—"

"No," Brittany said, interrupting his questions. "That's not the reason."

She paused, then said, "I wanted the house because it was willed to me by someone I've never met. My birth mother. She gave me up for adoption when I was born. Only thing is, I never got adopted. Most of the people who took me in did so for the extra income. I have to say I was treated decently the majority of the time, so I won't complain."

She paused for a moment before continuing. "Six months ago…in fact, it was the same day I saw you and returned from New York. When I got home, I discovered I'd gotten a letter from a woman informing me that she believed I was the daughter she'd given up for adoption twenty-eight years ago, and that I would be hearing from her again soon with arrangements for us to meet if I wanted to do so. There was no return address and that's all the letter said. I anxiously waited, and last week I received a letter from an attorney letting me know that my mother had passed away and had left her house to me."

She paused again. He'd come to a traffic light and glanced over at her. She was staring straight ahead. "It was only when I got here and met with her attorney that I found out about the back taxes on the house. Her taxes got delinquent because she used the money to hire a private investigator to find me. She had been diagnosed with cancer and was given five years to live. She found me, but we didn't get the chance to meet face-to-face."

She drew in a deep breath and glanced over and met his gaze. "So now you know the reason I want that house."

Yes, he knew, Galen thought. He'd known all along. At least the part he'd overheard when he should not have been listening. He was silent for a long moment and was grateful when the traffic light changed and the car moved forward. He needed to concentrate on his driving and not on the woman sitting beside him. She was doing strange things to his emotions and Galen wasn't so sure he could stop them.

Brittany swallowed hard and her heart beat furiously in her chest when Galen brought the car to a stop in front of the house that used to be her mother's home. She couldn't move, so she just sat there and gazed at it through the windshield. The first thing she noted was that the windows were no longer boarded up.

She glanced over at him. Her brow furrowed. "You've been here already?"

"No. Once I got your call yesterday afternoon I contacted someone to come take the boards off the windows. This is my first time seeing it."

She nodded. He'd said from the first that the only reason he'd bid on the house was because she'd wanted it. Galen Steele had proven that he definitely had an ulterior motive for owning this home now.

"Ready to go in?" he asked.

Her throat closed and she could barely get out her response. "Yes."

By the time she had unbuckled her seat belt, he had already gotten out of the car and walked around to open the car door for her. She was discovering that Galen used good manners and could be the perfect gentleman when it suited him.

They didn't say anything as they headed down the walkway. The moment she stepped onto the porch she saw up close what she hadn't seen from a distance. The house could use a paint job and the screen door needed to be repaired. She couldn't help wondering if these repairs, too, had taken a backseat to hiring a private investigator to find her.

Brittany paused for a moment to take in the enormity of what she was feeling, the emotions deep within her that had risen to the surface. Would she find answers to all the questions she had? Would she ever know why she'd been given away? Who was her father? Had he even known about her?

"You okay?"

She glanced up at Galen. She might have been mistaken, but was that concern in the depths of his green eyes? "Yes, I'm fine. Thanks for asking."

He reached into his pocket and pulled out a single key. "Here, the house is yours."

She raised a haughty brow. Did he assume because she was here at the house today that she would be in his bed tonight? "Jumping the gun, aren't you?"

He gave her an arrogant smile as he removed his Stetson. "No, I don't think so. Come on, let's go inside."

* * *

For a moment Galen stood back and watched as Brittany entered what had been her mother's home. He then followed her inside, closed the door behind them and glanced around. The interior looked a lot bigger than the exterior but everything inside, from the Early American–style furniture to the heavily draped windows, had a sense of home.

His gaze moved over to Brittany. She was no longer standing in the middle of the floor but had moved over to a vintage-looking desk and was looking at a picture in the frame. Deciding not to stare, he glanced around again.

It was evident that although the outside showed signs of deterioration and neglect, the interior did not. Everything looked well cared-for and maintained, even the hardwood floors. It was clear that the person who lived here believed in being clean and neat. The place gave off a feeling that its owner had merely stepped out a minute and would be returning momentarily.

"Nice place," he said to Brittany, mainly to get her talking again. She'd gone too quiet on him and continued to stare at that picture frame. Was it a picture of the woman who had been her mother?

When she didn't acknowledge his remark, he knew she had effectively tuned him out, although not intentionally because her manners wouldn't allow such a thing. Emotions had taken over her, and he wasn't used to dealing with emotional women. Usually that was when he would cut and run like hell. But he wouldn't be going anywhere today. He felt as if he had a vested interest in this woman, which really didn't make much sense. All he wanted was to get her in his bed so she could soothe the ache in his pants. What he didn't understand, and what he was trying like hell to figure out, was his insane fascination with her.

And at the moment he didn't like her wandering around this place sinking deeper and deeper into a maudlin state of depression he refused to accept for her. He'd rather have her mad than sad. But right now he wanted her talking.

She glanced over at him and the look in her eyes was like a kick in the gut. It was as if he felt her pain. She hadn't known the owner of the house, nor would she recognize her if they'd passed in the street. But none of that mattered. The woman who used to live here had been her mother. The woman who'd given birth to her.

The woman who, for some reason, had given her away.

He waited for her to say something. The look in her eyes said she was ready. He wasn't Dr. Phil by any means, but he figured she needed to express her feelings, get them out in the open.

"I think I look like her," she said, holding the picture out for him to see.

He moved away from the door, crossed the room and took the picture frame she offered. He studied the image of the woman standing beside a tall man. She looked younger than Galen had expected, which meant she'd had Brittany at an early age. Probably a teen pregnancy. "Yes, you do favor her," he said honestly. "I wonder how old she was when she gave birth to you."

"Sixteen. According to her attorney she died at forty-four."

He nodded as he handed the picture frame back to her. "You want to check out the other rooms?"

"Sure."

She walked slowly and he did likewise beside her.

The kitchen was nice and the bay window provided a view of a lot of the land. It seemed to go on for miles. And the view of the mountains was just as impressive as the one from his place. No wonder those men at the auction mart wanted to demolish the house and build a hotel on the land.

He walked around the kitchen to the table. Just like the rest of the house, the table and chairs were Early American and fit perfectly in their setting.

Brittany then moved to the window and was looking out at the mountains and all the land. He decided to keep her talking.

"Do you know if she had any other relatives?"

She turned around. "According to her attorney, Mr. Banyon, she didn't. She and her husband never had any children. I'm not even certain he knew about me."

She moved away from the window and placed her hands on her hips and his gaze was immediately drawn to that area of her body. He liked how she looked in that skirt and figured he'd probably like her even better without it. Without a single stitch on her body. Okay, he would admit he was an ass, without a lick of manners. Here she was mourning the loss of her mother and his mind was in the bedroom.

"I guess we need to see the rest of the place," she said, lacking enthusiasm and reclaiming his attention. When she crossed the room to pass by him he got a whiff of her. Her scent had nearly driven him crazy on the drive over and it was playing havoc with his senses again.

There were two bathrooms, both of which he'd consider remodeling if the house was his. But it wasn't. He recalled her reaction when he'd handed her the key and told her the house was hers. Of course he'd meant it because legally it was. But the look she'd given him told a different story. She'd no doubt figured he'd given it to her because of the terms of their agreement. She was so far from right it wasn't funny.

"Thanks for having those boards removed, Galen. The view from every window is fabulous."

The midday sun was pouring through the windows of every bedroom they passed and seemed to hit her at every angle. There was just something about a beautiful woman. Now they stood in the master bedroom. It was a little larger than the other bedrooms and it did have its own bath. Brittany was standing next to the bed. The king-size and oversize furniture seemed to take up most of the space, making it tight to walk around much. Just as well. It wouldn't take much to tumble her onto that bed about now. It looked so inviting and she looked so damn enticing.

"Do you know what your mother did for a living?" he cleared his throat and asked, deciding to stay where he was standing in the doorway.

She looked over at him. "Mr. Banyon said she'd been a librarian within the public school system for years."

He nodded. "That doesn't surprise me. She was probably prim and proper just like you."

She tilted her head and met his gaze. "You think I'm prim and proper?"

"Yes. Don't you?"

She frowned. "No. I just believe a person should display good manners."

He glanced around and then looked back at her. "And I'm sure you're going to think I have atrocious manners when I say that I feel we've been here long enough and that I'm ready to go."

"But we just got here. You could leave me for a while and return for me later."

He could but he wouldn't. He wanted her with him, if that didn't sound crazy. It wasn't that he didn't have anything to do. He had Sniper to work on. But right now the only thing he wanted to work on was her. Tomorrow he'd probably feel differently and would give her a chance to come over here by herself to go through her mother's stuff. But today he couldn't handle her sadness any longer.

"That's not our agreement, Brittany. I brought you here so you can check out the place and we've done that. It's past time for lunch. Do you have a taste for anything in particular?"

He could tell from the expression on her face that she hadn't liked being reminded about their agreement. "No, wherever you decide is fine."

He was glad she wasn't pouting or pitching a fit because they were leaving. There had been enough gloom for one day, and he wanted to take her someplace to put a smile on her face.

Ten

An hour later they had returned to Galen's home and Brittany was rubbing her stomach. "I can't believe I ate that much. It's all your fault."

Galen chuckled. "It was my fault that you made a pig of yourself?"

"That's not a nice thing to say."

He rolled his eyes. "Okay, Miss Manners, it might not be nice but it's true."

She dropped down on his sofa. "Maybe next time you'll think twice before taking me to an all-you-can-eat place that serves barbecued ribs that fall off the bone."

He shrugged. "Then I'm not a good man," he said as if the thought didn't bother him in the least. "Earlier you schooled my manners on being conceited. Do you have any other lessons for today?"

"There are a couple I'd like to interject."

He took the armchair across from her. "Go ahead."

He was sitting right in her line of vision and a part of her wished he wasn't. Her reaction to him today wasn't good. She had handled it pretty well at her mother's house, because her mind had been filled with so many other things. But at the restaurant, she had been filled with images of him. So much so that her nipples pressing against her blouse had throbbed through most of the meal. And now there were these nerve endings inside her that seemed pricked, painfully stretched, whenever those laser green eyes lit on her.

He was leaning back in the chair, his legs crossed at the knees in a manly pose. His thighs were taut and his abs sturdy, masculine and ripped beneath his shirt. She felt a tingling in her fingers. They itched to reach out and touch his bare skin. She'd bet his flesh would be warm. How would it taste? Heat drenched her face. She'd never thought of putting her mouth on a man before.

She cleared her throat and forced her attention back to business. "Your cell phone," she said.

He lifted a brow. "What about it?"

"You answered it in the restaurant."

A smile touched his lips. "I answer it wherever it rings. That's why they call it a mobile phone. It's a phone on the go."

She rolled her eyes. "Proper etiquette dictates that you should turn your cell phone off in a restaurant just like you would do at church." From the look on his face she got the distinct impression that he didn't turn his phone off in church, either. Or maybe the look meant he didn't go to church.

"And if I miss a call?"

"You'll know it and you can call the person back once you leave the restaurant. Was it someone you couldn't call back later?" In a way she didn't want to know. What if it was a woman he was interested in?

"It was Mercury being nosy."

"Mercury?"

"My brother."

She nodded and tucked her legs beneath her on the sofa. She noticed his gaze followed her every movement. "You have a brother named Mercury?" she asked.

"Yes, and before you ask, the answer is no, he wasn't named after the planet or that Roman god. He was named for Mercury Morris. Ever heard of him?"

"Of course. I'm from Florida. He was a running back for the Miami Dolphins in the seventies, during the time they were unstoppable, undefeated one season."

She watched him smile and wanted to roll her eyes. Did men think they were the only ones who knew anything about football?

"My father was a huge Dolphins fan while growing up," he said. "He still is. In fact, he got drafted right out of college to play for them, but a knee injury kept that from happening before the start of what should have been his first season."

"How sad."

"Yes, it was for him at the time." He paused a moment and then said, "Okay, I get the 'no cell phone in the restaurant' rule. What's the other?"

She shifted in her seat when his gaze drifted down to her breasts and she wondered if he'd noticed her hardened nipples through her blouse. "The other is toothpicks. I didn't see you use them and I'm glad for that, but several others in the restaurant did. You don't stick a toothpick in your mouth after finishing a meal."

"We had ribs."

"That makes it worse," she said.

"But they're on the table."

"I noticed. Usually there're at the cash register on your way out. There's nothing nice about a person using a toothpick to pick their teeth at a restaurant, especially when others are still eating. You should take the tooth-pick and use it in the privacy of your own home."

He leaned forward in his seat. "And you know all this stuff, how?"

She smiled. "I studied it in college. I got a degree in history, but I took every course offered on etiquette and even saved my money for Emily Post Finishing School a couple of summers."

He nodded and stood up, and her gaze traveled the length of him. He was tall, well over six foot, muscular and his body was honed to perfection. He had an abdomen with a six-pack if ever there was one. She was so enraptured by him that she barely heard him say, "So I read on the Internet."

She raised a brow. "You looked me up on the Internet?"

He smiled. "Of course. You said you had a business and I wanted to check it out to make sure you were legit. I was impressed. So now I know for sure that you know what you're talking about."

He glanced at his watch. "I have some things to do in my garage. You can decide on dinner when I return in a few hours," he said as he was about to move away.

"Wait," she said. "Is that it? That's the manners les-son for today?"

His gaze then swept over her and she felt the heat emanating from the dark orbs wherever they touched. A sardonic smile then touched his lips when he said, "Yes, but there's always tonight. You can get prepared for whatever manners you want to go over with me then."

She lifted her chin. "That sounds like a proposition."

She saw irritation flash in the depths of his green eyes. "The proposition was made days ago. You accepted and as a result you're here under my roof. Mine for seven days to do as I please. And nothing will please me more than to have you naked in my bed beneath me every night while I breathe in your scent and make love to you until we both reach one hell of an orgasm."

She gasped at his words and she suddenly felt breathless. Her knees weakened and she was glad she was already sitting down or she would have fallen flat on her face. An image of her naked in bed beneath him flashed through her mind, and she was filled with a wanting she'd never known before.

His voice had deepened to a husky tone and he'd spoken promises he intended to deliver. He evidently didn't believe in holding back on anything, even words that a true gentleman wouldn't say, words that put her out of her comfort zone. She'd never dealt with a man like him before. He not only stated what he wanted, but he was letting her know he intended to have things his way.

And maybe that's exactly what she needed.

A man who was arrogant, sure of himself, a pure alpha male through and through. One who had manners when they counted and refused to display them when they didn't. She fought the inclination to cross the room and kiss him, which at that moment seemed the most natural thing in the world for her to do. Her, of all people. A woman who before meeting him would never have considered doing such a thing.

But Galen Steele had a way of pulling something out of her, and like Nikki, she was now convinced if there were hidden pleasures lurking somewhere beneath her surface, she would know about it before she left his home seven days from now.

She slowly stood up and placed her hands on her hips, tilted her head back and gave him what she hoped was one hell of a haughty look. With a man like him, a woman needed to be able to hold her own. "Talk is cheap, Galen. We'll see later how well you are on delivering."

She inwardly smiled. The effect of her words was priceless. Although he tried to keep his emotions in check, she read the look of startled surprise in his eyes. He hadn't expected her to goad him.

Brittany pulled in a deep breath when he began walking toward her, but she refused to step back or move away, although her heart was beating a wild rhythm in her chest. He didn't need to know her hands were trembling on her hips and heat had gathered at the juncture of her legs.

"You're right, Brittany, talk is cheap," he said when he came to a stop in front of her. The sound of his deep, husky voice made those already-hardened nipples get even harder.

"But I won't be doing much talking and neither will you. I believe in action."

She swallowed. "Do you?"

"Very much so. And just so you know, I want you. I wanted you in New York and I definitely want you now. And I'll give you fair warning. Tonight is taste-you night. I want the taste of you in my mouth, all over my tongue and embedded in my taste buds when I wake up in the morning."

Brittany's stomach clenched. This man of Steele was making her hot merely with his words. He hadn't touched her yet. And now he would taste her? Just the thought was filling her with more desire and longing than she'd ever felt before. She suddenly became fully aware of something that was new and exciting to her. Carnal greed.

She swallowed. "Like I said. Talk is cheap."

He smiled in a hungry way. "And like I said, I'm a man of action."

Then he leaned in and captured her mouth, not giving her a chance to stifle the moan that immediately rose in her throat. His arms wrapped around her, and his hands stroked her back at the same time his tongue stroked every inch of her mouth.

She had long ago decided his kisses were unique, full of passion and capable of inciting lust. But she was also discovering that each time they kissed, she encountered a different effect. This kiss was tapping into her emotions and she was fighting like hell to keep them under tight control where he was concerned. This was all a game to him. Not for her. For her, it was about finding herself in more ways than one. Discovering her past and making headway into her future.

He deepened the kiss and she felt his hands move downward to cup her backside and pull her more fully against him. She groaned again when she felt his hard erection press into her at a place that was already tingling with longing. Unfamiliar sensations were floating around in her stomach and she was drenched even more in potent desire.

And then he suddenly broke off the kiss and took a step back. She watched him lick his lips as if he'd enjoyed kissing her and then he thrust his hands into his jeans pockets, looked at her and asked, "Did I make my point?"

Oh, he'd made it, all right, but she'd never admit it to him. "Kind of."

She quickly scooted around him. "I think you should get to work now. I plan on setting up my laptop and answering a few e-mails. And then I plan to work on tomorrow's manners lesson for you." She headed toward the stairs.

"Brittany?"

She stopped and turned around. "Yes?"

A smile touched both corners of his mouth. "I like you." His face lit up as if the thought of it was a revelation to him or something.

She rolled her eyes. "Should I be thrilled?"

He gave her an arrogant chuckle. "The thrill will come later."

She turned back toward the stairs and damn if she wasn't looking forward to her first orgasm ever.

Eleven

Galen shut off the lamp on his worktable. Surprisingly, he had gotten a lot done once he'd been able to put Brittany to the back of his mind.

He liked her.

He had told her that earlier and had meant it. There were no dull moments with her around. Just when he thought he had her figured out, she would do or say something to throw him off base, literally stun him. His Miss Manners was becoming a puzzle he needed to put together, but there were so many pieces, he wouldn't know where to start. One thing was for certain, she was definitely keeping him on his toes.

Just like he had plans to keep her on her back starting tonight.

He smiled at the thought and leaned back in his chair as he recalled their meal at the restaurant earlier today. There was nothing like a buffet that included mouthwatering ribs and the best corn bread you'd ever want to taste. Jennie's Soul Food drew a lot of truckers, businesspeople and just plain everyday folks. Brittany hadn't been bothered by the mixture of clientele. The last woman he'd taken there had complained all through dinner, saying she'd felt out of place. That had been their first and their last date. He hadn't looked her up afterward, not even for a booty call. Personally, he didn't like women who whined or who felt they had a reason to complain about everything. Brittany was definitely not that type of woman.

He glanced at his watch. It was six already, which meant he'd been holed up in his garage for at least four solid hours. He'd still managed to get a lot done while anticipating tonight's events. He wondered if Brittany had taken his advice and was prepared. Probably not. He had pretty much spelled things out to her earlier. Laid them on the table, so to speak. Given her the real deal. If there had been any doubt in her mind just what his proposal had been about, now she knew. But he was certain she'd known all along that her being here was not just about teaching him manners. Oh, he was enjoying her little tidbits and would certainly keep them in mind, but manners weren't all he intended for them to cover over the next seven days.

He wondered where he would be taking her for dinner. Wherever they went he wanted to make sure she again ate well because she would definitely need her strength for later.

Galen stood to stretch his body and immediately felt his erection kick in. He was hard. He was ready. And it was time to find his woman. *His woman?* Okay, it had been an unwitting slip. He didn't think of any woman as his. But in a way Brittany was his—at least for the next seven days. After she left, his life would get back to normal. He was sure of it.

It was a romantic setting straight out of a movie. Brittany drew in a deep breath as she glanced around the bedroom. She'd taken all the advice the Internet had to offer. After checking e-mails from her staff, she'd searched several Web sites on what to do for a romantic night. Then she'd put the bedroom together.

She had every reason to believe Galen would deliver tonight and if he did, it would be her first orgasm ever. She wanted more than just the bells and whistles; she wanted drums and several trombones, as well. She would have a lot to celebrate after twenty-eight years, and she just hoped and prayed things came through for her. The thought that she was emotionally damaged from her teenage trauma was a lot for her to take in.

She glanced at the clock on the nightstand and wondered how much longer Galen would be working in his garage. A couple of times she had started to go find him, but figured he might not appreciate the interruption. Besides, she'd needed to prepare for tonight.

Deciding she wouldn't be kept a prisoner, she had scribbled him a note and given him her cell-phone number so he would know how to reach her. And she'd taken off to shop for everything she needed for tonight. Because he hadn't tried reaching her, chances were he hadn't known she'd left.

In addition to purchasing scented candles, she'd also bought a bottle of wine and a dozen red roses whose petals she'd strewn over the bed. Then there was the racy new outfit guaranteed to escalate her seduction.

She felt a deep surge of nervousness as she glanced down at herself. Talk about being bold. She'd never owned a pair of stilettos until now. And red of all colors. She had paid good money for them, although she figured she wouldn't get much use out of them after tonight. According to the online article, men wanted sex frequently and they liked seeing their women looking sexy—preferably naked and wearing stilettos.

Brittany had decided she could go with the stilettos, but she would definitely not be naked. Instead she'd purchased the short red dress she'd seen in one of the stores' window. Like the shoes, it was a first for her. She had the legs to wear a hemline halfway up her thighs, but she worried that if she were to bend over in this dress, Galen wouldn't miss seeing much. Including her new red lace panties.

She drew an unsteady breath, wondering if perhaps she'd gone a little too far. But then she had to remind herself there was a reason for her madness. Not only had she gotten her mother's home out of the deal, but she would also find out tonight whether she was frigid.

She shuddered at the use of that word but knew she had to call it what it was or could possibly be. According to the research she'd done on the Internet today, that word described any woman who didn't have a sex drive. She fit into that category.

However, she believed all that would change tonight. Already she felt a deep attraction to Galen and he had been able to get her juices flowing, literally. But the last thing she wanted was for him to question why she was so eager to become intimate with him now after she'd resisted his offer initially. He didn't need to know that in addition to wanting her mother's home she had a hidden motive for accepting his offer. A secret she'd shared only with Nikki and one she would take to the grave with her.

In addition to turning his bedroom into a seduction scene, she'd made a pit stop at the grocery store after discovering his pantry bare. Another rule of manners he'd broken. She wasn't Rachael Ray by any means, but she didn't do so badly in the kitchen. And just in case the sex thing with her was a total flop, at least she'd have the meal as a consolation prize.

Her ears perked up when she heard the sound of a door closing and figured it was Galen coming out of the garage. She nervously nibbled on her bottom lip knowing at any moment he would be coming up the stairs for her. She knew what happened after that would determine her fate.

Whatever it took—even if it was every ounce of resolve she had—she would get through it. No matter the outcome.

Galen sniffed the air the moment he closed the door from the garage. He had to be at the right house, but couldn't remember the last time he'd encountered the smell of food cooking.

He walked into his kitchen and glanced around. He'd been living here for four years, and this was probably the first time his stove had earned its keep. And the only thing his refrigerator had been good for was to chill his beer because he ate out one hundred percent of the time. Getting a home-cooked meal at his parents' place was one of the reasons he actually looked forward to Thursday nights.

He glanced over at his table. It was set for two with elegant china, silverware and glasses. He then glanced back at the stove and saw all stainless-steel pots. He could only assume all this kitchenware belonged to him. Was it a house-warming gift from his mother when he'd first moved in? Now that he thought about it, he was sure of it.

Whatever was in those pots sure smelled good and he couldn't wait to get into it. But then he frowned. If for one minute Brittany assumed a home-cooked dinner would replace the sex they were to have later, then she had another thought coming. He could get a meal from just about anywhere.

Galen turned toward the stairs, bracing himself for what he figured would be opposition to keeping her side of their agreement. She had been the one who'd tossed the "talk is cheap" challenge out there, and he was so looking forward to hearing her give one hell of an orgasmic scream. He could just imagine his hard body intimately connected to her soft one, her arms wrapped around his neck or her hands gripping his shoulders. All that mattered was getting inside her, thrusting in and out. His penis, which had gotten hard from the moment he'd finished working that day, seemed to have taken on a life of its own. If he didn't know better he'd suspect it had Brittany's name written all over it.

He'd never been this hard up for a woman. Each step he took up the stairs, closer to her, made his erection surge in anticipation. The lust that had been eating at him, nipping at his heels, from the first time he'd set eyes on her had overtaken his senses, was devouring his control and intoxicating his mind.

Galen wasn't sure what he would do if he'd discovered Brittany had reneged. He didn't expect her to be already naked waiting for him in his bed, but he didn't expect for her to come kicking and screaming, either.

He moved toward the hall that led to his bedroom, not sure what he would find. It wouldn't surprise him if he found her sitting with her laptop still working on her e-mails. He knew there hadn't been any food in the house, which meant she had gone to the grocery store at some point. No doubt she wasn't happy about doing that.

He placed one foot in front of the other thinking this had to be the longest walk of his life, mainly because what awaited him on the other side could make or break him. He should never have allowed any woman to sink her claws into him this deep. But he'd been a goner the first time she'd frowned at him when he'd hijacked her cab. And he hadn't been right in the head since.

When he stood in front of the closed double doors to his bedroom, his eyebrows furled. Was that music he was hearing? He reached out to open the doors and then quickly remembered his manners. Although it was his room, for the next seven days they would be sharing it and he had to afford Brittany the courtesy of knocking before entering. Pulling in a deep breath, he tapped his knuckles on the door.

"Come in."

He lifted a brow. Was he imagining things or had he heard a tremble in her voice? Taking another deep breath, he opened the doors. What he saw made him blink and mutter in a shocked tone, "Holy crap."

Twelve

Galen was convinced his heart had stopped beating, his lungs had seized and his penis had doubled in size. He had to literally shake himself just to get his body back to working order.

Brittany stood there with a sexy smile on her gorgeous face, and the "come get whatever you want" invitation he saw in her eyes suddenly made him feel like Adam in the Garden of Eden. Only thing missing was the apple.

"It took you long enough to get up here, Galen."

He swallowed. If she hadn't said his name he would have wondered if she was talking to him. Was she saying she'd been waiting for him to make an appearance? What the heck was going on and why did he feel he had gotten caught in some sort of trap?

In his peripheral vision he saw that his room had been transformed into a setting he hadn't ever seen before. Candles, imparting the scent of vanilla, glowed all around the room, soft music was playing and red rose petals were sprinkled over his bed, giving the room an overall romantic effect. He'd never thought he had a romantic bone in his body—until now.

But what caught his attention and held it more than anything was Brittany herself. How in the hell had she known that a woman in stilettos was his weakness, especially if she had legs like hers? And if that wasn't bad enough, the stilettos were red.

It was her dress, however, that had his erection throbbing, his tongue feeling thick in his throat. Where in the hell had she gotten something like that from? It was red to match the shoes and it was short. The fabric crisscrossed at the top and tantalized at the bottom with its flirty hem that barely covered her thighs. What was she trying to do? Kill him?

That thought, quite seriously, sent all kinds of questions flying through his mind. But all it took was a whiff of whatever perfume she was wearing to lay them to rest unanswered. His main consideration was getting her out of that dress.

"So how did work go today?"

He blinked, realizing she had spoken, and then what she was asking. While heat drummed through him, he figured that he needed to move his tongue to answer. "I finished my goal for today. Just one or two more pieces to work on this week and I'll be ready."

None of what he said was making any real sense. His mouth was saying words that his body didn't comprehend. Finish what? Ready for whom? His mouth was merely responding to her inquiry when the rest of him wanted to respond in another way. Forget the small talk.

"I didn't know you were waiting for me," he said,

moving toward her, deciding to dispense with pre-
liminaries and anything keeping him from her. Manners be damned.

"Yes," she said. "You probably didn't notice, but I
left for a while to do some shopping. Because I'd found
your pantry bare, I also stopped by the grocery store to
pick up a few things to prepare for dinner. Rule number four is to never invite someone to your home as an
overnight guest without plans to feed them."

"I was going to take you out," he defended.

"For breakfast, lunch and dinner?"

"Yes."

"Don't you ever cook for yourself?"

"No."

"That can get kind of pricey," she pointed out.

"I can afford it," he said, coming to a stop in front of
her. "Is this dress real?"

"Touch it and see," she challenged.

"I think I will."

Galen smiled and for one heart-stopping moment,
Brittany suddenly realized he wouldn't stop at touching the dress. He reached out and his hands slowly made
their way down the front of her dress, tracing his fingers across the soft material. But as expected, his hands
didn't stop there.

They slid over the softness of her shapely figure, as
if molding her in a way that made her breath choppy.
When he took a step closer and cupped her buttocks,
rubbing his hands over their firm curve, she fought back
the moan from deep within her throat.

"What is this about, Brittany? Why are you all of a
sudden handing yourself to me on a silver platter?" His
voice was husky as his hands continued to roam.

She stared into the depths of his green eyes. "You

ask too many questions," she said in a voice that trembled even to her own ears. He was standing close. His body was pressed into hers. She could feel the outline of his erection through his jeans. His eyes were trained on her face, causing goose bumps to appear on her arms and stirring a hunger within her. A hunger that was all new to her.

Deciding it was time to be bold and take things to the next level, she wrapped her arms around his neck and molded her body to his. She felt her already-short dress rise up in the process. Air fanned her butt as she pressed her hardened nipples into his solid chest. Instinctively, she shifted her body, causing her hips to move against his rock-hard thighs and his very aroused penis.

The thought that he wanted her filled her head with an excitement she'd never felt before. It made her bolder. Made her want things she'd never desired before. Made her want to do things she'd never done before.

She decided not to fight anything tonight, to just roll with the flow. Let loose. Be something she'd never been before—one of those sexually needy chicks. And with that thought in mind, she stood on tiptoes and offered her mouth to him.

He took it, and the thrust of his tongue between her lips made her quiver. At the same time that his mouth ravaged her, his hands took advantage of her raised dress and began caressing her backside and then slipping under her lacy panties to touch her bare skin.

He continued to kiss her in a way that made her moan and spread heat through all parts of her body. The juncture of her thighs tingled. Nothing she and any other man had done in the bedroom could equate to this. A mere kiss. Never had she gotten fired up to this degree. Or to any measure, to be honest. She hated admitting she used to pretend in the bedroom. Actually she'd gotten pretty good at faking it. But there was nothing bogus going on here.

Their lips clung and she wasn't aware until now a mouth could actually make love to her. It was as if he was determined to know her taste, emerge himself in her scent. He seemed content just to stand there, feel her body wherever he liked and explore her mouth. And she was pretty much content to let him. They had kissed before, but never like this. Never with this much hunger, greed and intensity.

He suddenly broke off the kiss and the sound of his breathing—rapid successions of quick, hard breaths—matched her own. He met her gaze and held it and she noticed his lips were wet from devouring her.

"You do know this dress is coming off, don't you?" he asked in a deep, throaty voice.

"And what if I said it was glued to my body?" she teased.

He smiled. "Then I would have to prove that it wasn't. Stitch by stitch. Inch by inch." And he began doing just that as his hands slowly moved over her body, tugging the dress off her shoulders and down her hips.

She heard his sharp intake of breath when he saw her red lace bra. And with a flick of his wrist he undid the front clasp and let the bra fall, setting free her twin mounds. His mouth immediately set upon them, drawing a nipple into the contours of his mouth to begin sucking.

Brittany grabbed hold of his shoulders when she felt weak in the knees. She hadn't known her breasts were so sensitive. Hadn't known they could ache for a man's mouth, until now. He had moved his mouth to the other breast, and quickly he had latched onto the other nipple, sucking profusely, and causing her stomach to tighten with every pull.

Holding her nipple hostage, he tilted his head to gaze up at her and she saw a flicker in the depths of his eyes as his hands remained clenched around the curves of her buttocks.

He lifted his head, touched his lips to her neck when he whispered, "Remember I told you it was 'taste you' night." And without waiting to see if she recalled it or not, he dropped to his knees in front of her. "I want the taste of you in my mouth. We're going to see just how cheap talk is, baby."

Brittany tried to ignore his term of endearment when she lifted her heels to step out of the dress that had tangled around her feet. He tossed it aside and glanced up at her wearing nothing but red lace panties and red stilettos.

"Damn, you look sexy. And tasty," he said, leaning forward, his hot breath right there at the crotch of her panties. He reached out and slowly began easing them down her legs and over her shoes to toss them aside.

He leaned back on his haunches. She was standing in front of him naked except for her high heels. When she made a move to take them off, he said, "Leave them on."

She looked at him questioningly, but only for a minute. His hands had slid up the backs of her thighs, while his face had moved close to her stomach. He was licking the flesh around her belly button. The feel of his tongue on her stomach sent unfamiliar sensations through her, flooding all parts of her. And then, in a simultaneous invasion, his hands cupped her backside at the same time his mouth lowered to her womanly folds. He slid his tongue between them, and Brittany let out a deep whimper.

Never had any man tasted her there. But he wasn't

just tasting her. He was devouring her. She grabbed hold of his shoulders as his mouth seemed intent to make a meal of her. She deliberately rolled her hips against his mouth, instinctively pushed forward as blood rushed to her head, making her dizzy.

His hands held her buttocks, determined to keep her pressed to his mouth as his tongue filled her, sent widespread shivers through her. She continued to whimper as he ravaged her womanhood, openmouthed and thrusting deep, as far as his tongue could go.

This was what other women had experienced. Why they kept wanting more. Why they'd looked at her like she was crazy when she seemed oblivious to what an orgasm was about. Now she was finding out firsthand. She felt it building, right at the juncture of her thighs, under the onslaught of Galen's mouth and tongue.

The throbbing between her legs intensified until it was downright unbearable, and then suddenly her entire body ignited in one hell of an explosion and she cried out his name and catapulted in a free fall. This was pleasure. One of those hidden pleasures that Nikki had warned her about. The intensity of it held her captured within its grip.

How had she gone twenty-eight years without experiencing this? The cells in her body felt pulverized and she succumbed to every novel feeling, soared higher than she'd ever thought possible.

When she thought she would crumble to the floor, he pulled his mouth away, stood and swept her off her feet into his arms. He moved up the steps to the bed and placed her on it, right on those rose petals and among the scented candles. And then he moved back, stared at her stretched across his bed. Naked, except for her shoes.

At the questioning look in her eyes, he said, "Keep them on. It's my fantasy."

And then she watched as he began removing his clothes.

Thirteen

Galen unbuttoned his shirt thinking there was no woman he wanted to make love to more than the one stretched out on his bed, naked except for those sexy red high heels he dreamed about.

He'd asked her to keep them on because he'd never made love to a woman with her shoes on, and because the ones she was wearing looked so damn hot on her. Too hot to take off. He'd seen women in sexy heels a number of times and had always gotten one hell of a boner. But seeing Brittany in them was messing not only with his body but also with his mind.

He couldn't take his gaze off her. She was lying on her side facing him and her breasts were full, firm and high and the nipples he had sucked on earlier looked ready for him to feast on again. And then there were the dark curls between her legs, looking as luscious as anything he'd ever seen. He was getting harder just looking at that part of her. Using his mouth, he had made her come. And before the night touched the stroke of midnight, she would come plenty more times.

As he tossed his shirt aside he tried to come to terms with what was going on with him where she was concerned. Why was she so embedded under his skin that he was intent on screwing her out of it?

He swallowed hard at the thought of that tactic backfiring on him and instead of screwing her out of it, he might just bury her deeper into it. But for some reason that possibility didn't bother him. He breathed in deeply, feeling antsy, unreasonably horny. Maybe he ought to slow things down a bit.

For what purpose? his mind snapped back and asked. She was in a giving mood tonight, so he'd best just take what she was offering.

His erection had thickened and lengthened, and like a divining rod, it was aimed straight toward her, namely the juncture of her legs. He removed the rest of his clothes and when he stood naked in front of her, he let out a deep growl when her scent reached him. And from her scent, he knew she wanted him as much as he wanted her.

But something was nagging his mind, making him wonder why she was being so generous tonight. She had known when she'd accepted his offer that it would come down to this. Still, she hadn't been happy about it. Why had she done a one-eighty?

"Manners rule number five, Galen. Never keep a lady waiting."

Her words made his heart pound and his pulse race. And as he moved toward the bed he knew that she *was* a lady. The sexiest lady he'd ever met. "There's a good reason for this delay, sweetheart," he said, moving to the bench at the foot of the bed. "A must-do." He lifted the top and pulled out a condom packet and proceeded to sheath himself.

He knew she was watching his every move. When he finished, he braced one knee on the bed, held out his hand and said, "Come here, baby."

He thought her movement was as graceful as a swan, and she looked sexier than any woman had a right to be. When she reached him and placed her hand in his, he leaned toward her and began placing kisses up the side of her neck while whispering how much he wanted her.

He then began trailing kisses along the curve of her shoulders, liking the taste of her skin there just as much as he had the area between her thighs. The sweet taste of her womanly essence was still on his tongue and would stay there for some time. And then he kissed her deeply as they tumbled backward onto the bed together.

It was then that Galen pulled back and stared deep into her eyes. "I need to know," he whispered. "I need to know that tonight isn't a fluke and tomorrow you'll regret everything that takes place in this bedroom. And even worse, that you won't share yourself with me the next six days."

He outlined her lips with the tip of his finger. "Tell me that won't happen, Brittany."

Brittany stared deep into Galen's intense eyes and at that moment she doubted she could deny him anything. Not this man who'd less than twenty minutes ago given her the experience of her first orgasm. And for that she was exceedingly grateful. The last thing she would have tomorrow was regrets. Nor did she want to deny herself this pleasure for the next six days. She was a late bloomer where sex was concerned, but tonight she'd become a woman finding out how to lose herself in the heat of passion and pleasure.

"Tell me, Brittany."

She swallowed. A part of her silently warned she was getting in too deep. She should take tonight and be done with it. Anything beyond this could lead to some serious trouble. What if he discovered it had been more than the lure of her mother's house that brought her to his bed? That it had also been her quest to find out more about herself. Her need to know if she could enjoy an amorous relationship with a man.

He'd proven she could. Should she take that knowledge and run? Be through with it? Let him know there wouldn't be any more sensual interludes between them and all he would be getting from her over the next six days were lessons in manners? She knew she wasn't capable of running anywhere. Now that he'd revealed all her hidden pleasures, she wanted to spend as much time as she could and explore those pleasures with him.

"There won't be any regrets tomorrow, Galen," she said in a soft voice. "And I'm committed to keeping my end of our agreement, so there will be more nights like this one."

He frowned and she wondered why he was doing so. Hadn't she just stated what he'd wanted to hear? They both had their own ulterior motives for sharing this week. He'd been right when he'd said that he had something she wanted and she had something he wanted.

But what happened after the seven days?

A shiver ran through her, although the answer to that question was simple. He went his way and she went hers. She would have her mother's home and he'd get his week of sexual enjoyment. What more could either of them expect?

She tilted her head and studied Galen, wondering the reason for the heavy silence. "That's what you want, isn't it?"

"Of course."

Still, she continued to look at him, wondering if she was missing something. She shook off the possibility that she was. Before she could dwell on it any more, he lowered his mouth and captured hers again.

Galen, she decided, was a perfectionist when it came to kissing. Some of the things he did with his tongue should be outlawed. Even now he was sucking gently on hers, while his hands were touching her everywhere, squeezing her breasts, teasing the hardened tips of her nipples. And then he lowered his hand between her legs and inserted a finger into her.

She pulled her mouth back and drew in a deep breath before burying her face in the warmth of his hairy chest. He smelled good. He smelled of man. And his intimate touch was driving her sensuously insane. When his free hand moved to caress the slope of her back she lifted her head from his chest and met his intense gaze.

"Make love to me, Galen."

She whispered the words not caring that her request probably lacked manners. The protocol was changing, and women were bold enough to ask something like that. Still, such an audacious request sounded strange coming from a female. However, at the moment the only thing she cared about was the deep ache in her stomach that had been there for a while and had become unbearable the moment he'd removed his pants to reveal the thatch of dark curly hair at his groin. There was just something about seeing him exposed and the thickness of his erection that had heat radiating to her lower limbs. She wanted him in a way she'd never truly wanted a man. With Galen she could be herself. She could be the woman she'd never been.

She wanted him. He wanted her. And for now that was all that mattered.

"Be careful what you ask for, sweetheart," he whispered as he gathered her close to the warmth and solid hardness of his body. She felt his arousal pressed against her belly and was compelled to reach down and grip his manhood in her hand.

She remembered touching Gilford once and the harsh words he'd said when she did. He'd reminded her that she was a lady who was above doing such things. Instead of being turned off by her actions, it was evident Galen had no such problem with her touching him, if the sound of his heavy breathing and deep guttural groans were any indication. Empowered by his response, she began stroking him, liking the feel of the thick veins that outlined the shaft of his penis, and the warmth that emitted from the tip of it.

"Damn, Brittany," he growled. "You're about to make me lose my manners."

She smiled thinking he just had. A true gentleman would never swear in front of a lady. Instead of pointing that out to him, she decided to inflict her own brand of punishment by sinking her teeth into his shoulder blade and then licking the bruise with her tongue.

"Payback, Brittany."

He shifted their positions and she found herself flat on her back with him looming over her, sliding in place between her open legs and red stilettos. And she knew whatever patience he'd been holding in check had gotten tossed to the wind. She glanced up at the see-through ceiling. It had gotten dark and there were stars in the sky adding to the romantic effect she'd created.

That effect stirred everything within her and when she felt his manhood at the entrance of her mound, nudging her womanly folds apart trying to seek admittance, streaks of anticipation flooded her.

Then she felt him, the heat of him sliding inside her wet channel, stretching her, taking her, preparing to mate with her. Her muscles clenched him, gripped him, needing something only he could give. She knew she had to relax, stop being greedy, but this was all new to her and she wanted it all.

He remained still when he was inside her to the hilt and then he glanced down at her and whispered, "Wrap those legs and high heels around my waist. I want to feel you. I want to feel them. I'm about to do the very thing to you that those shoes stand for."

And he did.

He began moving in and out of her, and the throbbing between her legs intensified with each stroke. She did just as he suggested and wrapped her legs around him, stilettos and all.

He lifted her hips to receive him deeper and she could actually feel blood rushing through her veins. And then in a surprise move he lowered his head and captured a nipple in his mouth and began sucking while his body rode her hard. She bit her lips against a moan and then gave up and screamed out his name when a mass of sensations ripped through her.

She pressed closer to him, tightened her legs around him as he continued to pound into her. Heat burst into flames and she tightened her grip on him when he bucked several times with whiplash speed. They held nothing back. They shared passion, pleasure and possession. Tonight he was hers and she was his. He kept thrusting inside her until he had nothing left to give, and then finally he moaned her name and collapsed on top of her.

When his breathing returned to normal, he shifted his weight off her. She cuddled closer to him as if that was where she belonged.

He laid a hand across her thigh as he met her gaze, breathing in deeply and then saying, "That was simply amazing. Incredible." He then reached down to remove her shoes and tossed them across the room.

She lay there, completely sated, as she tried to catch her breath. She totally agreed with him. She wondered what he would think if he knew tonight was the first time she'd made love and considered it a pleasurable experience.

He wrapped his arms around her and pulled her closer. "Let's sleep a while. Dinner will keep until later. Besides, I doubt either of us has the strength to get out of this bed right now."

He was right, she thought, laying her head on his chest and giving in to her body's exhaustion. She felt drained, yet at the same time flagrantly and passionately pleasured. She moved her head to look at him, and when she did their eyes locked. He had been looking at her. At that moment something passed between them. Just what, she wasn't sure.

Sensations rippled through her all over again and she knew at that instant that Galen Steele was every woman's fantasy.

He was certainly hers.

Fourteen

Brittany woke up the next morning, shifted her body and stared up into the sky. She could even see birds flying overhead through the bedroom ceiling. Amazing. She closed her eyes thinking nothing was as amazing as making love with Galen last night.

She had lost count of her orgasms. After they'd taken a nap and awakened to make love again, they had slipped into their clothes and gone downstairs to eat, totally famished.

Galen told her more than once how much he enjoyed her spaghetti, which she'd served with a salad and garlic bread. He had even asked for seconds. Then he had helped with the cleanup. The next thing she knew, she was swept into his arms and taken back upstairs where he'd made love to her again several more times.

She'd come close to telling him what last night had meant to her and how her better judgment had warned her against the indulgence. But Galen was a man used to sleeping with women who know the score, and although she wasn't a virgin, her experience left a lot to be desired. In the end, she kept the secret.

She shifted in bed and wished she'd stayed put when her muscles ached. The intensity of Galen's lovemaking last night had made her sore, which would no doubt slow her down a bit today. At least until she took a hot, relaxing bath. Then she would go over to her house. After yesterday she finally allowed herself to label the house as hers, especially after Galen had given her the key.

She wondered where he'd gone. Although today was Saturday, he was probably downstairs working in his garage. She had yet to see that part of his house and knew he considered it his private domain where he allowed his creativity to flow. She smiled thinking his creativity had done a pretty good job flowing right here in this bedroom last night.

Easing out of bed, she went into the bathroom. If Galen intended to work all day today, then she could very well revisit her house. If he thought she would be at his beck and call, then he had another think coming.

Galen's heart began racing when he heard Brittany moving around upstairs. Although he'd been tempted to wake her early this morning to make love again, he'd figured she needed her rest, especially because he'd kept her up most of the night.

He probably should feel like an oversexed, greedy ass, but he was too damn satisfied, far too content, to find fault in his behavior last night. Besides, he knew although Brittany might not have expected to go as many rounds with him, she'd enjoyed each and every one of them. Her screams were still ringing in his ears.

Something about her screams, though, hadn't been right. Not that he thought she'd been faking them, mind you, but he'd made love to enough women to recognize the tenor of a scream. Listening to Brittany's, one would get the impression she'd never screamed during a climax before. It could very well be that she assumed screaming displayed reproachful behavior, definitely a lack of manners. But still, lack of manners or not, some things couldn't be held back. And letting go while gripped within the throes of passion was one of them.

He moved away from the sink to open the refrigerator and again was taken aback by the sight of the items inside. Milk, eggs, cheese, fruit… The meal Brittany prepared last night had been off the charts. But he hoped she didn't assume she had to cook, because he'd made it clear he had no problems with their eating out. And then there was dinner at his parents' home on Thursday night and—

Holy crap! Brittany would still be here on Thursday night. According to the terms of their agreement that Eli had drawn up, she wouldn't be leaving his place until next Saturday morning. There was no way he would take her to his parents' place for dinner. He didn't want anyone getting the wrong impression, and knowing his mother, she would. It was not the norm for women to hang around his place on a frequent basis. Although several had spent the night, he didn't waste time helping them to the door bright and early the next morning. And it went without saying that he'd never taken a woman to his parents' dinners.

"Good morning."

He hadn't heard Brittany come down the stairs. But then why would he have been listening for her? Talk about irregular behavior…

He drew in a deep breath, closed the refrigerator door and turned around. The moment he did so, a fine sheen of perspiration touched his brow. Some women looked better than others in the morning and he quickly decided she fit in that category. She had taken a shower, which was probably the reason she looked so fresh in her top and jeans. But a shower hadn't put the glow on her face. He had posted enough notches on his bedpost to know only a night of earth-shattering sex could do that to a woman. He inwardly flinched at the thought of her being a notch on anyone's bedpost, including his.

"Good morning, Brittany." There was no need to ask if she'd gotten a good night's sleep because thanks to him she hadn't.

Instead he asked, "Where would you like to go for breakfast?" He had showered and shaved earlier and was ready to go. And getting out of the house wasn't such a bad idea; then he wouldn't have thoughts running through his head of taking her back upstairs.

"I can prepare something for us. Won't take but a minute. At least, if that's all right with you because it's your kitchen."

Yes, it was his kitchen, and as far as he was concerned, everything in it was his, including her. He then heaved a sigh, wondering how his mind could think such a thing. There was no woman alive that was his. He borrowed them for the time it took to get his pleasure and then he returned them to where they'd come from. It would be easy to tell Brittany she could go upstairs and pack, and that starting today she could stay at her mother's place, but for some reason he couldn't fix his mouth to say those words.

Instead he said, "I don't have a problem with it. I just don't want you to assume I expect it of you."

He watched in fascination when her lower lip started to quiver. Call him sick but he had missed seeing that, although he knew she was vexed with him for some reason. "Trust me, Galen. I know your expectations where I'm concerned."

"Do you?"

"Yes."

A sudden smile touched his lips. "In that case…" He moved toward her. As soon as he reached her, he picked her up off her feet and placed her on his kitchen counter and moved between her jeans-clad legs. Already he missed seeing her in those sexy high heels.

"What do you think you're doing, Galen?" she asked, staring at him with a frown on her face.

That elicited a laugh from him. "I bet you won't ask me that in a couple of minutes." He then swooped his mouth down to hers.

Brittany wondered why after a night like last night, they were at odds with each other this morning. And why did it take this, another Galen Steele mind-blowing kiss, to put things in perspective?

Instead of thinking about the answers to those questions, she decided to concentrate on the kiss instead. Might as well, because it would have snatched her focus anyway. Heat always sizzled between them whenever their lips locked and this morning was no exception.

His hands reached up to cup both sides of her face, making her feel the intensity of him making love to her mouth. And that was exactly what he was doing. His tongue was ravaging her, leaving no part of her mouth unscathed.

His mouth continued to move against hers with a hunger she felt all the way to her toes, and she couldn't resist returning the kiss with equal fervor. All she could think about was how last night this same mouth and this very naughty tongue feasted at her breasts and between her thighs, driving her over the brink of madness and lapping her into orgasm after orgasm. Neither could she forget his powerful thrusts into her, over and over, in and out, making her scream more times than she could count. It was a wonder her throat wasn't raw this morning.

He pulled back, breaking off the kiss, and she stared into his face, saw that arrogant smile on his moist lips and she swallowed hard. It was either that or grab his shirt and make him kiss her again.

"Now, you were asking?"

She blinked. *She'd asked him something?* Oh, yeah, she'd asked what he thought he was doing. He'd given her an answer in a tongue-tangling way. Brittany considered saying they should take this to the bedroom but decided not to. Instead she said, "Breakfast. What are we going to do about breakfast? This is Saturday, so I'm sure most breakfast places are crowded and it's after nine already."

He nodded and she noticed his gaze was glued to her lips. "So what do you suggest?"

"I suggest I prepare something. Afterward I'm sure you have your day planned."

"I had thought about putting in more time on Sniper today."

"And I plan to go over to my mother's place for a while."

He lifted her off the counter and placed her back on her feet. "It's no longer your mother's place. It's yours. I gave you the key yesterday and she willed the house to you, so you might want to start thinking of yourself as the owner."

She rubbed her arms where his hands had touched. "I know," she said smiling faintly up at him. "But no one has ever given me anything before." And that had been the truth. Even during the Christmas holidays when she'd received presents from her foster parents, she'd known the gifts had been donated by charity.

He took a step toward her and reached out and traced the curve of her mouth with his thumb. "But all that's changed now, hasn't it?"

He was standing close, so close she could feel his erection through his jeans pressing against her. She couldn't stop the stab of sexual sensations that spiked through her veins.

His question made her realize that yes, it had changed. Her mother may have given her away when she was born, but before Gloria McIntyre had left this earth she had found her and had tried making things right. Not that they had been wrong. A part of her had always figured her mother had been a teenager who'd wanted the best for her. She'd had no way of knowing that what she'd wanted for her daughter and what her daughter eventually got were two different things. But then maybe she did know once she'd gotten the investigator's report.

"Do you need my help?"

She gave Galen a reluctant smile. What she needed was for him to leave the kitchen so she could concentrate. "No, I can handle things. Why don't you go to the garage and start working," she suggested. "I'll call you when I'm done."

"And you're sure you don't need my help?"

"I'm positive."

"All right. And you don't have to come to the garage looking for me. I'll be back up in fifteen minutes or so. I'll lay out my supplies and come back."

He turned to leave, then, catching Brittany off guard, he pulled her against him and covered her lips in a kiss that sent her pulse racing. When he released her, he whispered against her moist lips, "I like you." And then he moved toward the door that led to his garage.

"Tell me about your brothers, Galen."

Galen glanced across the table. When he had returned from the garage, it had been just in time to see Brittany place the pancakes she'd prepared on a platter. Then there were the eggs, bacon and orange juice. Everything he would normally get at Flynn's Breakfast Café where he ate most mornings. But he would be the first to say the meal Brittany had prepared could hold its own against Flynn's any day.

He lifted a brow. "My brothers?"

"Yes."

She had asked about his brothers before, a couple of times, and he'd always avoided her question. His family was his family, and most people living in Phoenix knew the Steele brothers. Most women he'd dated didn't ask about his brothers, because Tyson, Eli, Jonas, Mercury and Gannon had managed to carve out reputations around the city on their own. He had to remember Brittany wasn't from Phoenix, though, which could be a good thing. She wouldn't know about the Steele brothers' reputation. She had no idea some women considered them the "Bad News Steeles." Nor would she know they liked women in their beds, but had no plans to keep them in their lives.

"I mentioned I'm the oldest," he started off by saying.

"After me there's Tyson. There's only an eleven-month difference in our ages. At thirty-three he's the doctor in the family, a heart surgeon and a damn good one."

He took a sip of his coffee, thinking it tasted just as good as any he purchased from Starbucks. "After Tyson there's Eli. As you already know, he's the attorney in the family. He's thirty-two. Then there's Jonas, who's thirty-one. Jonas owns a marketing firm and has some top names as clients. After Jonas there's Mercury at thirty. He's an ex-NFL player turned sports agent. And last but not least is Gannon, the youngest at twenty-nine, but he's definitely not the smallest. He took over the day-to-day operations of my father's trucking company and even gets behind a rig himself every once in a while."

He leaned back in his chair. "So there you have it, the Phoenix Steeles."

She smiled and lifted a brow. "There's more?"

He chuckled. "Yes, mostly living in North Carolina. Have you ever heard of the Steele Manufacturing Company?"

"Yes."

"That's those Steeles."

"You're close to them, as well?"

"Of course, they're family."

"Of course."

He looked down into his coffee cup as he recalled that Brittany did not have a family, and he remembered what she'd said about never feeling a part of any of her foster families. He wished he could have changed that for her.

"So tell me about Galen Steele."

He glanced up thinking he'd rather not. But he would, because talking was a lot safer—he wouldn't be tempted to take her upstairs and communicate in a different way. "What do you want to know?"

"Anything. Everything."

He couldn't help but smile at the thought of that. Either could get the both of them in trouble. "I like sex." He thought the blush on her face was cute. Just as cute as the quivering of her lips when she got angry.

"I know that already. What else do you like?" she asked.

"You. I like you," he said honestly, even though he knew such an admission would rattle her.

He watched her bite her lip. "Yes, I think you've said that already, too," she said. "What else do you like besides sex and me?"

"I like auto racing. The Steele Manufacturing Company sponsors a car for NASCAR, so I travel to the races quite a bit."

She nodded. "When our paths crossed in New York, you were there for a wedding, right?"

He chuckled. She'd made it seem like it had been a casual meeting when it had been anything but. He'd swiped her cab. "Yes, my cousin Donovan. There wasn't supposed to be a wedding."

She lifted a brow. "There wasn't?"

"No, because Donovan wasn't ever supposed to marry. He was supposed to be a bachelor for life."

"Is that what he'd said?"

"Yes. Always."

Galen stared back into his cup of coffee, which was almost empty. Donovan used to say it and was quite serious about it, but a woman had come along and changed his mind. Galen was certain that he would never let that happen to him, and to this day he didn't understand how it happened to Donovan. His cousin had had everything going for him. Any woman he wanted. And then Natalie came along and whammo, he'd fallen in love and the next thing everyone knew, he was talking marriage.

Deciding they'd sat at the table and chitchatted long enough, he stood to clear his plate. "You sure you don't need me to help do anything over at your place?"

"Yes, I'm positive. Today I plan to go through her things and see what I need to pack up and what I want to keep."

"You don't have to do everything in one day, you know."

"Yes, I know. But I want to get it done."

"Well, call me if you change your mind and need my help," he said, taking his plate and cup to the sink.

"You have your own work to do."

Galen was about to say that he didn't care how much work he had to do; if she needed him, he wanted her to call. She came first. But he quickly clamped his mouth shut, wondering why on earth he'd think something like that. No woman came before his work…except his mother and most of the time that couldn't be helped. His father had basically spoiled Eden. She'd been the only female in a houseful of males and she'd been treated like a queen. Unfortunately, she hadn't pulled off her crown yet.

"Just call me if you decide you need me. And don't wash the dishes. Just put everything in the sink. You cooked breakfast, so I'll clean up on my next break."

Growing frustrated over what seemed to be his mounting fascination with her—memories of their night together weren't helping matters—he said, "I'll see you later." And then he left the kitchen.

Fifteen

Brittany moved around her mother's home. In a way she was glad Galen hadn't come with her this time. She needed space from him to think. For some reason he'd appeared guarded this morning. Although he'd kissed her when he'd sat her up on the counter, from then on he seemed cool. Not cold but cool. She hoped he wasn't thinking she wanted something beyond this week because she didn't. All she wanted was full ownership of this house, fair and square, and then she would decide what she would do with it.

She moved toward her mother's room and pulled out several drawers. There were more pictures of Gloria McIntyre and a man Brittany could only assume was her mother's husband. They seemed like a close pair.

Brittany had decided if she didn't find anything to give her a clue as to why her mother had decided to look for her all these years, then she would go talk to the private investigator she'd hired. Maybe the man could shed light on a few things.

She pulled out another drawer, thinking like the others she would find more pictures, and was surprised to find a journal. Her heart rate increased as she pulled out the journal and closed the drawer. It was thick and she could tell it contained many entries.

Moving quickly to her mother's bed, Brittany kicked off her shoes before lying down on the bed. One of the first things she'd done when she arrived this morning was strip the bed and put on fresh linen. The washer and dryer were going and she intended to have the sheets back in the linen closet before she left. It was still early yet, not quite four o'clock. More than likely Galen was working and hadn't noticed the time.

The first entry she came to was written eighteen years ago on January tenth. Brittany's tenth birthday.

I tried to bring up the subject of the baby I gave away, my beautiful little girl, but Walter doesn't want to talk about it. He'd said he could handle it when I first told him about her last year, but now I'm not sure I did the right thing.

Brittany quickly sat up. Her mother had told her husband about her? Quickly she scanned ahead to another entry, recorded on her thirteenth birthday.

Today my daughter becomes a teenager. I hope the family that adopted her loves her as much as I do. It was so hard for me to give her up, but I wasn't given a choice. I couldn't abort her like Mom and Dad wanted. Especially after Britton drowned. She was to be our baby. Britton and I had so many plans, and when he died he left me all alone.

Brittany's heart jumped. Her father's name had been

Britton and he'd drowned. A knot formed in her throat when she kept reading.

I cried for days and Mom and Dad refused to speak to me for months, but I wouldn't back down about the abortion. They finally sent me away to Phoenix to live with Uncle Milton and Aunt Pauline. I agreed to give my baby up for adoption since everyone said she would go to a couple who wanted a baby but couldn't have one. They would love and cherish my baby like I would have done. When I met with the people at the adoption agency a month before my due date, I thought they were nice, and they said I could even name the baby. I decided to name him Britton if he was a boy and Brittany if she was a girl. She was a girl so I named her Brittany. I got to hold her for only a little while and I thought she looked like Britton. She was a beautiful little girl with a head full of curly black hair. I noticed two of her fingers were crooked and her feet were turned in but the nurse said they would eventually straighten out. Happy Birthday, Brittany, wherever you are. I hope you're happy.

Brittany wiped a tear from her eye. She hadn't been happy. While her mother assumed she was somewhere being loved and cherished by some nice couple on her thirteenth birthday, it had been just weeks after that when Mr. Ponder had tried to molest her. And those fingers never changed, and as a child she had to wear heavy metal braces that fit into her shoes until her bones straightened out. Both birth defects made her a flawed baby nobody wanted to adopt.

Brittany looked down at her hand. All her fingers were straight now because one of the first things she'd done after making a profit at Etiquette Matters was to have surgery on her fingers.

She drew in a deep breath and continued reading.

Seconds turned into minutes and minutes into hours.
The entries came to an end and Brittany was so full of
her mother's love that she couldn't stop the tears that
poured from her eyes. All those years when she thought
nobody loved her, nobody cared, here in this house located thousands of miles from where she lived in Florida, Gloria McIntyre had loved her. She had made an
entry in memory of her on every birthday she'd had.

Brittany couldn't do anything but drop back down
on the bed and cry her eyes out. She understood why
her mother had given her up thinking she would get a
better life, but still...

"Brittany? What's wrong?"

Brittany snatched her head up and through the tears
she saw Galen. Where had he come from? She pulled
herself up and by then he was there, pulling her into his
arms, and she went willingly, circling her arms around
his neck.

"What is it, Brittany?" he asked, his voice soft and
filled with concern as he sat down on the edge of the
bed with her in his arms.

And then the words came pouring out and she knew
to him they probably made no sense and ran all together.
"My mother loved me. My father's name was Britton and
he drowned when he was eighteen, leaving my sixteen-
year-old mother pregnant with me. My grandparents
wanted her to get an abortion but she wouldn't, so they
sent her here to live with her uncle and aunt. The people
at the adoption agency let her name me after my father,
and promised to give me to a nice couple who would
love and cherish me. But nobody wanted me because
two of my fingers were crooked and I had to wear those
metal leg braces until my bones straightened out. And
then when she thought I was doing fine on my thir-

teenth birthday, that was the year Mr. Ponder tried to molest me, which is why I've never liked sex. And I paid a plastic surgeon to fix my fingers. She wanted to find me but had to wait until her husband died and then she died before I could meet her."

There, she'd said it all and then she cried even more. And Galen just held her.

It wasn't supposed to be this way, Galen thought as he stared into space while holding the woman in his arms. She wasn't supposed to wiggle her way into his heart so easily. Now he fully understood what had happened to Donovan.

He glanced down at Brittany. The sound of her crying tore at his heart. But he was letting her get it all out—all the pain, heartache, heartbreak, loneliness, the feeling of belonging to no one. And as she cried he gently rubbed her back, held her in his arms and whispered over and over again that everything would be okay.

He doubted when it was over she would remember even half the stuff she'd told him just now, but he would never forget it. She thought she'd never liked sex? A part of him inwardly smiled knowing she'd certainly enjoyed it last night. Was that what last night had been about? Testing the waters to see if perhaps, considering all the sexual chemistry between them, she could possibly enjoy it with him?

And what was all that about her fingers and legs? Was that why she hadn't gotten adopted as a baby? Most people wanted newborns instead of an older child, and for her not to have gotten adopted meant that someone thought something was wrong with her. So, she'd had a couple of crooked fingers and weak legs, big damn deal. Was that a good reason not to take a baby into your home and love it? And he would love to be in the same room as this Ponder guy about now. He'd put both his feet up the man's rear end.

Pulling in a deep breath, he continued to rock her and kept whispering that everything would be okay.

Earlier that afternoon he'd begun getting concerned when she hadn't returned, and when she hadn't answered her cell phone, concern turned to worry. A first for him over a woman.

All he could think was that she was alone in a house on a secluded road. He'd driven like a maniac to get here. And now that he was here with her, there was no need to question why his heart was filled with so much love for her.

Damn.

And with that realization he could only shake his head. No need to ask how it happened, where it happened or when it happened. Those logistics really didn't matter. All that mattered was that he had fallen hopelessly in love with Brittany Thrasher. Especially when it had been just yesterday he'd assured himself his fascination with her was bound to wear off. Today he realized he had no intentions of letting her go. Ever.

When she finally pulled her face from his chest and tried wiping away any traces of tears, he asked softly, "Where's your cell phone, sweetheart? I tried calling you a hundred times."

She didn't look up at him, pretending interest in the buttons of his shirt. She was probably trying to recall just how much she'd told him. No doubt she figured she'd given him too much information.

"It's in my purse on top of the washing machine. I guess I didn't hear it ring."

"Okay, we'll grab it on our way out." He then swept

her into his arms. At her gasp of surprise he looked down at her and said, "And before you ask, I'm taking you home."

She really didn't have a clue just how much he meant it.

"You are mine," a raspy voice whispered as Brittany felt her clothes being removed from her body. She couldn't stay awake. She felt so sleepy.

She recalled Galen bringing her back here and leaving her car at her mother's place. The drive over here was a blur, but she did remember him carrying her into the house and then up the stairs to his bedroom.

She had the faintest memory of him giving her a glass of wine to drink, but only because the sweet taste of fermented grape was still on her tongue. And now Galen was whispering to her, letting her know he was removing her clothes and getting her ready for bed. That only made her want to cry even more because no one had ever really taken care of her. But tonight he was.

"Hold up your arms, Brittany, so I can slip the T-shirt on you."

Like a child, she did what she was told, because all she wanted to do was sleep. And she shivered when she felt the cotton material sliding over her head and past her shoulders to hardly cover her thighs.

Through barely opened eyes, she watched as he tossed the covers back and then, reaching his hand out to her, she took it and slid beneath the covers. When he tucked her in, a tear fell from her eye. No one had ever tucked her into bed before.

"You're going to read me a story?" she asked, trying to tease but barely getting the words out. She had a feeling she'd taken too many sips of wine.

"Do you want me to?" he asked, and she felt his callused fingertips brush across her cheek. So gentle.

"Yes, but nothing sad."

She felt the bed dip and knew he'd slid in bed beside her, fully clothed, to gather her into his arms. She inhaled his scent and took comfort in his nearness.

"This story has a happy ending," he whispered close to her ear.

"All right."

"There once was a man name Drew, who had so many women he didn't know what to do. And he thought he was happy until one day he saw this girl named Eden, and figured he would make her another one of his women. But he soon realized Eden was special. She couldn't be like his other women. Because this girl had done something the others couldn't do. She had captured his heart. And then he and Eden got married and lived happily ever after."

She snuggled closer to him and his warmth. "Hmm, nice." And then she drifted off to sleep.

Sixteen

Brittany opened her eyes and stared up at the gray clouds in the sky. It was supposed to rain today, wasn't it? She closed her eyes, not sure what day it was. Sunday, she believed.

Parts of yesterday floated through her memory. She remembered going to her house and washing the bed linens and then finding her mother's journal.

She opened her eyes. The journal. She recalled reading the journal and the parts that had made her cry. And she remembered Galen showing up and holding her while she cried and bringing her back here.

Brittany threw back the covers and glanced down at herself. She was wearing one of his T-shirts. The details of last night were sketchy, but she did recall him undressing her and tucking her into bed. He'd even told her some story, although she couldn't exactly remember it. Hopefully, it would all come back later.

She eased out of bed and stretched. She needed to shower, put on some clothes and go apologize to Galen for her actions yesterday. It was not good manners for a woman to get all emotional on a man.

As she headed toward the bathroom, she promised herself that she would make it up to him.

"So, Galen, where's your houseguest?"

Galen stared across the table at Jonas. This brother had asked the very question the other four were wondering but hadn't the nerve to inquire about. Galen was no fool. He'd known the moment he had opened the door to them that they had visited for a reason. He couldn't recall the last time they'd dropped by bringing him breakfast.

"Brittany's upstairs," he said as he continued eating.

"Nice name," Gannon interjected.

Galen nodded. "She's a nice girl."

"Classify nice."

That had come from Tyson. Eli, he noticed, wasn't saying anything. He was just looking, listening and eating. "She's not anyone I'd typically mess around with."

"Then why are you?" Mercury asked.

Galen smiled. "Because I like her." He thought about what he'd just said and decided these five men deserved his honesty, even though what he was about to say would stun them. "In fact, I'm in love with her."

Their reaction was comical at best. Only Eli had managed to keep a straight face—one of those "I told you so" expressions. The others looked shocked.

"What do you mean you love her? The way Drew loves Eden or the way Colfax loves Velvet?" Mercury asked.

Everyone was familiar with Mercury's friend Jaye

Colfax. He claimed he was in love with Velvet Spencer; however, he wasn't in love with the woman, just the sex because it was off the chain.

"It's like Drew and Eden."

That confession was like a missile going off in his kitchen, and with it came a blast. Colorful expletives were discharged in different languages because he and all of his brothers spoke several foreign languages. In fact, maybe that was a good thing considering Brittany was upstairs. He hadn't heard her moving around, but that didn't mean she hadn't awakened. The last thing she needed to hear was the Steele brothers discussing her.

"Let's speak German," Galen suggested.

English or German, what his brothers were saying was scorching his ears. He was being called everything but a child of God. Now he knew how Donovan felt, because Galen had been one of the first to read his cousin the riot act, as if falling in love was something he could have avoided.

When he felt they'd pretty much gotten everything off their chests, and probably every filthy word they could think of out of their mouths, he stood and said in German, "Okay, you've all had your say, now get over it."

It wasn't just what he said, but the tone he used that made his kitchen suddenly get quiet. Five pairs of green eyes stared at him. And then he said, "What happens to me has no bearing on the five of you."

He knew it was a lie even as he said it. Eden Tyson Steele wouldn't see it that way. She would think one down and five more to go.

"And you truly love her? This woman you met…less than a week ago?" Jonas asked, looking at him like he ought to have his head examined.

"We didn't just meet. I met her in New York six months ago."

"Hey, wait a minute," Gannon said, as if something had just clicked inside his head. "Is she the one who got away?"

Galen couldn't help but smile. Gannon had a tendency to remember everything. "Yes, she's the one, which is why I don't plan on letting her get away again."

"So when is the wedding?" Jonas asked. "If I'm going to be in a wedding, I need to know when. My schedule is pretty crazy for the next few months."

Galen shrugged. "Don't know because she hasn't a clue how I feel. And chances are she might not return the feelings."

His brothers looked aghast at such a possibility. After all, Galen was a Steele and all women loved the Steeles. "So you're going to have to work on her? Convince her you're worthy of her affections?" Tyson asked, as if the thought of Galen doing such a thing was downright shameful.

"Yes, and I intend to win her over."

"And if you don't?"

An assured and confident smile touched his lips. "I will."

Brittany was halfway down the stairs when she heard the sound of male voices…and they were speaking in a different language. German, she believed, but wasn't sure. The only other language she spoke was Spanish. Why would they be doing such a thing? She stopped walking, wondering if she should interrupt.

She shrugged. A few days ago when she'd asked about meeting his brothers, Galen had said they'd come around sooner or later, when word got out about her.

They were here, so evidently word was out and she might as well get it over with and make an appearance.

She walked into the kitchen. "Good morning."

The room went silent and six pairs of eyes turned to her. Her gaze immediately latched onto Galen's as the other men just stared at her. The one thing she did notice was that they appeared to be sextuplets. All six had the same height and build and those Smokey Robinson eyes. And all were handsome as sin.

Galen walked over to her and she felt a semblance of relief because his brothers just continued to eye her up and down. She was glad she looked pretty decent in her knit top and skirt.

"Okay, guys, I want you to meet Brittany Thrasher," Galen said, wrapping one arm around her waist. "Brittany, from left to right, that's Tyson, Eli, Jonas, Mercury and Gannon."

She smiled warmly, then said, "Nice meeting all of you."

But the men didn't reply. They just continued to gawk. "It's not polite to stare."

Simultaneously, their faces broke into smiles and Brittany knew Nikki's warnings about these brothers were true. They were Phoenix's most eligible bachelors, heartbreakers to the core. Even the one standing close by her side.

"Sorry. Please forgive our manners," the one introduced as Tyson said. "Your beauty has left us speechless."

Yeah, right, she thought to herself. This one, Dr. Tyson Steele, was the epitome of suave and sophisticated, exuding an aura of self-assurance and confidence. Instead of saying what she really thought about his compliment, though, she decided to accept it graciously. "Thank you."

"My brothers brought breakfast. Please join us," Galen invited.

She shook her head. "That's okay. I didn't mean to interrupt."

"And you didn't," Eli said. "Please join us. We insist."

Her gaze lit on the man who looked like he could easily grace the cover of *GQ*. In fact they all did, including Galen. She allowed herself a moment to size up the brothers the same way they were doing with her. They were probably trying to figure things out between her and their brother. Evidently, Galen hadn't told them much and now they probably wanted to pump information out of her.

She'd never had siblings, so she didn't know how they operated collectively. But she had a feeling those Steeles were rather unique when it came to looking out for each other. She wondered if they saw her as a threat to Galen for some reason.

Deciding to go along with the invitation, she said, "Thanks. I'd love to join you for breakfast."

She glanced up at Galen. His arms were still around her waist, but he had an odd look on his face. Had he expected her to turn down his invitation? Sometimes she could read him and sometimes she could not.

This was one of those times.

Galen leaned back in his chair watching Brittany. She conversed and joked easily with his brothers and they had definitely warmed up to her. Over breakfast she had told them about her business and in kind, they told her about theirs. That unfortunately extended their stay. He was about to suggest they think about leaving when Jonas remembered their golf game at noon, and the five reluctantly left.

"I like your brothers," Brittany said when Galen returned after walking them to the door with strict orders not to come back anytime soon.

"They're okay." He had sat there and watched her interactions with his siblings, thinking of just how well she would fit in with his family. His parents would adore her; especially his mother. Brittany said she'd never had a family before; well, she had one now. His brothers didn't take to people easily. They were usually guarded and reserved. But they had taken to her.

"Did you sleep well last night?" he asked, walking over to her.

He saw the blush that stained her cheeks when she said, "Yes. I didn't mean to be so much trouble. I see you got me ready for bed and tucked me in."

And I told you a story you probably don't remember, he thought. "You weren't any trouble. I didn't mind taking care of you."

"But you shouldn't have had to. That wasn't part of our agreement, Galen."

Damn the agreement, he wanted to say. Instead he said, "So what are your plans today? We left your car at the house. Do you want to go back and get it now or do you want to wait until later?"

"I'll wait until later, if you don't mind. Do you usually work on your video games on Sunday, as well?"

"It depends on what I have to do to it. Sniper is relatively finished except for a few components. Would you like to see it?"

He could tell by her expression she was surprised he'd asked. "Can I?"

"Sure. Come on."

She followed him to the door that led to his garage. He opened it and then held it for her to precede him through it and down the steps. "Is this a garage or a dungeon?" she threw over her shoulder to ask.

He laughed as he closed the door and followed her downstairs. "In a way it's both. My house is built on a high peak, but the driveway is on a slope, which means you have to drive down to the garage. It's a six-car garage."

"You have that many cars?"

He chuckled. "Not yet, but I'm working on it. I collect vintage cars, specifically muscle cars," he said when they reached the bottom.

She glanced over at him. "What's a muscle car?"

"It's a high-performance automobile that was manufactured in the late sixties and early seventies. I own three now and I'm always looking to add more to my collection."

She glanced around. "This is a huge area and I've never seen a garage floor that's tiled, and with such nice stone pavers."

He smiled. "Thanks. Come on. I'll show you my cars and then I'll let you watch me work with Sniper."

Brittany followed Galen and admired the vintage cars he had in his collection. They were beautiful, all three of them—a 1967 Camaro, a 1969 GTO and a 1968 Road Runner. They went along with his everyday cars, the late-model SUV, Corvette and Mercedes sedan.

"Where did you get your interest in muscle cars?" she asked, admiring the sleek design and craftsmanship of each vehicle. She didn't know a lot about cars, but she could tell these were in great shape. A collector's dream.

"My father. He has his own collection," he explained as he led her over to his work area.

She couldn't believe how spacious his work space was, and how neat and organized. She could see why he preferred working in his garage instead of an off-site office or warehouse. Everything was at his fingertips here.

He offered her the seat next to his and then proceeded to explain how the video game would work and what he needed to do to get it ready for the Video Game Expo in the spring. She could hear the excitement in his voice when he told her about it. She was touched that he was sharing his work with her. He hadn't invited her in here before and she wondered why he was doing so now. Still, it felt good knowing he had allowed her into his private space.

Brittany scooted her chair closer as he talked her through the assembly of one of the components of the game. Everything was being designed on a huge computer screen in front of him. She was amazed at how much graphic art expertise went into the creation of a game, as well as the game engine. The more she watched, the more she admired his skill, proficiency and imagination.

She glanced over at him. His face was set with determination and concentration. But he was her focal point as she studied him, scanned his features with the intensity of a woman who wanted a man.

She liked watching his hands move and remembered those same hands moving over her as his fingertips caressed the curve of her breasts, cupped her backside or slid between her thighs. A rush of heat hit her in the chest as her body responded to the memories. She let out a slow breath.

"Getting bored?" he asked, glancing over at her.

"No, not at all. I enjoy looking at you work." And I enjoy looking at you.

She watched him save whatever program he'd been working on and then turn to her. Galen had a way of looking at her that left her breathless, made her hot. Made the area between her legs tingle.

"You ever make out in the backseat of a car?"

She clamped her mouth shut to keep it from dropping open. Was she really supposed to answer that? Evidently, because he seemed to be waiting on her response. "No."

"You want to try it?" There was that arrogant smile on his face. The one she both loved and detested.

"Before you answer, let me tell you how it will work," he said, leaning closer so that his heated breath came into contact with her skin. "The backseat of the car will be the ending point. We will actually start here in my work space. I want to take you all over it."

His words sent a surge of anticipation through her. Adrenaline pumped through her bloodstream; visual imagery danced in her head. "I'll start off by licking you all over and then going inside you so deep, you won't know where your body ends and mine begins."

He reached out and with the tip of his finger he caressed her arm. She could feel the goose bumps forming there. "And after we make love over in this area a few times…"

A few times? Mercy.

"Then we'll move to the cars. You can take your pick."

Boy, was he generous. In more ways than one. His fingers had moved from her arm and had dropped to her thigh and were now slowly sliding beneath her skirt. One spot he touched made her quiver inside. And she was convinced her panties were getting wet.

"So, Brittany Thrasher, what do you say?"

She couldn't say anything. She wasn't capable of speech. As an intense ache spread all over her body, she reached up and wrapped her arms around his neck. She decided to let her actions show him what she couldn't put into words.

Seventeen

Galen didn't have a problem with Brittany taking the initiative with this kiss after he'd planted a few sensuous seeds in her mind. He would use any tactic he thought would work. He was determined to bind her to him and they might as well start here, because they did enjoy making love.

And today he intended for there to be plenty of foreplay. When it was all said and done, Brittany would know without a doubt that she was his. Permanently and irrevocably.

While her tongue tangled with his, she began kneading the muscles in his shoulders, heating his blood to flash point. He pulled her out of her chair and into his lap, scooting his own chair back from the table so that her body was practically draped over his.

And then he took over the kiss and decided to seduce her Galen Steele–style. The exploration of her mouth was intense and he intended for his tongue to leave a mark wherever it went. He was on the verge of getting intoxicated just with a kiss and a touch. Then he slid his fingers into her womanly folds, and her groan sent spirals of intense longing right to his crotch, making his erection press hard against the zipper of his jeans.

With her in his arms he stood and stripped her naked in record time, for desire consumed him in a way it never had before. When he was done with hers, he removed his own clothes and noticed her staring down at his erection.

"You want it, Brittany?"

She glanced up at him. "Yes, I want it."

"Then take it."

He didn't have to say the words twice. She eased down in front of him.

"I've never done this before," she said, looking up at him, "but I want so much to do it for you."

He smiled down at her. "Practice makes perfect."

"And if you don't like it?"

"I'm going to like it. Trust me."

She held his gaze for a moment and then said in a soft voice, "I do trust you, Galen."

And then she dipped her head and took him into the warmth of her mouth. Every part of his body, every cell and molecule, quivered in response. Her hand gripped him while her mouth drove him crazy. Using her tongue she covered every inch of him, from the tip all the way to the base.

He reached out and tightened his hand in her hair and let out a deep guttural groan. Had she actually thought he wouldn't like this? How could he not like the feel of her hot tongue gliding over him, and then pulling him inside the sweet recesses of her mouth? When he felt a deep throbbing about to erupt, he quickly pulled her up and swept her into his arms and placed her on his work desk, spreading her legs in the process.

He sheathed himself with a condom and made good his threat to lick her all over. With erotic caresses his tongue covered every inch of her, intent on giving her the pleasures she thought she could never enjoy. And he didn't let up until he had her on the verge of a climax. But then he didn't really let up; he delved in deeper, using his tongue to deliver powerful strokes. She moaned and writhed beneath his mouth.

And then she screamed, shuddered uncontrollably and clutched the sides of his head as the intense sensations erupted inside her. Sensations Galen felt in his mouth. He hadn't been prepared for a woman like her. He hadn't been prepared to fall in love with her.

But he had.

When he pulled his mouth away while licking his lips, he leaned forward and whispered in her ear, "Now we make out in my car."

Galen knew for the rest of the day he would continue to assault her mind with desire and fill her body with pleasure. He couldn't imagine ever being inside any other woman but her for the rest of his days.

And as he picked her up into his arms and carried her toward his 1969 GTO, he knew that sex between them would never be enough. But he intended to make it a good start.

Brittany stepped out of the shower and caught her reflection in the vanity mirror and couldn't help but smile. For someone who'd started out the week with hidden pleasures, Galen had done a pretty good job of uncovering them.

Her smile slowly faded when she remembered they

had only two more days and then their week together would end. She thought of her mother's home as hers, and had even gone so far as to order repairs to those areas that needed it. And she would be interviewing a painter later today after having lunch with Nikki.

She would leave Saturday morning to fly back to Tampa with plans to return to Phoenix in a week's time. She had finished reading all of her mother's entries in the journal and continued to feel the love her mother had for her. She'd thought about expanding the house and using it to open a home base for Etiquette Matters. She had discussed the idea with Galen, who thought it was a good one.

The only problem she saw—and it was her problem—was how she would handle it when she returned to Phoenix and ran into him with another woman. She knew they didn't have any hold on each other; they weren't even dating. Their agreement was for her to live with him for a week and she was only two days short of fulfilling her terms. But she knew leaving here would be the hardest thing she'd ever had to do.

Because she'd fallen in love with him.

Every time he touched her, made love to her, she fell deeper and deeper in love with him. Emotions washed over her and they were emotions she had no right to feel where Galen Steele was concerned. He hadn't made any promises, hadn't alluded to the possibility that he felt anything for her. To a man like him, sex was sex. When their affair ended, his affair with another woman would begin. Her heart ached at the thought, but she knew it to be true. She had fallen in love with him, but he hadn't fallen in love with her.

She pulled in a deep breath. That was the story of her life. None of the couples wanting to adopt a child had found her worthy, either. But deep down she believed she had a lot to offer a man. That man just wasn't Galen.

She lifted her chin as she proceeded to rub lotion on her body. As far as she was concerned it was his loss and not hers.

"Have you told Brittany how you feel?"

Galen glanced up at Eli. He had stopped by his brother's office to sign papers for SID. "No, I haven't told her."

One of Eli's brows rose. "What the hell are you waiting for?"

Galen leaned back in his chair, thinking Eli's question was a good one. The only excuse he could come up with was that the last few days with Brittany had been perfect and he hadn't wanted to do anything to mess them up. He had no idea how she would react to such an admission on his part, especially because she seemed content with how things were now.

In the mornings she was over at her place taking care of her mother's belongings while he worked on perfecting Sniper. Then in the afternoon she would arrive home and they'd spend time together. One afternoon they'd gone hiking, another time they'd shared his hot tub, and still another day he'd given her lessons on how to properly use a bow and arrow. He enjoyed having her in his space and spending time with her.

And at night he enjoyed sleeping with her. Making love to her under the moon or the stars overhead. She was so responsive that they had to be the most intense lovemaking sessions of his life. Even the breathless aftermath made him shiver inside just thinking about it.

He also enjoyed waking up with her wrapped in his arms every morning, and making love to her before either of them started their day. And they would talk. She trusted him enough to share her secret with him about Mr. Ponder and why making love to Galen had been a crucial step to overcoming her inability to enjoy sex.

He was well aware that Brittany assumed that in two days she would be leaving, walking out of his life, and he hadn't a clue how to break it to her that that was not how things were going to be.

"Galen?"

He glanced up to find Eli staring at him. "What?"

"When are you going to tell Brittany how you feel about her? Doesn't she leave in a couple of days?"

"Yes, but she'll be back."

"Back to Phoenix but not to your place. She thinks when she leaves here Saturday morning what's between the two of you will be over."

Galen pulled in a deep breath, not surprised Eli knew as much as he did. Brittany had sought him out to handle a couple of legal issues regarding her house. She was trying to get the area rezoned to open the headquarters for Etiquette Matters.

"Nothing between us will be over. I love her," Galen said.

"Then maybe you ought to tell her that. She needs to know she's worthy of being loved."

Galen ran his hand down his face. Over the last few days, even though he'd warned them to stay away, his brothers had revisited anyway and had grown attached to Brittany. They were now her champions and wanted to make sure he would do the right thing by her, although he'd told them from day one what his feelings had been.

"She's never been part of a family and I want so much for her to feel a part of ours."

"Then tomorrow night will be perfect. Thursday-night dinner at Mom's."

Galen's head jerked up. Damn, why hadn't he thought of that? Eli was right. Galen had never brought a woman home to meet his mother before. None of them had. She would have to know the importance of that, wouldn't she? And if she didn't, he would explain things to her.

"That's a good idea."

Eli grinned. "Thank you."

Galen eyed his brother suspiciously. "And just what's in it for you?"

Eli's features broke into a serious expression when he said, "Your happiness."

Galen held his brother's gaze and then nodded. He and his brothers might have inherited Drew's horny genes, but they'd also inherited Eden's caring genes, as well.

"Okay, there's no way after tomorrow night Brittany won't know how I feel."

Once Galen had left his brother's office and slid behind the steering wheel of his car, he pulled out his cell phone and punched in a few numbers.

A feminine voice picked up on the second ring. "Hello."

"Mom, this is Galen. And I'm keeping my promise that you'd be one of the first to know." He couldn't help but smile. His brothers had been the first to know, but there was no reason to tell Eden Steele that.

"Know what?"

"There's a woman I'm interested in." He shook his head and decided to go for broke. "I'm in love with her and I'd like to bring her to dinner tomorrow night."

Eighteen

Brittany checked her lipstick again before putting the small mirror back in her purse. She then glanced over at Galen as he drove to his parents' home for dinner. "Are you sure I look okay?"

Without taking his eyes off the road, he said, "You look great. I love that outfit, by the way."

She smiled. "Thanks. Nikki and I went shopping yesterday and I bought it then." She had introduced him to Nikki a few days ago. She had been helping her with packing up her mother's things. She felt so very blessed having her best friend back in her life.

"So this is a weekly event for you and your brothers with your parents?" she asked.

"Yes. Just for our family. No outsiders."

Brittany frowned. Then why had she gotten invited? She shrugged. Evidently Galen felt he would lack manners if he were to not include his houseguest. She felt bad knowing the only reason she'd been invited was because he'd felt compelled to bring her.

"What time do you fly out Saturday morning to return to Tampa?" he asked her.

"Eight." She couldn't help wondering if the reason he was asking was because he was eager for her to leave. Her heart ached at the thought.

"Well, here we are."

Brittany glanced through the window and saw the huge house whose exterior was beautifully decorated for the holidays. It was twice the size of Galen's home. "And this is the house you lived in as a child?" she couldn't help asking.

"Yes. We moved in here when I was in the first grade. My parents knew they wanted a lot of children and went ahead and purchased a house that could accommodate a large family."

Brittany nodded, thinking that made perfect sense.

Galen brought the car to a stop among several others and she said, "Looks like your brothers are here already."

"Yes, it looks that way."

She felt relieved. Over the last few days she'd gotten to know Galen's brothers and truly liked them. She wouldn't feel so out of place with them around. She could just imagine what Galen's mother was going to think when she walked in with him.

"Ready?" Galen asked, glancing over at her.

She released a deep breath and said, "Yes, I'm ready."

Brittany took a sip of her wine thinking it odd that Galen's parents hadn't asked how they met or how long they'd known each other. It seemed the moment she and Galen had walked in and all eyes turned to them, she'd felt a strange sort of connection to his mother. It was as if beneath all her outer beauty was a heart of gold. Someone beautiful on the inside as well as the outside. And Eden Tyson Steele was beautiful. She didn't look as if she should be the mother of six sons. The woman didn't look a day over forty, if that. And it was plain to see her husband simply adored her.

It was also plain to see that although Galen and his brothers had their mother's eyes, the rest of their features belonged to Drew Steele. The man was tall, dark and definitely handsome, and Brittany could just imagine him being a devilish rogue in his day, capturing the hearts of many women but giving his heart to only one.

She'd asked Galen how his parents had met and he'd said his father owned a trucking company and was doing a run one night from Phoenix to California, filling in for a sick driver, when he came across Eden, who'd stowed away in the back of his truck at a truck stop, in an attempt to get away from an overbearing agent.

The moment Brittany had walked in with Galen, Eden had given her a smile that Brittany felt was truly genuine and the woman seemed pleased that Galen had brought her to dinner with him. Galen's father was kind as well, and it was quite obvious that he loved and respected his sons and was proud of the men they'd become.

Brittany had never been around such a close-knit family.

"You okay?"

She glanced up at Galen and smiled. "Yes, I'm fine."

He'd rarely left her side and when and if he had, one or all of his brothers had been right there. Except for the time his mother asked if she wanted to see how she had personally decorated the courtyard for the holidays.

Brittany had figured the woman had wanted to get her alone to grill her about her life and discovered that had not been the case. They had talked about fashion, movies and things women talk about when they get together. Brittany found herself talking comfortably, and had told Eden about the home she'd inherited from her birth mother. She had found it so easy to talk to Galen's mother and a part of her wished things were different between her and Galen. Eden would be the type of mother-in-law any woman would want to have. But she knew she would never be hers because she and Galen didn't have that sort of relationship. For some strange reason, though, Brittany had a feeling his family thought otherwise.

"So what do you think of my parents?" he leaned close and asked her.

"I think you are blessed to have them. They are super."

"Yes, they are," he agreed. "And what do you think of my mother's courtyard?"

Brittany grinned. "If I wasn't in the holiday spirit before arriving here, I would definitely be now."

Galen threw his head back and laughed, and Brittany couldn't help herself when she joined in with him. His mother's courtyard looked like a Christmas wonderland. Beautiful as well as festive.

"Christmas is her favorite holiday," he said, placing an arm around her shoulders and bringing her closer to his side.

She lifted her glass to her lips and smiled before taking a sip of her wine. "I can tell."

It didn't take a rocket scientist to see his parents were taken with Brittany, Galen thought. From the moment she walked into their home, Drew and Eden had begun treating her like the daughter they'd never had. Galen could tell that at first Brittany was overwhelmed, didn't know what to make of such an overflow of love and kindness, but then he figured she assumed that's just the way his parents were.

Not really.

He would be the first to admit his parents were good people, but even he had noticed how solicitous they were toward her. And his brothers were no exception. They flocked around her like the caring brothers they would become once they married. He had thought of that word a lot lately and he knew he truly wanted to marry Brittany. He couldn't imagine his life without her.

They needed to talk, he knew, and he'd start that conversation in earnest when they returned to his place. Now he crossed the room to where Brittany stood talking to his parents and brothers.

"Time to go, sweetheart," he said softly.

She smiled over at him. "All right." She then turned to his parents. "Thanks so much for having me here tonight."

Eden beamed. "And we look forward to you coming back." She then shifted her gaze to her oldest son. "You will bring her back, Galen, won't you?"

Galen grinned. "Yes, whenever she's in town. If I come, she'll be with me."

"Wonderful!"

Galen noticed on the way back home that Brittany seemed awfully quiet. He knew for sure something was bothering her when they arrived back at his place and he saw her lips quivering. She was mad about something. What? He found out the moment he closed the door behind them.

"How could you do that, Galen?" she asked angrily. "How could you let your parents assume I meant something to you and I'd be back to have dinner with them again when you don't want me? Do you know how that made me feel?"

Yes, Galen thought, leaning back against the door. He knew precisely how she felt. She had gone through life assuming no one wanted her. In her eyes, she had been the flawed baby no one wanted to adopt. Not worthy of anyone's love. Well, he had news for her and he might as well set her straight right now and not while making love to her later tonight as he'd planned.

He moved away from the door and crossed the distance separating them. When he came to a stop in front of her, he saw the tears she was trying hard to hold back and promised himself that he would never let her shed a single tear for thinking no one wanted her.

"It should have made you feel loved, Brittany, because you are. My parents treated you the way they did tonight because they knew what you evidently don't. Granted, I've never said the words, but I'd thought my actions spoke loud and clear. I love you."

He could tell she didn't get it for a moment because she just stood there and stared at him. And then she spoke. "What did you say?"

He had no trouble repeating it. "I said I love you. I love you so much I ache. I believe I fell in love with you that day in New York when you saw me at my worst. And when I saw you again here in Phoenix, I knew I would do whatever it took to have you with me, even concocting a plan to bid on the house you wanted just so you'd stay a week here with me. Of course I didn't think you would go for it, but I wanted you to have the house anyway. In fact, when you get back to Tampa you'll have the packet Eli sent giving you the house free and clear *before* you decided to take my offer."

Brittany blinked. "But, if that was the case, then why did you still make me think I had to stay here for a week?"

He gave her an arrogant smile. "Because I wanted you in my bed. I'm a Steele."

She just stood there and stared at him for a long moment and then a smile trembled on her lips. "Your conceit is showing again," she pointed out.

"Sorry."

"I'm not. I love you just the way you are. And I do love you, Galen. I was so afraid you couldn't love me."

Another smile touched his lips, this one filled with care, concern and sincerity. "You are an easy person to love, Brittany. If there is any way I could redo your childhood, I would. But I think you're the person that you are because of it and the challenges you had to face," he said, reaching out and caressing her cheek with his thumb.

"But for the rest of your days, I will make up for all the love you didn't get. I will love you and honor you."

"Oh, Galen." Tears she couldn't hold back streamed down her face.

It was then that Galen swept her off her feet and into his arms to carry her up the stairs. "I told my brothers how I felt about you that day they met you and advised my parents yesterday. Tonight they treated you just as they should have—as a person who will soon become an official member of our family."

He looked down at her and paused on the stair. "Will you marry me?"

Brittany smiled up at him. "Yes! Yes, I will marry you."

Galen grinned as he continued walking up the stairs to his bedroom. "Just so you'll know, I'm having your ring specially designed by Zion."

Brittany's mouth dropped open. "I'm getting a ring by Zion?"

Galen threw his head back and laughed when he placed her on the bed. "Yes." He knew any jewelry by Zion was the rave because Zion was the First Lady's personal jeweler.

She beamed. "I feel special."

"Always keep that thought, because you are."

Galen glanced down at the woman he had placed on his bed. His soul mate. The woman he would love forever. The thought nearly overwhelmed him. "And just so you'll know, I've cleared my work schedule. I'm going with you back to Tampa."

Surprise lit her face. "You are?"

"Yes. I don't intend to let you out of my sight." He dipped his knee on the bed. "Now come here." When she lifted a brow, he added, "Please."

Brittany chuckled as she moved toward Galen and when he wrapped her in his arms and kissed her, she felt completely loved by the one man who had discovered all her hidden pleasures. "How could things be this way for us this soon?"

He understood her question and had a good reason for what probably seemed like madness. "My mother has always warned her sons that we're like our father in a lot of ways," he said. "We're known to be skirt chasers until we meet the one woman who will claim our hearts. You are that woman for me, Brittany. I realized just how empty my life has been until this week while you were here with me. I love you."

She fought back tears in her eyes when she said, "And I love you, too."

And then Galen kissed her and she knew a lot of people would think their affair had been rather short, but she knew it had been just like it was meant to be. Now they would embark upon a life together filled with romance and passion.

Epilogue

Four months later

Galen glanced around the room at all the Steeles in attendance. The last time they'd all gotten together had been at Donovan's wedding in New York. Now they'd all assembled here in Phoenix to watch the first of Drew's boys take the plunge. And very happily, he might add.

Nikki had been Brittany's bridesmaid and his father had been his best man. They'd wanted it simple and decided to have a wedding on the grounds of the home Brittany's mother had left her. Brittany felt her mother's presence there and wanted to start their life off surrounded by love.

"So, what were the nasty things you said to me when I told you I was getting married?" his cousin Donovan said, pulling him out of his reverie.

Galen smiled. "Okay, that was before I knew better.

Before I understood the power of love." He glanced over to where Brittany stood with his mother and his heart expanded twice the size.

"You have a beautiful bride and I wish the two of you happiness always."

"Thanks, Donovan."

Deciding his mother had taken up enough of his wife's time, Galen crossed the room and when Brittany glanced up and saw him, she smiled. She had been a beautiful bride and looked absolutely radiant. And when he opened his arms, she stepped into his embrace. They would be leaving later that day to fly to London where they would catch a ship for a twelve-day Mediterranean cruise.

"I love you, Mrs. Steele," he whispered, holding her tight in his arms.

She smiled up at him. "And I love you."

Over his shoulders he saw his mother eyeing his brothers, who seemed oblivious of her perusal. Galen knew exactly how their mother's mind worked. She was thinking, "One down, five to go."

His brothers would deal with Eden Steele as they saw fit. Galen knew he would have his hands full with the beautiful, sexy woman in his arms. She would continue to teach him manners and he intended to make sure her pleasures were never hidden again.

"Are you ready for your wedding gift now, Galen?"

He arched a brow. "I have another one?" A couple of days ago she had given him a new digital camera. And she'd given him a book on manners. He had given her a gold bracelet with the inscription "Galen's Lady." And he'd given her a toy yellow cab to replace the one he'd taken from her that day in New York.

"Yes, you have another one. I'm not going to blindfold

you but you must promise to close your eyes and keep them closed until I say you can open them."

"All right."

He closed his eyes and felt himself being led no telling where, and after a few minutes, Brittany instructed, "You can open them now, Galen."

He did and sucked in a quick breath when he saw the car he'd wanted, the 1969 Chevelle, parked only a few feet away from where he stood. He couldn't believe it. It looked beautiful, but then when he glanced over at Brittany, he knew she was the most beautiful thing in his life.

"But how?" he asked, barely able to get the words out past his excitement.

She smiled. "After you confessed to eavesdropping on my and Nikki's conversation that day, I felt bad that you missed out on the chance to bid for this car because of me, so I gave your brothers the job of locating it for me. Luckily, they did. I hope you like it."

"Oh, sweetheart, I love it, but not as much as I love you." He pulled her into his arms intent on showing her how much. He took her mouth in a lingering kiss, not caring if his brothers or any of the other wedding guests could see them.

She was his and he was hers. Forever.

* * * * *

SPECIAL EXCERPT FROM

 HARLEQUIN®

 *Desire*

A sneak peek at

STERN, *a Westmoreland novel*

by New York Times *and* USA TODAY *bestselling author*

Brenda Jackson

Available September 2013.
Only from Harlequin® Desire!

As far as Stern was concerned, his best friend had lost her ever-loving mind. But he didn't say that. Instead, he asked, "What's his name?"

"You don't need to know that. Do you tell me the name of every woman you want?"

"This is different."

"Really? In what way?"

He wasn't sure, but he just knew that it was. "For you to even ask me, that means you're not ready for the kind of relationship you're going after."

JoJo threw her head back and laughed. "Stern, I'll be thirty next year. I'm beginning to think that most of the men in town wonder if I'm really a girl."

He studied her. There had never been any doubt in his mind that she was a girl. She had long lashes and eyes so dark they were the color of midnight. She had gorgeous legs, long and endless. But he knew he was one of the few men who'd ever seen them.

"You hide what a nice body you have," he finally said. He suddenly sat up straight in the rocker. "I have an idea.

HDEXP73264

What you need is a makeover."

"A makeover?"

"Yes, and then you need to go where your guy hangs out. In a dress that shows your legs, in a style that shows off your hair." He reached over and took the cap off her head. Lustrous dark brown hair tumbled to her shoulders. He smiled. "See, I like it already."

And he did. He was tempted to run his hands through it to feel the silky texture.

He leaned back and took another sip of his beer, wondering where such a tempting thought had come from. This was JoJo, for heaven's sake. His best friend. He should not be thinking about how silky her hair was.

He should not be bothered by the thought of men checking out JoJo, of men calling her for a date.

Suddenly, he was thinking that maybe a makeover wasn't such a great idea after all.

Will Stern help JoJo win her dream man?

STERN

by New York Times *and* USA TODAY
bestselling author Brenda Jackson

Available September 2013
Only from Harlequin® Desire!

REQUEST YOUR FREE BOOKS!
2 FREE NOVELS PLUS 2 FREE GIFTS!

H HARLEQUIN®

Desire

ALWAYS POWERFUL, PASSIONATE AND PROVOCATIVE

HD13R